A Verse to Murder

PETER TONKIN

For:

Cham, Guy and Mark

As always.

TABLE OF CONTENTS

Chapter 1: The Poisoned Poet

i

'When shall we three meet again?' asked Will Shakespeare, last to arrive but nevertheless in a hurry to leave, Tom Musgrave observed; still uncertain as to why the other two had called him here in the first place.

In the heartbeat of silence that followed Will's question a talon of lightning clawed the leaden sky outside the garret window, flooding the cramped room with an instant of brightness no sooner there than gone. It froze the three men in place: Will Shakespeare glaring impatiently out at the storm, Tom Musgrave looking down at the bed and John Gerard the herbalist bending over it. The instantaneous bolt illuminated the shabby walls of the bedchamber above the Golden Lion tavern on King Street hard by Westminster. It gilded the rickety furniture, the crazy desk laden with manuscripts, scrolls and letters.

But most of all it lit up the dead man.

The corpse was that of the late Chief Secretary for Ireland and current Sheriff of Cork, the poet Edmund Spencer. It lay on its side atop the piss-soiled, rumpled blankets, facing away from the window and looking across the bedding towards the inner wall. *Looking* was the right word, thought Tom, for the dead poet's eyes were wide even though they obviously saw nothing. What had so recently been a man, a client at his school of fencing and a friend had been transformed by death into an object; into something that was no longer a person but a puzzle. One needing an urgent solution for this death was neither natural nor accidental. The eyes suggested this but the ear proved it.

The Master of Logic in Tom's keen mind devoured the scene narrowing his own eyes and seeking the tiniest detail that might help solve the deadly conundrum which he had been called upon to investigate. To which John Gerard in turn had been summoned. John was more than a mere apothecary - he was an expert on all things toxic and had helped Tom overcome more than one attempted poisoning. John, moreover, had been treating Spenser for the discomfort caused by a burst eardrum and had dispensed a range of herbs to the poet, designed to ease pain, aid restful sleep and hasten recovery. Drugs which were only safe when taken in controlled doses, for, as with many medicines, large quantities could be lethal.

The pair of them were too late to prevent the death in this case and were working to explain exactly what had been done to cause it. Later, Tom would examine why the murder had been committed and, finally, who was guilty of the lethal act. Working independently of any legal authorities called upon to perform a more formal investigation; fighting almost as actively as the murderer to stay well clear of the clutches of the law, especially as those enforcing it were all-too often swayed by fractured and mutually antagonistic politics rather than by evidence adduced or proof presented.

The pupils of Spenser's staring eyes gaped cavernously. Tom recognized that as a sure sign the dead poet had taken a great deal of belladonna. An effect confirmed by Will, whose company of actors used belladonna to widen the eyes of the boys playing girls and women; young Robert Goffe's eyes had been swimming in the stuff as he played Juliet to Burbage's Romeo for instance. But belladonna was a potent poison as well as a useful piece of stagecraft and an effective sleeping-draught. Had Spenser consumed sufficient quantities to kill himself, Tom wondered. If so, why so? If not, what other more lethal poison might have been employed to snuff out his life? In any case, pouring the concoction into his ear instead of down his throat - as appeared to have been done here - was suspicious to put it mildly, and seemed to Tom to rule out accidental overdose.

*

Beneath its staring eyes, the cadaver's shadowed mouth was agape. A thread of vomit escaped from the lower corner to ooze through moustache and beard and soil the pillow as the excess of urine dampened the blankets below. Spenser's whole slight frame seemed to be locked in a rictus like his face - as though it had been turned to cold stone by some witchcraft, as Tom had already discovered the instant he tried to move it. But it was that darkly crusted ear that made the situation so remarkable.

The well of Spenser's uppermost ear was caked with some thick liquid most of which seemed to have seeped into the dead man's head; in the absence of any other likelihood, thought Tom, certainly put there to kill him; he could think of no other reasonable likelihood. The cold calculation of the murderous act was further emphasized by the bandage lying on the pillow behind the dead head. For the bandage had been tightly bound over the damaged ear itself the last time Tom had seen it. Tom's observation confirmed by John Gerard who had bound the bandage in place himself twelve hours ago when the poisoned poet had still been alive and visiting the apothecary for treatment and more medicine.

But Spenser had clearly collapsed onto the bed too exhausted to remove any of his clothing other than his shoes, thought Tom. Too worn out even to use the chamberpot and crawl beneath the blankets. So what could have prompted him to go through the complicated process of taking the bandage off his ear then pouring his medicine into it? If, in fact, he had taken it off himself; if indeed, he had been capable of achieving the difficult task of pouring anything into his ear without slopping it all over the side of his head, his shoulder and his bedding, all of which were reasonably clean. In any case, that was something which seemed disturbingly unlikely. Trying to apply the pain-killing medicine directly to the seat of discomfort might be logical were the place easy to reach but Tom could not conceive of Spenser, too fatigued to remove his clothing doing such a complicated thing. Besides, there was the matter of the floor.

ii

Immediately after the flash of lightning came the crash of thunder, which was instantly followed by the fearsome drumming of the downpour. Tom glanced up at the ceiling which seemed sound enough even beneath this almost Biblical battering. There was not the slightest sign of a leak anywhere. And yet there was dampness on the floor - the ghost of a sizeable puddle close by the bed-head suggesting that someone wearing wet clothes had lingered there. Someone other than Spenser who had so obviously kicked off his shoes and collapsed directly into bed; whose upper clothes were, in any case, quite dry as well as quite clean. Which was a remarkable fact in itself for an icy Christmas had been succeeded by rain-storms of singular ferocity, last night's succeeded almost immediately by this morning's. Someone else had lingered, dripping, long enough to remove the bandage from the drugged victim's ear. And, logic suggested, to pour in the poison.

Furthermore, Tom observed, there was a trail of smaller marks leading back and forth between the dead man's bed and the door opening out into the modest parlour; patches of dampness that he and John had been careful not to obliterate with their own dripping cloaks.

Below Spenser's waist, however, things were different. He had emptied his bladder forcibly and his clothing and bedding were sopping wet - a fact that seemed somehow to have disturbed John.

Tom raised his voice over the noise. 'The tavern-keeper's boys were off to summon the constable as well as to guide us here. The constable will have summoned the Queen's Crowner or the Earl Marshal by now, for Spenser is certainly important enough to warrant a full, formal *postmortem* investigation and The Golden Lion is well within The Verge.'

'Less than a mile from Westminster Palace,' said Will. 'Certainly nowhere near the thirteen miles from Her Majesty's person covered by The Verge.'

'Just so,' agreed Tom. 'We may therefore expect the Queen's Coroner or Earl Marshal's men; and when they arrive there will be all hell let loose…'

'Let us meet when that hurlyburly's done then,' suggested John as he finished collecting samples of the dark stuff round Spenser's ear and the vomit on his pillow. 'You should both come home to me and we'll test whatever this liquid is and the vomit it appears to have generated.'

'You go on, Will,' suggested Tom. 'John and I will deal with The Crowner or the Earl Marshal's men. They will be here for much of the day I would judge. Or at least it will be if they suspect foul play as sharply as I do. So, look for me by sunset.'

*

'Look for you where? Where's the place?' asked Will, distracted by the corpse on the bed and deafened by the thunder-clap, the raving wind and pounding downpour alike, and yet keen to be gone. Still, Tom calculated, not quite sure why he had been called here in the first place - his acquaintance with the dead man was social: little more than rivalry between two master poets, each jealous of his reputation and wary of any challenge from the other. Though Tom was well enough aware that such rivalry could prove fatal if it grew bitter enough. It was not yet a year, after all, since Ben Jonson had only escaped hanging by pleading benefit of clergy for the murder of rival Gabriel Harvey committed over just such a matter.

But Will was called away from the room and the corpse by the immediate responsibilities that filled his mornings under normal circumstances - as a Sharer in the Globe Theatre part-way through construction on Sir Nicholas Brend's field in Southwark; as the playwright responsible for generating a new play to open it; as the soon-to-be occupant of a lodging south of the River as close to the new theatre as possible; and as the would-be lover of Rosalind Fletcher, the woman he was planning to share that lodging with while his wife Ann and their family stayed in distant Stratford.

'Meet us at High Holborn at set of sun as John suggested,' said Tom more loudly, 'where we can look further into this matter. Spenser was less than fifty years old. He was fit and healthy apart from his ear when we last saw him. And now look at him. If it's not poison it's witchcraft; if not witchcraft then it's poison.'

'Poison poured into his ear as he slept,' said Will, shaking his head at the horror of it. 'That will haunt my nightmares for some time to come.'

'It will be among the last of my thoughts before I go to sleep, certainly,' concurred Tom and John Gerard nodded silent agreement as Will vanished through the door.

Moments later the playwright was little more than a ghostly grey figure lost beneath a hooded cloak, hurrying eastward along King Street. Tom and John stood shoulder to shoulder, looking down through the trembling, rain-spattered bedroom window as they watched him vanish into the deluge.

'You're certain?' asked Tom

'My apprentice Hal is certain,' answered John Gerard. 'I have interrogated him thoroughly and there can be no mistake. Even though he did not see the face of the man who purchased the belladonna and the hemlock, he is absolutely sure about the name he gave and will swear to it if called upon by Queen's Crowner or Earl Marshal. The man who bought all that deadly poison yesterday evening was William Shakespeare.'

iii

Moments after Will disappeared, a troupe of horsemen came thundering up King Street from its eastern end to rein to a stop outside the Golden Lion. The leader glanced up before dismounting and heading for the street door immediately below. Tom only got a glance at the man's face but it was enough for him to identify the impatient visitor. 'It's our namesake, John,' he said grimly. 'Sir Thomas Gerard the Knight Marshal.'

'The right hand of the Earl Marshal,' nodded the apothecary.

'And the Earl Marshal is Robert Devereux, the Earl of Essex. Whose main mission as Earl Marshal is to protect the Queen against Jesuit assassins,' added Tom. 'So Earl Marshal Essex thinks that if Spenser has been murdered, there's a Catholic plot behind it because of Spenser's links with Ireland. Though it serves his ends to say so because he is all afire to take an army westwards and crush the Catholic rebellion in Ulster. Especially as Her Majesty has promised him the post of Lord Lieutenant of Ireland and has only to sign the commission for him to get under way.'

But the Earl Marshal could be right, thought Tom as Sir Thomas and his men came pounding up the stairs. For Spencer had recently found himself at the heart of a murderous mystery involving not only the bitter rivalry between Essex and Walter Raleigh but also Irish Catholic assassins, secret messages, riots in the City and attempts on the lives of Raleigh, his family and household - all of which had only been resolved six days ago at the Queen's Twelfth Night festivities.

Tom usually dealt with Queen's Crowner Sir William Danby when his path crossed those of Her Majesty's many law officers. But he knew all about the tall official striding through the door into the dead poet's bedroom. Sir Thomas Gerard was a Staffordshire man, already a star rising steadily at Court though still only thirty five. Home tutored from childhood, he had been accepted into Caius College Cambridge at the age of sixteen, completing his studies swiftly - able to enter Parliament as MP for Lancashire at twenty. Now, having become an accomplished soldier in the mean-time - following Essex to war in France and knighted by him before the walls of Rouen - he represented Staffordshire, where Robert Devereux, already the Earl of the county of Essex, was building yet another power-base. This one bestriding the path he would have to take when he led the army he was already assembling, arming and training into Ireland as Lord Lieutenant.

Moreover, as well as being Earl Marshal Essex's deputy and MP for a county he coveted, Sir Thomas had been Captain of The Isle of Man for the last four years. Man, which reared out of the Irish Sea to stand half way between Staffordshire and Dublin. Whose mighty Castles of Rushen and Peel were already filling with the sorts of supplies, arms and armaments such as Essex might require as he faced the rebellious Hugh O'Neill, Earl of Tyrone in Ulster. Or - as increasing numbers of powerful men were beginning to suspect - when he brought his army back to England and tried to snatch Queen Elizabeth's throne.

*

Oddly, for one of Essex' faction, Sir Thomas favored the swashbuckling style of sweeping moustaches and arrogantly pointed beard made famous by Drake, Hawkins and Raleigh rather than the long beard of square Puritan cut favoured by the Earl himself. He had every bit of his superior's arrogant abruptness, however. 'Who are you Sirrah? What are you doing here?' he demanded as his men crowded into Spenser's bedchamber behind him, filling the modest space to overflowing.

'Thomas Musgrave, Master of Defence, Sir Thomas. Master Spencer came to me for lessons in the art of rapier-play. We became friends, as the people at the Golden Lion know.'

'And you?' Sir Thomas glared at John.

Before John could answer, one of the men at Sir Thomas' shoulder spoke for him. 'That is John Gerard, Sir Thomas. Calls himself a herbalist and apothecary. Little more than a country bumpkin with a little learning such as a wise woman or a midwife might impart.'

'A choice pair,' sneered another of the Knight Marshal's retinue. 'Friends to Will Shagsberd, who poor Robert Greene rightly called *upstart crow*.'

Tom recognized these speakers too. The first, a slight, almost dwarfish, figure had a high, lined forehead, the hair swept back into rats' tails on his collar, the sunken eyes, the venal lips not quite concealed by the oily fringe of his moustache, the spread of beard falling across his upper chest; it was Simon Forman, astrologer, occultist, serial seducer of innocent maidens, hanger-on of Raleigh's notorious School of Atheists, which Will had characterized as The School of Night. Not so much a school of learning as a sinister group who met to discuss forbidden subjects. As well as Raleigh, The School of Night comprised Henry Percy Earl of Northumberland, Thomas Harriot the astronomer, Simon Foreman, seemingly - a late arrival perhaps. And Christopher Marlowe, poet, playwright and spy, atheist and blasphemer, dead these six years - murdered in Deptford as efficiently as Spencer here lying dead on the bed. A dagger thrust through the eye for one poet; poison dropped into an ear for the other.

The second speaker, his beard cut roughly in Essex' puritan style was the man who completed dead Marlowe's poem *Hero and Leander* which had been published little more than a year ago; one of Will's greatest competitors and most implacable rivals - especially now that Marlowe and Greene were both dead. This was the poet and playwright George Chapman. His eyes blazing feverishly, his cheeks lank, his neck scrawny, his frame too slight for the ill-fitting clothes he wore. A man desperately near to starvation, thought Tom.

'Whatever your reasons for being here, they are done now,' snapped Sir Thomas. 'If you wish to have any further involvement in this matter, you may report to my prison, the Marshalsea, and discuss it with my aide the Pursuivant Marshal or the Keeper of the Keys there.'

After a moment of silence, he turned. 'Clear the way,' he ordered. 'These two are leaving.

Tom allowed John to go first, following his friend across a floor now puddled with water from the new arrivals' cloaks, pausing to turn as he himself went through the doorway, just in time to see Simon Forman standing in the largest puddle of all beside the bed-head with Chapman at his shoulder, closing those staring eyes and carefully replacing the bandage over Spenser's ear. Then, frowning suspiciously, he turned and followed John across the little parlour and down the narrow stairs, wondering why Simon Foreman was rearranging Spenser's corpse instead of examining it as John Gerard and he had done.

iv

The two men paused in the empty vestibule between the stair foot and the street door which stood half open revealing a bedraggled groom holding the Knight Marshal's horses. 'He was speaking in jest was he not?' whispered John. 'He does not want us down at the Marshalsea?'

'A grim enough jest, but a jest in truth,' answered Tom, who relished the idea of visiting the notorious prison no more than did his friend, though Sir Thomas' mention of his assistant the Pursuivant Marshal raised something in Tom's capacious memory. He dismissed the thought as he turned to more immediate concerns, first amongst them the manner in which the areas south of the River were policed and who had the power to arrest and detain John and himself if they wished to do so.

Tom's longtime associate Talbot Law policed the Liberty of the Clink on the south bank of the Thames, enforcing the laws against drunkenness, violence, robbery, card-sharping and all the other illegal pastimes popular in the area owned by the Bishop of Winchester outside the walls and jurisdiction of the

City of London. The Liberty of the Clink being the most famous of the traditionally lawless areas forbidden to the Lord Mayor, his various district constables and their City watchmen.

The Liberty of the Clink lay immediately across the River from the City and on the South Wark. But further south still, down by the Borough, stood the prison manned and run by the Earl Marshal and his associates the Knight Marshal and the Pursuivant Marshal. It was a grim place with such a fearsome reputation that Wat Tyler had burned it to the ground two hundred and twenty years earlier during the Peasants' Revolt. But it had been rebuilt almost immediately, such was the demand for its use. It currently housed anyone suspected of carrying Catholic sympathies too close to treasonous action or such as could not pay the fines for failing to attend Protestant services dictated by the Recusancy Acts. Traitors such as members of the Babington plot, though they were questioned in the Tower by the terrifying torturer Topcliffe before being hung, drawn and quartered at Tyburn. Drawn and quartered, at the Queen's personal command, while still alive.

At least, so said Robert Poley, spy, spymaster, sometime associate of Tom's; the man who broke the Babington plot and saw the conspirators die in September 1586, witnessed the execution of its centre - Mary, Queen of Scots - in February 1587; and, apparently coincidentally, held Christopher Marlowe still on the evening of Thursday, 30th May 1593 with Nicholas Skeres while Ingram Frizer ran his deadly twelve-penny dagger into Marlowe's right eye.

Jesuit priests passed through the Marshalsea on their way to their martyr's Heaven via Tyburn or The Tower. As did pirates, such as captains Wickens, Woodes and Venables - who had used the Isle of Man as a base for their maritime depredations and lived to regret it courtesy of Sir Thomas Gerard in both of his roles. As had any sailors from Philip of Spain's several armadas unlucky enough to have been wrecked on the shores of sternly Protestant England or brutally Calvinist Scotland as opposed to staunchly Catholic Ireland - where they interbred with more welcoming Catholic locals. And finally, increasingly, so did those who could not meet their financial obligations in Elizabeth's progressively debt-ridden society. Men like the desperate, impecunious and unlucky George Chapman.

*

Tom and John lingered in the doorway at the foot of the stairs, looking glumly out at the deluge that neither man was as powerfully motivated as Will Shakespeare to brave. In any case, thought Tom, he needed to visit the Golden Lion before going with John to interrogate Hal his apprentice who had identified Will as the purchaser of so many poisons. Like Romeo in the play that was named for him. What had Will's character so aptly said? *A dram of poison, such soon-speeding gear/As will disperse itself through all the veins/That the life-weary taker may fall dead.*

Tom had to interrogate Hal rather than merely question the boy, for his evidence seemed to prove that Will was involved in the deadly matter at the very least, Romeo's words suggesting some expertise even beyond Will's acquaintance with belladonna and its uses on the stage. Perhaps even that Shakespeare was the murderer himself. Though, allowed The Master of Logic, Will had shown shock and horror at the sight of Spenser's body but not a trace of guilt. He had been motivated to leave the death-chamber by impatience and responsibility, not by the desire of a murderer to flee the scene of his crime.

Tom had been watching his friend closely because it was what John had revealed about Hal's evidence that caused Tom to call Will to the dead Spencer's room in the first place. But then, admitted Tom to himself as he pushed wide the inner door leading directly to the Golden Lion, Will was an actor as well as a poet and playwright; an actor schooled in making his face betray only the emotions he wished it to present to the world.

On that thought he and John stepped through into the tavern's parlour. Even before the arrival of the first customers, which would be soon - as midday was approaching - it was a bright, warm room with a fire blazing in the wide grate, a haunch of Kentish mutton spitted there beginning to cook. The men and women who rented and ran the place were all assembled in the golden glow as though the warmth could cure the nervousness they all plainly felt at being associated, even by mere proximity, with such a dreadful occurrence. Tom wondered whether they yet suspected that their guest had been murdered. But someone must. No matter who had discovered the body, the innkeeper would have gone up to check matters out; must have seen as much as Tom of the wet floor, the staring eyes, the disturbed bandage, the dark oil round the ear.

'I have a question or two,' he said. 'First for whoever discovered the body and then for whoever summoned myself, Apothecary Gerard and the authorities.'

The men and women crowding round the fire looked nervously at one another. No-one spoke but no-one needed to. A pale young parlourmaid was seated on a three-legged stool clutching a tiny glass of amber liquid that looked like French brandywine, recovering from the shock of her discovery no doubt. And two strong boys on the cusp of manhood were glowering as they dripped onto the floor beside her and steamed in the heat of the fire. They were all looking at the barrel-bellied tavern keeper, whose normally cheery countenance wore a thoughtful frown as he calculated the odds between open honesty and a more careful version of events. No doubt balancing the possibility of profit on the one hand against that of prison on the other, thought Tom. So no-one said a word in the mean-time.

'Remember,' said Tom, 'I am the Master of Logic not the Pursuivant Marshal. You cannot do any damage to yourselves by being open with me. And, at the very least you can test your stories in preparation for Sir Thomas Gerard's arrival amongst you. Which is imminent.' He glanced meaningfully upward to the ceiling that was echoing to the footsteps on the floor immediately above.

A point well made to himself as well as to them, thought Tom, who was all too vividly aware that he needed to question the staff of the Golden Lion as swiftly as possible, for Sir Thomas had warned him off in no uncertain terms and if Tom and John were still examining the people who had first found the body when the Knight Marshal and his men came back downstairs, then he and the apothecary would almost certainly see the interior of the Marshalsea prison whether they wanted to or not.

v

'Let us start with last night,' prompted Tom. 'Did anyone see or hear anything untoward last night?'

The tavern keeper gave a bark of humourless laughter. 'Think, Master Musgrave. The Lion is a popular tavern, full and frantic even on a midsummer's night, as well you know, for you have supped here often enough. On winter evenings such as last night, all wet and freezing, you'd be hard-put to pack an extra body into the place! No sir. Master Spenser came in - after attending West Minster, seated in a draughty corridor awaiting the attention of the Council all day, he said. Having come via Holborn where he collected medicines from Master Gerard there and had the bandage on his bad ear changed. He sat close by the fire as his cloak and clothing dried. He supped his ale...'

'As he should not have done,' interrupted John. 'I warned him strictly against mixing strong liquor with the medicines my apprentice prepared for him. It was nothing as weak as small beer I suppose?'

'No sir. Not the best - that was too expensive he said - but a good strong Kentish ale for all that. Then he broke his bread so to speak - taking a lusty piece of a good fish pie. Once he was full-bellied, dry and warm he went aloft - because the noise in the parlour made his ear hurt and his head ache as he said. And that was the long and the short of it. No further interruptions. No sinister strangers. No new faces to be seen at all in fact. And as to hearing unusual sounds - why the Earl of Essex could have led his Irish army up the stairs and we'd never have heard a footstep or been any the wiser.'

'Very well,' said Tom. 'This morning then. Margery, is it?'

Margery the parlourmaid looked up from her empty glass. The brandywine had restored her colour and her confidence. 'I went up to awaken him at dawn as is my duty, sir. I took him a fresh-baked manchet loaf and some butter, a glass of milk and some water. I put them on the table in his little parlour and knocked on his chamber door. He had been sleeping so soundly of late because the herbs Master Gerard prescribes him to soothe the pain in his poor wounded ear and help him rest seem to put him in the deepest swoon.'

'Especially if washed down with strong ale,' added John grimly. 'Much of which seems to have come out again sometime in the night.'

Margery glanced at him, her eyes wide, then she resumed her story. 'I often have to shake him by the shoulder to awaken him. But this morning I found him stiff and cold when I did so.'

'What did you do then, Margery?' asked Tom gently.

'Why I came out again, took up the bread and milk and brought them back to the parlour here. Mistress Murrel was about and I told her what I had found and she went to tell Master Murrel.' The fat tavern keeper and his lean wife both nodded agreement with Margery's story.'

'Then she swooned dead away on the floor,' added master Murrel weightily. 'As though clubbed.'

'A sudden shock will do that,' observed John. 'I have seen it happen. Especially in young women of a nervous and hysterical nature.'

'And you took over matters then, Master Murrel?' asked Tom.

*

Murrel glanced at his wife. 'I did, sir. That I did.'

'By visiting the room yourself?'

'Just so, Master Musgrave.'

'And you observed…'

'Well, neither the outer door nor the bed-chamber door was properly closed - and Margery insists that she left them just as she found them. So Master Spencer either left them open last night or whoever entered his rooms left them open when they left. Though in truth, neither door has a lock.'

'The outer door at the foot of the stair leading from King Street up to Master Spencer's rooms was unlocked when I arrived this morning,' said Tom. 'Had you unlocked it?'

'No, Master Musgrave. As far as I know, no-one in the Lion came or went through that door at all. But you are right. It was unlocked though fast-closed when I checked it after examining the body.'

'So Master Spenser must have failed to secure it when he came home last night.'

'He often does, sir, and has done so more often since the hurt to his ear and the medicines he took.'

'I see. Well, proceed.'

'There was wetness on the floor both of the parlour and the bedroom which Margery again swears did not come from either the milk or the water she had carried. And there was wetness also on the stairs leading up from the street door. It was that convinced me someone must have come up into the room, for although Master Spencer was wet enough when he first arrived in the Lion last night, he was warm and dry when he went to bed. And, from the state of him I'm certain he could not have crept out into the storm then back again himself. Not that he had any reason to do so that I can conceive of. I saw the body just as it was and took the liberty of shaking it quite hard - with no effect of course - except that I moved the bandage that had been lying on the pillow a little further from master Spencer's head…'

'Margery, did you shake Master Spenser firmly enough to move the bandage? To uncover Master Spencer's wounded ear perhaps?'

'No, sir. The bandage was on the pillow.'

'Very well. And you, Master Murrel, reacted very properly by looking over the situation then sending Romulus and Remus here out to summon the authorities.' Tom nodded towards the two glowering boys.

'Well…' Murrel frowned in confusion.

'Their names are Nathaniel and Nicholas,' said his wife, glancing at the two dripping youngsters as Murrel floundered, failing to understand Tom's classical allusion. 'And yes, he sent them out, Nate to yourself, sir, as being the poor man's closest acquaintance, via Holborn not ten minutes from your door to alert Master Gerard who gave Master Spenser the medicines that he took last night. Then you sent him on to Bishopsgate to summon Master Shakespeare in turn. The other lad, Nic, went to alert the constable but by Nic's own account he was sent on further with one of the constable's men to Essex House and the

Earl Marshal, which explains why Nate and Master Shakespeare arrived before Sir Thomas and his men.

'Is that so, Nic?' Tom looked at the youth who was shifting from foot to foot, none too happy at being the subject of discussion.

'Aye,' he answered gracelessly. 'But as soon as I said who the dead man was, the constable ordered I should go straight and report to the Earl Marshal as the matter likely involved some Catholic plot him being the Sherriff of Cork and such. And besides the Master Spenser had been an associate and sometime pensioner of the Earl of Essex'.'

'And the Earl Marshal summoned the Knight Marshal having sent you back. Tell me, did you speak with the earl himself?'

'No! As you might expect the constable's man and I were kept hanging about in a little room after they finally deigned to admit us to Essex House. Kept us waiting for well over an hour I should judge but offered neither food, drink nor welcome of any sort. Eventually I spoke not with the earl but with two other men. A large man as looked like a soldier and had precious little patience and a slighter, slimmer man dressed in black with dark hair swept back and a pointed beard.'

'Sir Gelly Meyrick and Sir Francis Bacon as like as not; young Francis the lawyer rather than his elder brother Sir Antony the sickly secretary and spymaster,' mused Tom. 'Essex' right-hand man and one half of his chief intelligencer - at least the one Bacon brother who can get out of bed, up and about…'

But even as he entertained the thought, the footsteps on the stairs outside warned him that his interrogation was at an end.

vi

Tom and John stood in the shadowy doorway of Master Christie's book-shop opposite the Golden Lion. The rain had eased as noon passed and the storm wind lightened so that they had no need to shelter from the elements. They lingered there, sharp-eyed, to observe what the Knight Marshal, his astrologer-apothecary, the starving poet and their men were up to.

Sir Thomas was in the parlour with a couple of strapping assistants, no doubt wringing out of the men and women there much the same story as Tom already knew. Simon Forman was clearly in charge of the corpse, however, though George Chapman was busily making himself useful. No sooner had Tom and John taken up residence in the doorway and Sir Thomas vanished into the tavern than one of his men appeared, mounted up and galloped away eastward towards the City. Now, as Forman led a little cortege out onto the street carrying a sheet-wrapped bundle about the size of a slight man's body, the horseman reappeared with a carriage close behind. Giving a furtive glance up and down King Street - which apparently failed to notice the two witnesses opposite - Forman gestured to his men. The carriage door swung open, revealing the shield with its broad band and three red circles which formed the arms of the Earl of Essex. The corpse was loaded into the carriage. Foreman followed it. Chapman followed Foreman. The telltale door slammed but over the sharp sound, Tom heard Forman order 'Essex House!' The driver obediently whipped up his horses, executed a tight turn and rattled away back towards The Strand and Essex House.

Tom and John lingered until Sir Thomas and the rest of his men emerged, mounted up and trotted away.

'Is there more you wish to ask Master Murrel and the folk at the Golden Lion?' asked John.

Tom shook his head. 'No. My next task is to examine Hal your apprentice and see can we discover more about this hooded, muffled and all-but faceless stranger who bought such suspicious amounts of questionably legal poisons and who called himself Will Shakespeare.'

John's premises in Holborn were a half-hour walk from King Street. As they followed the road towards Charing Cross, the weather moderated further. By the time they were hurrying along Cockspur Street past St Martin's Field towards Shaftesbury Avenue which took them in turn above Long Acre and into St Giles, the sun was shining pallidly through the skirts of the departing storm.

St Giles led them past the right-turn into Drury Lane with Southampton House on their left. Tom looked across the private grounds to where the great mansion stood bathed in strengthening brightness. Will Shakespeare had been intimate with those chambers and corridors, he thought, not so long ago when Henry Wriothesely the third Earl of Southampton was supporting his rise to poetic notoriety, much as George Chapman was currently hoping that Essex would do for him. Southampton was the dedicatee of Will's poems *Venus and Adonis* and *The Rape of Lucrece* - and the subject, it was suspected, of some of his more extravagant love sonnets: perhaps, therefore, Will's lover. Whatever the truth of that, Southampton was certainly Essex' closest friend and supporter. This mysterious element in the playwright's history stopped Tom from ever trusting him absolutely, no-matter how amicable they were, irrespective of what deadly matter they were facing.

*

St Giles led Tom and John into High Holborn and soon after that they reached John Gerard's house. To be fair, thought Tom, it was more than a simple house. He knew it well for he had visited before, making use of the herbalist's knowledge in more than one case of death like that suffered by poor Edmund Spenser. There were simple living quarters upstairs and a kitchen downstairs in which meals could be taken. But that deceptive room could be used for much more than heating and eating, for apart from this one relatively usual chamber, the lower floor was split into the shop at the front where herbal remedies of all sorts were dispensed and sold while behind the shop stood the areas in which the herbs were dried, crushed, boiled, distilled and concocted into the pills, powders, oils and unguents that might be purchased in the shop.

The kitchen, therefore doubled as a *laboratorium* and manufactory. Its rear door opened into one of the most extensive herb gardens in England where, behind the brick hovel containing the privy, row upon row of plants stood, all carefully and individually labeled; and behind them, bed after bed of shrubs and saplings all equally precisely named culled by the herbalist, his friends and contacts from as far afield as India and the New World so recently explored by Raleigh in search of El Dorado. The thick hawthorn hedge at the rear opening through a gate into Red Lion Fields and, a few yards further north, the red-walled buildings of Grays Inn.

This Inn was not a hostelry or tavern of any kind but the most powerful of the four Inns of Court where, since the reign of Edward III, the brightest and best graduates of Oxford and Cambridge, sons of the most powerful men in the land like William Cecil and Nicholas Bacon studied for the law and, like Anthony and Francis Bacon, prepared themselves to stand for parliament and take the reins of political power in their turn.

Side by side Tom and John walked up to John's house. The door was, as usual, unlocked; they were entering a shop after all. The chamber that greeted them seemed tidy enough - the shelves behind the counter well-stocked with a range of packages, boxes, and jars all containing dried herbs, powders, pills and liquids of various colours and consistencies. Tom saw nothing amiss except that the apprentice he had come to question was absent.

'Hal?' called John, crossing to the counter and raising a section of it, leading Tom through into the back of the shop where his chemical equipment stood and the section of the kitchen where the concoctions were made and tested. '*Hal*!'

The immediate answer came from several children who came thundering downstairs and into the room, followed by a harassed looking woman who Tom recognized as their mother. 'Mistress Ann,' he greeted her with a bow. He knew her and the children slightly - the children ranging from a babe in arms, through four or five growing youngsters to Elizabeth who was nigh on eighteen now, and for once not here to help her mother with the youngsters nor to help Hal with the shop.

'Master Musgrave,' Ann Gerard curtseyed as best she could with a somnolent baby swaddled in her arms.

'Ann, my dear, where is Hal?' asked the apothecary gently as his younger children gathered round him - those nearer Elizabeth's age out at school, thought Tom; the boys at least..

'He's gone out about some business,' Ann answered. 'Left soon after you were summoned.'

'I gave him no commission,' frowned John. 'Did he say where he was going?'

'To Billingsgate, I believe.'

'Billingsgate! Do we need fish?'

'No. He went on no errand of mine, husband.'

'Well enough. But Billingsgate - you're sure?' he continued to speak as she nodded. 'What is there at Billingsgate?'

'More than fish, certainly,' said Tom.

'What more?' demanded John, his face an almost grotesque mask of confusion.

But even as Tom drew breath to answer, a great peal of bells rang out from St Andrews in Holborn which stood just across the road and, behind it, peal after peal from the bell-tower of every church in the City, carried northwards on a southerly breeze.

'What in God's name...' said John, swinging round to look towards the city, overwhelmed by the cacophony of ill-tuned campanology.

Tom's eyes were closed, counting the chimes of St Andrews' peal. 'Nine tailors,' he said at last. 'Nine tailors and forty-six chimes. The bells are being rung for the death of a man aged forty-six - and someone important at that to set every bell in London jangling.'

He paused for a heartbeat, meeting John's confused gaze. 'They're sounding Edmund Spenser's death knell,' he explained.

.

Chapter 2: The Arcane Astrologer

'Simon Forman lives in Billingsgate,' said Tom.

'He does. But what of it?' John's eyes slid away from Tom's direct gaze.

'It seems a strange coincidence to me that the apprentice of one apothecary should visit - for no apparent reason - the place where a rival apothecary lives. It's as though George Chapman should suddenly frequent Will Shakespeare's new lodgings in Southwark.'

'But why would Hal go there? What reason would he have? He is my apprentice not Forman's.' *Was John protesting too much*? Tom wondered, unused to the blustering tone in his old friend's voice.

'Is he ambitious, perhaps?' he probed.

'He works only for me,' insisted John. 'I pay what I can though I am not obliged to do so and I am training him in my craft. But yes, he is young, ambitious, impatient.'

'Is he bound to you by articles like a normal apprentice?' asked Tom.

'He is and has been for a number of years, though he is coming to the end of the term. He has much to be taught but he has also learned a lot. I let him weigh, prepare and pack the medicines I prescribe. When I am absent, he is in charge of the shop - notionally under Ann's eye. Or under Elizabeth's if Ann is otherwise occupied. I furnish him with bed and board but I am happy to let him come and go a little more now he is a grown lad. He has always been reliable.'

'"Under Elizabeth's eye,"' echoed Tom. 'And has he eyes for your Elizabeth? Such things are not unknown.'

'He does not - and no matter if he did, for she has set her sights far above young apprentices. Her head has been turned by some of my more aristocratic clients…'

'And she might well look higher than Hal,' observed Tom, 'for she is a pretty young woman.'

John nodded proudly, mollified by Tom's calculated compliment.

'So young Hal "comes and goes",' mused Tom. 'Where does he *go* to?'

'Never to Simon Forman,' said John, his voice ringing with shock. Perhaps too much shock. Unlike Will Shakespeare, thought Tom, John was no actor.

Both men were speaking with raised voices in spite of the fact that they were in John's private chambers above the shop. They talked not only over the sound of the bells but over the remains of a light lunch which they had consumed as they spoke, with Ann and the children in the kitchen below. The steady rhythm of the chiming bells seemed to penetrate the walls as easily as it came through the shivering windows.

'I'm certain sure,' insisted John.

Unconsciously he ran a nervous finger along one wing of his moustache, brushing away a crumb of cheese. Tom's old friend was wearing the same sweeping moustaches and pointed beard as Drake, Hawkins, Raleigh - and Sir Thomas his namesake - emphasizing a similarity in their faces as well as their names - though John Gerard's beard and moustaches were growing silver now. Whereas Tom's, also cut in the same swashbuckling style, were coloured a virile red-blond, several shades darker than his flaxen hair.

*

'He has gone off like this once or twice recently,' the apothecary admitted, sounding a good deal more truthful but suddenly looking his age, which Tom calculated to be rising fifty five. Twenty years more than Will, twenty five years more than Tom himself. Ten years more than poor Spenser had achieved in the end. 'I had thought perhaps there was a sweetheart - I do not give him enough to afford beer or wenches.'

Tom nodded, waiting for John to add more thoughts. Being careful not to repeat his assertion nor the reasons for it which seemed so plain and indisputable to him - Hal was somehow entangled with Forman, probably recently so - conceivably only immediately so - perhaps even at John's instigation. But what could be so vital that it spurred John to send an apprentice to his greatest rival and then lie about it to one of his closest

22

associates? Yet Tom felt certain that, whatever the case, John knew more than he was saying; more than he had so far let slip.

Tom liked John Gerard and found him too useful an ally to risk alienating him. Especially as the pair of them needed to try and work out precisely what had been poured into Edmund Spencer's ear and where it had come from - samples of which now lay in John's work-room awaiting their attention once the more pressing matter of the missing apprentice had been settled. After all, the poisoning was done - its origins, type and effects appeared to be of less importance than the possibility that the apprentice was under arrest and explaining to the Knight Marshal, the Pursuivant Marshal or their henchmen that a heavily cloaked and muffled customer calling himself Will Shakespeare had purchased suspicious amounts of various poisons on the night the poet died.

Tom sat back, his eyes hooded with speculation, his mind racing; his memory of Forman and Chapman loading Spenser's corpse into the Earl of Essex' private carriage vivid. Chance, coincidence - or something more sinister it seemed - tied these two apothecaries together through the seemingly reliable but suddenly absent Hal. Who, now Tom thought of it, had prepared the medicines that had put Spenser into such a deep sleep - whether or not assisted by good Kentish ale - while his master tied the bandage over the poet's ear more than eighteen hours ago. Whose evidence was all that implicated Will Shakespeare in a situation that was rapidly gaining artistic, social and political importance: the City's bells did not knell for every dead ruffler, roaring boy or beggar.

'Ah, I see,' he purred at last. 'Young Hal could become a potent secret agent, collecting information from Foreman that might be of use to you. Like the intelligencer Robert Poley pretending to be imprisoned in the Clink, the Marshalsea or Newgate jail, listening for sedition and treason amongst the genuine inmates there and bringing his information home to The Council. And Foreman does not mind this canker in his bosom? Or does he not suspect?'

'NO!' John Gerard sat up straight, outraged. 'I have no need of anything that charlatan says he has discovered! No, he's worse than a charlatan, he's a… He's a…'

'No matter *what* he is, I know well enough *where* he is for the time-being at least,' said Tom, rising and glad to be in action once again. 'I'm for Billingsgate to search Forman's premises in the hope he still lingers at Essex House, just in case Hal has looked for something we cannot yet guess at down there. One way or another, it is young Hal I need to question first and soonest.'

'If you go in search of Hal then I will come with you,' decided John, all uncertainty and hesitation vanishing. He rose and crossed to a cupboard near the reverberating window, opened it and pulled out the trappings he would need to hang a sword at his hip.

ii

Holborn curved southwards as it ran east and less than ten minutes after leaving John's premises the pair of them were pushing through the bustle at the New Gate in London's wall, and elbowing past the prison of that name, paying scant attention to the calls of bankrupt prisoners begging through the gratings at their feet. One of whom at any time might be the impecunious George Chapman, mused Tom, always assuming he did not end up at the Marshalsea instead.

As they approached the precinct of St Paul's, however, Tom turned abruptly southwards into Blackfriars. 'I was called betimes this morning,' he bellowed in explanation, 'summoned with some urgency as you may imagine and so I came out naked, as you did.' He struck his left hip where his rapier normally hung. John had armed himself with an old-fashioned short sword, the preferred weapon of an older generation which matched his outmoded clothing with its bright russet doublet tight against chest; its small ruff above with short breeches below, puffed out above long tights. The colour and style those of ten years ago when tobacco and its particular autumnal shade were all the rage. His outfit was in striking contrast to Tom's fashionable boat-bellied doublet with its slashed sleeves through which silk puffed, galligaskins that reached to the knee almost meeting the Spanish leather boots, all in the expensively modish black.

Within a few minutes they were at the shop owned by the Haberdasher Robert Aske and Tom bounded up the stairs beside it, through the door that led into his own dwelling, school-room and fencing *piste* above the merchant's shop as John laboured up behind him. While Tom was strapping on his favorite rapier, his friend and assistant the Dutch gunsmith Ugo Stell came out of his workshop. 'They say the bells are for Edmund Spenser,' said the Dutchman. 'Is it true?'

'It is. I was called to see the body and summoned John here in turn.'

'Jesu! How did he die?'

'We calculate by poison poured into his ear. It has given Will Shakespeare nightmares and will no doubt turn up in one of his plays. Beyond that, we are hunting for facts.'

'And where is Spenser now?' asked Ugo.

'Simon Forman has him at Essex House. He's assisting the Knight Marshal in post mortem matters.'

'Forman! And at Essex House? Is that where you're going?'

'No. We're going to Forman's premises in Billingsgate. There's something mysterious going on - besides the fact that Spencer has likely been murdered. We might find some answers down there.'

The phlegmatic Dutchman blinked as the news that Spencer had probably been murdered hit him fully. He had known the politician and poet almost as well as Tom. Then, ever practical, he said, 'Murdered was he, with poisons dropped in his ear? If there's murder afoot then maybe I'd better come with you. Wait a moment and I'll get a brace of my new snaphaunce pistols.'

*

The quickest way the three men could take on foot would lead them eastwards from Blackfriars along Carter Lane and Knightrider Street into Old Fish Street then via Cloak Lane down College Hill into Thames Street which ran parallel to the River right across the city until Thames Street crossed New Fish Street which led down to London Bridge, then pushed further on until it turned right into the wide opening of the Romeland coal market and the public well standing beside it and so down to Billingsgate itself.

They had little enough to discuss as they set out along this route, each one prey to his own thoughts. Besides, they were armed to the limit of the law - with Ugo's pistols almost certainly illegal in public - so their main focus was in keeping their cloaks tight about their waists. Tom tried to converse at first though, for he could not see what young Hal hoped to learn from Simon Forman that he could not learn better and deeper from John. He bellowed his question and could have worked out what the answer would be before John's loud reply.

'Astrology. Foreman is a great one for seeing the future in the stars. He says it gives him almost magical power. Power he seems to use in the seduction of every woman with pleasing looks who comes to him for a potion or a prediction. The gossip goes that he practices other, darker arts. Though he keeps close company with such men as Essex, and even with the Queen, so there is never any talk of blasphemy or witchcraft. Merchants flock to him for assurances as to the safety of their argosies, soldiers - such as Essex himself - for the result of their proposed campaigns, bankers for the reliability of their investments, lovers for the outcomes of their affairs - and the potions and philtres that make such outcomes certain; youths and lasses for astrological information about whether they are beloved and by whom...'

'I can see how such power might appeal to an ambitious lad,' added Ugo. 'And the promise of the elevated company - the circle of his rich and influential clients and acquaintance must almost equal yours.'

'An ambitious and a lusty one,' added Tom. 'Is your Hal inclined to the sins of the flesh, John?'

'He is young and full of fiery humors,' answered John. 'His hand is forever in his codpiece when he thinks I am not looking.'

'Unlimited power over women,' said Ugo. 'That would indeed be a great temptation and a powerful motivator to a youth who believed in it.'

'And the very thought of it enough to coax a lad into mastrupation,' nodded John sadly.

'Yet you have kept your Elizabeth safe from all this fiery lust?' wondered Tom.

The question was enough to stop the conversation, which would have been difficult to pursue much further in any case, as the nine tailors continued to toll in every church they passed - and they passed a lot, for there were more than a hundred in the City. The noise of Spencer's passing-bells was enough to ensure that the crowds of citizens they moved through, who did need to talk to each-other, did so with voices raised to a shout. And then of course the speakers found they needed to shout louder still to overcome the combined cacophony of bells and bellowed conversations.

The crush and the noise grew worse still as the followed Thames Street across New Fish Street with the church of St Magnus on the corner where the cross road ran southward onto London Bridge and away across the South Wark onto the South Bank. But at last the three of them passed St Mary's At Hill and came down past the Romeland coal market and the public well into Billingsgate where Simon Foreman lived and did his business.

iii

There was a deep-water channel reaching up into the north bank of the Thames at Billingsgate, the first downriver of the Bridge and therefore the first available to tall ships too impatient to wait for the draw-bridge to be raised. It was broad enough to allow ocean-going vessels to tie up and unload their cargoes which usually consisted of fish. On the downriver side of this the Billingsgate pier stretched out into the River with the steps on the far edge of it where the wherries nestled. Boats and the occasional ship lay round its farthest reaches but the afternoon was wearing on so the fish-market was all but done for the day. Beyond the pier-end away to Tom's right London Bridge stepped massively over the Thames with the steeple of St Mary Overie standing on the South Bank beyond it. The wind backed, bringing the roar of the water-wheel and the rush of the falling tide between the starlings to mingle with the clangour of the bells - and an eye-watering stench of fish.

Tom turned his back on the scene as well as the stink and looked up the hill. The houses here were tightly packed but he knew the one he was looking for. Cheek by jowl with its neighbors, nevertheless it contrived to stand alone. Something emphasized by the fact that the buildings to the south of it were little more than hovels hardly one full storey tall. Narrow alleys ran up either side of it leading, Tom knew, to Forman's smaller version of John's herb garden. Like John's, the rooms nearest the street were a shop front with - no doubt - the kitchen and the *laboritorium* or preparation area behind. But what lay above? John's house on Holborn was two storeys high but reached further back, allowing room for the Gerard family. Forman's was maybe three rooms deep but had tell-tale garret windows in the roof suggesting some kind of accommodation on the third storey as well. Hardly enough for the man, his wife and family though. Not, as far as Tom knew, that Foreman had either. Moreover, it all looked closed and shuttered. Dark, even on a bright winter's afternoon, and the place seemed to give off a chill that rivaled the coldest night of the season so far.

'Should we try the shop door?' wondered John, looking towards the front of the house hard up against Billingsgate Street with broad windows beside the solid-looking front door and even broader ones on the floor above.

'I think so - just to discover whether the shop is open and the house full of customers and servants,' answered Tom, 'or whether Forman has yet returned from Essex House. Then we will move into the side alley and proceed with caution. We want this visit to go unremarked as far as possible. Does Forman have any apprentices?'

'I don't think so,' John shook his head. 'He likes to pursue his studies and so-forth in private.'

'So *forth* meaning potions, spells, predictions and seductions…' growled Ugo.

'If reputation speaks true,' nodded Tom.

'Best go in by the rear then,' said John.

'Something else he likes to do by all accounts,' added Ugo.

The shop was closed, the front door locked and a moment or two of hammering on it proved that the whole establishment was almost certainly deserted. The three of them vanished into the alley on the southern side of the house, trying to look as inconspicuous as possible. Tom led them forward through the unexpectedly dark shadows, his eyes everywhere, his breath clouding on the air.

*

The wall of Forman's house was sheer above their left shoulders with windows marking the ground floor and the upper floor before the overhang of the roof with its garrets. The ground floor windows were high in the wall and tiny - for all that they faced southward, seeking to gather whatever light was coming across the reach of the River. Those on the upper floor were wider, probably affording a view of the river-docks as well as letting in a good deal of brightness. The front of the place showed its broad, mullioned facade to the west across Billingsgate Street seeking the sun in the afternoon and evening.

Immediately beyond the side wall of the house, ancient brickwork continued, defining the edge of a long garden. The garden wall was twelve feet high, perhaps more - there was no way over it without a ladder, decided Tom regretfully dismissing the idea that he could stand on Ugo's shoulders and reach up. The top of the brickwork, outlined against the pale sky was a mantrap of broken glass and sharp-edged rusty metal.

The back gate was almost as formidable as the walls, which was logical, thought Tom, and it boasted an ancient but effective lock. But he had foreseen this eventuality. While Ugo was collecting his pistols, Tom had been slipping another highly specialized set of instruments into his pouch. He had heard quite a lot about Forman's fascination with the Black Arts, he mused with wry amusement. Now it was time to practice some of his own. He had learned the black art of picking locks under the tutelage of a master, Nic o'Darkmans, one of the foremost *charms* in Romeville as the thieves' fraternity called London, *charm* being the thieves' cant term for a lock-picker and *black art* what they called his particular skill. The gate yielded as easily as a Southwark virgin and creaked open to reveal a regimented herb garden as carefully laid out and labeled as John's own. Tom led the little troupe along the central path, pausing only to ensure Ugo had closed the gate behind them.

iii

As with the path in John's garden, Forman's led directly to his back door past a solid, brick-walled privy - the nightsoil it contained far too useful a fertilizer simply to be dumped into the street from a chamberpot. Tom would have pushed on with their mission rapidly, but John was too easily distracted by what he saw around him.

'Look!' said the apothecary, his voice urgent enough to stop Tom and make him turn. 'Look at this hemlock!' Tom did as the herbalist suggested. The plant was about a foot tall, the first of a line of identical herbs, all ringed with straw against the winter chill, most looking bedraggled, near frozen but still alive. The nearest seemed the strongest - what was left of it. Tall stems of vivid green spotted with purple marks that reminded Tom unsettlingly of the rash which accompanied the plague. Its flowers and leaves were all gone.

'It has been stripped to the branch,' continued John. 'And see, the state of the plant makes it plain that this was done some time ago! I had been wondering...'

'Wondering how it is that the hemlock in your garden, apparently culled last night for the stranger Hal says called himself Will Shakespeare, could have been used in Spencer's murder. Because the concoction poured into his ear, whether or not mixed with belladonna, must have taken the better part of a week to extract, distil and concentrate. Yes, I have been wondering that too and was hoping to discuss it when we examined the oil from Spenser's ear more closely. But I doubt that the Knight Marshal will worry too much about such subtleties before he hands Will over to Torturer Topcliffe in the Tower.'

This was as far as the conversation got, because as Tom turned back, Ugo stepped past him and tip-toed on down the path past a new brick privy to the back door. 'Tom,' called the usually placid Dutchman. There was a strange note in his voice Tom could not remember having heard before. It was sufficiently unusual to make him turn away from the privy and hurry to his friend's side.

'What?'

'Here.' Ugo pointed with the long barrel of his right-hand pistol.

The door had been secured by another lock - not a particularly reliable one by the look of things; certainly not in Tom's experience, nor in Forman's, apparently, especially as the upper section of the door had several panes of glass in it. Moreover, Tom's first touch revealed that it had been broken - just as that first touch on Spenser's shoulder had confirmed that he was dead. But the magician had overcome the weakness of the lock and the fragility of the door. He had done this by clearly understanding how superstitious the London brotherhood of thieves and felons actually was.

*

Nailed on the inside so that its long-dead, mummified face screamed out at anyone trying to enter, hung the corpse of a cat crucified against the wooden frame. Its hollow eye-sockets seemed to stare at each man individually, the ears above them disturbingly like demonic horns. The black lips shriveled back from white, needle-sharp teeth. An equally black tongue stood a little higher than the gape of the lower jaw. Above it, a piece of parchment had been pinned in place for all to see - and for those who could read to read:

'*Best leave this place inviolate*
Or the beast that watches here
Will hunt thee straight.'

The three would-be burglars exchanged a lingering look, each one seeking to discern whether his companions were convinced or moved by the supernatural threat. '*The beast that watches*,' said Tom after a moment. 'That's a good one. You think George Chapman penned it? Forman is no poet as far as I know.'

And he pushed the door inwards, doing a little more damage to the broken lock.

The unsettling curse and the crucified cat were only the start of things. The door swung inwards at his first push. As it did so, its hinges gave the scream the mummified cat was no longer capable of giving. Ugo had cocked his pistols and John pulled his sword half out of its scabbard before they were fully in the kitchen and even Tom felt his hair stir at the ghastly sound. But they swung the door closed behind them and crept on. The room was warm - a low fire smoldered in a wide grate, heating an oven beside it.

Forman was apparently not a tidy worker but he had a lively enough sense of self-preservation to keep his foodstuffs and his poisons well separated. Even so, there were herbs of all sorts everywhere, hanging drying from the ceiling or piled on work surfaces waiting to be bound in bundles and suspended. 'It's a wonder the place isn't alive with rats,' whispered Ugo, gesturing at a pile of succulent flowers.

'It is,' said John grimly. 'Well, perhaps not *alive...*' he used the blade of his short sword to move the stems aside. There were several dead rats and mice lying beneath them. He prodded one with the point of his blade. It was as stiff as Spenser had been.

'Do you think,' mused Tom, 'that the cat on the door died because it ate a rat that had just consumed one of Forman's potions?'

'Who knows?' shrugged Ugo. 'It could have been alive when it was nailed there for all we know.'

'No,' whispered John. 'Surely it would have made too much noise as it died...'

'Unlikely,' said Tom. 'The thing has been long dead, mayhap centuries dead. I saw such things in Italy. Wonders discovered in Egypt, preserved in tombs of sand and gigantic tombs called *pyramides.*' As he spoke, Tom swung open the inner door and unleashed a series of screams and howls that would have drowned any sounds the dying cat could have made.

iv

They all froze. Then, as the shrieks died back and nothing further happened, Tom stepped through into the hallway still echoing with the demonic noises, breathing through his mouth as he gasped with shock. A moment later he stepped back into the kitchen. 'It's alright,' he said. 'There are some birds in a cage here. Giving notice of our invasion like the sacred geese warning the ancient Romans about the Gauls secretly invading their city.'

'Oh very literary!' snarled Ugo. 'And is there a record of how many Romans died of fright at the noise?'

'Or Gauls come to that!' added John.

'Well,' said Tom, 'at least we can be fairly certain there's no-one in the house or they would have reacted to such a commotion!'

'Unless they're setting traps or ambuscades,' countered John nervously. 'But if Hal was here, surely he would have heard such an uproar as well and be seeking whoever caused it - or calling out at least…'

'Always supposing,' said Tom grimly, 'that he is any condition to call out or come seeking in the first place.'

The screaming birds settled, croaking and muttering as the intruders whispered together immediately below their cage. When silence returned, Tom pushed forward once more as his breathing settled and his heart rate fell back towards its normal steady pulse. He reckoned that the crucified cat was only the first ambush. The birds as much another trap as very efficient watch-keepers, for they were likely to frighten anyone entering uninvited as well as warning the household. And a frightened man is much less likely to act calmly, quickly and sensibly in a crisis or a confrontation.

But he feared as much for his immortal soul as for his mortal body. The mummified creature and the curse clearly relied for their effect on superstition and magic. Yet the strange birds flapping and screaming in their cage suggested a breadth of approaches to the house's security; but not necessarily a wide one. The demonic birds were of a breed he had never seen before. They looked like black falcons but their brutally clawed red feet and markings at the base of their hooked bills were completely new to him. He would not be surprised to find that they were not native to England or even Europe - perhaps not to the mortal world. He half expected to discover some sort of satanic leopard or demonic hell-hound companion to them shut in one of the rooms waiting silently to attack body and soul.

As Tom entertained these misgivings, he crept forward along a short dark corridor. On his right, a flight of stairs mounted to the next storey. On his left the first of two doors was closed but, as he discovered, not locked. He opened it carefully, allowing a slit of no more than an inch, still half convinced some monstrous demonic creature might be waiting in there. But no. A narrow window high in the south-facing wall illuminated what was clearly a *laboratorium* as the Latin had it - the word laboratory only just beginning to come into English. He pushed the door wider, revealing benches on three sides of the room laden with vessels of all sorts - glass beakers, conical flasks, boiling flasks, retorts for distillation, wax candles for heating and boiling rather than illuminating, clay crucibles for collecting and containing, marble mortars and pestles for grinding; metallic equipment that at first looked like bullet moulds which he soon realized was for making pills. The stink of the place was even worse than that of Billingsgate wharf.

*

Above the benches stood more racks of glass vessels full of multicoloured liquids, all labeled. John, his sword sheathed once more, pushed past him and walked into the room as though entranced already. This was clearly the first time he had been in Forman's laboratory, and it looked to be at least the equal of his own. But there was one major difference. His wide eyes soaked up the rows of bottles with their labels. He turned towards Tom and Ugo at his shoulder. 'There are no medicines that I can see, only potions and poisons,' he said, his voice awed. He gestured at a retort half full of golden liquid, bubbling gently. 'Apart from this one where I judge, he's trying to distil gold out of urine, it's all potions and poisons.'

'Love and death,' growled Ugo. 'That's where the money is. And gold boiled out of piss of course.'

'There is some logic in that,' allowed John. 'Man is at the pinnacle of animal creation after all just as gold is at the pinnacle of mineral creation. The possibility that it could be gold that colours urine, therefore, has been an area of alchemical speculation for centuries…'

There was a door in the wall which led straight on through from this room to the shop, though that could also be accessed by the door from the passage beyond the foot of the stairs. The door between these two rooms, Tom noted, could be securely locked, though it stood open now. According to John after a swift examination, the more public emporium was stocked with less potent and lethal versions of what was stored in the laboratory. And no retorts half full of super-concentrated urine. The main door to the shop opened into this room, with windows on one side and a more social area on the other. This area was near a fireplace where yet another low-banked fire gave off welcome warmth. Forman clearly made good use of the Romeland coal market at the upper end of Billingsgate. The fireplace was surrounded by chairs and stools with a table where customers could wait to be served while the shop was open and where Forman and any guests could take their ease when it was closed. That, thought Tom, explained the lock on the inside of the door connecting the two rooms: Forman did not want nosey guests or casual shoppers coming through into the laboratory where he kept his more lethal and experimental wares unless they were invited.

The shop front, looking directly out into Billingsgate, was also bolted from the inside with bolts so strong that there was no need for extra curses to be added. The front door was locked but not bolted. Forman clearly had no worries about people breaking in that way thought Tom, for the whole of bustling Billingsgate would be watching them. Once John declared himself satisfied with the relative inoffensiveness of what was displayed in Forman's shop, he led them back out into the corridor and began to mount the stairs.

v

The disturbing atmosphere of the house seemed to gather around them as they climbed higher. Ugo had already primed and cocked his pistols. Now John pulled out his sword once more, the hiss as the weapon came out of its sheath and the bell-like ringing of the steel blade suddenly emphasizing the fact that Spencer's death knells had stopped. Silence gripped the place and the men within it like dark shadows. Abruptly Tom could hear his heartbeat hammering in his ears once more and it took all his self-control not to slide his rapier out of its sheath like John's short sword.

'I'm growing bored with this tip-toeing around,' said John suddenly and before Tom or Ugo could stop him, he bellowed at the top of his voice, '*HAL*!'

And very faintly, someone called, '*Help me…*'

The three of them froze in place. The cry was not repeated. 'Did that sound like Hal?' asked Tom.

'No. To be honest it sounded more like a woman,' answered John. 'It seemed to come from upstairs…'

'But it may even have come from outside in the street,' added Ugo.

'I can't be sure…' John concluded.

'It has all the marks of another trap,' warned Tom. 'When we proceed we must do so with absolute caution. If there is someone there it is unlikely that waiting an extra few moments while we ensure we are safe ourselves will make much difference to them. But if it is some kind of trap, then the only thing likely to protect us is caution.' The others nodded and gripped their weapons more tightly. Still disdaining even to touch his rapier's hilt, Tom led them onwards and upwards. Once they had all stepped off the top stair, Tom nodded at John and the apothecary called again, '*Hal*! Are you here?'

This time there was no reply.

Tom turned slowly, looking around, alert for trickery and danger. The landing they were standing on led back into a small chamber at the rear of the house and then turned, leading on to two larger rooms and turning yet again to climb to the next level. This upper staircase was a much narrower, apparently flimsier affair, giving access to the loft at the very top of the house; but not for the heavily built or the faint of heart. It was topped not by a landing but by yet another closed door designed to open immediately from the topmost step.

A glance into the small room at the back revealed nothing more than a basin and cloths for washing and drying; but the room was above the kitchen and would likely be warm when there was work being done downstairs. There was also a wide fireplace full of ashes and a wooden hip bath. A large *laver* vessel hung in the fireplace, waiting to be filled with water which the flames would eventually heat before it filled the bath for use. Baths were by no means usual in ordinary houses such as this and its presence here was almost sinister. But then, thought Tom, so was everything else about the place. They gave it a cursory inspection, however. The fire was out, the laver was dry and the bath was wet. A reddish scum line marked the upper limit that the water had reached last time the bath was used.

The next large room was a kind of library and study. Daylight coming through a wide south-facing window illuminated a large but littered desk so tall it could only be used by someone standing up, a fact emphasized by the absence of any chairs. Tom crossed to it and glanced at the papers. There were calculations of some sort - apparently to do with the orbits and conjunctions of celestial bodies. There were lists of strange half-familiar names. There was a slightly larger piece of paper which showed signs of having been folded in half and in half again. One corner of it was marked with deep red.

'John,' he called. 'Is any of this familiar to you?'

John came over and glanced at the arcane calculations. 'I believe it is a birth chart,' he said. 'Such as astrologers make in order to reflect a person's character, catalogue their strengths and weaknesses, advise as to their lucky and unlucky actions and relationships - ultimately to predict their future. This one seems to be for someone born under Virgo - between late August and late September, like my Elizabeth. Here is the sign, you see, like a letter M? It has been prepared for a young woman too, by the look of things, though there is no name. It seems to describe someone who is modest, hardworking and kind, yet desirous of making a match above her station in life - no doubt why she has come to Forman for advice. There's a deal more in it I daresay but it would take some time for me to interpret and I could by no means promise insight or accuracy.' He turned away but Tom lingered looking down, frowning. Date of birth September 4th - by the old calendar planned by Julius Caesar and Cleopatra's Greek mathematician Sosigenes of Alexandria rather than Pope Gregory's more recent revision. The date as it had been in the dark ages when such magics were being codified. The place of birth, London, and the time of birth…

'Well,' said Ugo. 'If Elizabeth's come to Forman for guidance, let us hope that she is still a *Virgo*, eh?'

The three of them moved away from the chart to look at other things. There was what appeared to be some sort of diary. Idly leafing through it, Tom found he was thoughtlessly looking for the names of young women, especially that of Elizabeth Gerard. But in any case, all the names and many personal details seemed to be in code. When he realized this, Tom closed the volume, put it aside and looked up, realizing that the sunlight also illuminated shelves full of other, older volumes. He could just make out the titles of some - which he had heard of but never seen before, let alone read. They exercised sufficient fascination to stop the search for a moment or two, even though there might be someone needing help in the next room or further upstairs.

*

'John, are any of these books familiar to you?' asked Tom.

'I know their titles but not their contents in any detail.' John sounded shocked; shaken. 'I practice botany not astrology, and certainly not the sort of magic contained in some these *grammaries*.'

'But they are familiar?' persisted Tom. 'In name at least?'

'I know John Dee had several of them in his library at Mortlake before it was vandalized. Such as *The Aldataia* here and *The Book of Soyga* which I understand particularly fascinated Dee and which he spent years studying. Apart from that and what remains of his library - which as far as I know is with him in Manchester now that he is Warden of Christ's College there - this is one of the most extensive occult libraries I have come across.'

'Some of these books may have come from John Dee's Mortlake house in any case,' mused Tom. 'Forman could have bought them from the thieves who wrecked his library.'

'Or indeed bought them from Dee himself,' said John 'I believe he sold some books off so he could afford to keep the rest.'

'*The Mithras Liturgy*,' Tom read. 'What is that?'

'A volume of papers in Greek and Latin originating in the worship of Mithra, a powerful Eastern god who the Romans assumed was derived from Persian Zoroastrian religions. It is by its very nature dangerously heretical. The teachings are similar to those followed by the Albigensians or Cathars in the South of France more than three centuries ago. They postulate that God as the embodiment of light and Satan as the embodiment of darkness are equal in power and locked in an eternal battle for control of the world and mankind.'

'I imagine that sort of thinking would get you into trouble with the Church pretty quickly. What happened to them?' asked Tom.

'Pope Innocent III called a crusade and wiped them out.'

'I see,' said Tom. 'What else is there?'

'A great deal,' answered John nervously, 'and most of it much, much more dangerous.'

Chapter 3: The Occult Chamber

i

'The *Corpus Hermeticum*, for instance,' supplied John. 'From the ancient Greek of Hermes Trismegistus. Again, utterly heretical - a catalogue of methods to gain power by moving beyond what is revealed in the Bible or allowed in the Commandments.'

'The *Arbatel de Magica Verum*, the arbatel of true magic - no more explanation needed,' continued Tom. 'The *Pseudomonarchia Daemonum* the royal rule of demons - I hardly dare touch it! *The Book of Aramelin the Mage*, *The Book of Secrets*, *The Key of Solomon*, *The Lesser Key or Lemegeton* - which lists the seventy-two most puissant devils and their powers - *Three Books of Occult Philosophy* by Heinrich Cornelius Agrippa, *The Picatrix or The Aim of the Wise...*'

'That is enough,' said John, his voice even more nervous than before. 'They are all dangerously heretical volumes detailing how to access ungodly power, many of them revealing how to summon and control Satan and his legions out of Hell, either individually or in any numbers. That last one, *The Picatrix* is one of the most powerful books ever written if it lives up to its reputation. Have you not seen Marlowe's play of *Faustus*? It would have been a book such as that which gave Faustus the knowledge how to raise the devil Mephistopheles; how to control such an awesome power and yet to stay safe from him. Some say the play is a guide as to how to do such things. There have actually been demons and devils seen at various performances, so the gossip goes.' He looked around the room which seemed icy in spite of the bright sunshine. 'Who knows what hell-born creatures may be close at hand simply because these volumes are collected all together here?' He shuddered.

'*The beast that watches*?' suggested Tom breezily, earning an icy glare from his superstitious friend. Though, to be fair, his tone belied the nervousness he felt being in the presence of so much demonic wickedness.

'And yet look here,' said Ugo seemingly unaware of the atmosphere brewing between the others. 'Here are books about fighting and defeating witchcraft: *The Maellus Maleficarum - The Hammer of Witches*, and *Daemonologie* by King James VI of Scotland...'

'Soon to be King James the First of England if some of the dark powers at Queen Elizabeth's court get their way,' added Tom.

'That's as may be,' shrugged Ugo, 'but look here. There are books by modern writers. Here is George Chapman's *Shadow of Night* and Mathew Roydon's *A Friend's Passion*. Work by Thomas Lodge, Thomas Hariot, Sir Walter Raleigh; Sir Philip Sidney's *Astrophil and Stella*. And by Christopher Marlowe as we have already discussed - both parts of his *Tamburlaine*, *The Jew of Malta*, *Edward the Second, The Massacre at Paris*, and, as you already mentioned, *The Tragical History of the Life and Death of Doctor Faustus*...'

*

'All these men, living or dead, were, with Ferdinando Stanley Lord Strange and, some say, Edmund Spenser, not to mention John Dee and Simon Forman themselves, members of Raleigh's circle though many have moved to Essex' circle in the meantime,' mused Tom. 'At one time or another they were with Raleigh, though. Men who met at Raleigh's London home Durham House and dabbled in occult matters and atheism, questioning the truth of the Bible, the group that Will Shakespeare christened *The School of Night*.'

'Standing in opposition - intellectual opposition at the very least - to the more stoutly Protestant faction gathered at Essex House,' added John, regaining control of himself. 'With Essex, Southampton and - although a youngster in those days - William Shakespeare. However, as you observe, many of them have changed their allegiances since.'

'And Marlowe's *Doctor Faustus*,' concluded Ugo grimly having apparently paid no attention to the other two once more. 'Is right here beside the German *Faustbuch* which, as I remember it, gives even more details of the spells Faustus used to raise and control the demon Mephistopheles.'

'*These metaphysics of magicians/And necromantic books are heavenly*,' quoted Tom. 'As Marlowe's Faustus observed, *A sound magician is a mighty god...*'

'*See, see where Christ's blood/Streams in the firmament*,' countered Ugo. '*One drop would save my soul/But half a drop. Oh spare me Lucifer; I'll burn my books!*'

'And so, like Faustus, everyone who tries to use these *grimoires* will be damned,' said John, the certainty of unshakeable faith ringing in his voice as powerfully as Spencer's funeral bells. Tom nodded his agreement then led them out of the sinister chamber.

ii

The next room, the front one above the shop, was the largest so far and, in keeping with the magician's lewd reputation, it was the bedroom. There was no adjoining door leading through from the library, so they approached it from the corridor. As soon as he opened the door, Tom discovered broad windows that looked out westward across Billingsgate towards the westering sun on his right; windows which filled the entire chamber with light. And, straight ahead, narrower casements facing southwards towards the River added a breath-taking view over the Billingsgate pier and London Bridge. On the wall behind the door hung a full-length mirror in a gilded frame whose clarity and quality exceeded even the mirror Tom had on the wall beside his *piste* so his students could observe and perfect their duelling style. However, this mirror was clearly designed to reflect love rather than war.

The walls were further hung with carpets and tapestries from the furthest corners of the world - some, thought Tom, almost certainly brought back by Raleigh or Gilbert from their explorations in Guiana together with the creatures, plants, beliefs and ideas that made them question the veracity of the Bible as well as the teachings of both Catholic and Protestant elders. Amongst these, and more discretely displayed in the shadier corners, hung paintings and stood statues from less far afield. The Trojan prince Paris, painted by an unfamiliar probably Flemish hand, lingered over his Judgement of the three graphically naked goddesses Hera, Athena and Aphrodite. In another, rather more risky picture given the situation, a couple of demons guided a line of sinners - all as naked as Paris' goddesses and mostly women - towards the gates of Hell. In a third, Zeus, disguised as a swan, ravished an all-too willing Leda whose every feature was rendered in life-like detail; and again, in the last, Zeus again, this time disguised as a buxom Aphrodite, frolicked with an equally nude Callisto. In every corner stood Greek or Roman statues of the naked Venus, some modestly if ineffectively trying to shield their virtue, some stepping rather less self-consciously into or out of their baths.

At the centre of this disturbingly sexual chamber stood a great four-poster with richly tapestried hangings on which rampant fauns and satyrs pursued voluptuous nymphs. Tom crossed to it, his mind fastening once more on that faint, possibly feminine, call for help. He lifted the heavy cloth to reveal a tumble of sheets, pillows and blankets unsettlingly reminiscent of Spenser's death-bed.

'Nothing,' he said. 'Except that Simon the satyr seems to have caught a nymph here relatively recently - which explains I suppose why he needs a convenient bath.' Then, looking up at John's expression, 'What?'

'If Hal has seen this room...' said the apothecary, at his most outraged, paternal and protective.

'It would certainly explain why he fiddles with his codpiece,' nodded Ugo.

Goaded into a flash of rage, John turned and bellowed '*HAL*! Are you here boy?'

And whatever came by way of reply, if indeed it came from the earthly plane rather than the demonic, seemed to emanate from whatever lay above that last, rickety staircase.

*

The corridor and the last staircase seemed to catch and concentrate the atmosphere from the library like an apothecary distilling poison. Or perhaps it was just their imaginary forces, thought Tom. Imagination abetted by every creak and groan the flimsy staircase gave beneath three sets of footwear. The stair-foot was stained, a darkness reaching across the floorboards that reminded Tom of the wet patch on the floor beside Spenser's head. The lower treads were unstable, one or two dented; the banister bent and broken in a couple of places. Tom would have lingered over these but Ugo and John pushed impatiently upward. Imagination or not, by the time he reached the door at the top of the staircase he found that his rapier was in his hand and he had no memory of having drawn it. He hesitated, mind racing. Ugo and John crowded behind and below him. He paused a moment longer, studying the portal as though it was an enemy. The panels heavy and black, the jamb and lintel slightly lighter, the sill on the threshold paler, slightly splintered. Then he took a deep breath to steady himself, reached up and turned the handle - itself something of a rarity on internal doors in private houses. His own doors latched and bolted - or were replaced with hangings. Only the main door and the door to his school room with its mirror and fencing *piste* were as solid as this one. The fact that this was so heavy simply added to the atmosphere of danger. What was in this room that required such a solid barrier to contain it?

Tom pushed it inwards an inch and waited. Silence; stillness - underpinned, perhaps emphasised, by the whisper of distant conversation from the street and by the breathing of his companions close behind. By the faintest stirring as though there was something alive in here. Something alive but not, he was sure, human. Certainly not the apprentice apothecary Hal no matter how well bound and gagged. And yet there had been that strange call for help. That weird noise as they exited the library.

Tom pushed the door a little wider. The garret windows he had seen from the street faced west and south. They were curtained, but sufficient light from the cloudless afternoon came round their edges to illuminate the place.

What first struck Tom was the size of the room. Then he began to make out some of its contents. He lingered in the doorway with Ugo and John pressing forward as they strained to see in. But he refused to move as he took stock of the disturbingly bizarre contents of the place. There was a stuffed crocodile hanging from the ceiling. It was massive, the better part of fifteen feet from nose to tail-tip as near as he could judge. It seemed scarcely better preserved than the cat crucified on the back door. Yet it glared balefully out of the shadows, its empty eye-sockets seemingly brimming with malignity, its mouth partly agape, teeth the length of fingers gleaming. And wrapped around it, scarcely in better condition, was the longest snake that Tom had ever seen. Something of that size and power, he thought, must have come from Eden fresh from seducing Eve. Even part rotten as they were, the monsters were enough to hold him still as he continued to look around the strange room while his eyes adjusted to the gloom. And his nostrils adjusted to the strange, musty smell.

The next thing to strike him was a looming presence in the corner nearest the west-facing windows. At first he thought it might be a cloaked and hooded figure nearly seven feet high standing there and the impact of the thought shortened his breath, speeded his heartbeat and caused his rapier to thrust towards it almost of its own accord. But no. A moment's reflection made him realise that it was some tall piece of furniture draped in black cloth. He lowered his blade and stepped up into the room, his body nevertheless falling into Capo Ferro's *terza* guard as though a master swordsman was just about to attack him out of the shadows. Eyes as busy as they would have been on a duelling *piste* or, indeed, a battlefield, he moved further into the room.

Along the back wall there stood a waist high shelf that doubled as a table. In the middle of it there was a human skull. It was fleshless, scraped or scrubbed white - except that on the top of it stood a black candle whose meltings spread over the ball of the cranium. Beside it, a severed hand stood apparently balanced on its square-cut wrist, fingers spread and reaching upward, pale as white wax. Beyond that there were three wooden stands. On the first lay the mummified remains of some kind of dog, on the second, those of a monkey looking disturbingly like the remains of a child. Only the fact that they were labelled ANUBIS the JACKAL and BABI the MONKEY proved what they were. The third was empty but it was just possible to read BAST the CAT.

There were more books piled there but after seeing what was in the library downstairs, Tom had no desire to look more closely at them. A mortar and pestle sat beside a pile of dried herbs, jars and cups full of other ingredients and a flask of crimson liquid beside them. Tom prayed that it was wine or vinegar but it looked for all the world like blood. There were phials that seemed to contain oil and water, each marked with a crucifix. A cross nearly three feet high leaned against the wall nearby. A massive pair of compasses with arms well over a yard in length leaned beside it. There was an orb of some kind - perhaps a globe, a long pointer, even bigger than the compasses. A sizeable box came next and, at the far end by the south-facing window, a wardrobe whose part-open door revealed dark folds of cloth hanging within it.

Fascinated to see what was in the box, Tom stepped further into the room. But then his progress was stopped by both his companions speaking at once.

'Where's the person who called out?' wondered John, his voice trembling slightly - clearly fearing that the voice must belong to some invisible creature or occult power.

And Ugo said '*Stop*!'

iii

Tom glanced at the Dutchman. Ugo was pointing downwards with one of his pistols. Tom's gaze followed the gesture to look down at the floor immediately in front of his feet. His black leather toecaps were standing on the outer edge of a circle that had been drawn across most of the floor. There was another circle a foot or so inside it. The space between the two was split into sections and each section contained what could only be a magic letter, sign or sigil. Tom counted eighteen. Then he realised there was a third circle inside the other two, the gap between them filled with words in a language he had never seen before. And within the third circle there was a man-sized five-pointed star whose apexes somehow fitted into the over-all pattern.

Tom shivered and stepped back at once. He knew nothing more about the occult than he had learned from Kit Marlowe and the plays he had written before Poley, Skeres and Frizer murdered him. But he knew what this was - a pentacle. An occult wall of magic force designed to keep demons away from anyone foolish enough to perform the rituals in the books downstairs. Either to keep them out while the diabolist who had summoned them stood safe within - or to keep them caged within while the thaumaturge who called them out of hell went abroad through the rest of the house, the city or the world.

John also followed Ugo's gesture, and realised that he was standing much further within the magic circle even than Tom. Without thinking, he leaped back and as he did so he collided with the seven-foot shape near the western window. The whole thing juddered, rocking back and forth. Something within it gave an unearthly howl, a sound that would have suited a demon very well indeed, thought Tom as John jumped away from the snarling monster, colliding with Ugo who, having stepped back out of the magic circle himself nearly went backwards through the door and down the stairs. Only Tom's speedy reactions saved him. Even so the pair of them wavered dangerously in the doorway for a moment, Tom looking over his friend's shoulder down the rickety staircase. And just for that moment, all the little things that he had noticed on the way up seemed to fall into a pattern. It looked to The Master of Logic as though someone had recently done what he had just saved Ugo from doing: fallen headlong backwards down the stairs, splintering the sill with his boot-heels, breaking the banister as he clutched the balusters but failing to stop himself; denting the lower steps with the back of his head before spreading blood - and maybe brains - across the floor at the bottom. Then, he realised, whoever it was had been kept in the bath for some time as Forman cleaned up the mess and decided on how best to proceed.

'*Bedankt mijn vriende*,' said Ugo, breaking Tom's train of thought as he stepped forward to steady himself and level his pistol at the growling monster.

'Ugo! Stop!' called Tom. He strode across the room, paying no more attention to the marks on the floor or those on the stairs and sheathing his rapier as he moved. He grabbed the cloth

47

wrapped around the creature and pulled it clear revealing a tall stand with a large cage hanging from it. A shaft of sunlight stabbed in round the curtain he disturbed as he pulled the cloth aside to reveal the most garishly colourful bird he had ever seen. Its breast was dazzling yellow which darkened to orange on its head. The wings it flapped and the tail-feathers it spread were green. Its bill was black and powerfully hooked, gaping at the moment as it emitted growls and snarls like those of an enraged hound. Then, abruptly, it stilled, settled and glared at all of them. '*Help me*,' it shouted clearly, in the voice of an impatient woman. '*Help me unloose this shift or I shall be forced to tear it off! Help me quickly Simon or I shall expire with lust!*'

*

'The bird is possessed!' said John, staggering back in genuine terror. Only Ugo's steady hand saved him from pitching headlong back down the stairs as Ugo himself had so nearly done. 'Asmodeus the spirit of salacity has entered it!' whispered John, still tensed to take that one fatal step backwards.

'No,' said Tom. 'I have heard of birds such as this. Sir Humphrey Gilbert gave one to William Cecil Lord Burghley nearly fifteen years ago. It could mimic many sounds including human speech. And, now I think of it, this creature fits in with the crocodile and the monstrous snake hanging above us which are both also from far distant places, especially those explored by men such as Gilbert, Raleigh and Drake. It is not this creature that is possessed by the naked lust of Asmodeus, it is whichever woman said these words so forcefully or so regularly that the bird learned to imitate them!'

'However that may be,' said John, beginning to recover his equanimity as he stepped forward out of the doorway, 'Hal's not here.'

'I agree,' said Tom. 'Let's cover the cage once again and make our way out of this place.'

'Leaving no trace of our visit,' said Ugo. 'Just in case he can send the *beast that watches* after us.'

'Good idea,' said John.

Tom forbore to remark that if *the beast* was real then it had been watching them all along and would have no trouble hunting them no matter how few clues they left. He just shook his head at their superstitious gullibility, replaced the cover over the cage and its strange, colourful occupant then he followed them, reaching out to close the door, planning to creep down the rickety stairs immediately behind them. Before he did so, however, he turned and scanned the room one more time. The light struck across the floor, illuminating the pentacle at the heart of the double circle. The floor itself was layered with dust - clearly not the sort of chamber that would welcome much in the way of cleaning, a matter further compounded by powdery filth drifting down from the crocodile and the snake. The slanting light revealled patterns in the dust filling the pentacle and it seemed to him that the patterns showed the outlines of bodies that had lain there, arms, legs and heads straining towards the points of the star itself. Thoughtfully, he stepped out and pulled the door closed behind him. They all tip-toed down the main staircase and arrived in the corridor that led to the shop on the one hand and the laboratory, kitchen and back door on the other. As they reached the kitchen door, the grey birds in the cage hanging there flapped and croaked but made nothing like the commotion they had caused when the three housebreakers first entered. It was almost enough noise, however, to cover the grating of a key turning in the front door's lock and the grinding of the handle turning. The door into the shop from the corridor stood wide. Anyone entering was bound to see them.

iv

As the front door began to swing inwards, Tom bundled his two companions into the kitchen and pulled the door to behind him. His immediate thought was to lead them through the back door past the crucified cat - with a prayer that the hinges would not shriek again - and escape down the garden. However, the conversation between the newcomers made him hesitate.

'Tuesday,' the first man was saying - Tom recognised Forman's voice.

'So soon?' asked a second - who sounded like Chapman.

'The Earl was adamant. The passing bells have pealed at his command. He has sent notification to the court. He will put everything in motion for Tuesday. The sooner, he said, the better. He, Gelly Meyrick and the Bacon brothers were all there and bursting with ideas.'

'Well! Things are moving even faster than I anticipated.'

'Just so.'

The voices lingered as the newcomers removed their cloaks, then moved away but remained easily audible as they went through into the shop. Chair-feet scraped on the floor and there was a rattle as the fire was stoked. Tom imagined the two men sitting beside the table before the fire there, as the conversation continued with Foreman still speaking. 'The Earl has a task for each of us to move matters to that planned end. I will arrange for the body to be cleaned, coffined and hearsed. It must be done at Essex house, apparently, so I will be hither and thither over the Sabbath and Monday. The Earl will clear matters with the Dean and with any other authorities in the Abbey. He is to be buried as close to Chaucer as can be arranged.'

'But I understood,' said jealous Chapman, 'that Chaucer earned his place there by being Clerk to the King's Works leasing a garden beside the abbey - not because of his reputation as a poet.'

'That's as may be,' answered Forman. 'The Earl has decreed that, as Spenser is the New Chaucer, they must lie together, cheek by jowl, as comparable poets.'

There was a brief silence and Tom could almost have sworn he heard Chapman grinding his teeth with jealousy.

'And me?' demanded Chapman at last. 'What is my part in this grand scheme? What does the Earl want me to do?'

'You are to rouse all the greatest poets in London,' explained Forman. 'They will carry the coffin and lay it to rest.'

'That should present no problem,' agreed Chapman. 'There will be many, both known and unknown, who will see a fine chance for advancement in this. Spencer's death will do a good number of men a great deal of benefit.'

You among them, thought Tom cynically.

'If you call more than are needed for that purpose,' Forman continued, 'they may follow as mourners.'

'I will get them each to write an elegy to be read over the grave,' enthused the poet, his suddenly cheerful tone and ready planning bringing a frown of distaste to Tom's face. 'With quills all of black. And they will cast the quills and the papers themselves into the grave along with him in place of kerchiefs or flowers. It will be an act that garners fame for those who participate - and those who arranged it. I will call on John Weever, Nicholas Breton, Francis Thynne, Charles Fitzgeoffrey, William Alabaster...'

'None of whom are your equal - as poet, playwright or translator,' Tom murmured to himself. Perhaps only Will and Ben Johnson were. But Chapman was going to garner the greatest part of the glory by the sound of things.

'Ha!' Forman interrupted the poet's cheerful flow and the master of Logic's cynical thoughts. 'For a moment there I supposed you were about to say "William *Shagsberd*"!'

'No. I will call everyone *except* him - whose absence will strike everyone as strange, *suspicious...*' The tone seemed to Tom to reflect a knowing wink.

*

'A good thought, and convenient to what is planned!' Forman agreed. 'However, take care not to over-extend yourself, George. It must all be ready by Tuesday.'

'And the other matter?' asked Chapman, his tone darkening once more.

'The fates were against us there. What did Ben Jonson say in the play of *Every Man in his Humour*? "Care killed the cat?" well in this case we may fairly say that "curiosity killed the cat". Either way, the cat is dead. But I believe we can still make use of him. As a mute witness if as nothing more. But we will need to move him soon - I cannot have all the servants away for much longer. Still, in the mean-time, I believe I can manage to make us a hot posset...'

Footsteps approached the kitchen door. Tom gestured to the others and they ran silently to the back door and the crucified cat.

'No,' called Chapman. 'If I may impose on your generosity, have you no *aqua vitae*?'

'I have both French brandy and Holland gin,' answered Foreman, his footsteps hesitating then retreating once more. 'From the look of you it is Dutch courage that you need...'

Tom eased the back door open. Thankfully the hinges did not scream.

'No, old friend. Brandy,' said Chapman distantly. 'I gained a taste for it following Sir Francis Vere in the Low Countries. Give me a good measure of brandy if you would be so kind...'

'Well, we will share a measure. I have it in my *laboratorium* with all my other spirituous liquors, medicinal and cordial.' The footsteps faded as Forman turned aside into his laboratory. Tom ushered his companions out, exited himself, turned and eased the door shut.

Then they were off at full pelt down the garden, Tom's one lingering regret was that he dared not allow himself time for even the quickest glance into the garden privy. For by the sound of things there was more than one dead cat in Foreman's house - and this was the final place where the body might be concealed.

As they leaned against the outer panels of that tall garden gate, catching their breath while an icy evening gathered around them, John said, 'Well, at least there was no sign of Hal there!'

Nor of your Elizabeth, thought Tom, though I'd hazard that was her birth chart being drawn. One part at least of the secret you are trying to hide from The Master of Logic.

'But much talk of Will Shakespeare,' mused Ugo. 'Almost as though someone in this coil wants him blamed for Spenser's death - and it was murder, you say? Murder. Tell me, Tom, does Will have the slightest idea of the dark forces that are being secretly ranged against him?'

Chapter 4: Dead Man's Place

i

'Dead Man's Place?' said Rosalind Fletcher, her breath clouding on the late afternoon air. 'You want me to live in *Dead Man's Place*? Will Shakespeare have you run mad? I would rather live in a Bankside brothel. There are a good number close at hand you must admit!'

Will looked at her in horror. She was tall enough so that her face was level with his but her profile was hidden by a tumble of chestnut hair, all except for the point of her turned-up nose and the thrust of her determined chin. He needed to read her eyes and see the set of her lips to be certain whether she spoke seriously or in jest. He hadn't loved her for long enough to read her tone of voice with any accuracy. So he took her at her word. 'No! No, I promise! We but cross Dead Man's Place on our way to view a property I have found on Maiden Lane.' He gave a sweeping gesture that covered both Dead Man's Place on either hand of them and the opening of Maiden Lane a little further on.

But she did not relent. 'Hum. Well, Maiden Lane sounds somewhat more suitable I'll allow, though the way down here from the Mary Overie Steps seems deep enough in mire both physical and moral.'

'The house is clean and the rooms much larger than my lodging in St Helen's,' he offered, too well aware that he was beginning to sound like an anxious schoolboy.

'At least this one does not overlook a graveyard like your rooms behind St Helen's church, you say…'

'It overlooks the Globe - or will do so when the Globe is finished. It overlooks Sir Nicholas Brend's field and a promising partial erection at the moment. It is owned by an honest widow…'

'Not that honest if she is happy to accept couples moving in together outside the banns of wedlock…'

He was almost certain her tone was teasing now. However… 'She is happy to believe that you are my cousin come up from the country and recently orphaned,' he said. Then he could have bitten his tongue for she was indeed recently and brutally orphaned. She turned towards him, delicately arched eyebrows raised. He focused on the dimple in that determined chin because he saw the look on her face and floundered into silence.

'That is a truth which has got me safe haven in my cousin Martin Fletcher the carter's home,' she agreed, her tone darkened by sadness. 'But cousin Martin has a wife and family so I share a room with his daughters - unutterably cramped but entirely respectable. Until I come visiting wayward poets and playwrights in St Helen's that is, which is likely to get the pair of us whipped or pilloried for concupiscence.'

'But things are different south of the River,' he persisted desperately. 'And besides, like most property owners near here, she actually lives in Winchester and lets her agent look after things. And he is, what shall I say? *Amenable*.'

'And the law? What does the law say about such things? Is the law also *amenable*?' She was being serious now - and he realized that most of their earlier conversation had been teasing after all. Or it had been until he mentioned her father's murder.

'As I said, things are different south of the River,' he repeated.

*

The pair of them continued side by side westward along the muddy pathway that ran parallel to the Thames, behind the backs of the inns, brothels, theatres and baiting pits that lined the South Bank. 'There seem to be fewer churches, certainly,' Rosalind allowed after a moment. 'And fewer parish constables I suppose; fewer pillories, stocks or whipping posts despite the fact that you seem to have The Clink, the Borough Counter and the Marshalsea in which to house felons, financial, legal, religious and moral. So no fewer sinners I'd wager; a goodly sum more than in the City if the quantity of taverns and brothels is any measure.'

'And you would not be happy to find a bed amongst them? Why, Tom told me that you…'

'Let us leave master Musgrave and what he may have told you out of this - and Robert Poley for that matter, for it was Poley who was my master in such matters when I worked for him and his intelligencers at my father's inn The Crown in Saffron

Walden teasing secrets out of those on their way north to Edinburgh via Cambridge and south with word from the Scottish court and Mary Queen of Scots' son King James.'

There was a moment of silence as she returned to that painful subject once again. Will knew that the inn was burned and her father beaten to death by Gelly Merrick and his bullies working for the Earl of Essex during their successful attempt to kidnap and interrogate her, for she had told the truth about her reason for boarding with her cousin Martin in his already crowded tenement behind Three Cranes Wharf. 'Well, let us look at these rooms you have secured,' she suggested quietly.

'I have secured them only if you approve of them,' said Will.

'Well, I'm sure I shall approve them and I will need to do so speedily or we will find ourselves locked out of the city at curfew.'

Rosalind was as good as her word and approved the rooms on Maiden Lane so that they could get back before curfew. The owner's agent was a sober, sensible man whose steady professionalism was not tainted by puritan disapproval. The paperwork was ready. The paperwork was signed and the deposit paid. So all that needed to be arranged was the carting of Will's and Rosalind's necessaries from one side of the Thames to the other. His consisted of his clothing, his papers, his travelling trunk which doubled as his writing desk, his wardrobe and his bed; hers consisted of little more than the clothes she stood up in. And her cousin Martin was a carter by profession so it seemed that there were no obstacles remaining to complicate their plans.

ii

Although they had taken a wherry to the south bank from Three Cranes Stairs, the quickest way to return to St Helen's was across London Bridge. Side by side they hurried up the slope of the South Wark and under the arch of the southern gatehouse, the tarred and mummified heads of traitors on their pikes high above outlined against a clear blue evening sky that would not have been out of place in a stained-glass window. It was not yet sunset but Will had completely forgotten that he was due at John Gerard's house then in any case. Rosalind filled his mind for the moment, to the exclusion of everything else.

The constricted bustle of the Bridge closed around them at once. It was nine hundred feet long and thirty feet wide. But there were houses on either hand, nearly two hundred of them, some rising to seven stories, many almost joining together above their heads. At bridge level, most of them opened into shop-fronts selling everything from fish to furbelows, jackets to jewelry, leather to lace. There was a lively crush here as last-minute shoppers mixed with farmers driving their sheep through for tomorrow's early markets and even the occasional wagon or coach travelling northward or southward through the throng. Every now and then there was an open space - for the drawbridge, for example, designed to let tall ships run further upstream - and in front of the public toilets though these were little more than boards with holes cut in them that conveniently overhung the river.

'Perhaps we'd have been better on a wherry,' shouted Will a little nervously. He was a private person and was uneasy in crowds and gatherings of all sorts - except for dramatic ones.

'Nonsense,' answered Rosalind, her eyes shining. 'You forget, sir, that Saffron Waldon has nothing to offer that equals this, not even on market day!'

At last the crush eased as they came out into the open area in front of Nonsuch House, the residence of Sir Thomas Walsingham, patron of poets and master of spies in succession to his late uncle Sir Francis, and current employer of Ingram Frizer as the earl of Essex employed Nicholas Skeres and sometimes it seemed that the Devil himself employed Robert Poley, the three intelligencers responsible for Kit Marlowe's murder.

Nonsuch House was the point at which Will developed an unsettling feeling that Rosalind and he were being watched. By the time they came out past the northern latrines and under the gatehouse exit where the planks beneath them vibrated unsettlingly as the watermills between the northernmost starlings were vigorously turned by a falling tide, he was certain that they were being followed.

'Do you feel there are eyes on us?' he whispered to Rosalind. As an ex-employee of Robert Poley she was likely to be even more acute in such matters than he.

'Those of a small man,' she replied. 'Twenty-five years of age I'd guess, straight nose, frog's eyes, thin beard, big hands; no great peacock in his dress but no poor beggar neither. He was lingering outside Nonsuch House but fell in behind us as we passed.'

*

'If he knew to follow us then he likely knows who we are. So it takes no Tom Musgrave, Master of Logic, to calculate that he knows where we are likely going no matter where we chose to visit on our way thither.'

'Spoken like a true intelligencer,' she said. 'And doubly true if he is actually employed by the owner of Nonsuch House.'

'As you say. Sir Thomas Walsingham knows almost all there is to know about me. His wife Lady Audrey and sister-in-law Kate Shelton know all there is to know about Tom Musgrave too. So there is no point in trying to lose any spy he sets on us.'

'I agree,' she said decisively. 'We either allow him to follow us or we find some convenient alley and kill him.'

'I would not see him killed until we discover why he dogs our footsteps as well as the truth of who actually set him on to do so and for what reason.'

'Again, spoken like an old intelligencer,' she said approvingly. 'I might almost be talking with Robert Poley except that Poley would likely have a third way at hand - use a convenient alley to render him helpless or unconscious then hand him over to Torturer Topcliffe to see what information the Tower's racks could pull out of him, whether he's Walsingham's man or not.'

'Agreed. But there is yet another possibility…'

'I have foreseen it, Will. What if our dwarfish friend actually *works for* Poley rather than for Walsingham. Then any damage we might do him is likely to land *us* in the Tower stretched on one of Topcliffe's racks.'

'A terrible fate, as befell poor Thomas Kyd racked as part of the investigation into Kit Marlowe's doings. He died a cripple in consequence aged only thirty-six.'

'And I have heard tell that a woman dressed in nothing more than a shift for interrogation, may be stretched on a rack at about waist height, convenient to her torturer's lusts. Step into the frame, pull up her hem and there she lies, wide open to any desires and helpless to resist. Poor Anne Bellamy was neither the first nor the last by all accounts; I hear Topcliffe made her pregnant then gave her as wife to one of his henchmen.'

'Truly. In this as in so much, women have so much more to fear than men.'

'Nothing more than womankind's just deserts. Our sex are the originators of the original sin, according to the Good Book and elders in almost every church. Had Eve not listened to the Serpent and so caused Adam's fall we would all still be living in Eden.'

'Truly?' The inflection with which he said the word betrayed his surprise that she should admit so much - or at least seem to do so.

'Well, here am I, another Eve, with or without the Serpent's prompting, tempting you out of Eden - or St Helen's at least, hard by the churchyard and an edifice of absolute rectitude - down to the Land of Nod. Which I have to admit is south of Eden rather than east of it, but every bit as replete with all the sins of spirit and flesh.' Her tone had lightened from mock-seriousness to cheerful irony as she spoke.

'Oh do not fear for me,' answered the playwright, joining in her game with relief and alacrity. 'I met another, earlier, Eve in paradisiacal Stratford where I was born and raised, though I must admit that it was quite another type of *serpent* that caused my troubles. And I am indeed come east of Eden in consequence.'

This conversation, witty though skirting impiety if not blasphemy, took them up Fish Street past the cross-roads with Thames Street and into Bishopsgate which ran northward into the parish of St Helen's. And the animated manner in which it was conducted covered - as it was designed to do - the fact that every now and then one or the other of the conversants would look back to check on the slight man with frogs' eyes who continued to follow them through the crowds like a hound coursing a pair of hares. But neither the hares nor their courser realized that there were more men involved in the pursuit and the hunter himself was being hunted.

iii

As Will stoked the fire into a blaze that could heat his room in St Helen's, Rosalind went round tidying. They had peered out of the window as soon as they arrived, pausing only to shrug off their cloaks, and knew that their mysterious shadow still lingered outside, shivering in a shady corner by the churchyard. But the fact that he was obviously so cold made then crave warmth even more. So Will took up the poker while Rosalind began to take up the papers.

'Take care with those,' ordered Will turning, poker in hand, as she started piling his documents together.

'I'm only clearing the bed,' she answered, apparently innocently, her words robbing him of his breath for a moment. 'The skirts of my dress are thick with mud from Dead Man's Place and will need to be dried and brushed before I return to Three Cranes Warf so I will avail myself of the security and warmth of your blankets as we hang it in front of the fire. And the blankets will also assist my shift in protecting my person from your prying eyes and the serpent that caused your troubles in Stratford. Besides, why can I not make a neat pile out of these chaotic scribblings?'

He put the poker down then strode across the room frowning. 'These are not *scribblings*, they are three part-completed plays. The one you are holding is my updating of the ancient play of Hamlet as possibly originally penned by Thomas Kyd. This one here is a part finished presentation of the murder of Julius Caesar and the third, as yet untouched, is my *History of Henry the Fifth*.'

'You are working on three at once? Surely that is madness! How do you hold them all separately in your head, even though you are taking two from old plays and one, from the look of things, straight out of Sir Thomas North's translation of Plutarch's *Lives*.'

'I do so because I have to.'

'But why?'

'Because one of them must be ready for performance at the opening of The Globe. A new theatre requires a new play. I have just not yet decided which one is best to proceed with.'

'Proceed with the one you can complete most swiftly.'

'That's a logical thought and worthy of Tom Musgrave himself but not as simple as it sounds. There is an impediment in each one which I have not yet managed to overcome. Take the *Caesar* for instance. I have written everything past the scene of his brutal murder and showed it on the stage which is unusual but effective I believe. It flowed as sweetly as the Avon right up to the spoken *duello* between Brutus and Mark Antony as each tries to sway the crowd to his will. But now I need to polish their speeches before I work out a final act when Brutus and Cassius die in the battle at Philippi. *Hamlet* requires further work too - in the original the old king is stabbed in his orchard and that's too simple, too pat. He must die in some shocking, insidious manner - the more unnatural the better. If he is to return as a ghost he needs clearer and more powerful motivation...'

'And *Henry*?'

'In some ways the most difficult. I wrote it originally to follow my plays of *Henry the Fourth* but I am rewriting it removing the character Falstaff because Will Kemp - who played him to such great acclaim - actually damaged the drama with his incessant clowning. So he is no longer with our troupe and I have therefore written him out of the drama. I have made up the missing Falstaff lines with speeches from a Chorus - that proved so successful in my play of *Romeo* - but there is still something missing. It is all too easy for Henry. His character is too simple, his actions too heroic. Without the comic relief it is all... What did Robert Poley say when we discussed it just after Christmas? It is all just tennis balls, Harfleur and Agincourt. As though Henry never hesitated, worried, doubted; as though he could never be overcome. Not a man but a kind of god or super-man.'

'I see what you mean. Even Achilles had his heel - and that weakness makes him more interesting. But…'

'But what?'

'Is there not another element that might be borne in mind? Could not your play reflect events that are happening now?' She sat on the edge of his bed and began to remove her filthy shoes. Then, seemingly forgetting his presence she pulled up the muddied hem of her skirt and began to remove her wet-footed hose and the garters holding them in place.

'I have been accused of using Falstaff to unmask the way that Captains like Sir Thomas North have fleeced the exchequer,' Will continued in a rather constricted voice. 'They do so by supplying fewer, worse trained and ill-equipped companies of soldiers than those they were paid to supply, and yet take full pay and pocket the difference. The Earl of Essex believes that is part of the reason no-one else has been successful in Ireland. Something he is hell-bent on overcoming.'

'Ireland - there's your focus!' she said, lowering her hem once more. 'Why not work on your play of *Henry* and try to have it open The Globe just as the Earl of Essex leads his army into Ireland: Henry the Fifth re-born, marching away to victory!'

*

As Rosalind arranged her shoes and hose in front of the fire, leaving room for a chair on which she proposed to place her dress as well, Will piled the sheets of paper comprising the three plays on top of each-other, with *Caesar* lying sideways in the middle to separate *Hamlet* and *Henry*. After Rosalind's suggestion, he thoughtfully made sure that *Henry* was on top.

Then they turned their attention to her soiled dress and he began to unlace it down the back. After a few moments he pulled it wide at her direction; she shrugged her shoulders and it slid to the floor. She stepped daintily out of it, stooped, lifted it and crossed to the fire, holding it high and then laying it over the chair-back. She did all this slowly and carefully, apparently unaware that the firelight shone through the fine linen of her smock effectively rendering her naked.

She turned, wide-eyed, and her gaze fell upon his straining codpiece. 'Why Master Shakespeare…' she said in tones of theatrical outrage.

What she might have said next was interrupted by a fist hammering on the door.

Rosalind gave a tiny scream and dived for the bed. Will crossed to the door, grabbing the handle and holding it securely shut. 'Who's there?' he asked.

'It's Tom, Will,' came the answer. 'I've brought you the man who followed you and Rosalind from Nonsuch.'

Will swung round. 'Shall I let him in?'

'Yes!' she answered. There was nothing to see of her but her head as the blankets even covered her arms and shoulders. 'Tom has seen me wearing less than this and the other man would need the eyes of Argus to see through your blankets.'

'Let's hope he's not a churchwarden, then, or we'll both be shamed at services tomorrow!'

As he said this, Will released the handle and Tom opened the door, pushing the slight man into the room, following close on his heels.

'This is John Weevil,' he said. 'A friend of George Chapman's and a kind of poet, I understand.'

'*Weever*!' snapped the frog-eyed man. 'It's John Weever!'

iii

'I know of Master Weever,' said Will. 'Are you not employed on producing epigrams in preparation for a volume?'

'I am,' answered Weever.

'But you are a Cambridge man…' added Will.

'Queen's College,' supplied Weever proudly.

'Not quite the nest of spies that Corpus Christi is,' supplied Tom. 'But even so…'

'I am no spy, sir!' snapped Weever, outraged.

'So, Master Weevil,' purred Tom, 'then perhaps you would be kind enough to explain to Master Shakespeare here why you were following him.'

'I was not following him!' spat. Weever.

'Ah,' said Tom. 'So it was a kind of concurrence that you should be waiting outside Nonsuch and yet planning to come here to St Helen's. And that you did so by dogging Master Shakespeare's footsteps. All this for no reason?'

'Yes!' spat Weever. 'No! I was not following him. I was following *her*!'

'You were following Mistress Fletcher? In God's name, why?' demanded Will.

'I was commanded to do so. Mistress Fletcher has eyes on her - more than she knows, perhaps.'

'More than she knows for certain!' snarled Rosalind. 'Who set you on me and why, you bull's pizzle!'

Weever, very much the pale, slim animal's member she had just likened him to, looked at the outraged woman, at Will, who towered over him threateningly and at Tom who terrifyingly towered over them all. 'Bacon,' he said. 'Sir Anthony Bacon, secretary to the Earl of Essex. His concern is simple. Your father was killed and yourself taken forcibly by the Earl's men and interrogated by Sir Francis, Sir Antony's brother. But you are a creature of Robert Poley's and a limb of The Council and therefore of Secretary Cecil, the Earl's greatest enemy at court. He had determined you will be overwatched until he can discern your intentions and decide how best to proceed with you.'

Immediately the conversation Will and Rosalind had had about what to do with the man following them gained new and unsettling significance. If they did in fact damage or dispose of this pizzle of a poet, the Earl of Essex had almost limitless ways of proceeding with them in which ravishment on the rack was likely one of the least uncomfortable.

Ten minutes later, Tom was leaning back with his shoulders against Will's door forming an extremely efficient barrier. Not that Essex' no longer very secret agent John Weever showed much inclination for escape. 'But why should the Earl be so interested in me now?' wondered Rosalind.

'He's on the point of being confirmed as Lord Lieutenant of Ireland,' Tom pointed out.

'A poisoned chalice if ever there was one,' observed Will.

'But a chalice nevertheless that he himself has asked for,' emphasized Rosalind.

'The Earl is well aware of the dangers,' said Weever. 'But he is also well aware of the possible rewards.'

'Which might include the throne,' said Tom.

'No!' said Weever. 'Such a thought is treasonous and voicing it surely high treason; best beware, all of you. The prize he seeks is most likely to include elevation in the eyes of Her Majesty and therefore in those of her successor if he settles a dangerous situation so close to our shores and also to both their hearts.'

*

Had Weevil revealed too much? Tom wondered. Certainly his unguarded observation explained why Antony Bacon on Essex' behalf wanted a close watch kept on the woman who knew more than many - perhaps more than anybody - about negotiations with that successor: Mary of Scots' son King James the Sixth of Scotland.

'So,' he purred, 'the Earl is willing to risk everything on success against Hugh O'Neill and his catholic armies in Ireland while all too well aware that his absence fighting in Ulster gives his rivals at court - men such as Secretary Cecil and I would judge, Captain of the Queen's Guard Sir Walter Raleigh - the chance to further ingratiate themselves with Her Majesty, while also courting King James in Edinburgh, though I hear tell that Raleigh may have spread his nets wider. Sir Antony Bacon sees this as clearly as anyone and is also well aware that the lady of Nonsuch House, Lady Audrey Walsingham, has managed to forge a friendship, not with King James but with his wife Queen Ann. It was therefore no coincidence that you were hanging round Nonsuch when you fell in behind Mistress Rosalind here. Sir Antony will soon be so worried about all this going on behind the Earl's back as he marches off to Ireland that he might actually get out of bed and come to look for himself!'

'Not while he had eyes like Master Weevil's here to spy out the situation for him,' said Rosalind.

'Spoken like a creature of Robert Poley's!' sneered Weever. 'And once again, as you slander your betters, you sail dangerously close to treason. Remember, all of you, that my

Lord of Essex is Earl Marshal. Together with the Knight Marshal and the Pursuivant Marshal he has an army of pursuivants at his command, whose sole mission is to police Her Majesty's subjects, seeking out Catholic plots against her. Each one a trained seeker after those of Jesuitical leanings - who have been known to measure houses outside and inside as they seek hiding places and priests' holes. There is no end to their power when confronted by those suspected of recusancy. The Earl Marshal can have you in the Marshalsea or the Tower with a snap of his fingers.

'But I spoke truly nonetheless,' she countered, 'whether I spoke here, in the Marsalsea or the Tower as you suggest. But I am no Catholic or Recusant that you threaten me with the pursuivants. There are no priests' holes here, sir!'

'It is not you that I refer to in this case, woman, but your swain and paramour there, Master Shagsberd. If the pursuivants have not yet come hammering on his door, it is only a matter of time before they do, for along with everything else, he is known to have gained employment in Popish houses before he came to London and may still harbor Popish sympathies!'

iv

'"Along with everything else",' said Will a little while later. 'What did he mean by that?'

'Shall I fetch him back and ask him?' offered Tom 'He went off like a hunted hare but he shouldn't have made it through the Bishop's Gate quite yet.' He was talking in jest, but although his tone was light, his brows were pulled close together in a frown. For he suspected that John Weever was referring to Hal the apprentice's testimony that Will had bought the poisons which could have been used to murder Edmund Spenser. And the way the situation had developed so far, the only people who should have known about that accusation were John Gerard - who had sworn Hal to silence for the moment at least - and Tom. But also, it now occurred to him, it was just possible that whoever had silenced Hal more permanently might also know. Other than that, of course, whoever had pretended to be Will and given his name to Hal as he purchased the poisons would know as well. However, Tom could see nothing but trouble ahead if he broke that news to Will now, particularly as Hal had vanished, as he believed, forever. Under normal circumstances he would have talked things through with Ugo, but the Dutch gunsmith was escorting John Gerard home.

However, Tom needed to talk to someone, for there was a deal of untangling still to do, he thought. And the possibilities he had just ranged through showed all to clearly how Gordian the knot of suspicion had become. If Will had not bought the herbs and not, therefore, murdered Spenser, then who had? Who had bought the herbs? Who had poisoned Spenser? Did they have to be one and the same person? Could they not be two in confederacy? And why had the man who bought the herbs dragged Will Shakespeare into the matter?

As Cicero himself observed, quoting the respected judge Lucius Cassius, *cui bono*? Who would benefit? What had Spenser and Shakespeare in common that killing one and blaming the other might benefit a third party? That they were increasingly famous and successful poets? Was the benefit of their absence motive enough to motivate a competitor - Ben Jonson, perhaps, recently released from the Marshalsea and sent thither by Topcliffe himself but last heard of to be languishing in Newgate for killing Gabriel Spenser in a jealous rage immediately on his release and equally jealous of men at liberty to build their reputations while he was forbidden to do so. Would Ben dare to go to such an extreme? Or might someone like him?

'What did he mean, Tom?' repeated Will.

'I don't know, Will, but it seems clear to me that your name is being bandied about in dangerous places. The threat of the pursuivants seemed serious enough. When is the soonest you can move south of the river where you are less well known and may be harder to find?'

'As soon as Martin Fletcher can cart my possessions.'

'After services tomorrow,' supplied Rosalind. 'He rarely takes any business on the Sabbath. It jars with his beliefs to do so, but he is no great Bible thumper so he is likely to agree if I ask him.'

'Very well,' said Tom. 'If your clothes are dry enough, put them on and I will escort you to Three Cranes Warf. It is on my way to Blackfriars, though we will take a small detour to High Holborn. Whither you do not need to accompany us after all, Will - for I see the assignation has slipped your mind entirely. Be quick, Rosalind. I will go down and secure the services of a link boy with a torch for it is close to sunset and we will borrowing a dark hour or two before we both get home.' And he vanished.

'He did that to spare my blushes,' said Rosalind as she scrambled out of bed. 'What is at High Holborn that slipped your mind?' she asked as she scurried across the room.

'John Gerard, the herbalist. He is looking into matters to do with Edmund Spenser's death.'

'I see,' she said, lifting her dress off the back of the chair. 'Will, give me something to brush off this mud with. Come on, sir, look sharp and stop trying to peer through my shift. We will sleep apart tonight. And tomorrow we shall see. I am reliably informed that things are different south of the River…'

*

'What was that all about?' demanded Rosalind almost the instant they set out for Three Cranes Warf via Holborn.

Tom looked across at her as he turned over a range of facts in his mind. She might be Will's lover but as Weevil had observed, she was still Robert Poley's creature. Though that in itself was no great matter - his own mistress Kate was younger sister to Audrey Walsingham and the pair of them were deep in the mire of spycraft. Indeed, the fact that Rosalind had worked for Robert Poley - and did so still if the bull's pizzle of a poet could be believed - meant that he could take certain things for granted with her. Though he must never forget how careful he must be - she had slept with him on their first acquaintance, ordered to do so by Poley to show Tom how easily she could extract secrets from him during those deliriously unguarded moments. But he also felt some guilt that she was orphaned and her late father's business ruined. Essex' henchman Sir Gelly Meyrick fired The Crown, killed the old man and ravished away Rosalind because of an investigation that Tom had been pursuing. Furthermore, she was about to move in with Will and from the sound and state of things she had best not do so blindly, unaware that someone - for some as yet undisclosed reason - was trying to put the blame for Spencer's murder squarely on the playwright's shoulders. And as Antony Bacon had already set some of Essex' spies to watch her, if Will went down then so would she: down to the Tower, as like as not, and into the hands of Rackmaster Topcliffe.

'Come, sir,' she prompted, less than happy at his protracted silence, as they turned out of Bishopsgate Street into Wormwood, following the still pallid spark of the linkboy's torch as he in turn followed the directions Tom had given him together with a fourpenny groat while awaiting Rosalind. 'If anyone knows what is going on it is you.'

'It is me. But it is also Anthony Bacon, Sir Francis his brother who interrogated you, and Robert Poley.'

'Well, of all the alternative founts of knowledge as listed, only you are currently available. So tell me all.' Wormwood gave way to Moorgate as she spoke. 'You know I know that you insisted on walking home with me because you had things to share that were not for Will's ears either as innocent playwright with his mind full of the adventures of Henry the Fifth, or as the slightly less unworldly ex-lover of the Earl of Southampton, Essex' closest friend and, therefore, possibly a secret agent for that camp himself.'

'A matter I had perhaps better discuss with Robert Poley after services tomorrow while you and Will are moving…' he said.

'To Dead Man's Place, aye.' Silence fell once again.

They followed the brightening light of the torch through gathering shadows as Moorgate gave way to London Wall, north of which, outside the city, Houndsditch ran parallel. Houndsditch with Hog Lane a little further north still where Robert Poley had rooms with Master and Mistress Yeomans; Mistress Joan Yeomans being his one weakness.

'To Maiden Lane at least,' he said, dragging his mind back to the present. 'But there may be dead men enough placed at the centre of this.'

V

'The first dead man, I assume, being Edmund Spenser,' said Rosalind. 'And I'd hazard, he met no natural end if you are involved in the matter. And so, Will informs me, is John Gerard.'

'As you say. It seems he was murdered by having poison poured in his ear. Something the murderer was able to accomplish because Spenser was deep in drugged slumber.'

'How so?' her tone seemed distant, suddenly, and he looked down at her, eyebrows raised. Her face was folded in a thoughtful frown as she glanced with evident approval at the section of the city they were passing through. He recognized the substantial houses and the wider, less littered, thoroughfare. It. was Silver Street, though the rooftops high above them in the sunset were golden.

'He was being treated by John Gerard for the pain in his ear as you may remember,' he reminded her, recapturing her attention as they went into Noble Street approaching St Martins and The Shambles beyond. 'Gerard's apprentice Hal made up the mixture that Spenser took last night. Moreover, either before or after he took his medicine, Spenser consumed a fair amount of strong ale, which Gerard fears would have compounded its effect.'

'So your next move is to talk not only with Gerard but also with his apprentice Hal.'

'Aye. But there's the rub. I have more than one matter to discuss with young Hal, but Hal seems to have vanished and it is my firm belief that he too is dead, though possibly not murdered.' Aptly enough on that word, they came past Newgate Jail and exited the city through the New Gate itself.

'Young but dead - and *possibly* not murdered,' she echoed. 'I believe I need to converse with the Master of Logic over that supposition.'

So, as Snow Hill gave onto Holborn Bridge over the stench of the open sewer that was Fleet River and proceeded on to Holborn Hill and then Holborn Bars, Tom exercised the Master of Logic for her benefit. 'Hal is apprenticed to Master Gerard as you know. It was he who prepared the herbs that Spenser took, as strengthened in their effect by strong ale. But what you do not know is that Hal also testified - to Gerard at least - that a customer bought deadly poisons soon after Spenser left and while Gerard was out of the shop. The customer was cloaked and muffled, his face invisible, but he gave his name as Will Shakespeare. What he purchased may well be the poisons used on Spenser. That is the second matter on which I wish to question Hal.'

'But Hal has vanished…'

'Perhaps a mere correspondence of chances for Hal was also involved in a matter that John Gerard has been reticent to discuss with me. Gerard's daughter Elizabeth is comely and of marriageable age. Hal, whose favorite toy lies within his codpiece, is likely in love with her. But she has higher ambitions, spurred on no doubt by the elevated clientele who call at her father's shop. She therefore visits Simon Forman in secret, asking him to draw up her birth chart in which she might discover whether she would be better suited with young Hal or with some scion of aristocracy.'

'If Simon Forman can predict that, perhaps I will visit him myself.'

'If you do so, you would be best to keep your wits about you and your legs crossed. He has the reputation of being a *rakeshame*, seducing every comely woman who comes to consult him. This explains why John sent Hal to spy on Forman to ensure as best he could that Elizabeth was not compromised. And that was a fatal mistake.'

*

'How so?'

'Ugo, John and I have visited Forman's house this afternoon. It is a strange and fearful place. But there was a pattern that seemed to speak to me. To begin with there were no servants present and the house seemed to have been empty for some time, therefore we can assume either that the place was empty when Hal visited - or Hal waited until it was so. Then he went down the side and managed to climb over the gate at the end of the garden. The back door was locked but in the force of his desire to enter and find out the truth of Elizabeth's situation, he broke the lock and entered. We can assume he scouted through the rooms downstairs and found nothing of interest, but upstairs was another matter.'

'Things were different upstairs, as they are south of the river,' she murmured.

'Just so. Upstairs, he discovered a library in which lay a part-completed birth-chart for someone with the same name, birth date and birth location as Elizabeth Gerard. This, as well as the range of occult books beside it, must have prompted him to explore further. But I believe he took the chart, folded and re-folded it then put it in his jerkin first. The next room - Forman's bedroom - must have undone in a couple of heartbeats all the Church's teachings about chastity and self-control. Don't ask why - just take my word for it. But the sight of the bedroom merely served as a spur to further exploration and up he went again. The room at the top of the house - at the head of a narrow and treacherous staircase - is the most disturbing of all. There are evidences of black magic and witchcraft there and, perhaps most dangerous of all, a bird which is apparently possessed. It speaks in clear English and its screams very nearly pitched John Gerard himself down the stair with horror that such a thing exists. Only Ugo and myself saved him. Hal, alone, would have stood no chance.'

'So, fearful of this monstrous bird, he pitched headlong…'

'Headlong but backwards,' nodded Tom. 'The staircase bore all the marks of a body falling backwards down it, trying fruitlessly to catch the banister at first, but hitting his head on the edges of the stairs as he tumbled. Breaking his neck as like as not, and splitting open his skull when he finally landed.'

'And the Master of Logic has reasoned all this out?'

'All this and more: I believe that Forman arrived home to find his back door broken open, a body lying at the foot of the stair leading up to his devil's shrine. With Elizabeth Gerard's birth chart sticking out of his jerkin marked with blood. Proof enough of who the dead boy was and why he had come hither. And could Forman be certain that John Gerard, for whom the dead boy evidently worked, might not be related to Sir Thomas Gerard the Knight Marshal? Too deep an inspection - perhaps even by the pursuivants - would have him in the Marshalsea, the Tower or at the stake for witchcraft - even if he is friends with half the court and most of their wives or mistresses. So he lugs the body to his bathroom and puts it in his bath as he cleans the place of bloodstains. Then he bundles it down the stairs and out through the broken door into the outside privy in his garden. He has scarce completed this when Essex' messengers come beating at his front door summoning him to attend the Earl Marshal. He takes time to run upstairs and catch up the mummified cat that should stand with his jackal and his monkey beneath the serpent and crocodile in his magic room. He nails it to the back door and pens a curse in doggerel to go above it. As effective as a good strong lock against most would-be burglars I should think. Then he's off to Essex House as though nothing has happened - and no-one any the wiser.'

'And whoever put him up to giving evidence against Will is thwarted of his design - unless Forman can raise the dead to testify.'

'Forman and Chapman, thick as thieves together, seemed to discuss that very matter just as we were leaving the Billingsgate house. But they talked in code - if not in riddles.'

'So there is more to discover there…' she said as darkness closed over the link boy making his torch seem to burn more brightly.

'And the man with whom to talk the matter through is…' prompted Tom, enjoying her quick thinking and acuity.

'Robert Poley,' she concluded.

'Robert Poley,' he confirmed.

Chapter 5: The Pursuivant Marshal

i

'Still no sign of Hal?' asked Tom as he led Rosalind into John Gerard's laboratory.

'None,' answered the apothecary, his expression and tone showing how worried he was.

'And Elizabeth?'

'Helping her mother in the kitchen. She knows nothing of Hal's whereabouts either.'

'Well, I will not disturb her now but I may want to talk with her later.'

'You are welcome to stay to dinner - both of you - if you can get back through the New Gate after curfew.'

'That should be no trouble. I'll get another link boy on the corner and the gate's watchmen know me well enough.' He tapped his purse, making the coins in it jingle.

'So be it. Now, as you see, I have arranged a simple experiment.' On John's bench there sat two cages, each containing a scrawny street cat, both of them restless with hunger. 'We have to use cats,' John explained, very much in his element. 'If we used mice we would be hard-put to see the symptoms as they unfold. I would prefer to use dogs, or even man-sized pigs, as the Roman physician Galen did, and get a clearer view still but the little sample we are testing might not present a clear effect in larger animals.' He gestured to a small bowl which contained everything he had managed to retrieve from Spenser's ear and pillow.

'I have just enough here to split into two in case the first experiment is unsuccessful,' he said. 'But we have been given a pointer both in my garden and in Forman's for it was hemlock that was taken from both.'

'With what objective?' wondered Rosalind. 'Surely it would be wiser to take different poisons from each of you - then use a third one altogether, to confuse detection. To suggest belladonna and hemlock, for instance, but actually make use of arsenic.'

'Only if evading detection was the objective' said Tom, turning towards John. 'In a situation I resolved only recently, the use of the murder weapon - the Irish *bata* or club - was done to announce who the murderers were and to put their opponents in fear of them.' Rosalind nodded - she had been involved. Tom continued, 'But here, I admit, such a procedure might well serve different ends; to assign blame to an innocent bystander, for instance - a carefully selected gull such as Will Shakespeare, *per exemplum*.

'Well,' said John. 'Let us see. We are looking for the effects of belladonna, which are dilated pupils, sensitivity to light, loss of balance, staggering, flushing, severely dry mouth and throat, urinary retention, confusion, delirium, and convulsions; as much as might be discerned in a cat. Or we look out for those of hemlock poisoning which are as follows: stimulation followed by paralysis, vomiting, trembling, problems in movement, rapid respiration, salivation, plenteous urination, nausea, convulsions, coma and death.'

'To translate that,' said Tom, 'a poisoned cat should first run madly round its cage but suddenly slow and stumble as though blind - for the pupils of its eyes will dilate as wide as any bathed in belladonna. It may vomit and shiver convulsively. It should pant and drool. It will go into convulsions, losing control of its bladder, then slide into a coma and so die. If memory serves the whole process should take one hour depending on the dose.'

John opened his mouth to question or further explain part of Tom's description, but he was interrupted immediately.

'You have done this before,' said Rosalind harshly.

'We have,' answered Tom, 'and with poisons even more deadly than hemlock.'

*

As Tom was speaking, John turned away and put half of the oil he had taken from Spenser's ear in a small bowl, added a tiny amount of milk, mixed the two together and slid it up to the nearest cage. The caged cat thrust its head out eagerly and lapped up the milk at once. 'One hour,' said Tom.

'One hour until it is dead,' confirmed John, 'if that really is either belladonna or hemlock at any rate. If Hal were here I would trust him to record the process so we could be certain. But he is not, so I will do so myself.'

'If the lady Ann can be persuaded to send dinner in here I will keep you company,' offered Tom.

'And I,' added Rosalind.

So it was arranged. The three of them sat round the table and positioned themselves so that they could keep an eye on the poisoned cat. One of the children brought a bowl of water and they all washed their hands - John most carefully; then he placed a pile of paper and a pen convenient to his elbow so he could record the stages of the cat's demise.

The child who brought the water replaced it with a loaf of bread and a pat of good yellow butter. Then Elizabeth brought in three bowls of eel stew with horn spoons and a knife to spread the butter. While she was passing them all out a jug of small beer and three cups arrived.

Elizabeth turned to go but Tom prevented her. 'A question for you, Elizabeth, answer truly and I will not detain you long.'

Elizabeth turned, shooting a guarded look at her father who refused to meet her eye. In the brief moment of silence that followed, Tom assessed her. Eighteen and full grown, blonde hair that would not do her bidding, blue eyes below arched brows and dark lashes, pink cheeks and pale peony lips - a little thin for his taste but set in a resolute line. A chin every bit as determined as Rosalind's but giving the effect of wilfulness rather than strength.

'How long have you been consulting Simon Forman?' he asked.

She paled, her eyes wide with shock. 'Who told you? Did Hal betray me?'

'I have seen your birth chart in his house,' said Tom equably. 'How long have you been consulting Forman and for what purpose?'

'If you measure up to your reputation in my father's eyes at least you should be able to exercise your logic and answer that for yourself,' she snapped.

'It was the precise element of your future you wanted to know that interested me,' he said. 'Were you assessing outcomes with Hal or with other, more elevated, members of society?'

'Hal!' she sneered. 'He follows me like a spaniel and is ever more faithful the crueller I treat him! If he has betrayed me...'

'So.' Tom cut off her fulminations firmly. 'It is the offspring of some courtier who has turned your head, for I assume you have no designs upon any of the great men for whom your father works, many of whom are old enough to be your grandsires.'

'I would wager,' struck in Rosalind suddenly, 'that there is no one particular lordling. They would hardly know that the apothecary's girl even exists! She has Simon Forman drawing up her chart in the hope that he will guide her towards one or another so she may scheme to turn his head. With philtres or love-tokens I'll be bound.'

'Not so!' snapped Elizabeth. 'There is a widely-travelled young man in the household of Sir Thomas Edgerton, Lord Keeper of the Great Seal in York House, has a burning affection for me. He is chief secretary...'

'Dear God in Heaven,' said Tom, 'you do not mean *John Donne*?'

ii

'John Donne,' Tom repeated, staring Elizabeth straight in the eyes. 'Why the man is a rakehell and besides, I am certain he has designs upon young Anne More...'

'That's all you know, Master of Logic! John has told me of his love for me!'

'And where did you meet this Master Donne?' demanded her outraged father.

'At St Paul's. Mother sent me on an errand but Hal could not go with me so I went alone. She urgently wanted fruit in despite of the season, with child yet again I'll wager, and there's a fruit stall hard by St Pauls with some booksellers beside it. I was buying winter apples and he was looking at some poem books there. Then he came up and we fell to talking. He told me of himself and his adventures. Such places he has been to, such things has he seen and done. Such great men as are his acquaintance, Sir Walter Raleigh, the Earl of Essex...'

'And so you started meeting more regularly?' asked Tom, his voice deceptively gentle once more.

'I got Hal to help,' she tossed her head. 'He will do anything for me. When Mother told me to run errands, Hal would come with me and I would meet John in St Paul's Churchyard while Hal looked sadly on.'

'But you were never alone?'

'Never other than that first time. But he loves me. He has written poems to me...'

'And to half the young women in London!' said Tom, more firmly. 'A rakehell recusant from an infamously Catholic family. His brother died in Newgate, imprisoned for sheltering the Jesuit Priest Harrington as was hanged, drawn and quartered at Tyburn three years ago after the pursuivants took him to the tender mercies of Rackmaster Topcliffe!'

'He has told me all this. He looks to me as his angel who will redirect his footsteps into the purer Protestant path...'

'He will direct his footsteps and more straight beneath your petticoats if you are not careful of him!' answered Tom. 'And to go to Simon Forman of all people to assess the likelihood of your snaring John Donne. That is fighting fire with fire with a vengeance. If one doesn't have you, the other assuredly will!'

Tom's words echoed in the room for a moment as everyone remained rigid with shock: John at the revelation, Elizabeth at the fact that no one had ever spoken to her like that in all her life and Rosalind at the behaviour of the poisoned cat.

Rosalind spoke first. 'Look!' she said. The cat was throwing itself from side to side. Its wide eyes were almost entirely black, their pupils yawning wide. Its mouth was agape, drool spraying from its lolling tongue. And even as they all swung round to see exactly what she was talking about, its legs gave out and it collapsed, quaking, onto the floor of the cage. A yellow pool of urine spread across the bench.

'That did not take an hour, surely,' said Tom, the outraged Elizabeth forgotten. He rose and crossed to the cage as John swiftly recorded the symptoms and their sequence. The shuddering animal was fighting for breath, emitting the faintest mewling sound as vomit dribbled out of a mouth that seemed frozen in a rictus. The black-pupilled eyes stared helplessly as the creature's ribs gave up the struggle to keep it breathing and all of a sudden it was dead. Tom inserted a careful finger between the bars of the cage and prodded the corpse. It was warm, but every bit as rigid as Spencer's had been.

'Hemlock,' said Tom and shook his head sadly.

'Definitely hemlock,' agreed John, looking up from his note-taking. 'One of hemlock's symptoms is the expanded irises - just as with belladonna. But one of the symptoms of belladonna is inability to pass urine. Hemlock, however, causes piss in abundance. Whatever herbs of mine Hal gave him to aid his sleep, it was a powerful distillation of hemlock that the murderer poured into his ear.'

'And Hal's herbs held him fast asleep as the hemlock did its work, said Tom. 'So he could not run madly round his room but suddenly slow and stumble as though blind. He did vomit and may have shivered convulsively. He certainly panted and drooled. He may well have gone into convulsions - the blankets were well enough disturbed and he certainly did lose control of his bladder. Then, I assume, he slid ever deeper into a false sleep, which the Ancient Greeks called a *koma* I believe - and so died.' There was a short silence as the others considered the terrible truth of his words. 'Well,' continued Tom after a few moments more, 'speaking of Greeks, at least poor Spencer shared his death with Socrates. That might have been some consolation, had he known it.'

*

'But the hemlock must have been distilled and concentrated to a terrible degree,' John shook his head. 'To have killed the cat so swiftly.'

'Who would make such a horrible concoction?' wondered Elizabeth, shaken out of her righteous rage and the only one in the room who did not know.

'Simon Forman for one,' answered her father shortly. 'And if I hear that you have visited him or that rakehell poet Donne again, I will take a rod to you, girl, that will make you skip and whimper! Ask your mother if you doubt me, for I have taken one to her in the past as is a father's right and a husband's duty.'

Elizabeth turned on her heel at that and stormed out. The others returned to the eel stew while it was still warm, though in truth none of them had much appetite left. They ate in silence - there seemed nothing more to say. Until John started, apparently a propos of nothing, 'I did not order him to go.' He looked up at the others. 'Hal,' he explained unnecessarily. 'He told me he planned to visit Foreman's house and see could he recover anything Elizabeth had left there. He loved her you see and wanted to protect her. I should have stopped him, especially as he was now a witness to Will Shakespeare buying poisons and therefore likely to be asked some hard questions by the Queen's Crowner or the Earl Marshal's men. But I didn't think - so I did not forbid him. He's dead, isn't he?'

'Fell down those stairs, frightened by the bird which seemed demonically possessed, just as you almost did yourself,' confirmed Tom. 'With no-one there to catch him as Ugo and I caught you.'

'Where is he now do you think?'

'In the brick privy in Foreman's garden as like as not. But as near as I can reckon from what we overheard, he won't be there for long. Forman, Chapman and - who knows - the Earl of Essex himself seem to have other plans for him.

iii

Early afternoon next day found Tom fresh from Sabbath worship and a bite of luncheon, with belly full and soul as clean as it would ever be, strolling apparently casually along Hog Lane. He could afford his apparent nonchalance because yesterday evening's clear weather still lingered with no sign of rain or snow returning. The day was frosty, fair enough, but even that worked in his favour by keeping the lane's thick mud solid so that his boots weren't even soiled. As he strolled eastward from Bishop's Gate, north of Houndsditch and the city wall, he turned over in his mind the conversation he was likely to have when he arrived at the Yeomans' familiar door. So deep in thought was he that he hardly registered the bustle of citizens heading the other way towards the Spital Field Butts and the Artillary Yard beyond - required by law to continue their weapons training each Sunday. As a member of the Guild of Masters of Defence, Tom was excused. It was assumed that if the Spanish did invade his mastery with his rapiers would be immediately and effectively employed without constant weekly honing. And Poley was excused because his work against the Spaniards - and indeed all the enemies of England - was on another level altogether.

With his planned conversation still unfinished in his mind, Tom turned off Hog Lane and onto the path leading to the Yeomans' door. Three brisk raps brought Bess the serving maid. 'Good morrow, Bess,' he greeted her as she peered round the edge of the door. 'I seek master Poley. Is he aloft?' he asked. Poley's rooms were immediately beneath the eaves - in a similar room to that in which Forman kept his black magic paraphernalia and his demon-possessed parrot. Aptly enough, thought Tom, for Poley was also a master of dark arts.

'No, Master Musgrave,' whispered Bess. 'Master Poley hasn't lain here for the best part of a week.'

'Do you know where he is?'

'No, Master Musgrave. My Mistress might know, but she is not to be disturbed.'

'At prayer or Sabbath study, I expect,' said Tom. Bess's eyes widened and she choked on a giggle.

Then her countenance became perfectly demure; suspiciously so, thought Tom. 'Just so, sir I'm sure,' she said and closed the door in his face.

Tom hesitated for a moment before turning away. He had known Bess for as long as he had been visiting this house and he had never seen her behave quite like this. So, his interest piqued, he wandered off down Hog Lane as though deep in thought. He half wished he had taken to the fashion for smoking - a pipe now would explain why he lingered even though it was unusual to see anyone applying its undoubted medicinal benefits outside a tavern or smoking house. He paused, raised his foot onto a low wall and seemed to be attending to some mud clinging to his boot. He had to be careful, though. Loitering was at least frowned upon and in some areas illegal - especially on the Sabbath when so many folk had so much to do between Matins and Evensong.

*

But luckily he did not have to wait too long. Less than ten minutes after Bess shut Joan Yeomans' door, she opened it again. Bess and her mistress swept out, dressed for a lengthy walk, laden with covered baskets whose contents were impossible even for the Master of Logic to guess with any certainty. But it looked like food and drink to Tom.

The two women marched purposefully back toward Bishopsgate Street, then they turned south and hurried along it through the Bishops Gate itself. Tom followed them, unnoticed, into Gracechurch Street then on into Fish Street, crossing the City in its entirety, and so into the thinner Sunday afternoon bustle of London Bridge. He still had almost no idea where they were heading for, but he had a shrewd idea who they were planning to meet: Robert Poley. And if Poley had not slept in his own bed for a week it could only mean that he was working undercover, probably in some prison, trying to tempt his fellow inmates into indiscretions that would reveal sedition or treason and fit them for Tyburn or The Tower. Which of the nearby jails he was currently resident in, was difficult to ascertain until the women marched down off the South Wark and continued straight into The Borough without turning right into Clink Street and the Clink Gaol or left into Tooley Street and the Borough Counter. As they continued straight on, it was clear that they must be heading for the Marshalsea.

Tom followed, fascinated; his mind no longer turning over what he would say to Poley but how he would actually get to him. At last the women turned left into Angel Place and followed the edge of the churchyard behind the church of St George The Martyr until they reached the forbidding frontage of the Marshalsea. Tom paused, uncharacteristically hesitant. Should he push forward and pretend to be part of their party or should he hang back and await events?

Joan Yeomans knocked on the door and spoke to the man whose face appeared behind the grille set at head-height into it.

After a moment, the door opened and the two women vanished inside. Still in a quandary, Tom hesitated - what he would say to the door keeper now all intermixed with what he wished to say to Poley. But all too soon he ran out of patience. He crossed the street and knocked on the jail's forbidding door. After a moment the section behind the grille opened. A battered countenance with scar-thickened brows and a flattened nose appeared. 'Yuss?' if demanded.

'I am come with Mistress Yeomans,' he said. 'I have a message for Master Poley. It is vital that I speak with him.'

'Mistress Yeomans, ye say?' demanded the battered face. 'With a message for Master Poley?'

'Yes! It is most urgent that I give it to him...'

'Well ye don't just walk in here, cully, message or no.' The lips, almost as thick as the battered brows. parted in a mocking grin to reveal the brown stumps of random teeth and to release a breath that seemed to have issued straight from the nearest dunghill. 'Mayhap ye'd better get yourself taken up by the pursuivants, then ye'll be in here quickly enough. Master Gauge is to hand and he'll be happy to oblige...'

There was a moment of silence as Tom tried to think of a riposte to this. But then matters moved on. The man at the door turned to glance over his shoulder. There was a stirring behind him and he turned right round. 'Ho Mistress Bess,' he said, suddenly the most courteous gallant. 'I did not see ye there. Is everything satisfactory?'

'It is, thank'ee. But my mistress wishes me to return home.'

'Of course.' The key turned, the door opened and Bess appeared. 'Why Master Musgrave,' she said with a low curtsey as she saw him waiting there. 'What do you do here, sir?'

'A message, Bess,' he said. 'For Mistress Yeomans and Master Poley.'

Bess's eyes widened. The shadow of a conspiratorial grin flitted over her face then she turned to the turnkey. 'This is Master Musgrave,' she said. 'You should let him enter and show him to Master Poley at once. And no need to disturb Master Gauge nor any other of the pursuivants for if they aren't at evensong they will be on their way.' She hurried on out, pausing only to curtsey once again. And, before the bemused turnkey could shut the door again, Tom stepped in to the Marshalsea prison.

iv

The turnkey looked at Tom, clearly less than happy with what was going on. But then, pretty little Bess knew this tall, well-dressed stranger and had recommended him. So the turnkey gave a mental shrug and decided to do as she had asked. 'Master Poley,' he concluded, 'and don't disturb master Gauge'. All of the thoughts were reflected in his battered countenance, each one following the other so slowly that Tom had time to look around the jail's reception area, which was little more than a stone-walled room with a desk where the prison records could be kept - by someone who could write and therefore not the turnkey, he thought; perhaps by the mysterious master Gauge. The desk had a torch blazing above it. Opposite, in the shadows, was a bench, clearly for prospective inmates. A strong wooden strut ran the length of it at ankle height, worn and splintered, clearly from gyves and chains. Beyond that, a corridor opened into near darkness, no doubt leading also to the cells. 'Master Poley,' said the turnkey, recalling Tom's attention. You clearly didn't need to be Aristotle's intellectual equal to earn the post of turnkey at the Marshalsea.

'Lead on Master Turnkey,' said Tom breezily, as though he was used to making free of more prisons than the Clink, which was run by his old friend Talbot Law.

'Master Poley,' muttered the turnkey once more and ambled into the shadowy corridor, the stench of his breath replaced by various noxious odours emanating from other orifices about him. Tom followed, more closely than he wanted to - particularly than his nose wanted to - but the darkness left him little choice. 'Master *Poley*...'

By God's good grace it seemed to Tom, the turnkey stopped at the first door on the right. Tom was so preoccupied that the Master of Logic hardly stirred or he would have reasoned a great deal of information from this. Independently of the fact that there was a sign on the door which a combination of the turnkey's shoulder and the shadows made it impossible to read. The turnkey rapped on the wooden panel. 'What is it?' called a familiar voice impatiently.

Taking this as an invitation to enter, the turnkey opened the door.

Tom pushed past him, opening the door wider still. There were two people in the room. They sat behind a table amply supplied. At a glance, he saw a pie, some winter salad, the winter apples like those Elizabeth bought at the price of compromising her innocence in St Paul's beside John Donne and a good-looking bottle of wine. He saw all this at a glance because he his attention was focussed on the pair behind the table. Poley was bedraggled, ill-shaven and filthy, and yet Joan Yeomans was seated happily on his lap, her bodice gaping just enough to establish that his hand had been snatched out of its depths an instant or so ago.

'Master Poley...' began the turnkey.

But Poley cut him short. 'That will be all, *Dick Dull*,' he grated, leaving Tom uncertain whether Dick Dull was the turnkey's name or an insult. 'Show Master Musgrave in and then depart, disappear, decamp. Get OUT!'

The turnkey stumbled backwards as though struck in the face by Poley's angry words. Tom glanced over as he left and reached to close the door. So that at last he was able to read the sign.

PURSUIVANT MARSHAL

*

'Dear God in Heaven, Poley,' he said, his mind literally reeling as he closed the door behind himself. 'Don't tell me you are not only Chief Intelligencer to the Council and Secretary Cecil but Pursuivant Marshal working for his greatest rival Earl Marshal Essex. How in the Good Lord's name do you know who to stab in the back?'

Poley reacted to none of this. Joan Yeomans made to rise from his lap, fussing with her bodice as she did so but he held her firmly in place.

'Master Musgrave,' he said after a moment. 'I had not looked to see you here.' His face folded into a slow, thoughtful frown.

In the centre of the wrinkled forehead there was just the faintest dark mark - the last sign of a wound that robbed him of his memory some time ago - and came close to robbing him of his life. It was only really visible if you knew where to look, thought Tom, who had been there when Poley was assaulted and for some time thereafter. It was mostly covered now with dirt and an oily fringe.

'Nor I you, Master Poley,' he said. 'As I believe my astonishment has made clear. That is, I knew you were likely in the Marshalsea when Mistress Yeomans came hither. But to find you are Pursuivant Marshal! Can it be true?'

'Making free of the Pursuivant Marshal's office at any rate,' said Poley, never one to answer a straight question with a clear answer. Politic to his fingertips, thought Tom.

'Are you saying you are not the Pursuivant Marshal?'

'I am saying nothing. Except, perhaps, what brought you hither? And have you any expectation of leaving in the near future? I have many cells and many positions in the largest of them convenient to this office, most of them full but I'm sure I can find room. At the moment I am contemplating chaining you in one of them, awaiting transfer to the Tower and Rackmaster Topcliffe.'

Unlike Poley, Tom was willing to answer questions. 'What brought me hither was my search for you. I tried Hog Lane without success but was lucky in that I could follow Mistress Yeomans. I have a lively expectation of leaving to return to Blackfriars rather than The Tower because I believe you will be interested in what I have to say. It is about Spenser, the poet and Sherriff of Cork City.'

Poley frowned. 'Spenser.'

'As was found dead in his bed yesterday morning, who lies at the moment in Essex house, who is due to be washed, shrouded and coffined tomorrow, hearsed on Tuesday and buried next to Chaucer in Westminster Abbey.'

'With all the foremost poets in the city reading elegies over him.; yes, I know it all.'

'Except, perhaps, that Spenser met his end by having a potent distillation of hemlock poured into his ear as he slept,' said Tom.

Poley blinked. 'Are you telling me he was murdered?'

'As surely as Kit Marlowe was,' Tom answered.

Poley was so shaken that he didn't even rise to Tom's bait.

'Murdered, you say. Who by?'

'There was a witness said Will Shakespeare bought a great deal of hemlock early on Friday evening.'

'Which explains your involvement, at least in part,' observed Poley. 'But if it was a distillation that killed him, the hemlock would need to have been bought days in advance, perhaps more. Who is this witness?'

'John Gerard's apprentice, a young man name Hal.'

'And where is this Hal now?'

'Missing, believed dead.'

'A murdered poet, a missing witness and one of your closest friends standing accused. Well, here's a coil indeed! And why am I not surprised to find you caught right at the heart of it?'

v

'But I am surprised, I must admit,' answered Tom, 'to find that the Pursuivant Marshal - if you are truly the Pursuivant Marshal - remains in ignorance of the fact that Spenser was murdered. Sir Thomas Gerard, the Knight Marshal led the men who came for the body. He had apparently consulted with Essex, Gelly Meyrick and the Bacon brothers before he left Essex House. He had Simon Forman with him as I had John Gerard. Both men, whatever their faults and differences, could have seen that this was no natural death. John did and therefore I assume Simon Forman did. There must be some sort of investigation going on. But why keep it secret from one of the men who should be most actively involved in it?'

The three of them were seated at the table now, Joan Yeomans and Robert Poley pausing between mouthfuls of pie to talk to Tom, who was nibbling some cheese and nursing a goblet of wine.

'Perhaps because my work here is too important to be disturbed,' suggested Poley. Joan Yeomans nodded, cheeks bulging, at this obvious truth.

'What! You have another Babington plot afoot?' asked Tom ironically. 'Someone is planning to hide a dunderbus beneath a Jesuit cassock and shoot the Queen? There are barrels of gunpowder stacked beneath White Hall or West Minster waiting to blow Her Majesty, her parliament and her council out of this life and into the next?'

'Even to suggest such things in jest comes dangerously close to sedition,' warned Poley.

'Really? How disappointing! I was trying for outright treason.' Tom took a sip of wine, watching Poley over the rim of his glass.

Poley gave a snort of exasperation. 'You will end up in the Tower yet,' he warned. 'And at the headsman's block on Tower Green if you don't take care!'

'That is a risk I will have to run. But the questions still remain, Master Poley. Are you the Pursuivant Marshal and, if so, why has neither the Earl Marshal nor the Knight Marshal told you that Spenser was murdered?'

'You are the Master of Logic. You work it out.'

'Because they do not trust you,' said Tom. 'Which brings us to the next question. If indeed you are the Pursuivant Marshal, how did you come by the post - you being, as we all know, Chief Intelligencer to The Council. Is the Earl of Essex trying to prove something to Secretary Cecil? Are you, so to speak, an olive branch? What is it that Essex wants so badly that he would accept you into his closest circle, knowing your true allegiance? Why, the Queen's signature on his commission as Lord Lieutenant of Ireland, of course. It is all that consumes him at the moment. Is that it? He accepts you as Pursuivant Marshal and Cecil agrees to prompt the Queen into signing Essex' commission. And Cecil is content to allow things to proceed because he has absolute faith in Essex - that he will fail in this mission as he has done in so many others, outrage Her Majesty and utterly destroy himself in Ulster. But in the mean-time, the cautious Master Secretary wants you - you of all men - just where you are because he has heard rumours that if he sees things going too terribly wrong, Essex might yet use his Irish Army to invade England and either replace the Queen himself or facilitate the succession by James of Scotland. Essex must be absolutely desperate or overweeningly confident even to consider countenancing such an arrangement. But then, as we know all too well, the compound of desperation and overweening confidence is the very essence of the man.'

'That and arrogant high-handedness,' agreed Poley.

'So,' concluded Tom. 'You have the post and, no doubt, the power of the Pursuivant Marshal, especially in your search for Jesuit assassins. But you do not have the confidence of the Knight Marshal who has not shared the facts of Spencer's murder with you; or, I would guess, of the Earl Marshal his master. So I would assume that it is you, Master Poley, who must beware a sudden and unexpected end like Spenser's. For the instant Essex is commissioned as Lord Lieutenant, he is likely to have you murdered, just in case you have learned too much while posing as Pursuivant Marshal.'

*

'My life to protect the Queen,' said Poley. 'To safeguard the realm? Do you think I would hesitate?'

'No,' said Joan Yeomans. 'Oh no!' her voice rang with ill-controlled emotion and heartfelt pride.

Tom looked at her. Her eyes were streaming with tears and glowing with admiration. He nodded. 'Why man,' he said, quoting something of Will's that he had read recently. 'You do bestride the intelligence world like a colossus.'

'A *colossus*,' said Poley, looking at Tom askance.

'You have a foot in either camp at any rate,' said Tom. 'But remember to stand firm when the earth quakes.'

Poley gave a grunt of cynical laughter, then he returned to the matter in hand. 'Hemlock, you say.'

'A potent distillation; thick and dark, almost like tar. A small scraping of it mixed with milk killed a cat in less than half an hour.'

'Poured in his ear...' Poley was clearly becoming interested. And only Rosalind had equal acuity in Tom's experience.

'He had been taking drugs to overcome pain and aid restful sleep. You remember that his ear was hurt by a blow from as club...'

'An Irish *bata*, yes...' Poley's hand rose towards his own forehead before he could control the gesture.

'Since then he has kept it bandaged and has taken doses of belladonna to help him sleep.'

'A large dose to hold him asleep while hemlock was poured into his ear.'

'Especially as it was the wounded ear and whoever poured the hemlock removed the bandage first. Was it Vesalius or Eustachius who first suggested that the ear is connected by a tube to the back of the throat? Pouring poison into Spencer's ear was just the same as making him drink it - but far easier and quicker under the circumstances.'

'Hmm,' said Poley. 'Even so, I'd guess that whoever prepared the sleeping draught must be party to the plot and made up a stronger dose than usual.'

'Perhaps, but Spenser also drank a good deal of strong ale which John Gerard says would have compounded the sleeping draught's effect.'

'So the murderer was fortunate as well as well prepared. But to the sleeping potion,' said Poley. 'It was of course prepared by...' Poley's eyebrows rose interrogatively.

'Gerard's apprentice...' said Tom.

'Who is missing, presumed dead.'

'Just so.'

'Is there any suspicion that pressure could have been brought on this apprentice?' asked Poley out of a world of experience in such matters. 'Anything he wanted? Anything he feared? Any secrets he was afraid of having exposed?'

'If he had secrets they are secret still, and likely to remain so,' said Tom. 'But he wanted Elizabeth, his master's nubile daughter. And he feared that either John Donne or Simon Forman would have her first - she met the former by accident at St Pauls but he courted her after a fashion so she went to the latter to have her future foretold.'

'If she was my daughter I would foretell her a future involving a well whipped arse!'

Joan Yeomans nodded in righteous indignation at the wilful child's behaviour and Poley's suggested cure for it.

'Which John Gerard has promised her if she persists.' Tom said.

'I'm glad to hear it!' said Poley. 'There's some hope for modern parenting yet. But the apprentice has vanished, you say. If he's alive that would seem like a sure sign of guilt.'

'He died at Forman's I am sure,' said Tom, and went on to tell Poley what he had experienced in Billingsgate and what he had deduced from it.

But then, just as he finished, another thought struck him. 'Now I think of it, Master Poley, it seems unsettlingly convenient that the post of Pursuivant Marshal should fall vacant just at the time Secretary Cecil needed you to fill it and keep an eye on Essex and his acolytes. Can I ask, what happened to the previous incumbent? The man who last called this office his own?'

'Dead,' said Poley. 'No mystery nor murder that I can discover, convenient though the matter proved. Fell off his horse and broke his neck, leading a squad of pursuivants in the examination of the notoriously recusant catholic Hoghton Hall up in Lancashire.'

Chapter 6: The Ancient Abbey

i

Tom and Joan Yeomans parted company at the South Wark. The disgruntled woman, robbed of what she had hoped to receive from her lover in return for feeding him, went straight up under the southern gatehouse an all-but empty basket in the crook of each arm. The bridge was less busy than usual - they had crossed it in less than half an hour coming south and it looked as though she would get back even more quickly now. Tom turned left into Clink Street and strolled past St Mary Overie steps ignoring the calls of the wherrymen offering to skull him across the river to the City. Their cries had hardly faded before he was passing the Clink prison itself and crossing Dead Man's Place beyond it.

He was walking like a blind man, so deep in thought that Essex could have marched his Irish army past and Tom would not have noticed. Though to be fair, the bustle of people going into and out of the taverns and brothels all around was lessened, as was the audience at the Bull- and Bear-baiting pits. Like the crush on London Bridge there were fewer people here because it was a Sunday afternoon. Which also explained why the Rose theatre was closed.

Tom's first thought was that Joan's carnal desires had been thwarted by more than his presence in the Pursuivant Marshal's office. What he had described to Poley had sent the intelligencer into an equally deep brown study. He had hardly seemed to notice when Joan rose, cleared what was left of the food into her baskets and headed for the door with Tom immediately behind her. There were no farewells, fond or otherwise. Dick Dull had let them out into the calm, chilly afternoon. And they walked silently towards the bridge, each prey to their own thoughts.

As they parted company, Tom was going over and over the logic he applied to the revelation that Poley was the Pursuivant Marshal, even if only temporarily and as part of a dark bargain forced on two mortal enemies and immensely powerful men. He could not fault his reasoning. The diminutive, hunched Secretary Cecil was secretly convinced that Essex had a plan in

which he would snatch the throne from the elderly and
vacillating woman who saw him as the son she had never had
and spoiled him in consequence - while the power-hungry Earl
regarded her simply as an increasingly senile impediment to his
plans. Essex in turn suspected that Cecil, although he had no
direct ambition to succeed to the throne, nevertheless planned
to control whoever sat on it like a puppet master with his
marionette.

Essex might well be desperate enough to accept Cecil's chief
spy as co-commander of his army of pursuivants if he got his
wish to be Lord Lieutenant of Ireland as an immediate
consequence. For Ireland represented so much to the upright,
manly, strapping and thoroughly spoilt thirty-three year old
Earl. It was where his father Walter Devereux, first Earl of
Essex and Earl Marshal of Ireland, had thrown away the
family's fortune fighting to bring peace to the troubled country
- and then been poisoned and died aged thirty five; only two
years older than his son was now. Ironically enough, thought
Tom, he had been poisoned with hemlock. The lethal dose had
been slipped into his wine at a formal dinner in Dublin Castle.
It was never discovered who had performed the lethal act,
though the Catholics against whom he was fighting had always
seemed the most likely culprits. Ireland was where Essex could
revenge his father, rebuild his standing in the country and at
court after years of failure and disobedience.

Essex had made his reputation for disobedience at the age of
23 when he sailed with Drake aboard his English Armada to
Spain against the Queen's direct orders, thought Tom. But then
at 25 he proved himself a more reliable - and able - leader while
fighting for the Hugenot King Henri IV of France whose father
had been assassinated by the same brand of Catholic extremists
the Earl Marshal of England was there to protect his Queen
from. But Henri had become a Catholic himself only a couple
of years later, cynically observing 'Paris is worth a mass'. Thus
almost all of Essex' good work on the continent was undone in
a flash. And in many ways, thought Tom, Essex had gone
downhill from there, with the exception of that one shining

moment of glory when he headed the raid that captured Cadiz three years ago in 1596.

His command of the naval expedition to the Azores two years ago had gone badly. Raleigh, his second in command, had followed the Queen's wishes and planned to attack the Spanish fleet which was bound for the Channel but Essex went after a treasure ship instead, against orders once more - so that the Spaniards, unopposed, were able to mount a new Armada against an undefended South Coast. Only another Heaven-sent storm had saved England from invasion.

Since then, matters had gone from bad to worse. Only last year the Queen had actually boxed Essex' ears when he insulted her at a meeting of the Council. 'Your conditions are as twisted as your carcase,' he spat and she, nearly knocking him off his feet answered, 'Go to the devil! Get you gone and be hanged!'

There was little doubt in Tom's mind that Essex had worked himself into such a tight corner that only a resounding success in Ireland would free him and re-establish his reputation. Success which he and his circle were sure he would achieve.

But that thought led onto another. With Essex successful and Ireland finally at peace, who would join men like Humphrey Gilbert and Walter Raleigh and own great, hugely profitable estates there? That was an important consideration because the largest and potentially the richest of all the estates was that one centred on Kilcolman Castle, the burned-out residence of the late Edmund Spenser. If Essex defeated the Irish rebels and brought peace to Ireland, Spenser's estates could be worth an almost incalculable fortune, which could be - at the least - a potent motive for murder.

But why drag Will Shakespeare into the matter?

*

Tom was still turning this vital question over when he reached Maiden Lane. He did not need to bestir the Master of Logic to deduce where Will and Rosalind were planning on setting up home. Martin Fletcher's wagon, pulled by the inestimable filly Titania was standing outside, the horse named for the queen of fairyland contentedly cropping grass from the edge of the rutted mud path. More than that, Peter Street the carpenter led a crew who had been working on reassembling The Globe, clearly helping Will take his necessaries up into his room and, no doubt, to reassemble his bed so that he and Rosalind would sleep comfortably tonight. Dick Burbage was overseeing the whole process, as his training as a carpenter permitted, though he was not the sort of leader who delegated all the work and ended up doing nothing himself. His sleeves were rolled up and he was working as hard as all the rest.

'Tom,' he greeted his friend as Tom came down Maiden Lane.

'Dick,' answered Tom companionably. 'Everything in hand?'

'Snug and settled. Will can even see The Globe from his window. A mixed blessing at the moment.'

'Why's that?'

'He's in a kind of race. He must finish the play we need for the opening before the thatchers get the roof on our new theatre. We need time to rehearse and perfect production and performance of course.'

'Of course. Any *duellos*, as there were so bountifully in *Romeo*? You know my rates for advising and training in swordplay are very reasonable.'

'Not as far as I know. But he has yet to vouchsafe which particular play he wishes us to perform. He tells me he's working on three at once and has yet to make up his mind between them. Should he fail us, we will have to go with *Henry Four Part One*, his most successful play so far. Though we have no Will Kempe to play Falstaff.'

'Armin could carry it, surely, though his clowning is more Terence than Plautus.'

'Certainly Armin is noted for his wit rather than his buffoonery, though I do not doubt he could carry Falstaff off if the need arose. But I would rather have a new play nevertheless.'

While they held this conversation, Tom and Dick worked their way through the street door and up the stairs to Will's new rooms. Here things were beginning to settle. The bed frame was erected and secured in the back room. The mattress was laid in place. The bedding was piled convenient to use. This was the smaller of the rooms and lacked a window - relying on light from the front room for brightness as well as the fire and a range of candles and lamps. Will's precious travelling trunk and papers were neatly positioned in the front room beneath the window which looked across Maiden Lane at Sir Nicholas Brend's field where The Globe stood part competed. A tall wardrobe had appeared and been erected in this room as the other one was too small. A table had also appeared and was laden with food and drink - almost as though Titania below had exercised some of her magic powers. The rooms both had fire-places and both were blazing, bringing warmth and dryness to accommodation that had clearly lain empty for some time.

'All well, Will?' asked Tom, for his friend was clearly finding all the bustle going on around him unsettling at the very least.

Will glanced up, frowning. Rosalind answered for him. 'All's well, thank'ee Tom. Though it seems we left St Helen's just in the nick of time. Apparently there were strangers there looking for Will earlier this afternoon.'

'Pursuivants?'

'No-one is certain but we fear so.'

ii

By an elegant exercise in irony, the whole of Monday's lessons in the art and science of defence with Tom Musgrave had been cancelled. Several had been booked by Edmund Spenser himself and the others by young men who were now keen to use the time in preparation for his funeral tomorrow. Tom had been working on Spenser's technique - especially the lunge. The poet had been a short man with a limited reach and he had been all too well aware that the thrust would not serve him against a taller opponent with longer arms - which seemed to include just about every adult man in London with the exception of Robert Cecil the Lord Secretary who was stunted and crookbacked. Tom, like the red-headed, brown-eyed charmer Sir Walter Raleigh topped six feet in height. Cecil barely made it past five feet and did not quite reach either man's shoulder. The only person he topped at court was the queen herself. Something that Tom made light of but which Raleigh rarely failed to snigger at. Elizabeth herself called Cecil 'My

Dwarf', 'My Elf,' and occasionally 'My Ape'. When she did so, Cecil made a show of sharing the jest - but Tom had seen the look in his eyes. It was bad enough that the enormous intellect Cecil owned was trapped in that twisted, simian body but the pain and humiliation were compounded by the fact that the aging Queen surrounded herself with tall, strapping and famously good-looking men. Her playful nicknames for Cecil were in his eyes just a continuation of a childhood and youth blighted by the insults of his peers and their parents and by the agonies inflicted by doctors employed by his sadly disappointed father to try and straighten his carcase, which was, in Essex' insulting words to the outraged Queen herself, 'twisted'.

It was ironic, too, that poor little Spenser was being given such a grand farewell at the expense of the equally impecunious but famously tall and good-looking Robert Devereux.

That thought prompted Tom's next action. He was at liberty because of Spenser's sudden death - therefore he would go down to West Minster and see how the preparations in the Abbey were going. He would be attending the funeral in some capacity himself tomorrow - perhaps merely as a spectator if it was to be the poets who carried the coffin and led the mourning. But there would be more than mere poets attending - his aristocratic students had started cancelling tomorrow's lessons as well as today's already for this was clearly going to be an important social event, even though the Queen was not likely to be present. He wanted to see the place before the crush began.

'Ugo,' he called. 'I'm going to visit Westminster Abbey to look at the preparations for tomorrow. Coming?'

'*Ja*,' said the Dutchman. 'It's a pretty morning, cold but clear. A good day to be out, especially if we go by the river.'

Side by side they walked down Water Lane to the Blackfriars Steps. Tom caught the eye of a ferryman, 'Westward Ho!' he called, 'to the Queen's Bridge steps.'

'Right you are masters,' the ferryman replied, easing his boat alongside. 'Queen's Bridge steps and Her Majesty's court it is.'

*

The wherry took them swiftly upriver to the west, easily avoiding the occasional block of ice left over from when the river was entirely frozen at the end of last year. On the nearby north bank they passed the stinking outwash of the Fleet River with the Bridewell beside it - once a palace now yet another prison. Then Whitefriars was followed by The Inner Temple with the Temple garden and Middle Temple steps. On their left, the more distant South Bank was just a series of low, field-covered hills with pasture for cows. The South Wark and its taverns, baiting pits and theatres was, like London Bridge, well behind them. Nothing more of note lay ahead until Lambeth Palace opposite West Minster - a short ferry ride for the Archbishop of Canterbury to go from his London home to the principal London place of worship although the Church of St Peter also known as Westminster Abbey, was not actually under his jurisdiction at all but under that of the Dean, and, above him, the Queen.

The north bank continued to be packed - though it was really the west bank now as the river had swung through a right angle to run south. Arundel Palace, Somerset Palace and The Savoy, stood cheek-by-jowl with Essex House, Durham House, York Place and Scotland Yard. Then the Court steps were succeeded by the Privy Steps leading up into White Hall, the Star Chamber Steps and the Queen's Bridge leading up into West Minster.

It was as they approached the top of the Queen's Bridge steps that Ugo suddenly demanded, 'How do you propose to get in? The Abbey isn't open to every Tom or Dick...'

'...Or Harry. I thought you'd never ask. I propose to use my most potent arts of persuasion and fabrication.'

'Lies and prevarication.'

'You never know - it might work. It has in the past.'

'Not that I can remember.'

This conversation brought them up to the east-facing rear of the Abbey with Henry VII's magnificent new chapel extending the building further toward the river. The whole area was a flurry of activity. Workmen and onlookers teemed around the west-facing front of the building but the Dean of Westminster's men oversaw who was permitted entry and who was doomed to stand outside and gape.

At first it seemed that Tom and Ugo were destined to remain amongst the latter, but then chance intervened. Tom spotted two unlikely companions in the Great West Doorway talking to the Dean's guards. An improbable pairing indeed - Sir Francis Bacon, Essex' secretary, and Sir Walter Raleigh, Essex' most bitter rival. Both men knew Tom and both were likely to be indulgent with him. He shouldered over to them with Ugo close behind.

'Good day, Sir Walter,' called Tom, keeping his voice quiet and courteous - Raleigh had an occasionally unpredictable temper, as was often the case with red-headed people, Tom had noticed. Though Raleigh's hair and beard were much darker than the red heads of freckled and bellicose Irish men and women, he thought, more foxy than anything else. Unlike the glorious waves that adorned his mistress' head - a delicious mixture or mahogany, auburn and deep copper. Raleigh's quick brown eyes sought him out at once. As did those of Bacon, standing like a weasel beside him. For a moment Tom almost felt himself to be in one of Chaucer's Canterbury Tales where animals and humans became one and the same. Chaucer was probably lingering somewhere in his mind because he knew of Essex' plan to bury Spenser beside the dead man's poetic hero; unless his ghost was hovering nearby.

'Master Musgrave,' said Sir Walter, breaking into Tom's thoughts amiably enough. 'What are you doing here?'

'Sir Francis, your servant, sir.' Tom bowed to both Bacon and Raleigh at once then straightened. 'Well, Sir Walter, Master Stell and I have come to scout out the Abbey in preparation for tomorrow. As you may know, Spenser was a pupil of mine, so we will seek to attend the ceremony. In fact it was I who was first summoned to view the corpse, before the Earl of Essex became involved and Sir Thomas Gerard the Knight Marshal took matters in hand.'

Raleigh and Bacon exchanged a brief glance.

'Then you had best come in,' said Sir Walter. And Tom had the strangest feeling that he and Ugo were like two chickens being invited into the fox's den.

iii

Side by side, Tom and Ugo entered through the Great West Door into the towering space of the nave. Columns reached heavenwards on either hand and stepped forward, one after the other into the dazzling distance. Widely travelled though they were, environments like this were few and far-between in Tom's and Ugo's experience. Only in wild forests had Tom come across columns anywhere near as tall as these; and when he glanced up, it was almost as though he was looking at the sky. There was a kind of hush about the place that belied the scurrying of the workmen and their overseers. Footsteps, whispered conversations and occasional clang of a dropped implement seemed to echo unnaturally. The whole experience was so overpowering that it took Tom an instant or two before he realised that the fox and the weasel were following hard on their heels, discuss ing - of all things - the removal of Sir Walter's household from Durham House to his newly furbished residence in Sherborne.

Tom and Ugo walked toward the altar and the choir screen straight ahead. Tom couldn't get over the difference between this magnificence and the interiors of the simple Protestant churches he was used to. He had only seen fretwork equal to that on the choir screen in Catholic chapels in Italy and Spain. It all added to the strange, unsettling feeling that was beginning to grow on him.

Following their ears rather than any clear notion of precisely where they were going, Tom and Ugo went to the right of the choir and crossed the great open space where the North and South Transepts joined the east-running Nave. Each transept was the better part of one hundred feet wide - three times the width of London Bridge, though from the North Door to the southernmost chapels it was less than a third of the Bridge's length. Still, to capture such height and distance within the shell of a building seemed simply miraculous to the pair of them.

The workers preparing Spenser's grave seemed almost miniscule in comparison with their surroundings. They had lifted a series of flagstones and were digging into the earth beneath. It was a hard job by the look of it thought Tom, for the clay soil had lain undisturbed for centuries, compacted by the weight of the flags and those numberless people walking upon them. But on the other hand, he realised as Ugo and he came closer to the grave, the hard earth meant that the sides of the grave itself stood almost as solidly as the walls all around them, the pit followed the outer edges of the missing stones and sank squarely to where the gravedigger and his assistants were labouring.

Having reached his objective, Tom straightened and looked around, wondering where he would be able to place himself tomorrow when Essex, his acolytes and his tame poets led by George Chapman would be surrounding the bier or the coffin, reciting their self-serving doggerel and pretending heartbreak when they would mostly be dancing with inner joy that the death of a rival gave them such an excellent chance to advance their own reputations. Forgetting that Bacon and Raleigh were still behind them, Tom said to Ugo, 'We had best search out somewhere to sit and bring a bucket for vomit if we are going to suffer interminable poetising and stomach-heaving elegies.'

'Now, Master Musgrave,' purred Bacon, 'How is it that you know so much of the Earl's plans? I had supposed them still to be secret.'

*

'I had supposed them common knowledge, Sir Francis,' answered Tom, schooling his face into a look of open innocence. 'Has not George Chapman contacted many of the leading poets in the city? If my Lord of Essex hoped to keep things secret, he could hardly have done worse than to order his plans passed out to the greatest collection of chattering magpies in the land! I can assure you, sir, that Alabaster, Harvey, Holland and Weevil at the very least - probably with Chapman himself - will be seated in various taverns, ale-pots at their elbows, scribbling their doggerel and testing it at the top of their voices on anyone who will listen and a good few who would rather not.'

'Hmmm,' said Bacon, clearly unconvinced. 'And that's Weever, I believe, not Weevil.'

'Well, master gravedigger,' said Raleigh, paying no attention to Tom or Bacon. 'You make slow progress. Will everything be ready for tomorrow?'

'Aye your worship, that it will. 'Tis hard ground right enough but holy. Your man will lie here most snug in a grave inside an abbey, and the ground harder and holier than a churchyard even.'

'That's good enough for me,' said Raleigh. 'I'm off to Durham House and then to the court. Sir Francis?'

'I'm off to Essex House, Sir Walter, and report the progress to the earl.'

The two men turned away and their footsteps echoed down the soaring nave. Tom looked at Ugo. 'Let's look a little deeper, shall we? I was only half in jest about finding somewhere to sit.'

'Sitting in a church,' Ugo chided gently. 'It's not right, Tom. It shows too little respect to The Almighty, like as if a woman should come to worship with her head uncovered. But I take your point about the sick buckets.'

'Very well, let us look for somewhere we can stand in some comfort with the buckets at our feet.' The pair strolled deeper yet into the body of the church, their aimlessness attracting the attention of one of the Dean's guards. As they passed the Sanctuary and the High Altar, the man came towards them, calling, 'Masters, what is it you do here?'

'We are looking for a place to stand tomorrow,' explained Tom.

'Well, you cannot stand here. This is the tomb of St Edward, also known as The Confessor.'

'Really?' said Tom, his interest piqued. 'And this one behind it? I see some bruised and battered weapons and armour hanging from the beam above it but the effigy itself has been robbed of its head and hands.'

'Ah,' said the Dean's man. 'I can see you're not a Londoner sir by more than your Northern speech. Why that is the tomb of good King Henry V. I'm, told that the effigy's head and hands were all of solid silver and that he held a silver sceptre, but they have all been stolen, so he lies there without head or hands. And, truth to tell, without his wife either for Queen Katherine's body was removed from her tomb during the reign of our good queen's grandfather Henry VII, and the tomb has stood empty to this day. Not a kind manner to my way of thinking, sir, to treat one of our greatest hero kings. But then, what do I know of such matters beyond what I see in the playhouses? I am but a poor scholar.'

As Tom and Ugo made their way back down the echoing nave, Tom said, thoughtfully, 'Will is writing his play of *Henry Fifth* even now. I wonder does he know how England's greatest royal hero has been treated?'

'He's lost his head,' answered Ugo sadly. 'Who would have thought such a thing possible?'

'Let's hope we don't share the same fate,' said Tom. 'And that the great and the good all around us keep theirs as well.'

iv

Freedom from students for the afternoon and the promise of more freedom tomorrow put Tom into something of a holiday mood augmented by the sparkling clarity of the frosty afternoon. The Thames had been a continuous sheet of ice less than three weeks ago but it had broken up and the waterway was fairly free now, consequently there was a good deal of waterborne bustle. Tom, relaxing in the stern of a wherry seriously considered telling the wherryman to row them over to the nearest steps to Will Shakespeare's new residence, but in the end, the thought of fighting their way across to Bank End then back again to Blackfriars Steps seemed such a waste of time that he decided simply to retrace the course Ugo and he had taken earlier.

This decision turned out to be a fortunate thing, for as the Dutch gunsmith and he strolled out of Water Lane and into Blackfriars itself, a pair of worried looking youngsters came rushing towards them. It took Tom an instant to recognise John Gerard's oldest offspring other than Elizabeth. A pair of twins seemingly identical save that one was a girl and the other a boy. And the fact that they were here suggested that Elizabeth was not at home before they even opened their mouths.

'Mother sent us, Master Musgrave,' they gabbled, one talking over the other in their hurry to deliver their message.

'Elizabeth has gone off in a huff...

'Mother doesn't know where to...'

'Father is out tending Lord Cecil's gardens and not expected before sunset.'

'If Elizabeth is not home by then Mum says there will be murder done...'

'Father swore to beat her within an inch of her life if she goes off again...'

'Do you know where she might be found, sir?'

'Do you think you can bring her back home before Father arrives?'

Tom looked at Ugo and shrugged. 'Ugo, can you take these two upstairs and give them some milk. I suspect I know where Mistress Elizabeth might be discovered, and if not in one place then likely in the other.'

Ugo obediently shepherded the young Gerard twins up to the rooms he shared with Tom while Tom himself turned on his heel and strode eastwards along Carter Lane.

St Paul's churchyard was even busier than the River, folk of all sorts and standing brought out by the break in the wintery weather. Even so, Tom knew where he was headed - the best place to begin at any rate. He recognised Elizabeth's description of a bookseller's stall just beside a fruit and vegetable stand. The bookseller's name was Jaggard. He printed and bound pamphlets and slim volumes, and he specialised in poetry old and new, much of which had recently involved various works by Will Shakespeare.

That was where John Donne had been when Elizabeth and he first met and of all the places in the churchyard it was the most convenient for an assignation for it stood at the heart of a constantly shifting sea of humanity and yet, rock-like, it was always there, standing against the tide. Jaggard and his son were friends of Will's and, consequently, of Tom's. If Donne and Elizabeth had already met up and walked on, one of the Jaggards, father or son, would have a fair idea of where they went.

But when Tom arrived at Jaggard's stall, Donne was there alone, poring over a battered-looking pamphlet as Jaggard looked on impatiently, clearly wishing to make a sale and less than pleased that his customer was reading the entire booklet without purchasing it first. 'Well met Master Donne,' said Tom, who had been introduced to the recusant soldier poet at Thomas Walsingham's Nonesuch House some time ago. 'I'm looking for young Elizabeth Gerard as you have been courting. At least that's what she says. Have you had an assignation with her this afternoon?'

Donne looked up, apparently perplexed. 'I am courting no-one,' he said. 'I am not here on any assignation - merely to purchase this volume before Master Jaggard here sells it to any other. For it is, by my reckoning, unique.'

Sidetracked for a moment, Tom asked, 'Why? What is it?'

'Mayhap it is the last copy of Edmund Spenser's *Prosopopia or Mother Hubberd's Tale* still in circulation,' answered Donne excitedly. 'You know it has been banned and proscribed not once but twice. On its original publication it was banned by Lord Burghley; and more lately on its re-issue less than a year ago by Secretary Cecil his son. It is, they say, a scurrilous attack on one generation of great men after another - first the father and now the son, though that is by no means all. There are some who see almost treasonous references to courtiers right up to and including the Queen herself!'

'If that is so, then I have no doubt it has been banned and burned! Are you certain you have not seen Elizabeth Gerard, a tall, slim blonde girl, pretty spoilt and wilful?'

'I may have seen such a woman now you mention it. But not today.'

*

'Are you at liberty for a stroll down to Billingsgate?' asked Tom.

'I am at liberty, by why Billingsgate?' wondered Donne.

'Because the girl you only just recall is likely down there in Simon Forman's house completing her birth chart so he can predict whether you will wed her or not - and get him to supply a love philtre or some other magic toy in order to win you to her if you are not likely to fall in love any other way.'

'Dear God in Heaven! This is madness or witchcraft? Is she insane? I hardly know the girl.'

'It is her plan to ensure that you know her better - and ideally for the rest of both your lives.'

'Then I believe I had better accompany you post haste.'

Donne paid for the pamphlet then he and Tom set off for Billingsgate at a brisk walk.

'So,' said Tom, 'tell me more about this twice-banned publication. Is it like one of Ben Jonson's satiric plays that get him locked in jail every now and then?'

'No. It is more subtle than *The Isle of Dogs* that got Topcliffe chasing Jonson and Nashe that wrote it so that Jonson ended up in the Marshalsea under the eye of the Pursuivant Marshal, lucky not to have been racked in the mean time as I understand it.' Donne said.

'*More* subtle, you say. It could hardly be *less* so than *The Isle of Dogs*. But tell me how,' asked Tom, fascinated.

'Spencer's poem tells of a sick man, one too ill to leave his bed.'

'I know of one of those,' said Tom. 'Sir Antony Bacon. He works for the Earl of Essex.'

'Really? Well in this poem, the ailing poet is entertained by various friends but none can hold his interest until an old lady, Mother Hubberd, arrives. And she tells him a tale that holds his interest and begins his cure. This tale is about a Fox and an Ape who decide they are going to rise in the world and make themselves rich and powerful. This they do through a series of schemes and tricks. They first get a position tending the sheep of an honest farmer but they kill and eat them all then run away on the day before they are to account for the flock. They pretend to be clergymen to rob the poor and steal benefices, having been schooled in how to proceed by a priest who has no learning in anything except self-interest. Then they go to the lion king's court and behave in a manner that courtiers are forbidden to do - they accept bribes, terrorise any creature who doesn't pay enough, do down their enemies and bring forward members of their families whether they are honest and able or not. Finally, they discover the lion, as King of Beasts, asleep and they steal his skin, his crown and his sceptre so that they can rule the kingdom in his place. In the end the great god Jupiter is forced to intervene. He sends Mercury to rouse the sleeping lion so that all is put to rights. The Fox is stripped and banished while the Ape has his ears cropped and loses his tail.'

'A fox and an ape do this,' said Tom. 'You're sure it is a fox and an ape?'

'Indeed,' said Donne. 'There is no mistake. A fox and an ape.'

'Do you go much to the Queen's court?' wondered Tom.

'Hardly at all, as yet. But I hope for preferment...' Donne frowned with surprise at this apparent change of tack.

'So you would hardly be aware that the Queen herself, an elderly lady fond of stories, gives her closest courtiers nicknames, often animal names based on personal traits and so-forth. For instance, she called Sir Francis Walsingham her 'Moor' because he was so dark of aspect.'

Donne stopped short. He looked down at the pamphlet and up at Tom, an expression of horror slowly creeping over his face. 'And are you telling me that there are men there of great importance, whom she calls her Fox and her Ape?'

Tom nodded.

'But how can that be? The poem was written years ago, published ten years since to great initial success - until it was banned by order of Lord Burleigh...'

'But if it's been re-published again now,' said Tom grimly, 'it will be because Spencer was so desperate for money. By the look of things it has been re-published just at the time that its satire bites deepest and its targets are most obvious, like my bed-ridden Bacon, even if they are of a younger generation than the original ones!'

'Mary, mother of God! It is fortunate, perhaps, that poor Spenser is dead after all. And something of a miracle, I'd say, that he wasn't murdered by the Fox or the Ape, whoever they may be.'

V

Tom was still calculating how best to answer John Donne's remark when the poet gave a start and stopped on the spot. There immediately ahead of them, shouldering her way through the bustle of Thames Street, her face pale with fury, came Elizabeth Gerard. No sooner had Donne and Tom seen her than she saw them. The ice white cheeks became brick red in a heartbeat and Elizabeth froze in turn.

Tom walked forward, calling 'Well met, Elizabeth. Master Donne and I were seeking you. Your mother needs you at home.'

Elizabeth looked around like a cornered rabbit but the heedless bustle of those around her simply walled her in. As he approached, Tom noticed that she was carrying an oft-folded paper. Her birth chart, he guessed. And she was wearing something on a leather lace around her neck, something that looked like an amulet which rested on the upper slope of her breast, a piece of wood or stone that contrasted with the coarse blue cloth of her bodice.

'Master Musgrave,' she said, looking past him at his dark-haired, hot-eyed companion. 'Mother sent you? And Master Donne?'

'Your mother sent the twins asking if I could find you. I found Master Donne as I sought you. Are you well? You looked pale when I first saw you.'

'I am... I am...'

'You are returning from Simon Forman's,' he said. 'With your birth chart and an amulet. How did you afford such things?'

Her eyes widened and her gaze returned to Tom. 'When Mother sends me on errands I do not always spend everything she gives me. She never asks for change or accounting.'

'Best not let your father know you steal from your mother or he will take the rod to you as sure as night follows day. Was the risk worth taking?' he gestured to the folded chart. 'Does Foreman predict great things?' he gestured at the amulet. 'That charm would lead me to think perhaps he did not assure you of your heart's desire, so he has supplied a way of getting it beyond the control of the planets.'

Her eyes flicked up to Donne once more and her blush deepened.

'Whatever you hoped to gain from this adventure,' he continued smoothly, 'you have lost it. Master Donne was passing pleasantries, not courting you. His heart is already spoken for and lies elsewhere. As he will confirm should you have the courage to ask him. Our only concern is whether master Forman took you to his bedroom, which is by no means fit for a virgin to behold - and if he did, whether you are virgin still!'

*

The colour drained from her face once more. 'I ran away,' she said, her voice little more than a whisper. 'Out of that terrible room before he could lay a finger on me. I nearly fell down the stairs and I called to the servants for help but there was no-one there when I reached the kitchen. I ran out into the garden and would have hidden in the privy there but it was locked and looking through the peep-hole in the door I saw someone else was in it who did not bestir himself in spite of my pleas. So I ran back through the house and out through the shop. He did not follow me thank the Lord.'

'So you have escaped. Your virtue is intact. Whatever your birth chart predicts and whatever Master Forman promised that the amulet would do, it cannot involve Master Donne. We had best get you home before your father returns. It will go hard on you when you tell your mother what you have been doing. I will not answer for what your father will do if ever he should hear of it.'

Tom turned and paused, surprised for an instant. Sometime during his conversation with Elizabeth, John Donne had disappeared. He had planned to get the poet to confirm what he had just told the lovelorn maiden. But Donne's absence spoke every bit as loudly and clearly.

Depressed and defeated, Elizabeth fell in beside him and he matched the pace of his walking to hers. In truth he felt sorry for the girl. He was used to determined women. His last two lovers had both been full of fire and character, each headstrong in her own way, each forceful and impatient of propriety. The first was the beautiful Italian adventuress Costanza D'Agostino who had come with him from Maestro Capo Fero's school of fencing in Sienna but who had returned to her homeland while *Romeo* was still the rage at The Rose and the Newington Butts theatres. Who had been succeeded by flame-haired Kate Shelton, sister to Thomas Walsingham's wife Audrey, both swimming as deep in the murky pool of political spycraft as anyone - even Poley.

'I would counsel you to hide the chart and the amulet as best you can, though it will be difficult to do so in a house of inquisitive children such as the pair we must collect on our way to your home. Be honest and open with your mother and she will protect you from your father's anger should the need arise. She will be relieved that you have come to no harm and that will plead your cause as eloquently as a lawyer at the bar. But I would suggest you leave aside any details that might shock or upset her more than necessary. Such as the appearance of Foreman's bedchamber.'

'Have you seen it? It will be forever printed on my memory!' she shuddered.

'So, keep it well clear of your mother's.'

'I will do so.' She was quiet for a moment then she added, shyly, 'You are a good friend, Master Musgrave.'

'I'm not sure I agree with that, Elizabeth. You are wilful and out of control. Perhaps I should be more open to your father in the hope that a sound whipping would mend your ways. But I have chosen another path and will not deviate from it now.' He paused, then he began to ask a question or two in the hope that she might have noticed something that he himself had missed on his equally hurried exit from Forman's house. 'But tell me, were you not frightened by the screaming birds by the inner kitchen door?'

'When they screamed I nearly fainted!'

'Was there still a cat upon the door into the garden?' he asked.

'And some sort of curse, though I could not stop to read it - and probably could never have understood it if I did!'

'And the mysterious stranger in the privy?' He came to the crucial point at last.

'I could not make him out,' she answered. 'The peep-hole is the only part that lets in light and I blocked it by looking through it.'

'So you didn't see enough to recognise the man in there?'

'No, I didn't. Why? Is that important?'

'It might have been, had you recognised him,' said Tom. 'But now, who knows?' he added.

Chapter 7: The Sin Eater

i

The great gates of Essex House stood wide revealing a cobbled yard and the steps up to the house-front. The hearse rested clear of the opening, hard up against the outer wall on the Strand. It was easy enough for Tom and Ugo to see past the black-painted vehicle into the area between the main door of Essex House itself and the street. It seemed that half of London was gathered around them in sombre silence, but the pair were tall and near the front. Their view was unobstructed, though it was more difficult for Rosalind and Will standing beside them to see precisely what was going on. Will didn't want to be here. He was uneasy in crowds and emotionally torn by the fact that he hadn't been invited to join the other poets while being well aware that he would have refused in any case. On top of that, he was, as always, impatient to get on with his writing. But Rosalind had insisted so he was sulkily making the best of it. Rosalind on the other hand was glowing with excitement. No-one had any clear idea of who would actually attend the funeral service but she was certain that she would spend much of the day surrounded by men and women from the pinnacles of society. Tom, Ugo and Will, all welcome at court, would be able to put faces to names she had heard spoken of with awe since childhood.

The front door into Essex House stood wide. Half a dozen steps led down from it to the cobbled yard within the outer gate. On either side of the steps, a brazier glowed, packed with coal and clearly giving off some welcome heat in the bitter January morning. At the foot of the steps, Spenser, wrapped in his shroud, lay coffined on a bier. The coffin lid stood beside the bier like a guard at attention. The shroud was open so that the dead man's head and shoulders were uncovered. His face was clean and shaven, his hair washed and brushed. His ears as clear as shells lately taken from the sea, Tom observed; both of them. Essex himself was standing in front of the coffin lid. Gelly Meyrick and, for a wonder, both the Bacon brothers, stood opposite them; Sir Anthony pallid and leaning on a stick.

Chapman and his regiment of poetatsters filled much of the rest of the walled square, all dressed in funeral weeds only slightly darker than the sky.

Beside the coffin, near Francis and Anthony Bacon, sat an old man. Considering where he was, and the occasion he was part of, he was shabbily dressed, ill-shaven and scrawny. And yet, thought Tom there was an air of unruffled calm about him; a sense that he knew his place in creation and was content with it; a man with a task at hand that he was happy and uniquely fitted to perform.

'Who's the old man?' asked Ugo.

'He's the sin-eater,' answered Tom, who had come across such men in the far north during his youth.

A servant came out of the front door of Essex House and down the steps to stand beside the Earl. He carried a tray on which was a manchet loaf on a wooden platter and a wooden cup foaming with beer. The earl took the platter and passed it over Spenser's corpse to the sin-eater who took it, put the platter on his lap, tore the bread apart and consumed it. Essex passed him the cup. He took that also and drained it with a single draught, then he handed both back. Essex passed them to the servant who carried them back towards the main door, pausing half way up the steps to place the platter in one of the braziers and the cup in the other. Everything stopped until the wooden vessels burst into flames, then Essex nodded. The sin-eater rose and followed the servant up into the house. Chapman led some of his companions forward. They covered Spenser's face and placed the lid on his coffin.

*

'What was all that about?' asked Ugo.

'Spenser died in his sleep,' Tom explained. 'He had no chance to confess his sins; no opportunity even to pray at the end.'

'Sent to his account with God,' said Will, 'with all his imperfections on his head. Horrible!'

'He died with all his sins upon him,' Tom emphasised to Ugo. 'So he is likely bound for purgatory, if such a place exists, or even hell itself, as it is far too late to hope for absolution. He is doomed to wander the night as a ghost while suffering untold torments in the day. So the superstition goes.'

'Until all his sins are burned and purged away,' emphasised Will again.

'Except,' said Tom with some force, 'that Essex has hired a sin-eater. The old man has taken the bread and the beer passed to him over Spenser's corpse, and as he did so he took all Spenser's sins upon his own soul leaving Spencer's soul as white as snow.'

'Do you believe in such things?' demanded Rosalind.

'Not really. Not now. Ask me again on my death-bed and I'll be begging you to bring me a sin-eater as like as not.'

'Hunh! Not even a regiment of sin-eaters would suffice!' mocked Rosalind. 'But I'm not going anywhere near your bed at any time, Tom. Death-bed or not!'

'Glad to hear it!' said Will.

As they spoke, Chapman and his poets finished securing the lid on Spenser's coffin. They all stood back except for Chapman who produced a piece of paper and held it up before his mournful face.

'Here we go,' said Tom quietly. 'The first of the funeral odes. I hope to God he keeps it short.'

'And that he has decided that he should only deliver one,' said Will. 'But I doubt it. One here and another at the graveside. Two audiences,' he explained. 'Two bites at the cherry.'

'*Rich tapered sanctuary of the blest*,' Chapman began,
'*Palace of Ruth made all of tears and rest,*
To thy black shades and desolation
I consecrate this wight and giving moan
Where furies shall forever fighting be
And adders hiss the world for hating thee
Foxes shall bark and night ravens belch in groans
And owls shall hollow thy confusions
Where we will furnish up thy funeral bed
Strewn with the bones and relics of the dead.'

The moment Chapman was finished, the five nearest poets stepped forward then the six of them shouldered the box and carried it slowly out through the main gate and laid it, with much weeping and wailing, on the hearse hard up against the wall.

The main reason they were able to put the hearse so near to the wall, observed Tom, was the fact that the traces were empty. The carriage was designed to be pulled by two horses but there were no horses there. Instead, after they laid the coffin in the back of the hearse, the poets gathered round it. Some of them fitted themselves loosely into the harness while others simply took firm grip on the long wooden struts then, on Chapman's order, they all heaved together and the hearse was in motion. As it proceeded slowly down the Strand, the Earl of Essex and his senior officers, followed by most of his household, fell in behind. And the rest of London, so it seemed, fell in behind them and filled the Strand like a river in silent flood. The only sound was that of Tom's and Will's voices as they whispered to Rosalind the names of all the most important people there.

ii

It took well over an hour for the funeral to process from Essex House past Somerset House and The Savoy, Durham House, York Place and Hungerford House down to Charing Cross. Here the cortege paused in the wide space beneath the towering cross itself as more crowds joined them out of Cockspur Street before the weary poets continued to pull the hearse into Whitehall. Ever more slowly, it seemed, they moved onwards, the poet-powered hearse at the head of a great crowd following it down through the Court Gate, which was normally forbidden to commoners, into the great complex of palaces comprising White Hall and West Minster. Down King Street they processed until at last they arrived at the Abbey itself. The hearse stopped. The poets relinquished their grip on it. Six of them stood forward, ready to shoulder the coffin. But there was a hold-up at once as the rest of them squabbled over precedence in the line. As they did so, Essex and his household walked past them and entered the Abbey itself. A fine, freezing drizzle began to fall. A wind whipped over the river and moaned in the ornamented buttresses as though the building itself was weeping and wailing.

The area outside the Great West Door was already crowded. As Tom and his little party edged their way forward it was just possible to see that the inside of the ancient building was also busy. The entrance of Essex and his associates made it busier still but there was still room inside - for those allowed to pass as easily as the earl by the Dean's men guarding the entrance. Tom did not hesitate. He walked up to the guards with the air of a man who has every right to be doing what he's doing and fortune favoured him. One of the guards was the scholar from yesterday with whom he had discussed the fate of Henry V's memorial. Their eyes met. The young man nodded and turned to his companions, so Tom and the others followed Essex through the Great West Door so closely that they could almost have been members of his household. As they did so, the Abbey bells began to toll.

The interior of the Abbey was almost as confused as the gaggle of poets outside. In more than a dozen increasingly heated conversations, precedence and position were being sorted out as there was no plan for the congregation. As was all too often the case, thought Tom, there was no real plan for something that Essex was in charge of. In fact, only Essex, as theoretical host, was clear about where he should stand: as close to the grave as possible. Tom and Ugo knew precisely where they were heading as well, and made straight for the tomb of Henry V. Then, with the headless, handless king and the empty tomb of his French wife at their backs, they moved forward until they could get a clear view of the open grave, the bier beside it and the upstanding flagstones which leaned against the front of Chaucer's monument behind it.

There was a stirring in Essex' household who were standing in front of Tom, keeping respectfully clear of the grave itself, where the sexton and his men stood ready to lift the coffin off the bier and lower it at the appropriate point during the service. A small man in chaplain's robes moved toward the graveside, Bible in hand. Inflated with self-righteous haughtiness, he stood beside the empty bier and stared around impatiently.

'Who is that?' whispered Rosalind.

'Abdias Assheton, Essex' chaplain,' Tom whispered. 'One element of the conundrum that is Robert Devereux.'

'How so?' asked Rosalind. 'He seems no more than an inflated, self-important little priest. The religious equivalent of the poet Weevil.'

'As with so many of the men and women we are dealing with,' said Tom, 'though perhaps not with Weevil, there is more to him than meets the eye.'

*

'Assheton is an increasingly influential voice. He is famous for his absolute reliance on the Bible as the fount of all knowledge. He believes - and preaches - that every question that anyone can ever ask is answered in the Bible. It is the word of God revealed...'

'An increasingly popular philosophy,' added Ugo who had seen Puritanism on the Continent in the past and recognised the manner in which Assheton and the men who shared his views were taking precedence in the Church's thinking. 'Especially amongst Puritans,' he continued, 'many of look down on ancient wisdom - of which they are often ignorant in any case - and believe that knowledge of the Bible is all a learned religious philosopher requires.'

'Essex inclines to that way of thinking to the tips of his square-cut Puritan beard,' confirmed Tom. 'But he also has contact - as we all know - with men such as Simon Forman, who seek for knowledge seemingly everywhere *except* in the Bible.'

'As we know from our visit to Forman's library,' confirmed Ugo.

'Forman, it seems to me, is a more comfortable bedfellow with Raleigh, who is endlessly exploring - intellectually as well as physically.' Tom added. 'As his School of Night demonstrates. What he believes he has learned from the natives of the New World has made him question some widely accepted biblical 'truths', like the calculation that God made the earth around 4004 years before Christ was born.'

'Really,' whispered Rosalind. 'Who calculated that?'

'Another Irishman, the Archbishop of Armagh, has been working on it I believe,' answered Tom.

'Are we expecting Raleigh?' wondered Rosalind excitedly.

'I should imagine Sir Walter will grace us with his presence,' said a new voice from behind them.

Tom swung round to find Sir Thomas Walsingham at his shoulder. The spymaster and patron of poets was accompanied by Audrey, his wife, and Kate Shelton his sister-in-law who was also Tom's current lover. In his train were one or two other poets who, like Will, had not made it onto George Chapman's list of mourners. John Donne, whose eyes just failed to meet Tom's but rested lingeringly on Kate. Thomas Watson was there, the man who introduced Sir Thomas to Kit Marlowe who was, perhaps there in spirit.

Ben Jonson bulked out the group, his normal massiveness somewhat reduced by his recent term in Newgate for killing Gabriel Spencer. He nodded at Tom companionably enough, for they had worked together in the past. Tom nodded back, the Master of Logic observing the way Ben stroked the ball of his left thumb where the letter 'M' of the murderer's brand still burned - spiritually if not physically. Though the brand itself had probably hurt less than the forfeiture of all his property, goods and chattels, which was likely why the notoriously proud young man was relying on Sir Thomas' bounty.

The *neck verse* ran through Tom's mind as he looked at Jonson - the verse from the psalms of David that the poet and playwright, who had admitted manslaughter, had to recite to receive benefit of clergy and a brand instead of a hanging: '*Miserere mei Deus secundum misericordiam tuam iuxta multitudinem miserationum tuarum dele iniquitates meas... Have mercy upon me, O God, according to thy lovingkindness: according unto the multitude of thy tender mercies blot out my transgressions*. But then all Tom's thoughts were simply overcome by the arrival at his side of Kate Shelton, the origin of all his most pleasurable transgressions. Tall, deep-bosomed, witty and as forceful as either Rosalind or Audrey, Tom often wondered whether his green-eyed, flame-haired mistress had made her way into Will's play of the *Taming of the Shrew* five years ago. Though he had to admit that if she was Shakespeare's shrewish Kate, he was certainly no cunning Petruchio. She

snuggled against him in a manner that would have had the
carved saints and angels around them averting their eyes had
they been able. His nostrils filled with the fragrance of her
recently washed and perfumed hair. His ears filled with the
throaty purr of her whispering. 'Well met, my Tom. We came
hither apart but what say we leave together?'

'Gladly,' he answered. But then he added, 'I see Sir Thomas
is moving close behind Essex.'

'All the better to see the interment. Spenser, remember, was a
client of his long before he went to Essex and Raleigh for
sponsorship.'

'Do you know why he did so?'

'He was well served by what Sir Thomas gave when it was
combined with his own income from his estates until the Irish
victory at the Yellow Ford and the anarchy that sprang from it -
which led to the burning of his castle, the death of one of his
children, the flight of his family to the city of Cork and the
ruination of his profits from his Irish land holdings which is also
what he was seeking to discuss with the Council.'

'And the reason he re-published a volume of his earlier
poetry, including some works that had been banned.'

'Ah. You refer to *Mother Hubberd's Tale*. Sir Thomas was
very much surprised that he dared let Jaggard reprint that. And
that Jaggard dared to do so. It has been banned and burned of
course and Jaggard's fortunate not to have Poley and Topcliffe
after him.'

'Not just Poley and Topcliffe but Raleigh and Cecil from what
I understand!'

'And who is it controls Poley and Topcliffe do you think?'

'Essex controls Poley for the nonce. Did you not know he is
Pursuivant Marshal?'

She gave a gurgle of laughter. 'Essex might *think* he controls
Poley but...'

'But what, Lady Katherine?' said a yet another new voice.
Kate and Tom turned to see that Robert Poley was standing
immediately behind them in the place which Will and Rosalind
had occupied a few moments earlier.

iii

This was the Poley Tom was used to - bathed, barbered, attired in black. Calculatedly at the edge of Essex' party but not really a part of it; the Pursuivant Marshal maybe, but also - and perhaps more so - the Chief Intelligencer to Secretary Cecil and the Council. Tom was tempted to raise the circumstances of Sunday's meeting in the Marshalsea, but he could see no good coming from irritating a man who, albeit temporarily, controlled almost all the law enforcement agencies in the country.

'Ah, Master Poley,' said Sir Thomas, glancing over his shoulder. 'A word with you...'

'But one word?' Poley ironically quoted the doomed Mercutio from Will's *Romeo* as he moved to Sir Thomas' side. Apt enough, thought Tom, for it was generally recognised that Mercutio was a pen portrait of Kit Marlowe, recently deceased at Poley's instruction and with Poley's direct involvement when the play was first performed. Will and Rosalind, he noted were further back, looking at the tombs of headless Henry and his absent wife Catherine of Valois. He turned back, watching the two spies moving forward side by side.

Tom watched as the two men moved further and further until they were standing at the heart of Essex' household, immediately behind the Earl himself. 'I wonder,' whispered Tom to Kate, 'whether the Earl has read Sir Thomas North's translation of Plutarch?'

'*The Life of Julius Caesar*, you mean?'

'I had more in mind the death of Julius Caesar.'

'They would make a fine Brutus and an excellent Cassius,' she agreed with a chuckle. 'The one all bluff honesty, full of family pride in spite of the fact that he dirties his hands with spycraft, the other the very personification of that devious profession. Heart one might say, versus head.'

'And who would you play if Will ever finishes his play of *Caesar*?' he whispered.

'Why, Portia, Brutus' faithful if not very clever wife. To stab yourself in the thigh as a way of proving fortitude and reliability! That was almost as mad as eating hot coals to kill herself.'

'So, your thighs would remain inviolate?'

'As columns of alabaster, sir,' she said. 'And any time you wish to satisfy yourself that this is so...'

'Tom,' interrupted Will, his voice full of excitement. 'Have you seen what they've done to the tomb of Henry Vth?'

*

Tom's answer was forestalled by the commotion made as the poets finally entered through the Great West Gate.

'*Mournfull Muses, sorrowes minions*,' bellowed a great voice that echoed the length of the Abbey effectively reducing everyone there to silence. '*Dwelling in despaires opinions*,' it continued.

Looking to his right and craning to see over the heads of the crowd, Tom saw the great mass of bodies part like the Red Sea before Moses and the Children of Israel as they escaped Egypt. The six pall-bearers and their load moved forward with slow and stately tread. And, judging by the number of poets following Spenser's coffin the comparison with the Children of Israel was pretty accurate.

'*Yee that never thought invented*,' continued that ringing voice. '*How a heart may be contented, But in torments alle distressed, Hopelesse how to be redressed, All with howling and with crying, Live in a continuall dying Sing a Dirge on Spencers death,Till your soules be out of breath*.'

'Dear Lord, who wrote this drivel?' demanded Kate. '*Til your souls be out of breath!* Since when do souls breathe?'

'I take it he means it metaphoric,' said Will.

'Don't defend it Will,' snapped Kate. 'Someone selected this buffoon to pen this stuff - which deserves to lie in a midden with all the other excrement or go floating down the open sewer of the Fleet River! And think, they did not ask you, Ben Jonson, Master Watson or Master Donne over there whose least word is worth a volume of garbage such as this!'

'*Bidde the Dunces keepe their dennes*,' the voice continued.

'Dear God, there's more!' whispered Kate.

'Hours more I should guess,' said Tom.

'*And the Poets breake their pennes*.'

'If only this one had - and before he wrote this!' said Kate. 'Will, do you know whose excrement this is?'

'Nicholas Breton, if I had to guess.'

'Remind me to visit Simon Forman for a good strong curse against this man Breton. May his teeth fall out! May his fingers wither! May his stones...'

'Kate,' spat Tom. 'You visit Simon Forman?'

'On occasion! Hush now, I want to hear more of this deathless dirge.' Tom knew Kate realised that she had revealed much more than she meant to and felt guilty about it. He gave an inward shrug and acquiesced. But his mind continued to test what she had said, like a child pushing at a bruise to see how much it hurt.

'*Bidde the Sheepheards shed their teares*,' the voice continued, slowly coming closer. '*And the Nymphes go teare their haires*...'

'Tear their hairs,' echoed Kate - to prove, no doubt, that she was actually listening.

Tom, however, was no longer paying attention. He could not just forget what Kate had said. That Kate should visit Forman! Why? When? What had he cast for her? Drawn for her? Sold to her in the way of charms or philtres? What in God's name might he have done to her? Visions of that bedroom rose unbidden to his mind's eye, his imagination adding her naked body to the Venuses carved in marble there. The reference to her alabaster thighs did not help.

But he was drawn back out of one element of his speculation and thrust into another almost at once. '*Fairy Queene, shew fairest Queene, How her faire in thee is seene*,' bellowed the approaching voice. '*Sheepheards Calender set downe, How to figure best a clowne. As for* Mother Hubberts Tale*, Cracke the nut, and take the shale*...'

iv

The mention of *Mother Hubberd's Tale* brought Tom up short so that he hardly heard the lines that followed, let alone try to make sense of them.

'Jesu!' whispered Donne, also shocked and surprised.

'We should have expected it,' whispered Tom. 'With *The Fairy Queen* and *The Shepherd's Calendar* it was one of Spenser's most popular publications.' But if his discussions about it so far were anything to go by - if Donne's summation of the piece was in any way accurate, he thought - then it came dangerously close to treason with its attacks on Her Majesty and her closest advisers. Ten years away from their original targets perhaps, but focused now with disturbing accuracy on the generation that followed those originals.

Tom looked over his shoulder down the packed nave towards Spenser's shoulder-borne coffin as it came on as inevitably as death itself. The black casket and the mourning-suited poets carrying it were suddenly laden with a disturbing weight of threat and danger. Even the lines being so loudly recited began to sound like a challenge to a duel, perhaps even a declaration of war.

'*Farewell* Arte of Poetry,' continued that abruptly disturbing recitation. '*Scorning idle foolery, Farewell true conceited reason, Where was never thought of treason: Farewell all in one together, And, with Spencer's garland, wither.*'

Tom found himself short of breath as things plunged from bad to worse. What did Nicholas Breton - if this indeed was his work - mean? *Where was never thought of treason* and yet the satire in *Mother Hubberd's Tale* did indeed seem to show thought of treason. Perhaps more than mere *thought* of treason. Tom suddenly began to see Spenser in an entirely new light. So far he had thought of the diminutive poet as a desperate suitor to the Council, willing to sit seemingly hopelessly and endlessly in draughty White Hall corridors with his proposal for the subjugation of Ireland- largely through the calculated use of starvation, an idea he modestly proposed with Classical support - as it was said of the Roman Empire by Tacitus: 'They make a desert and call it peace', which was very much Spenser's plan. He seemed such an unworldly, ultimately powerless creature, apparently helplessly adrift in this ocean of bureaucracy in spite of his brutal proposals. Running dangerously short of money in spite of the Queen's bountiful pension of £50 so recently awarded. Far removed from his responsibilities as Sheriff of the County of Cork; far removed also from his beloved wife and what remained of his young family. To top it all, Spenser had been the victim of a seemingly random attack which resulted in his burst ear-drum - all in all, a figure worthy of a great deal of pity. So desperate in the end that he was willing to reprint any or all of his earlier work in the hope of turning a penny to keep him from starving as he waited seemingly eternally for the Council to make up their minds.

But now Tom was abruptly presented with Spenser as a creature more akin to Poley or one of his spies. Like Marlowe and all the rest, a Cambridge man - who worked as Sizar at Pembroke College while Poley was Sizar at Clare College and Marlowe was at Corpus Christie. A dangerous man whose patience with these irresolute and dawdling old men had run out, as Essex' had with his inconsistent Queen. Who saw the potential of *Mother Hubberd's Tale* to embarrass and motivate the men who were so slowly deciding to answer his pleas. To show the two most influential courtiers Raleigh and Cecil - the Fox and the Ape - and any other men of power who might see themselves lampooned in the apparently innocent fable that he was not toothless after all. That he needed to be respected and, most of all, answered. Answered swiftly or else...

The only risk being, of course, that he might be answered in a manner he clearly did not expect. The way he had actually been answered in the end: with a lethal dose of hemlock poured into his wounded ear as he slept.

*

The mournful procession was close at hand now. The echoing voice louder than ever: '*And, if any Graces live, That will vertue honour give, Let them shewe their true affection, In the depth of griefes perfection,*'

Tom and his companions, which numbered Sir Thomas Walsingham's party now, drew back as the coffin approached. Between Tom, Will, Donne, Ben Jonson and Thomas Watson, they could see the faces of all of the pall-bearers and put names to them as they bore the coffin, feet-first, through the open area where the transepts met the nave. There was a muted flurry of whispering as they told Rosalind who they could see. George Chapman was one of the leading pair, beneath Spenser's coffined left foot. Breton was his opposite, bellowing the words of his elegy as they all moved. Behind Chapman and Breton came Francis Thynne and Charles Fitzgeoffrey, then William Alabaster and John Weever brought up the rear, their shoulders beneath Spenser's. The first pair of mourners behind them were Richard Harvey and Hugh Holland.

'*In describing forth her glory, When she is all most deepely sory;*' shouted Breton. '*That they all may wish to heere, Such a song, and such a quier...*'

'That at least was well done,' whispered Kate. For as Breton said the word '*quier*' - a most lamantable rhyme for '*heere*', thought Tom - the coffin had actually just come past the choir, so that last couplet and a little silence took the melancholy burden to its destination: the bier and the priest beside it. '*As, with all the woes they have, Follow Spencer to his grave.*'

The coffin was placed on the bier. The poets all stood back - the pall bearers forming the front rank.

Abdias Assheton stepped forward until he stood beside the bier. He rested his right hand gently on the top of the coffin, drew in a deep breath and waited for absolute silence. 'Man that is born of a woman is of few days, and full of trouble. He cometh forth like a flower, and is cut down: he fleeth also as a shadow, and continueth not,' he began, his tones deep and resonant. He took another breath and continued, 'I am the resurrection and the life: saith the Lord. He that believeth on me yea though he were dead yet shall he live...'

Tom's mind began to wander at once, for he was all too familiar with the Service for the Burial of the Dead, though Essex' chaplain had rearranged this one slightly to suit himself. He scanned the black-garbed regiment of poets, then let his gaze wander wider. He saw Sir Walter Raleigh almost immediately, standing with his russet head bowed as Assheton's mellifluous voice carried down the nave. Beside him, visible in the crush only because he was Raleigh's companion, stood Simon Forman. Thomas Hariot, having scientific rather than poetic pretentions stood beside Forman. Raleigh, however seemed to be on the edge of Chapman's group, with Matthew Roydon close by. Tom strained to see whether Raleigh was holding a written elegy and a black quill.

'We brought nothing into the world and it is a plain case that we can carry nothing out...' There was no point in telling Rosalind who Raleigh was - she already knew. He looked at Will with raised eyebrows - neither of them had any intention of identifying Forman, especially not to an attractive, independent spirited woman with an enquiring mind. Roydon and Hariot hardly merited Rosalind's attention.

So Tom continued to search as much of the congregation as he could see from, where he was. Having found the Fox, he was now looking for the Ape - though he was well aware that, unlike Raleigh, Cecil would not be towering over those closest to him. But it seemed that, other than Raleigh and Essex who each had their own reasons for being here, Her Majesty's Council was unrepresented.

Was that because of more powerful priorities? Work-load? Politics? Guilt at dragging their feet until the poor supplicant died? Or something more sinister altogether, he wondered.

v

Nicholas Breton, mercifully silent, stepped to the edge of the grave as soon as Assheton completed the burial service and the gravedigger's men went through the ritual of lowering the coffin. He waited for an instant then allowed his poem to flutter down onto the coffin top like the first leaf of Autumn. He threw his quill onto it and stepped back. George Chapman pushed forward once more and stood at the edge of the grave, looking down at the coffin lid, the other poets in a disorderly crowd behind him.

'Told you,' whispered Will. 'Much bigger audience this time. Let's hope for a better poem.'

Chapman began to recite:

'*Now to the nestful woods the broode of flight*
Have on their black wings brought the Night,
When Fame's friends ope the windows they shut in
To bar day's worldly light and Men's rude din.

Now let us whisper that our Colin Clout is gone
That was of English poets the pinnacle alone.
Though all Fame's brazen gates and windows stood
Ope day and night, now should her wild notes rude
Hold still and breathless - all darkness, all forlorn.
Silence and night do best fit how we mourn.'

Having delivered his second epitaph, he too threw into the grave the papers on which the poems were written and the black quill that had penned them. He stood back and was replaced by Hugh Holland, who recited his couplet quickly, then threw the paper and the black quill into the open grave.

'He was and is, see then where lies the odds
Once god of poets now poet to the gods.'

As Holland stepped back, he was replaced by William Alabaster who surveyed his audience with lofty disdain, his eyes resting on Assheton for a heartbeat longer than was necessary, then began to recite in Latin:

'Fors qui sepulchre conditur siquis fuit...'

Tom automatically translated in his head as the pompous quatrain echoed:

'If who is buried here you ask, Oh passerby, you deserve to hear that Spenser is buried here. If who is Spenser you then enquire, you do not deserve to know!'

Tom's attention was beginning to waver once again when John Weever stepped forward, drew himself importantly upward, 'Like a cock,' whispered Kate, 'getting ready to crow…'

'Colin's gone home, the glorie of his clime,' Weever read.
'The Muses Mirrour, and the Shepheards Saint;
Spencer is ruin'd, of our latter time
The fairest ruine, Faeries foulest want:
Then his Time ruines did our ruine show,
Which by his ruine we untimely know:
Spencer therfore thy Ruines were cal'd in,
Too soone to sorrow least we should begin.'

The way Weever started with 'home' and then repeated the word 'ruin' sparked off further uneasiness in Tom's mind. For the central cause of Spenser's misery and - as far as was common knowledge, death - arose from the ruin of his castle at Kilcolman in the County of Cork; the burning of his home, the murder of at least one of his children, the near-death of his wife and the rest of his family and the ruination of his great estate. Weever was clearly speaking for the common people, then. But just because he put the blame on Spenser's ruin by Irish insurgents rather than on hemlock did not make him entirely wrong. And, as Tom had already considered, that fact also added to Essex' potent motivation to take his army over there and avenge yet another friend - while also prompting the capricious Queen, who loved Spenser's poetry, to give Essex her formal permission to do so as soon as possible.

*

Then that thought led onto another. Breton's poem contained scarcely-veiled references to Spenser's satire *Mother Hubberd's Tale* as discussed with Donne, and its potential to be seen as treason. How neat might it seem to the Fox and the Ape to rid themselves of the satirist in the knowledge that in doing so they would also rid themselves of Essex - released from the court and all ability to influence the Queen at any rate; and likely to destroy himself in Ireland into the bargain. Now here was John Weever examining how the destruction of Spenser's Irish land holdings might have affected him. Fair enough, Alabaster's Latin tag was utterly unoriginal in terms of language and presentation, but what about George Chapman's? The proper manner of mourning Spenser would involve silence and night! What was going on here? Perhaps there were sins - committed by Spenser and committed against him - that the Sin Eater had not managed to consume after all, which might better be examined in silence and at night. Say, for instance, by reading rather than reciting the elegies - and retrieving them as soon as possible after dark.

He began to pay closer attention to what was going on, wondering whether there was, perhaps, more about Spenser, his doings and his motivations to be revealed in the writing of his artistic friends.

As poet after poet - many of them flattering themselves that they deserved the name - read out their badly-rhymed doggerel with its limping scansion and pathetic content, Tom began to formulate a plan. Because of the over-enthusiastic input of the poetasters and their interminable verse, the service was running badly over time. Tom observed that the Earl of Essex, Poley and Sir Thomas were getting restless, and suspected that this was not just a reaction to the tedium. All of them, after all, were used to interminably boring sermons of similar length to the poetic input. But the afternoon was drawing on. Evening threatened and then night. He suspected that Essex would have filled the space where the Sin Eater began the formal ritual of the funeral by consuming Spenser's sins with comestibles for more general consumption at the wake that would equally formally end it. If they didn't hurry up, the food would be wasted and the rituals of burial left uncompleted.

But then the inevitable march of time became the saviour of the wake Essex planned and so of Tom's plans as well. The Earl stepped forward just as Charles Fitzgeoffrey was about to begin on several pages of closely-scripted eulogy. 'The poetical offerings have been unrivalled in their number and effect,' he said, his voice ringing down the Nave. 'Those poets with yet more eulogies to read may remain and read them. Those of the congregation who wish to remain and hear them may also remain. I will arrange for the Abbey to stay open until all is done. For the rest, there is ample provision of funereal baked meats at Essex House which must be consumed before nightfall and those who wish to partake will be made welcome.'

'We shall go at once!' breathed Kate.

'No, my love,' responded Tom. 'I at least shall stay.'

'But you hate poetry - not that this deserves the name.'

'True. But there is more than mere versifying going on here and I mean to get to the bottom of it!'

'To the bottom of the grave as like as not,' she hissed.

'If need be,' he responded, thinking that that was where the tell-tale poems all would be lying, thrown in by their creators with the black quill pens that wrote them. 'To the bottom of the grave if need be.'

Chapter 8: The Silence and the Night

i

Sir Gelly Meyrick and the Bacon brothers accompanied Essex down the nave followed by Assheton and the rest of his entourage. After a moment - so as not to be too closely associated with them, perhaps - Poley strode after them. Sir Thomas's group, including Kate, left with Sir Thomas, closely followed by Ugo and the others who had arrived with Tom.

All alone except for the headless King Henry, the Master of Logic began to wonder if he had made a miscalculation. This uneasiness was compounded by the fact that many of the congregation and a good number of the poets also headed for Essex House and sustenance rather than lingering at the graveside in the hope of immortality. Perhaps there was no hidden agenda; perhaps all there was here after all was a lot of mediocre versifying and a little coincidence.

But the fact that the crowd in the Nave had thinned revealed one or two things which had been hidden earlier. Against Tom's suspicion, Secretary Cecil had actually been there, and he remained now, listening to the poems with apparent interest. Robert Poley, Chief Intelligencer and Pursuivant Marshal had gone with his new employer the Earl Marshal, but Cecil was still supported by Thomas Phelippes, Poley's opposite number in charge of codes and communications for the Council's section of Her Majesty's secret service. And, Tom realised with a start, Sir Richard Topcliffe, Rackmaster to the Tower stood beside the Secretary and the codemaster. Were the three of them secret poetry-lovers, Tom wondered, or were they, like him, listening for sedition in verse? Surely they could not, also like him, be listening for clues as to Spenser's murder in spite of the fact that so little had been made of it so far. Or could they? Automatically, he stepped back into the shadows beside Henry Vth's tomb, hoping they hadn't seen him - but then wondering why he should be concerned either way.

The answer to those questions lay simply in Tom's lingering certainty that this was not the innocent funeral of a man everyone assumed had died of natural causes if unexpectedly and tragically young, or, as Ben Jonson was apparently suggesting, of starvation. Whether or not the corpse's ears were now as clean as sea-shells recently cast ashore, there appeared to be a growing number of powerful people who seemed to know - or suspect - about the distillation of hemlock. But did they know - or was there anything in verse to tell them - about Hal the missing apprentice and his accusation that Will Shakespeare bought the poison on the evening Spenser died? Or, indeed, the unsettling coincidence of Poley's predecessor's fatal accident up in the most dangerous catholic nests of the north.

Tom took a step further back into the shadows and began to look around, formulating a plan. There were still several poets left with elegies of varying length and Charles Fitzgeoffrey was only a little way through his. The bier had been removed as soon as the coffin was lowered. Abdias Assheton had gone with his earthly master and there was no sign of gravedigger or sexton. The hole would obviously not be filled tonight with anything other than paper and feathers. He suspected that the Abbey would be secured, perhaps even guarded, by the Dean's orders and men. If he waited until all was done, there were plenty of hiding places close at hand, Queen Catherine's tomb if nowhere else. But the only problem with planning to wait undiscovered until the place was empty lay in the fact that it would also be absolutely dark - and Tom had not brought tinder or taper with him. It would be useless even to steal a candle, of which there were plenty, as he hadn't the means to light it.

He was so deep in these thoughts that he actually jumped when a heavy hand fell on his shoulder from behind.

*

'We raided the Earl's collation,' growled a deep voice. Tom turned to see Ugo and Kate standing just behind him. The Dutchman was holding a kerchief laden with patties and pastries while Kate held some winter fruit and a bottle of Rhenish.

'This should make even the poetry more palatable,' she whispered cheerfully.

They laid it out on Queen Catherine's tomb to eat and drink as they listened to the last of the poems. By the time they and the eulogizing were finished, night had clearly fallen, for there was nothing to see but darkness through either windows or doors; deepening shadows gathered around and - especially - above them. As Secretary Cecil and his sinister companions left, with the last of the poets trailing after them regretting, no doubt, that they had missed the funeral feast, the Dean's men began a sweep through the Abbey. It was the student who found them and moved them on. Tom went willingly enough, his plan almost perfectly formed in his mind. As they reached the wide space where the Transepts met the Nave, he turned right, leading Ugo and Kate to the North Door. A careful glance back as they were shown out and the door locked behind them was sufficient to show Tom that the smaller, more accessible portal also had a smaller lock than that on the Great West Doorway, one that would yield more easily to the dark arts of his lock-pick. And his ears told him that once the lock was secured, there were no bolts sliding home. Breaking back in should be easy enough.

Though as he began to walk down towards the river and a wherry home, he wondered a little superstitiously whether the locks to the Abbey had ever been picked before - and, if so, what revenge The Lord had taken on the *charm* responsible for the sacrilege. Something similar, he supposed, to whatever plague had been visited on the men who stole King Henry's silver head and hands.

Back at Blackfriars, the atmosphere grew tense at once. Kate wanted to become sportive but Tom had no time to indulge her. He and Ugo were too busy getting ready to return to the Abbey, break in and recover the poems from Spenser's grave. In the face of this, Kate decided that she would come with them. 'If I derive no enjoyment from this evening in one way, I will do so in the other,' she announced. Tom instantly forbade it. He had little idea of what dangers - physical or spiritual - they might face but he had no intension of allowing Kate to face them too. The proposals became discussions and discussions rapidly became arguments. The arguments drew out long past the moment he had planned to leave. Past curfew indeed, when Kate could not get back to Nonsuch on her own - and neither Tom nor Ugo could escort her without losing the chance to break into the Abbey altogether.

'You have drawn this argument out a'purpose,' he said at last, more amused than angry at having been outmaneuvered. 'You will not stay. You cannot go. Therefore, much against my judgment, I must acquiesce. You may come. But I warn you, My Lady Willful, you have at the least submitted yourself to a long march from Blackfriars down to Essex House and then along the route followed by the poet-drawn hearse of this afternoon. And if we are lucky, all that weary way back again laden with elegiac doggerel.'

ii

A little over an hour later, Tom knelt in front of the Abbey's North Door while the other two kept watch. He had talked his heavily-cloaked companions through Lud Gate, relying on a couple of friendly watchmen and parting with several silver coins. He guided them up Ludgate Hill to Fleet Street, then to The Strand and Essex House - and so along the route followed by Spenser's hearse. Beneath their capacious cloaks, Ugo, Kate and he were well supplied with flint and steel, tinder and a dark-lantern, but a freshening wind had blown the ragged clouds away during their brisk walk here and there was enough moonlight for him to see what he was doing as he went to work with his lock picks. To see also, though he said nothing for the moment, that someone else had been trying to pick the lock he was planning to charm. There were scratches on the ancient wood around the massive key-hole which were pale, recent and which had not been there when he looked back on leaving earlier. Whether or not the would-be burglars had succeeded in breaking in he could not tell, but as he felt the tongue of the ancient mechanism slide back he rose quickly to his feet and whispered, 'Wait!'

He took the great round handle of the latch and twisted it. The simple mechanism moved silently. The door swung open as he pushed. It moved smoothly enough but the hinges groaned - the sound behaving strangely as it moved out into the gusty night and into the echoing stillness of the Abbey. Tom found that he was holding his breath, straining to hear the slightest sound that might be out of place. At the same time, straining his eyes until tears began to come, seeking the merest glimmer of light in the absolute blackness of the massive space before them. But there was neither sound nor brightness, so he stepped cautiously in, signaling the others to follow. Five steps into the North Transept took them out of the wind but left them in the last of the moonlight. They stopped here and lit the dark-lantern before Tom pushed the door closed and leaned against it to ensure it stayed shut as the latch dropped back into place even with the wind rattling it.

Ugo held the lantern. It was a column of thin horn panes perhaps eighteen inches in height and six in diameter held together by narrow metal struts, one section of which was hinged to open, allowing it to be lit. On the circular base there was a simple oil lamp with a deep reservoir and a thick wick. On the top, an inverted cone rose to a shielded chimney. Above that, a wire handle carefully placed to protect the user's fingers from the heat escaping upward. Opposite the horn-paned door, an extra vertical strut joined the top to the base and held two metal wings that could be closed over the column of brightness, cutting down the illumination until only the thinnest blade escaped to light the way.

At Tom's whispered prompting, Ugo set the lantern to its darkest and then the three of them followed the sliver of light into the dark and echoing immensity. It had always seemed to Tom that darkness dampened noise, especially darkness as absolute as this. But the Abbey worked to rules far beyond those of nature. Every breath and footfall seemed to be amplified until the three of them appeared to be making as much noise as an invading army. Even when they stopped to shine the golden blade of light around to try and get their bearings, the sounds they had made just echoed on and on. Conversation was out of the question - they hardly dared whisper. Tom found that his fists were closed tight on the handles of his rapier and dagger. When Kate brushed nervously against him without warning he nearly drew on her.

At last they reached the Nave and the light from Ugo's lantern showed the Choir to the right of them and the Sanctuary looming on their left. Spenser's grave was straight ahead with Chaucer's tomb behind it, flag stones standing against it, just visible over the pile of earth from the grave. As Ugo swung the light from side to side a simple truth occurred to Tom which he had overlooked so far. They were surrounded by shadowy, half-seen figures whose faces stared more or less accusingly down at them. Even in the sepulchral darkness, some part of him must have been aware of their stony gazes, which had been more than enough to unsettle the three interlopers.

'There's the grave,' he said more confidently. 'Let's go.'

*

Even with his mind settled on what had made the adventure so far so disquieting; Tom approached the edge of Spenser's grave cautiously, as though some demonic monster might be waiting down there. Or, after his conversation this afternoon, as though the Sin-Eater had failed in his duty and Spenser's ghost was waiting to harrow up their souls with a description of his tortures during the day. He and Ugo approached the sharp edge of the black pit side by side with the blade of light probing ahead of them and Kate for once a little behind them. Tom saw the square of the far side beneath the piled earth and the slabs fronting Chaucer's tomb. The cliff of black mud reached down as perfectly vertical as any brick wall in London, as shiny as the marble sides of the tombs standing around them.

He knew what he expected to see, could almost summon it into ghostly vision he was so certain of it. Spenser's coffin lying covered in a snow-drift of paper, each flake covered with writing and accompanied by a dead-black quill. Beneath Ugo's cloak, a rope clung tightly-wrapped around his waist to steady Tom as he climbed downwards. He had no intention of jumping onto Spenser's final resting place or even of lowering himself over the edge and feeling for the wooden lid with his toes. Though he was by no means given to superstition, he was not about to make any noise or movement that might wake the dead. But he was going to retrieve those verses and gut them for hidden meanings that might explain the murders. Or go some way towards an explanation at least. That was why they were here and he was not going to leave with his mission unfulfilled.

But the light from Ugo's lantern showed something he had not been expecting at all. Lying on top of Spenser's coffin, revealed bit by bit as the three of them approached the edge and the light fell deeper and deeper, was the corpse of a young man. Tom knew in his bones it was Hal the missing apprentice though he had never met the boy before. The body lay on its back on top of Spenser's coffin. Its eyes were wide and staring in a face as white as the paper beneath and around it. It was clothed in the modest, unfashionable attire to be expected of an apprentice, especially one apprenticed to a slightly down-at-heel apothecary. The only thing that came as a surprise to Tom was the dagger pushed through the left breast of the brown fustian doublet. Buried to the hilt, in fact and doing more than skewering the young man's heart. It held in place yet another piece of paper.

'Another elegy, perhaps,' said Tom.

'Certainly,' Ugo agreed.

'But who penned it?' wondered Kate standing beside the pair of them on the lip of the grave looking dispassionately down at the corpse. Never had Tom been more grateful for the fact that Kate was not the fainting sort.

'I'll lay you odds,' said Tom thoughtfully, 'that it will appear to be from Will Shakespeare.'

iii

'*When in the chronicle of long-past time,*' read Tom slowly,
'*I see descriptions of the fairest wights,*
And Spenser making beautiful old rhyme
In praise of ladies dead and Lordly knights,
Then, in despite of ruin, sweet poesy's best,
Of Fairy Queene, Mother Hubbard, Colin Clout,
I see his antique pen would have express'd,
Even such a sadness as we master now.
We Aped his verse with all our Foxy wit
His ironic lines with burning satire season'd,
But Spenser's subtle style we never hit

135

Nor ever any thought of speaking treason.
So all our praises were but dull prophecies
Of parting from this Irish sire of phantasies.'

He was standing astride the corpse, his feet resting on the edges of the coffin, with the poem in one hand and the dagger that had been run through it in the other. His head and shoulders stuck bizarrely out of the grave, a fact emphasised because Ugo had opened both wings of the dark lantern and bathed the tomb with brightness.

'Could Will have written that?' breathed Kate. 'There's something of his style in it, but...'

'I agree. I feel I've read something of his like this before. But we'll need to show it to him in order to be sure.'

'Is that wise?' wondered Ugo.

'None of this is wise,' said Tom. 'But we can't just leave everything as we found it. Throw the rope here and we'll lift poor Hal out of the grave he seems to have invaded...'

'How do you know who the dead boy is?' asked Kate as Tom went about looping the rope beneath the corpse's chest, under his arms. 'Have you met this Hal before?'

'Never. But I have seen where he died and there could not be two such.'

'He died of a dagger through the heart surely, and there are many such!' argued Kate.

'No, Kate. He was dead before he was stabbed and he died far from here of a shattered skull and a broken neck from a tumble down some stairs. He has been brought here, furnished with the poem which was stabbed in place and left to do as a corpse what he could no longer do as a living person. To wit, make the Earl Marshal, his lieutenants and their pursuivants go after Will for murdering Spenser and now, for slaughtering the boy as well.'

'How have you come to these conclusions? Here, Ugo, let me help you draw the poor lad up.'

'As you do so, you will see plain enough the shattered skull and broken neck.'

'And so I do,' admitted Kate as she and Ugo laid the corpse reverently at the graveside, her voice beginning to tremble at last. 'But hois fists are lenched as though he would fight us still.'

'Leave well alone,' ordered Ugo. 'Fore the time-being atleast.'

'Further to which there is no blood,' continued Tom, paying no attention to this byplay, 'neither on the dagger nor on the poem nor on any of the other writings here nor on Spencer's coffin. Living men bleed copiously when stabbed. Only corpses do not. This one, I am certain, has been secreted for nigh on three days in Simon Forman's garden privy.' As he talked, Tom was kneeling on one knee gathering together all the poems from on and around Spenser's coffin.

'So Forman brought him here?' asked Ugo.

'Somehow to put blame on Will?' asked Kate. 'How might that be effected?'

'To an eye already open to such things, the poem would seem to be a most potent link. An admission of guilt, almost, by the man that wrote it. I would not go so far as to say Forman brought him here, but Forman is caught up in the plot to blame Will and distract attention from the actual culprit. Forman has to be involved, with George Chapman, in some part of this and certainly in arranging today's service. But I suspect they are just puppets under more powerful men who pull their strings. You see how the poem, fashioned to be like one of Will's also makes such pointed mention of all the most potent themes and motives we have discussed so far - Ireland and the lands over which he was lord until his castle was burned, *Mother Hubberd*, his new targets Cecil - Fairy Queen Elizabeth's Ape - and Raleigh the Fox. Moreover, when we have time to mull things over there may well be more here.' He held up the bundle of poems he had collected.

'In time we might,' said Ugo. 'But in the mean-time what are we going to do with Hal?'

*

'We could just leave him in the grave where we found him,' said Kate. 'That would be easiest and quickest.'

'And it would alert whoever put him here as to what has been done - for I will not leave without these poems - though at this stage it will not alert them as to by whom it was done.'

'Is that such a bad thing?' wondered Kate.

'It depends on who they send hunting after the truth, and whether the hunt comes to our doors. But still, I think if we just leave him here we will have missed a trick.'

'How so?'

'Missed an opportunity to sew confusion where there might have been more certainty and thus to give us time to begin a hunt of our own.'

'So. What can we do with him that will sew this confusion?' asked Kate.

'I can tell you what we can *not* do,' said Ugo, the practical man. 'We cannot carry him out of this place. Whoever brought him here must have planned to do so. They must have found some way of hiding him as they transported him - from Billingsgate if you are right about Forman's privy - and therefore likely bundled in a wherry. We have nothing equivalent to carry him away in. Whatever else, he must stay in the Abbey. All the alternatives are too full of risk.'

'And yet,' said Kate thoughtfully, 'to work your plan and sew confusion, he must vanish.'

'Indeed,' said Tom. 'And I have just the place in mind. Ugo, let down the rope once more and help me up. Then we can go to work.'

The top of Queen Catherine of Valois' tomb slid silently open to reveal the empty vault beneath. As Kate held it balanced with her back against husband King Henry's tomb, Tom and Ugo lowered Hal's battered body into it then the three of them slid the lid closed once more. As they did so, Tom explained more of his thinking to them. 'Whoever put the body on top of Spenser's was relying on the Dean's grave digger and sexton returning to find it in the morning. They would report it to the Dean's guards, who would report it to the Dean. The Abbey is a Royal Peculiar - although the Archbishop of Canterbury uses it for coronations and similar special occasions, it does not fall directly under his control, or that of any bishop. It is controlled directly by the crown. The Dean, therefore, would report either to the Council or - more likely - to Essex as the man who took charge yesterday and who is in any case Earl Marshal and already involved as such. Not that it matters - the next step is the same no matter who takes it.'

'Well...' Kate didn't sound altogether convinced. 'What is that?'

'The body is examined and murder pronounced. The poem is examined and its authorship assigned. The man who wrote the poem stands accused of pinning it to Hal's breast, thus murdering him, and putting him in Spenser's grave.'

'For what reason? What good could anyone hope to derive? To write a poem, kill a boy and place his body in a grave?'

'It will be suggested that Will Shakespeare wrote the poem. Therefore Will Shakespeare killed the boy and placed him here in the deluded hope that he would be buried with Spenser and no-one any the wiser.'

'That reasoning is fit for Bedlam,' said Kate roundly. 'You yourself said you were not sure the poem is Will's. What motive would Will have for killing the boy then posting a poem on his breast - and hiding him here of all places?'

'You do not see the grim subtlety of the plan, Kate. There is no real logic here - merely rumour and supposition, guilt by accusation. It is the *questions* that do the work, not the *answers*.'

'How so?' she demanded.

'Will does not have to have written the poem. Someone will tell the Earl Marshal or the Council that Will wrote the poem and that should be enough. If they seek for motive in the murder, why Hal had been telling folk that Will Shakespeare bought just such poison as killed Spenser on the night that he died, which fact compounds his guilt even though the lad is no longer alive to repeat the accusation. And as for why or how he hid the body here, that will be a matter for the questioning.'

'But Will would admit to none of this, surely...' said Kate, shaking her head in confusion.

'What Will admits to, whether it's true or not, whether it hangs him or not, will likely depend on how fiercely Rackmaster Topcliffe tightens the ropes on his rack as he seeks Will's confession to everything. And you know that just before his joints are torn apart like poor Thomas Kyd's, Will will tell them anything they want to hear.'

iv

Rosalind answered Tom's knock next morning wearing a shawl over her shift, looking so thoroughly dishevelled that Kate gave a knowing wink. 'A sportive night, mistress?' she asked. Although she and Tom had indeed sported until near dawn, not one red hair was out of place and her dress was fit to attend at court.

Rosalind gave a wry laugh. 'No,' she answered. 'You clearly do not know my Will. He has been up all night scribbling away. It seems that the state of King Henry's tomb has inspired him. His body has not been in the bedroom, let alone in the bed, and his mind has been centuries distant.'

'Well,' said Tom, 'we have brought bread, milk and cheese. Even Will needs to eat and drink - no matter what century his mind is in.'

'Come in then, and welcome,' said Rosalind, stepping back.

Will was scribbling away, seated at the travelling trunk he used as a writing desk in spite of the fact that he had a table now. He hardly glanced up as Tom, Ugo and Kate entered. 'Rosalind tells us you have become a soul inspired,' said Tom, strolling across the room to stand behind his friend as Ugo handed over the food and the women prepared breakfast.

'I shall make Henry much less certain of the rightness of his cause, of the inevitability of victory, despite the support of the Church in the matter of Salic Law. Of the responsibility he bears for the death of his men in battle. He will search his soul, wander the camp during the night before Agincourt seeking to settle matters with his army - many of them soon to die - his conscience and his God. He'll care nothing for his place in history or his monument - his battered arms will suffice if he wins and his bones unmarked if not. He'll see himself as just another soldier among soldiers, prouder of his scars than of his escutcheons. Then there is the attempted assassination by Cambridge, Scrope and Grey which will show him having to exercise kingly authority and dispense royal justice. My sources say Agincourt was fought on St Crispin's Day - I'm certain I can make good use of that! Moreover, I have some great speeches for him, like Antony's speeches to the citizens after Caesar's death in North's *Plutarch* which I am preparing for my play of *Julius Caesar*. Speeches to rouse their pride and their passion. And Henry will have good reason to utter them for the Dauphin is the villain of the piece, though his part is not large - like that of Don John in *Much Ado*. He sent the tennis balls, he sent the challenges, he led the French knights at Agincourt, he ordered the camp boys killed. While Catherine of Anjou is Henry's sweet Kate, though a modest and quiet one - not like your Kate or my shrewish Kate at all! I have it all in head now...'

'And lucky not to get my shoe in your head as well,' added Kate.

'And your problem with Falstaff now that Kempe has left the company?' asked Tom to change the subject before Kate carried out her threat.

'Solved! I do not know how I missed it! I shall use the Ancient Pistol - he was almost as popular as Falstaff in any case - and Armin shall play him! It will all work so well and should be ready soon enough to please Burbage...'

'Still, you must eat, Will. Come, you know you will not lose the thread if the interruption is short. And besides, I have something that I need you to see.'

'Write this?' said Will five minutes later looking down at the sonnet spread on the table just as it had been spread across Hal's dead chest. 'Well, I did and I didn't. It is taken from one of my sonnets. The first line of the original is "*When in the chronicle of wasted time...*". Whoever did this has changed that. Then the rest goes on as more and more changes are added. What is this? Where did you get it?' He was too surprised to be angry yet and so far had no idea of the dangers the verse might represent.

'In many ways it's the elegy to Edmund Spenser you never wrote.' Tom spoke to Will's back as the poet rummaged in his travelling trunk, emerging with a slim volume which obviously contained some of his poems - presumably the original of this one, thought Tom.

'Well, the original is about Spenser, certainly; but not the man so much as his style of poetry,' said Will as he straightened. He opened the volume and leafed through it until he found the sonnet he was seeking. 'You see? I use antique words such as he used, *wights*, *blazon*. I talk of knights and ladies from his *Fairy Queene*. The conceit on which the poem rests is simple - ancient poetry describing love and beauty is just a prophesy of modern loveliness which we have no poets worthy of expressing.'

'And the name of the beauty that it flatters?' asked Rosalind sharply.

'No-one real, my love. A creature of poetic fancy. I wrote it when I was under the patronage of the Earl of Southampton.'

'But what can you discern from the rewritten verse?' asked Tom quietly.

*

'Well, it's still a sonnet,' said Will, 'though it's nowhere near as well constructed as mine. However I have to admit the octave and the sestet break between lines eight and nine as mine does. And the sense moves on from one to the other. The new poem also has the same rhyme scheme as I use...' he was frowning now. 'This forgery is better made than it seemed at first. Where did you get it?'

'Later. What else can you see in it?'

Will's frown deepened, but he leaned forward, smoothing the paper across the table and pausing to study it long enough to take a bite of bread and cheese. He chewed meditatively. 'It is a fitting elegy to Spencer,' he said at last speaking round his mouthful, 'but a double-edged one like a dagger. It says his old-fashioned poetry is better than anything we modern men can compose in memory of him.

'But that being said,' he continued, 'it mentions everything that got *Mother Hubberd* banned and burned for satire so sharp that it was seen as treason in some quarters. On top of that, it mentions the destruction of his lands and income, which is what brought him begging to the Council. On the one hand this is an elegy but on the other it is a kind of accusation. Were it the certain case that Spenser had been murdered, this is a list of why, with decided hints as to who might have done it.' He looked up, suddenly pale 'If the Council, the Earl of Essex or

Sir Walter Raleigh were to see this and suppose I wrote it, I would be in chains by the end of the day.'

'A dangerous situation,' said Rosalind quietly, 'considering that the pursuivants may be after you as well.'

'Well,' he said with a weak attempt at humour, 'at least I'd get the choice between the Tower and the Marshalsea.'

'I'm not sure you would be alone however,' said Tom. 'This is a distillation of points made by other elegies read at Spenser's grave-side yesterday.'

'So it is. Where did you get it?'

'It was in Spenser's grave with the other poems.'

A kind of ripple went through the room. Both Will and Rosalind felt it and looked at Ugo, who was in turn looking at Kate, its source. 'What has moved you?' asked Rosalind.

'Tom,' said Kate by way of answer. 'It is time to tell the whole truth, surely. When we all know then we can all take action and confront this, perhaps even overcome it.'

'You are right,' said Tom. And he realised that she was. Steeped in duplicity and spycraft far deeper than he was himself - deeper perhaps than anyone of his acquaintance other than Poley; though Rosalind ran her a close second - she saw the way forward more clearly than he. But he still had to be careful how he broke the news. Ideally, he thought, he should make sure that his revelations also answered some important questions.

'Last Friday afternoon,' he said. 'Where were you?'

'In my old rooms,' said Will.

'Working on three plays at once,' supplied Rosalind. 'The Theatre is being rebuilt as The Globe, the Admiral's Men were at The Rose with Ben Jonson's comedy *The Case is Altered*. The Swan is closed for the Council are still vexed at Master Langley who owns it, there was a display of rapier-play at Newington Butts and Pembroke's men were at The Curtain reviving Kyd's *Spanish Tragedy*. There was no work for The Lord Chamberlain's men therefore. Besides, the weather was abominable, so there would have been no audience neither. Will was at home at work and I was with him, watching him work.'

'I was wrestling with the problems you know about - which my visit to the Abbey yesterday relieved. So if I can get back to...'

'You were named as someone buying poisons from John Gerard's shop late that afternoon. Belladonna and hemlock.'

'Well that is a lie. Who says I did so?'

'The apprentice. He said he did not see your face for your hood was up and your scarf wrapped tight but you gave your name.'

'A trick and a lie,' said Rosalind, knowledgeably. 'Philip of Spain could come thus muffled and say his name was Will Shakespeare and it would be no more true. Where is this apprentice. Let me examine him. It will go harder for him than if I were Topcliffe himself.'

So Tom told her where the apprentice was - and everything he knew so far about what was going on.

V

Will Shakespeare sat, white-faced and slack-jawed as Tom finished his summation. He had suffered brushes with the undercover world before, usually at Tom's side, but this was clearly beyond anything he had ever imagined, let alone experienced. And Will had quite an imagination, thought Tom.

It was Rosalind, far more experienced in these dark matters than her current lover, who went to the heart of the problem. 'So someone we cannot identify killed Edmund Spenser and covered the fact - either himself or through an associate - by buying poison in Will's name from John Gerard's apprentice, Hal, clearly expecting him to be willing and able to inform against Will when the authorities came after him. But how were the authorities to be alerted? What was to prompt them to ask Hal who had bought what?'

'The fact that Spenser was being treated by John Gerard, his master,' answered Tom.

'I see that. But this Hal went to Simon Forman's house in search of whatever Forman had drawn for his master's daughter Elizabeth. Seemingly he became curious, searched too far and fell to his death down the stair. Is this too large a coincidence -

that it should be Forman, who you suspect of supplying the lethal dose, who was also known to the girl and the ill-fated apprentice?'

'No,' said Tom 'I have been looking at the situation from the opposite angle. Perhaps it was Gerard's shop and the apprentice Hal that were chosen *because* Forman was already acquainted with the girl. I will have to ask how she came to go to Forman in the first place...'

'He is notorious for doing precisely what she demanded of him,' said Ugo. 'Predictions, love potions, elixirs to prolong performance in bed and such...'

Kate had the grace to blush, Tom noted.

'Still,' he continued, 'it would be interesting to discover whether he was already at work on her behalf before she met Donne.'

'Could Donne be part of the trap?' wondered Rosalind. 'Is there anything Forman could promise him for meeting the girl apparently by chance but actually by design?'

'There is,' struck in Kate suddenly. 'I have spent some time with him. No frolics, Tom, I swear! But he is in love with the niece of Sir Thomas Egerton, to whom he is chief secretary. She is Ann More, daughter of the Lieutenant of the Tower. Donne would likely do anything for someone who predicted a happy outcome between himself and Mistress Ann and could provide some magical tokens to make the outcome certain, as both her father and Sir Thomas are dead set against the relationship.'

'So,' continued Tom, 'for various possible reasons, Apprentice Hal was chosen and fed the name Will Shakespeare. Then the murder proceeded by administration of the poison...'

'Through Spenser's ear as he slept... *Horrible*...' whispered Will.

'But in the mean-time, Hal broke into the Billingsgate house while Forman was away...'

'Administering the fatal dose?' wondered Rosalind.

*

'Possibly,' allowed Tom. 'But for the reasons I have detailed Hal fell down the stairs and killed himself.'

'Probably,' inserted Ugo. 'But he could have been pushed and we'd be none the wiser.'

'I'll allow that,' agreed Tom. 'Then Forman, probably not alone, conceivably in company with George Chapman, came back to the empty house - as they supposed - and discovered a dead boy at the foot of the stair. They cleaned up as best they could, put the corpse in the privy - the house being well supplied with chamber pots and a kennel running to the river right outside.'

'Can we assume,' asked Rosalind, 'that it must have been one or the other of them who pretended to be Will if they knew who the boy was?'

'Because they saw him while buying the hemlock from Gerard's shop?' probed Tom. 'Perhaps. But Hal had Elizabeth's chart somewhere about his person - that would have identified him as clearly as a passport from the Council.'

'So,' said Kate. 'They had lost the witness set to swear Will bought the Hemlock on the night of Spenser's death.'

'Indeed. Therefore they came up with the plan - simple and effective, dealing with both their concerns. Write a poem in Will's style whose content and references border on treason, and leave it where it will most certainly be discovered and point to Will as murderer once more.'

'On Hal's breast in Spenser's grave,' concluded Ugo.

'Dear God in Heaven here's a coil,' said Will, shaken to the core.

'But why?' demanded Rosalind, her strident words riding over his.

'To blame me for the murder,' supplied her lover.

'But *why*?'

'To take suspicion away from the real murderer,' answered Will.

'I see that well enough. But why *you*? God's truth we saw poets enough yesterday to choke the muses and I personally could draw me up a list of more than a dozen I would see destroyed before you...'

'Only a dozen?' asked Kate. 'I could name a score...'

'So, the question stands,' said Rosalind. 'Of all the poets in London they could have blamed, why did they choose Will Shakespeare? Who do you threaten, Will? Whose jealousy do you bestir? What have you done that makes you deserve this in someone's eyes?'

'Someone,' Tom pointed out, 'who wanted Spenser dead in the first place. Have you offended any powerful Irishmen?' Will shook his head and continued to do so as Tom fired question after question at him. 'Someone likely to profit from his death - to take his lands, perhaps? Someone wanting his death to prick the Queen into action and send Essex to Ireland at once? Someone insulted by the reprinting of *Mother Hubberd's Tale*?'

'Stop!' begged Will. 'You have suggested half of London and many in Dublin, Cork and Tyrone as well. How will we ever make sense of it?'

'We need a clear head who knows this game and has contacts in every camp,' said Rosalind. 'A Master of more than Logic...'

'Well,' said Tom, 'I can do my best...'

'Not you, you gudgeon! Think! If we asked the Queen for help, as her favourite poet is the murdered corpse in question, who would she turn to?'

'Secretary Cecil,' he answered.

'Good. And if we asked Walter Raleigh - for his School of Night may be caught up in this through Chapman and Forman if through no-one else...'

'He would turn to Cecil too.'

'And who would Cecil turn to?'

'The Chief Intelligencer.'

'Good. And say we took another tack and asked Essex, who we know is already entangled in whatever this is?'

'He is Earl Marshal and would turn to the Knight Marshal.'

'And the Knight Marshal would turn to...'

'The Pursuivant Marshal.'

'So we, therefore, might best turn to those worthies first. The Chief Intelligencer and the Pursuivant Marshal. Also known as...'

'Robert Poley,' breathed Tom. 'Are you seriously saying we should take this witches' brew of poetry, poison, falsehood, magic and murder to *Robert Poley*?'

Chapter 9: The Master of Deceit

i

Rosalind insisted on coming with Tom to see Poley. He was happy enough to take her because she and her parents who had run an inn on the main road between London and Edinburgh via Cambridge, had worked as spies for him and had been trained by him; Rosalind still being, as Tom calculated, more Poley's creature than Shakespeare's lover. In many ways this was especially true as the inn had been destroyed by Gelly Meyrick and her father beaten to death by others of Essex' men when they kidnapped her for interrogation by Sir Francis Bacon on Essex' orders. If anyone stood against her enemies - in spite of his current position - Poley did.

As his beautiful lover went with one man to meet another, the ever-trusting Will was happy enough to be left alone in his new lodging overlooking the Globe as Richard Burbage, Peter Street and his carpenters slowly erected it. Will was fiercely focused on his play of *Henry* now, with *Caesar* and *Hamlet* in the background. Though, as far as Tom could see, the playwright was currently trying to pen the rousing speech Mark Antony would have given to the English army had he been in command at the siege of Harfleur.

Tom and Rosalind were seated by the table in Poley's room at the top of the Yeomans' house on Hog Lane where he lodged. Tracking him had been surprisingly easy in the end. Tom reasoned that it would take time for him to revert to the ill-shaven, filthy state in which he did his undercover work at the Marshalsea. Until he did so he would be fulfilling other duties - either as Chief Intelligencer or as Pursuivant Marshal, though both often required him either to travel to distant places or to disguise himself as a prisoner in one of London's many jails. Most recently - previous to his brief sojourn in the Marshalsea a few days ago - he had been on a longer assignment in the same jail just over a year back when he had spied on the imprisoned Ben Jonson to establish whether he had any seriously treasonous leanings after the debacle arising from the play of *The Isle of Dogs* which Ben had written with Tom Nash - a work almost as dangerous as Spenser's *Mother Hubberd's Tale* seemed to have become, thought Tom. But in the end they had found Poley in the first place they looked - at home.

Looking across the table now, Tom found himself considering Poley, his background and his work as one of the most successful spies in the country. He saw a gaunt hawk-faced man in his mid-to-late forties. Lean but whip-strong. Thick, wavy brown hair swept back from a high forehead. Deep-set, fiercely intelligent eyes, startlingly blue beneath overhanging brows; beak of a nose, thin-lipped mouth, usually down-turned with uncompromising lines astride a square-chin, grey with ill-shaven stubble now - so he planned on more undercover work, for he was usually punctilious in such matters. Brutally powerful hands that were surprisingly large, rivaling even those of Rackmaster Topcliffe, lay on the table-top like somnolent animals.

*

Poley's origins were as obscure as most of his doings, but by sixteen he had been a sizar at Clare College, Cambridge, twenty years before Armada year, working his way through his studies by acting as a servant to the richer students - just as the young Edmund Spenser was doing at neighboring Pembroke College. Soon after graduation, he had managed to make contact with young Sir Thomas Walsingham and, through his good offices, started working for Sir Thomas' relative Sir Francis Walsingham, the head of the queen's spy service. Sir Francis, nicknamed her 'Moor' by Elizabeth because his colouring was so dark, shared Poley with the Earl of Leicester, her 'Sweet Robin' who also ran an intelligence unit. Both Walsinghams were instrumental in placing him in Sir Philip Sidney's household when the dashing soldier-poet married Sir Francis' daughter Frances Walsingham - who was later to marry the Earl of Essex after being widowed by Sidney's death at the battle of Zutphen. Whose funeral was in many ways the paradigm of Spenser's, which was apt enough in turn because Spenser had added immeasurably to Sidney's memory and standing by writing his great elegiac poem *Astrophel*.

Released from Sidney's service, Poley was rapidly promoted into being the Council's most trusted domestic courier, carrying secret messages to Mary Queen of Scots, becoming a trusted agent of her Catholic coterie - which in turn allowed him to warn the Earl of Leicester of a plot to murder him; something that enhanced his already burgeoning reputation and fastened him to Leicester' side for some time. Tom had first met him at Leicester's shoulder during the Battle of Nigmegen, part of Leicester's campaign against Philip of Spain's catholic armies in the Low Countries.

But the backbone of Poley's work was completed at home. He was the double agent at the heart of the Babington plot to put the Queen of Scots on her cousin Elizabeth's throne. Some said he had become Sir Antony Babington's lover in order to seduce information out of him. A suspicion echoing the gossip that Will Shakespeare had been catamite to Henry Wriothesley the Earl of Southampton and written some of his loveliest sonnets to him. As for Poley and Babington, it was certainly well attested - if not absolutely true - that Babington's last words were, 'Do not hurt my sweet Robert…'

However he gained the knowledge, Poley betrayed Babington and his co-conspirators to Walsingham and was present when they were hanged, drawn and quartered, and later at Fotheringay Castle when Mary lost her head for her part in the plot. As a consequence, he became the Council's most trusted international courier - into Europe as well as up to Edinburgh - while also establishing himself as their best undercover man - in Newgate and the Marshalsea.

It was this combination which put him at the centre of the plot to kill Kit Marlowe, following him abroad and ghosting him and his friends from one jail, secret meeting and clipping house to another, and finally to a cramped room in Mistress Bull's residence in Deptford with Ingram Frizer and Nick Skeres. After Marlowe's successful execution, Poley had simply gone from strength to strength. So that now, if temporarily, he was right-hand man to all of the most powerful, mutually mistrustful masterminds in Elizabeth's fragmented intelligence service.

ii

'So,' said Poley as he stirred the bundle of papers Tom had rescued from Spenser's grave, 'you attest that in amongst all this scribbled drivel there is proof of a plot to murder Spenser as well as strong suggestions as to who might have been responsible if murder was in fact done. Someone other than poetry-lovers who found his writings almost impossibly boring and utterly endless; especially, Heaven help us, that infinity of antique excrement the *Fairy Queen*...'

'*If murder was done*,' echoed Tom. 'Surely you must know that murder was done. Spenser's body was taken and presumably examined by Simon Forman under instruction from the Knight Marshal - himself under instruction from the Earl Marshal as passed on by Gelly Meyrick and the Bacon brothers.'

'Taken, and prepared for burial, certainly...' Poley's tone was unusually hesitant, but perhaps only someone who knew him well would notice.

'They haven't discussed this with you, have they?' said Tom softly. Then he answered his own question. 'But of course they haven't. There is the matter of trust after all. You might be *called* the Pursuivant Marshal but the Earl Marshal and the Knight Marshal are all too well aware that you are also the Chief Intelligencer to the Council...'

'Put in place to spy on them,' added Rosalind. 'Or at least to keep close watch on them.'

'Because the Council - and Secretary Cecil above all - fears that Essex has ulterior motives for planning to invade Ireland,' added Tom.

'Especially as he is doing his utmost to recruit the best trained and equipped soldiers he can,' added Rosalind. 'Men whose first allegiance is to him.'

'Like the thirteenth legion who crossed the Rubicon with Julius Caesar,' added Tom. 'Or, indeed, the army who crossed into Wales with Her Majesty's grandfather Henry Tudor to stand against King Richard III at Bosworth Field.'

'My Will Shakespeare would probably be happy to explain about Caesar as he's studying Sir Thomas North's *Plutarch* even now,' said Rosalind.

'The same Thomas North as is training Essex' Irish Army,' observed Poley.

'The other reason they probably don't want you too closely involved and studying these poems in any detail,' said Tom, 'is that many of them seem to suggest that Spenser's satire *Mother Hubberd's Tale* might have been seen as seditious when it was first released but changing times and circumstances have made its re-issue dangerously treasonous now. Particularly against the men you normally work for as Chief Intelligencer.'

'The Fox and the Ape,' added Rosalind helpfully.

Poley's finger stopped its dismissive shuffling of the poems on the table in front of him. That piercing blue gaze rested briefly on Rosalind then switched to Tom. 'The Fox and the Ape…' he mused.

'Men who might well find in the poem itself a motive for murder,' said Tom. 'And we bring it all to your attention in the full knowledge that if the Fox and the Ape did indeed want the upstart poet slaughtered for publishing such treasonous satires, then you are the man they would come to, as they did in the case of Kit Marlowe.'

*

Bess the serving woman tapped on the door some uncounted time later and Poley called, 'Come!'

Bess entered carrying a tray of food and drink but was forced to stand helplessly looking down at the littered table while Tom and Poley tried to move the piles of poems out of her way without getting them all mixed up again. But the necessity to do this seemed to focus their minds further so that when Bess had deposited the tray and left the room, the three of them were able to have a pointed and insightful discussion that moved beyond the facts and speculations they had shared so far as they consumed mutton pie, manchet loaves with minted butter and small beer.

'So,' said Rosalind round a most unladylike mouthful, 'this first pile of poesy, with Chapman's first elegy on the top has no relevance to the problem.'

'No apparent relevance,' nodded Poley.

'None that we can see so far,' concluded Tom.

'The poems there, like Chapman's first one, are general work-a-day elegies that could have been written by almost anyone for any purpose. Certainly, Chapman's first, with its talk of Ruth's tears and hissing adders apparently has no direct reference to Spenser himself at all. Even the mention of the fox seems to be a part of a night time description symbolizing sadness. It is very different from the much more calculated epitaph from the grave-side which goes with so many of the others in the poetry-writing community.'

'If such a community can be said to actually exist,' said Poley.

'So this second pile, with Chapman's second elegy on top, has half a dozen poems that refer to *Mother Hubberd's Tale* being satire as possible treason, also to Ireland, the loss of Spenser's castle, lands and fortunes, and hint at something we know to be true but which we supposed only a limited number of people were aware of…'

'To wit, the fact that he was murdered,' concluded Tom.

'Which in many ways does suggest a community of poets,' said Rosalind. 'For I can envisage poets in twos or threes writing elbow to elbow and cheek by jowl in one tavern after another, but surely the similarity of the points raised in so many poems by so many poets must speak of a wider group, all sharing the same thoughts and fears.'

'None of them seems to be an admission of guilt, however,' said Poley.

'But that third pile, with Will's sonnet on the top, seems to contain mute and subtle accusations as to who is guilty of the murder, again from a wide range of poets.'

'Guilt apparently assigned to your friend Shakespeare,' said Poley.

'Who we know in any case,' said Rosalind quickly, 'was already the subject of false accusations.'

'*Possibly* false accusations,' said Poley.

'*Definitely* false, Master Poley,' said Rosalind so forcefully that Tom raised an eyebrow. 'For I was with him at the time he was supposed to be making his purchases of poison from Master Gerard's apprentice. And I will stand up and say so if I need to.'

'Hmmm,' said Poley. 'Let us not hasten down that road too quickly, mistress. For it may well lead to the Tower and the rack.'

'And Rackmaster Topcliffe's pleasure,' added Tom with calculated tactlessness as he wondered *was Rosalind telling the truth*?

iii

'Leaving aside Sir Richard, Master Will and their various pleasures for the moment,' said Poley, 'the poems act as keys that open various doors of speculation. First that there are men amongst the poets themselves who would have wished to see Spenser dead and their own poetry therefore preferred in place of his.'

'Men at the edges of the court circle with ambitions to move inwards and upwards. Such men might well also wish Will out of the way likewise, for his plays are preferred at Christmas and Twelfth Night - and other festivities into the bargain. Thus they strike down two rivals at once.' Rosalind suggested.

'For reputation - whatever that is worth,' said Tom. 'Because it must be admitted that neither Spenser nor Shakespeare has made their fortune by publishing their verse or playing to the Queen. Though Spenser has received a grant from the royal purse.'

'I can envisage men jealous of Spenser's reputation,' said Poley, 'for he is or was "the modern Virgil; the English Ariosto" was he not? But *Shakespeare*? Who could be jealous of Southampton's catamite, Shakespeare?'

'Was not Julius Caesar himself said to have played the woman's part with King Nichomedes of Bithnya?' enquired Rosalind. 'So Plutarch records in the volume Englished by Sir Thomas North that Will has at home - which I read while he writes. Which is often and at length.' She sighed.

'Even so,' said Poley. 'We make no allowanced for Roman perversities here. So I ask again, who would be jealous of the upstart crow? Though it is Spenser who's covered with borrowed feathers now.'

'Kit Marlowe might have been, were he still alive,' suggested Tom, which closed down that particular avenue of speculation.

'So,' said Poley after a moment of silence. 'Jealous poets. Who else?'

'Anyone with designs on Spenser's Irish land holdings,' said Tom. 'Currently worth little, I grant you. But, should the Earl of Essex prove successful in his Irish crusade…'

'A long shot,' said Poley dismissively. 'Anyone aiming their arrow in that direction is likely to find it blown off course or falling short of the target.'

'*We* might suspect the Earl is unlikely to succeed in that particular endeavour,' said Rosalind. 'But we are a tiny number with special knowledge. The rest of the country sees only a military hero riding to certain victory. Sir Francis Drake on horseback; Henry Vth reborn. Such a belief might well underpin a certainty that Spenser's Irish lands will soon be worth a fortune.'

'So, we have jealous poets and acquisitive if sadly ignorant land speculators. What more?'

'The Irish themselves, though they have no place in the poems that I can see as yet,' said Tom. 'However, Hugh O'Neil, the Earl of Tyrone and England's principal foe, is not above sending spies to London. Such men or women would find it a hard matter to reach Essex himself, or Raleigh, or most of the others who pose a threat to Irish independence. But Spenser? All they'd have to do was tip-toe up some stairs…'

'Bribe the apprentice Hal to make sure the medicines were extra-strong and to swear that Shakespeare bought the hemlock,' added the more practical Rosalind. 'It is a pity we cannot question young Hal.'

*

'Aye,' said Poley. 'If what you have told me of the matter is accurate, it would have been interesting to find out what form of bribery was used and by whom. The best guess at the moment to my mind arises from the apparent place and nature of his death. I agree that it seems he had gone to Forman's house seeking Elizabeth Gerard's birth chart and such predictions as it might contain. But what if he also had plans involving Forman's wares? If Mistress Elizabeth was purchasing love potions and amulets to win Master Donne by magic, why should not young Hal be seeking the same things to win the heart of Elizabeth in the first place? Forman's part in this is by no means clear, whether or not he kept the boy's corpse in his privy and prepared the distillation of hemlock poured in Spenser's ear by person or persons as yet unknown. No. I wish we could have questioned young Hal I do indeed.'

'But his sudden and unexplained absence is now likely to cause some consternation,' said Rosalind. 'Has he risen from Spenser's grave? Has someone else resurrected him and taken the poems too? Where has he gone and why? There is black magic involved in this as well as alchemy and apothecaries - is there any of it strong enough to unlock death's door? There will be fearful heads shaken amongst the men who put him there in the first place and find him missing now. Much fluttering and confusion.'

'Like a cat among pigeons,' emphasized Tom. 'But only among the lesser suspects.'

'Ah,' said Poley. 'Now we come to more dangerous waters. Well, let the good ship *Speculation* sail on regardless.'

'Like Odysseus facing Scylla and Charybdis, we plough straight ahead as you suggest into the deadly seas of *Mother Hubberd's Tale*. We proceed between the Fox, do we not, and the Ape as we have discussed. No matter who was to be interpreted as the Fox when the poem was originally published, the Fox is Walter Raleigh now,' said Tom. 'Lean, acquisitive, ruthless and red-haired.'

'And he is also closely associated with Ireland,' said Rosalind. 'He has holdings there, and history…'

'He was with Lord Grey at the siege of Smerwick, as you know Master Poley. He and Macworth were captains in the force that defeated the Spanish and Italian troops sent by Philip of Spain to support the Irish and trapped them there by the coast.

Whether Lord Grey gave his word that all who surrendered would be spared or not remains a subject of debate. But there is no doubt that as soon as they did surrender, Raleigh and Macworth beheaded them all. Famously made a pile of their heads - six hundred of them - only sparing the officers in hope of ransom, and when that was not forthcoming they shattered the bones in their arms and legs with hammers and left them crying and crawling for a night before they strung them up the next day and left them flapping and choking. Certainly there are men and women in Ireland, Spain and Italy who would move heaven and earth to see The Fox hunted to his lair and hounded to death.'

'Spenser amongst them?'

'His lands are close enough to Smerwick. It was his castle razed and his children murdered, none of Raleigh's touched - for Raleigh of course has his principal residence, wife and children safely at Sherborne in nice peaceful Dorset. It is a situation which might generate sufficient jealousy in a frustrated and heartbroken father to make Spenser keen on republishing his most stinging satire.'

'And tempt Raleigh to reply in kind?' wondered Rosalind.

'Who knows?' shrugged Poley. 'There's no doubt he's capable of it, six hundred heads at Smerwick Bay stand mute witness to the fact. But does he have the power? Or the influence?'

iv

'Of one thing I am certain,' said Tom, 'Raleigh would never go running to Forman demanding hemlock in person. Nor would he pretend to be Will Shakespeare, disguised or not - though his reputation as a poet does suffer in comparison with Will's. And there is not a jot of possibility that it was Raleigh who tip-toed up the stair to pour the stuff in Spenser's ear. That's not his style at all.'

'But he is surrounded by men who would do all these things if he ordered them to,' said Rosalind. 'Soldiers and sailors alike.'

'True. But is this work for a soldier or a sailor? I think not…' he looked at Poley unflinchingly.

'You're in the right,' said Poley after a moment. 'It is work for a spy. A clandestine assassin.'

'Which brings us to the Ape,' said Tom. 'When *Mother Hubberd's Tale* was first published, the Ape was generally taken to be Lord Burghley but in the mean-time the target has become his son, Secretary Cecil. And the passage of years has made the satire more biting still. For William Cecil, Lord Burghley may have been the Queen's creature, performing her every wish in his desire to make himself more powerful but he was a strong and upstanding man of considerable physical beauty. His son, however, *is* her Ape. Ape by name as well as by nature - in every regard that his father was but with the added burden of his physical appearance. She calls him her Ape because he looks like an ape with his twisted spine, hunched back and small stature. He hides his bitterness well, but he is the result of his father's constant disappointment that he never grew strong or straight. Of the endless hours in the hands of doctors who tried everything including racks worthy of Topcliffe himself in the endeavour to make him fit his father's wishes. His elder half-brother is as tall as their father and has inherited the titles as Earl of Exeter and Lord Burleigh as well as his sporting prowess and physical beauty. His cousins are the Bacon brothers, Francis and Anthony. Anthony at least is bed-bound which must be some relief. His years at St John's College, Cambridge were such a trial to him that he contrived to leave the place early and finished his education at the Sorbonne in Paris hard by Notre Dame where his hunched back was apparently less remarkable. But there is no doubt that he has inherited his father's political genius and understanding of the way power works, be it in the most magnificent court or in the filthiest gutter. And of course, as master Poley knows better than anyone alive, Cecil is surrounded by spies and assassins who would avenge the insult against him by some upstart poet without a second thought.'

'And have the knowledge, skills and motivation to cover their tracks,' said Rosalind. Then a thought struck her. She turned to

Tom almost accusingly, 'And Secretary Cecil is well aware of your habit of seeking out murderers as well as your friendship with Will. What if he has ordered Will to be made a part of this - not because of his poetry or his standing as a writer of plays, but as a way of distracting you from seeking out the truth!'

*

Poley did not laugh outright but it was clear that he was fighting to keep a straight face as he said, 'Mistress Rosalind, I fear you may have overestimated master Musgrave's ability and standing, particularly in the eyes of the most powerful man in the country.'

'Perhaps,' she said. 'Then again, perhaps not. I'll allow you know Secretary Cecil better than we do, but you'll also allow that Tom has been of direct and personal service both to you and to him recently. The kind of service that is likely to place Tom in Master Secretary's memory for some time. And place him there to the good.'

'Very well, mistress, I'll allow that,' nodded Poley. 'And I'll also allow that there may be ulterior motives in causing Master Shakespeare to stand accused of involvement through the witness of the apprentice Hal - at one time articulate and now mute. An apparently devious stratagem which you, with a little help from the Fates and a precipitous staircase, have thwarted twice. I wonder, however, if you have quite thought through all the ramifications resulting from your actions.'

'Meaning?' asked Rosalind.

'Meaning,' answered Tom before Poley could speak, 'that we may be jumping to conclusions about how and why Hal died. And also that in the absence of any immediate chance of removing Will to the Tower or the Marshalsea, whoever arranged all this might well decide it is time to remove him to the graveyard alongside the two that lie dead so far.'

'Surely that would entail some risk,' said Rosalind. 'To have one poet die in mysterious circumstances might well be unremarkable enough. To have two dying so close together must surely rouse suspicion.'

'Not to mention a great deal of relief, perhaps even joy, amongst genuine poetry-lovers,' said Poley.

'Only if his death were in itself suspicious,' interjected Tom. 'And only, indeed, if Spenser's death is recognized as being out of the ordinary.'

'All you would need is sudden flaring of tempers over reputation slighted, such as arose between Ben Jonson and Gabriel Spenser, for instance, and there you have it,' added Poley, still considering how poets died. 'Or you do after a little rapier-play, though I understand in Gabriel Spenser's case the fatal wound was given by one large body - unusually large for a poet and playwright, though not for an ex-bricklayer like Jonson - jumping onto the belly of the other when he was down and bleeding from a wound in his side. One dead poet and one claiming benefit of clergy. It could happen daily without arousing suspicion.'

Rosalind frowned. 'Your levity, Master Poley, only serves to make one thing clear.'

'My unimpeachable taste in verse and drama?'

'The fact that my Will may be in immediate and mortal danger.'

'Ah,' said Poley, a little more seriously.

'Some men whom the neighbors thought to be pursuivants were looking for him in St Helen's soon after we moved to Maiden Lane,' said Rosalind.

'If they were pursuivants, I did not send them,' said Poley.

'Might Sir Thomas Gerard have done so?' she wondered.

'The Knight Marshal has yet to share any confidences with me,' admitted Poley. 'Nor, in truth, is he likely to do so; any more than the Earl Marshal.'

'You may be presented as Pursuivant Marshal,' nodded Rosalind. 'But you are still Chief Intelligencer to the Council.'

'Achilles disguised as a woman is still Achilles,' nodded Tom.

Poley looked at him in silence, his eyebrows raised in surprise that Tom should pay him a compliment instead of a bantering insult - their usual way of talking to each-other. 'If you confuse the Marshalsea with the mythic island of Skyros,' he allowed. 'And If I am Achilles disguised as a woman to gain entry there, then who are you?'

'Odysseus his companion,' answered Tom without a second thought. 'The cunning one.'

v

Tom and Rosalind discussed what they had learned as they made their way south through the city. Poley had lent Tom a leather bag big enough to hold the poems which were still carefully organized. Tom was quiet; not because he was mulling over their conversation with Poley, but rather because he was still wondering about the oh-so-convenient death of his predecessor as Pursuivant Marshal up at Houghton Hall, for something about the name of the place nagged at his memory.

They paused in Old Swan Lane to purchase a couple of soused herring and a loaf of barley bread for Will's supper. 'He won't have thought to get anything for himself,' said Rosalind. 'He'll have spent the day so far scribbling away at his play of *Henry*, glad of my absence and enjoying the peace and quiet, as like as not.' There was a tone in her voice that showed a conflict between love and frustration, thought Tom with an inward smile. Well, the pair of them would either settle together comfortably or they would not. Only time would tell.

Tom and Rosalind ran down Old Swan Stairs to the tiny landing place, then Rosalind looked around wide-eyed while Tom gestured to the nearest wherry. He was not surprised either at Rosalind's wonder or her silence. There was still something of the country-girl about her. She was by no means used to London, its sights, sounds and smells. Old Swan Stairs provided all three in abundance. The landing on which they were standing was the closest of all to London Bridge. The Bridge itself towered on their left, stepping out across the river, reaching half way to the clouds. Its starlings, pointed like the bows of ships, tore the river to pieces, especially now that the tide was falling fast. There was a cliff of water beneath the bridge, Tom knew, that was taller than a man. The fearsome noise of the nearest waterfalls between the starlings was compounded by the rumbling roar of the water-wheels between the nearest ones and the creaking thunder of cart-wheels, hooves, trotters and feet in their hundreds passing along above. The shouted conversations

162

of the river of humanity flowing this way and that were only occasionally audible above the cacophony of Nature meeting the work of Man. The wind backed, bringing the stomach-churning stench from the communal privies that were merely planks with holes in them overhanging the thundering flood.

The wherry Tom had signaled pulled up beside the landing. 'You and the pretty lady looking to shoot the bridge, Master?' bellowed the wherryman. 'It's just the right time for it. A mortal exciting ride.'

'No thank you. Bank End Stairs if you please,' bellowed Tom in return.

'Should we not shoot the bridge?' asked Rosalind as she settled onto her seat beside Tom. 'I hear it is a fearful ride and deadly dangerous too. I could do with some excitement!'

'Get Will to take you,' suggested Tom. 'He's bound to be planning a play with a storm, a shipwreck or a drowning in it soon.'

The wherryman obviously overheard them, thought Tom an instant later, for he took them as close to the Bridge as it was possible to come without getting sucked down by the fearsome current. Rosalind clutched his arm and resolutely refused to scream, her face spotted with spray, her hair gleaming with it, her eyes wide and her lips apart as she panted. Will had better not be hoping to get much more writing done today, thought Tom. Or any sleep tonight.

*

The door to Will and Rosalind's new lodgings was on the latch as usual. Rosalind opened it and Tom followed her into the spacious hall, then up the stairs. The door into their rooms stood slightly ajar but Rosalind saw nothing strange in this, pushing it wider, and calling to her preoccupied lover, 'Will! We're home and have supper for you.'

She bustled through the shadowy bedroom and into the brighter room at the front. Then she stopped, surprised and confused. The room was empty. The table still bore the remains of a sketchy lunch snatched at random. The wardrobe door stood open. The travelling trunk beneath the window was piled with sheets of paper that were in the process of becoming *The*

Chronicle History of Henry the fifth With his battle fought at Agin Court France together with Ancient Pistol as it now said on the title page. The ink well and a pile of quills lay tidily beside them. Other than that, the room was utterly empty.

Tom crossed to the wardrobe and pulled the door a little wider. 'His cloak's gone,' he said. 'Likely he's been called down to the Globe over some matter of Burbage's.'

Rosalind put the packages of fish and bread on the table. 'Let's go and find out,' she said.

They left the room and the lodging house side by side, crossed Maiden Lane shoulder to shoulder and strode across Sir Nicholas Brend's field. The Globe was almost walled now - certainly they needed to enter through the door. 'That'll be a penny-piece each, groundlings,' called Burbage cheerfully. 'Though you'll have to wait a while to see the play.' He jumped down off the undressed boards that would become the stage to land in front of them. 'What's amiss?'

'Have you seen Will?' asked Rosalind.

'No. Is he not hard at work on his play of *Henry Fifth*? The roof goes on as soon as the thatcher can manage it and we will need something to show our public. Will promised...'

'No,' said Tom. 'Will is gone.'

'His play is there right enough,' confirmed Rosalind. 'But Will is gone.'

*

Poley looked at the pursuivant without much liking. He was a square man of early middle years, dressed in a black tunic and black breeches. His stockings were black and his black shoes set off with silver-coloured pewter buckles. But this was not the rich, expensive, velvety black favored by Tom Musgrave. This was cheap, cloudy black over shoddy and fustian favored by those of Puritan bent. His face was square and shiny, his eyes and mouth small and disapproving. His hair was cropped as though his wife had put a basin upside-down over his head and cut round the rim. It hung one lank inch below the line of his wide-brimmed hat - which he kept in place even when faced by his betters. Though of course, he would not admit to having betters outside his congregation, for he was God's man doing

God's work in this wicked world and anyone opposing him was bound straight for Hell. His name was Humiliation Gouge and he was, for the moment, under Poley's command.

'Is it done?' asked Poley quietly.

Humiliation Gouge stopped looking with marked disapproval round Poley's comfortable lodgings and allowed his gaze to return to his commander's face. 'Done as ordered, Marshal. I took half a dozen men but he came quiet enough in the end.'

'And he's safe?'

'His body lies secure in the Marshalsea, safe enough. His immortal soul is likely well on the path to everlasting hellfire if there is truth in what we hear spoken of him. A writer of plays. A poet. A fornicator and a sodomite...'

Humiliation's tone was equally disapproving of poets and sodomites, noted Poley. 'Well, brother Humiliation,' he said, 'you have done good work and may return to your duties. I will come to the Marshalsea tomorrow. Master Shakespeare and I have much to discuss...'

Humiliation Gouge turned on his heel and began to march towards the door where Bess, who had shown him up, stood wide-eyed. 'Oh, and Gouge,' called Poley.

Gouge turned round, his face a mask of enquiry. 'Marshal?'

'When a man called Thomas Musgrave shows up, especially if he is accompanied by a woman called Rosalind Fletcher, they are under no circumstances to be allowed access to the prisoner.'

'Shall we arrest them too, Marshal?' asked Gouge hopefully.

'No. Don't let them in. Don't keep them in. At least not until you've seen me in the morning.'

'Yes, Marshal. Musgrave and Fletcher are not to be arrested until after I've seen you in the morning.' Pursuivant Humiliation Gouge nodded approvingly and marched on out of Pursuivant Marshal Poley's room.

PETER TONKIN

Chapter 10: The Man in the Marshalsea

i

Will Shakespeare shifted his weight from one buttock to the other, cursing the cold stone floor on which he was sitting. He leaned back against the wall and tried to order his thoughts once more. He had absolutely no idea why he was here in the Marshalsea. But he was thankful for one thing - that Rosalind had not been there when they came. The pursuivants who had arrested him and brought him here had said little, and nothing at all about what laws he might have broken. But they had at least given him pride of place in the big dank room of the main prison chamber. He was so relieved that this was so that it did not occur to him to be suspicious.

What light there was showed a large, almost featureless place haphazardly broken into smaller cells by barriers of iron bars. These had walls, floors and ceilings of stone or iron but no doors. They needed none because their occupants, like Will, were chained to the solid bricks that lined the place, some by the neck, some by the wrists and some by the ankles. Will's ankle gyves were not too tight and with luck would not damage his leggings or shoes, let alone his ankles or his feet.

Will was seated closest to the main door beneath which a draft of cool clean air gusted strongly enough to give him some relief from the fetid stench of the place, though it could not blow away the lice and fleas that teemed in the rotting rushes on the floor and clearly viewed this newcomer as a mountainous feast. At least his chains had proved to be long enough to allow him easy access to the nearest of the buckets positioned down the centre of the room to act as chamber-pots. Though great care had to be taken in their use for they swarmed with cockroaches - or they did until the rats came a'hunting. And, for a wonder at this season, the whole place seemed to be filled with fat black flies.

The half-dozen other inmates had watched with a kind of dull envy as the pursuivant who arrested him watched impatiently while the turnkey chained him here. The only sounds after the gyve lock clicked shut were the rattling of the jailer's keys, and two sets of heavy footsteps and the slamming of the door as the

166

pair left, which had been followed by the deep breath Will took as he had settled - but for little more than a heartbeat. Almost immediately he had realized that his nervousness had gone straight to his vitals and he needed to piss more than he had ever done in all his life before.

He was just settling back with his bladder empty, his mind still a jumble of nervous confusion, when the closest of his companions began a surprisingly amicable conversation. 'Name's Esau Parrot,' he introduced himself. '*Charm* by profession as you might say. Caught using my black arts on the wrong door. What you in for, cully?'

'Will Shakespeare, playwright,' Will answered guardedly. 'I've no idea why I'm here.'

'Playwright eh? You written something seditious that's upset the Chamberlain and the Council? Like that *Isle of Dogs*?' suggested Parrot.

Something fell into place in Will's disordered thoughts then. He had talked to Ben Jonson about that episode - for Jonson and Nash had written the offending piece - and the time Ben had spent in the Marshalsea which resulted from its publication. Ben had mentioned specifically and bitterly two undercover agents playing equivocator and Devil's advocate there - Richard Poley and Esau Parrot, both past masters in the art of tempting others into deadly sedition by saying treasonous things themselves.

*

Before he could reply to the equivocator's question, the man on Parrot's other side started mumbling. A prayer, perhaps, thought Will. Parrot turned away, 'That sounds Jesuitical to me, Reverend,' he said, his voice no longer friendly but full of threat. The mumbled prayer faded into near-silence. 'We'll continue our little chat later on old man. I know you Jesuits and Blackwell's common Catholic crew ain't no bosom friends so you can each serve your individual Whore of Babylon by handing the others over. That was Master Robert Roe's approach while he was Pursuivant Marshal when he was still above ground God rest his soul, before Master Poley took over.'

He swung back to Will, without bothering to put back his mask of apparent friendliness, a decision no doubt strengthened by the look of suspicion Will was now wearing. 'And you, Master Shakespeare, you don't need to wonder whether some seditious entertainment like *Isle of Dogs* brought you here. We've known of your catholic leanings for long enough, before poor Master Roe's days in fact. We watched you in the North before you travelled south and became the Earl of Southampton's lapdog.'

'I was never in the North,' said Will wearily. 'Nor did I ever meet the Earls of Northumberland or Westmorland, their friends, kith or kin. I was five when the North rose against the Queen. By the time I attained manhood I was in the Low Countries as well you know for your colleague in this foul trade Robert Poley saw me there, saving the Earl of Leicester's army at Nijmegen.'

Parrot shrugged. 'If you say so, Master. I'm not saying every man called a saint is a saint - nor every man called a sinner is a sinner. But I know how long you lingered in the Low Countries and how much time you had besides to be running round the catholic houses posing as tutor to the Percy or the Hoghton children there. Master Shakeshaft, tutor at Hoghton Tower…'

'Believe what you wish,' said Will wearily. 'I was never there nor ever called myself Shakeshaft. Nor Shagsberd come to that - a not-very-amusing fantasy of the clown Will Kempe's who hates me for excluding him from our company and, indeed, writing the character of Falstaff out of my new play entirely to make sure he stays away, having no part to perform. You equivocators can lie from either side of a case, saint or sinner. But you'll all go straight to hell in the end I'll wager, for you're all guilty as sin yourselves.'

'Mayhap I will,' said Parrot. 'Mayhap I won't and others will take the primrose path instead. But I was speaking the truth nonetheless - for me and Robert Poley both. We're watching you, Will Shagsberd, have been since you started poaching deer at Charlcoate and getting older women with child in the water meadows of the Avon - and don't you ever forget it. And, while you're sitting here protesting your innocence in all things, chew on this master lapdog. It was that den of catholics Hoghton Hall that Robert Roe was examining when he died and Master Poley succeeded him.'

Will closed his eyes. Despite Parrot's interruptions and insinuations - or perhaps because of them - questions kept arising, each time more confusingly and worryingly than the last. Were the pursuivants trying to link him with Hoghton Hall, where he had never worked, even under the name of Shakeshaft, and this man Roe's death? What else had he done? Why was he here? Did the pursuivants really think him guilty of dangerously catholic leanings? Had they in fact been watching him from so long ago - or was this all just gossip gleaned from his loose association with the Secret Services; Phelippes and his code-breakers, Poley and his spies. Something spun out from the coincidence of names - if this Master Shakeshaft had ever actually been the tutor at Hoghton?

If they really believed all that Parrot said was true, then why had it taken so long for them to take him? Why had Robert Poley ordered it rather than his predecessor Robert Roe? And, come to that, why was Parrot sitting in chains beside him and not someone like the self-confessed recusant John Donne whose brother had been arrested and died in Newgate for shielding Jesuit priests who were in turn executed at Tyburn? Worst of all - what in Heaven's name was going to happen next?

*

Will got a grip on himself and tried to settle into more positive speculation. Tom and Rosalind would work out where he was in no time once they saw that he had disappeared. They both knew Poley; Rosalind had even worked for him as Kate Shelton and her sister Audrey worked for Sir Thomas Walsingham. They would be here before he knew it. They'd get him out.

The confidence he had in his old friend and his new lover allowed some further calming, and as his heartbeat slowed while his breathing settled, inevitably his mind returned to his work. He had been taken by the pursuivants half way through composing King Henry's speech at Harfleur: *Once more unto the breach, dear friends…* How effective it seemed to be that great leaders like Henry and Mark Antony, should see their men as friends, no matter how elevated and aristocratic they themselves were; that they should talk to them as equals - especially at moments of great danger. Perhaps he should try something similar when Henry addressed his troops at Agincourt on St Crispin's Day. Should Antony also call the Roman mob his 'friends' when he spoke at Caesar's funeral?

Calmer now, Will looked around his prison and began to wonder whether King Henry might also feel a little imprisoned; trapped by the reputation of his wild youth in spite of the fact that he had severed all ties with his evil angel Falstaff, the massive new responsibilities of kingship, the irresistible urge to carve out a place for himself in history. All of it leading, in the end, to that tomb in the Abbey with his French queen Kate, his silver scepter, his hands and even his head all stolen from him. Nothing left but a few heroic memories and some battered armour hanging up as a makeshift monument.

ii

The office at the Marshalsea had been stripped of all the ungodly voluptuousness Poley and Joan Yeomans had brought to the place. Now the table that had been laden with their food and drink carried a bible and a list of prisoners. The chair which had supported the Pursuivant Marshal and his concubine supported only the broad buttocks of the stone-faced pursuivant who apparently gloried in the name of Humiliation Gauge.

'I will not lie,' Gauge answered Tom's abrupt enquiry. 'William Shakespeare is here. You may not see him until the Pursuivant Marshal has questioned him on the morrow.' He licked his lips and allowed his broad countenance assume a sly expression. 'After the questioning is finished, you are welcome to return.'

'If you will not let us see him, will you at least give him this?' Rosalind put Will's lunch of pie and small beer on the table beside the prisoner list.

'I have not had any orders to the contrary,' said Gouge, guardedly.

'Very well,' said Tom, thinking the food and drink would tell Will that they knew where he was and were employed in seeking his release, as long as he actually got it. 'You swear you will take the food to him?' he insisted.

Gouge's eyelids flickered. 'I swear,' he said after a moment.

'Very well, we will return tomorrow.'

Tom and Rosalind walked out into the bitter evening. Gouge closed the prison door behind them. 'Do you think he will take the food through?' asked Rosalind as they turned out of Angel Place into the Borough and began following the High Street north towards the South Wark and the Bridge.

'He swore,' said Tom shortly.

'You know how easily such men break their word without seeming to do so,' she said. 'Like equivocators, they can tell any lie they like in expectation of Divine forgiveness - they are doing God's work after all. Or so they believe. Just like the Inquisition in Spain; and like any Jesuit murderer given license by the Pope to kill the Queen! Or he could take the food to Will but place it beyond his reach, or in a night-soil bucket, or beside a nest of cockroaches or rats…'

'Do not allow your imagination to grow too wild,' advised Tom, the ghost of a laugh in his tone. 'Remember, the main purpose of the food is not sustenance - Will can go hungry 'til tomorrow without much harm. It is the message that it carries - *do not fear, we know where you are…*'

'That will give him hope, I suppose.'

'It will. Now, as to you. Are you content to return to your new lodgings and remain there alone?'

'Given the possibility that the men who came for Will might also come for me or that some roaring boys might mistake our home for one of the nearby brothels and take their pleasure - with or without due payment?'

*

'Your imagination runs wild yet again. Make up your mind. If you are truly fearful then either I can stay with you in Maiden Lane or you can stay with me in Blackfriars. Or, indeed, I can see you safely back to your cousin Martin's house behind Three Cranes Wharf. Either way, you must decide. And soon. We are passing the Borough Counter jail now and will cross the South Wark soon enough. If you decide on Blackfriars or Three

171

Cranes Wharf, we will take a boat from the Mary Overie steps. If Maiden Lane, then we go past The Clink and Dead Man's Place.'

'To be honest, Tom, my desires are governed by my belly at the moment. I am less afraid of loneliness or rapine than I am of hunger. It is the thought of poor Will starving, I suppose. There are eating places convenient to Maiden Lane and I would wish to explore whichever has been best in your experience.'

'So, you suppose I frequent the Bankside brothels so regularly that I have a ready preference - as to the food at least?'

'Oh no! I know you are Mistress Kate Shelton's man to the end of your...' she paused. The tip of her tongue traced her lip.

'Yes, Madam? To the end of my...'

'...fingertips, Sirrah.'

'Hmmm. Well, you are an inkeep's daughter. Surely you can tell which will best suit your stomach simply by employing your nose - and perhaps your eyes. If you and Will are to live here, it is knowledge that may serve you well.'

'Very well, I will accept your challenge. Let us walk along Bankside and I shall decide on the best hostelry there.'

Luckily the wind was blowing from the south so as they walked along the Bankside, the odours from more than twenty establishments from The Castell nearest to the Bridge itself to the Cross Keys down by Paris Garden overwhelmed them. Rosalind chose The Rose tavern which was not far from The Rose theatre. In fact, Tom was a frequent client of the place himself, visiting it over the years in company with the mistress who had accompanied him home from Maestro Capo Fero's Italian school of defence, Constanza D'Agostino; and, after her, Kate Shelton. And even, indeed, with Robert Poley - though it was hard to imagine anyone less like a lovely woman than the sly intelligencer. But nomatter who came here with him, they always presented problems. The next one appeared immediately after he had followed Rosalind through the Rose tavern's door.

iii

Away to the right there gaped a huge cooking fire in front of which the bullock was roasting on a spit turned by a couple of sweating boys. In the brickwork on either side of the fire were capacious ovens full, no doubt, of loaves, pies and pastries. A team of half a dozen cooks and helpers were busy preparing platters and replenishing the ovens. Astride the fire hung great round-bellied pots full of fragrant stocks and soups. Beyond the fire was the counter where a busy team of bar-keepers was dispensing drinks with truly impressive rapidity into the experienced hands of a gaggle of barmaids who clearly doubled as the Winchester geese anathematized by men like Humiliation Gouge. The girls wove their way sinuously between tables which were well-peopled with customers of both sexes, swinging their hips as they went and leaning forward as they served their clients to display their wares. At least, thought Tom, Rosalind had chosen a tavern where the main amusements were feeding and fornicating - there were no gaming tables that he could see, no *cogging* or *coney-catching* here; no *rufflers* out to *cozen* the *country cousins* up for market out of their meager profits. No *barrators* or *barnacles*, accusations of cheating and *cozening* therefore. No fights erupting over hands dealt from the bottom of the deck or throws with bristle dice. All was peace and plenty.

The only elements that appeared to be out of place were one or two tables in the shadows right at the back where clients sat in threes and fours, shoulders hunched, heads together, whispering secrets that were likely dangerous - to someone other than themselves. Above the secretive figures, the roof sloped down to a set of windows overlooking a garden where, in the Summer, minstrels played and the girls took their clients for speedy assignations. Now the panes of thick green glass might just as well have been painted with pitch for all that was visible through them.

Rosalind plunged into the bustling throng, confident in her familiarity with taverns if not brothels. Tom had taken two steps forward in her wake when one of the secretive clients in the shadows close by the windows looked up. The movement of his head revealed not only his face but those of his companions. Tom froze, mind racing, calculating what best to do now that he was confronted by something he had never thought to see.

For the man who looked up was Robert Poley. And his companions at this clandestine meeting were Simon Forman, Francis Bacon and Kate Shelton.

*

Tom leaned forward, grabbed Rosalind by the shoulder and swung her round. 'We leave. NOW!' He spat into her shocked face.

'What...' She had never seen him behave like this and was clearly about to argue but he didn't have time or leisure to take the risk.

'*Now*!' he repeated. 'And with no fuss.'

Something in his expression or tone overrode her understandable confusion. She trusted him. She did as he asked.

Side by side, they left the tavern, Tom praying that none of that strange quartet at the shadowed table had noticed them. 'We'll go to the Little Rose next door,' he said as they stepped out into the chilly darkness. 'The food is almost as good...'

'What is going on?' Rosalind demanded.

'The table at the back in the shadows, closest to the window overlooking the garden,' he answered. 'There were Forman, Kate Shelton, Poley and Francis Bacon all together there.'

As he listed the table's occupants in careful order, he could feel her respond, for he still held her by her upper arm. Forman and Kate meant nothing to her. Poley had been her spymaster and she trusted him still. At the mention of his name she tensed to return and question him face to face. But the last name, Francis Bacon, brought her up short, for as she knew all too well, Bacon was Essex' man. It was Essex' men who had burned her father's inn, beaten him down and killed him while kidnapping her, all so that Francis Bacon could interrogate her, to discover what she knew about Essex' plans to raise an army to subdue Ireland and, in due time, to invade England as well. And even now she was surprised he had not used torture - and suspicious that he might yet do so. Therefore Francis Bacon's name stopped her in her tracks. It stunned her enough to let him guide her out of the tavern with no further trouble and into the Little Rose next door.

Here there was a side of mutton on the spit. Things were quieter and, Tom had to admit, that was because neither the food nor the drink were up to The Rose's standard. There was gambling of all sorts going on and that too was logical - the girls were willing enough but lacked a certain something that the girls in the Rose possessed. Allure. They were, by and large, as lean and lank as the mutton on the spit, which was being turned through a series of cogs by a trained dog running in circles.

Tom led Rosalind through the place, weaving between the tables, exchanging a word or two with those *barraters* and *coney catchers* keen for him to join their games or share his pretty little *mort* with them. He nodded to the landlord, with whom he was well acquainted, and with his wife who really ran the place, then he and Rosalind were out in the garden where, in summer, the *lank mistresses of the game* took their lean pickings one way or another, mostly standing against the trunks of the sturdier trees nearby.

In early January the place was mercifully untenanted, though Tom wryly reckoned that his reputation for desperation and Rosalind's for willingness would both be enhanced by their speedy exit. However he had brought her here not for sport but for spying. The gardens behind the Rose and the Little Rose were separated by a meager hedge as well as by the occasional trees. It was the work of a moment for them to push their way through and creep unobserved and unsuspected up to the window nearest to Poley's table.

iv

'...but he is safe,' Kate Shelton was saying.

'Safe enough,' Poley assured her. 'Until we decide how best to proceed with him.'

'How can it be,' wondered Forman, 'That such a simple matter should go awry not once but twice? That the boy, ready to testify, should come to such an end...'

'Gratis of my lady impatience here,' inserted the one voice Tom did not know - Bacon's therefore.

'Howsoever that might be,' continued Forman, 'that the boy's body should vanish before the message could be delivered is almost inconceivable. Have you no notion, Master Poley?'

'Oh I know well enough who removed it but as yet remain ignorant as to where they put it.' He paused for a heartbeat and Tom found himself wondering why Kate did not tell him where the body lay - because she had helped put it there. But then Poley continued, 'And in any case it is no longer of any use, for the poem you caused to be so carefully forged, Master Forman, has been removed and is currently with all the others. At least I know where that is and can reclaim it at any time for all the use it will be to us by then.'

'But the stratagem,' insisted Forman. 'How can that be maintained?'

'We have time to reconsider,' said Poley. 'What do you advise, Sir Francis?'

'If we have time, then we should use it,' answered Bacon, 'to the advantage of ourselves and our masters.'

'How can that be?' demanded Kate. 'Are we not all met here to speak for those who could never come to any accord in anything save in this? Master Forman speaks for Sir Walter, Sir Francis for the Earl, Master Poley for the Secretary and myself for Sir Thomas. Except for Philip of Spain and Henry of France, Rudolph of Germany the Holy Roman Emperor and of course Pope Clement, our masters are the four most powerful men in Europe.'

'Don't forget Albert, Archduke of Austria,' said Poley. 'At the moment he is merely Emperor Rudolph's younger brother but he is betrothed to the Infanta Isabella of Spain, who is likely to become Queen of England if certain factions in the North centered round Hoghton Hall get their way. Especially as Lady Arbella Stuart remains unattached and currently out of the running for the succession. That would make Albert even more powerful than Isabella's father, Philip II of Spain our late Queen Mary's husband, who never gave up on his claim to the English throne as consort to our Queen even though she was dead and replaced by her sister Elizabeth.'

'The four of our masters wish to *remain* amongst the most powerful of men,' purred Bacon, 'despite what vagaries are likely to overwhelm us all in the not-so-distant future.'

'But to return to the matter in hand,' said Poley. 'We as their creatures may say what they may not, discuss what they cannot and propose what they would never countenance...'

'In public, at least,' said Kate.

'As the mention of Archduke Albert and the Infanta have already suggested, such matters ultimately hinge upon the Queen and the succession,' said Poley after a short silence. His tone, thought Tom, was that of a man wading into uncharted waters likely to be full of man-eating monsters. 'The Queen herself - who has refused to name a successor - and how My Lord of Essex wishes to approach this problem in one way, despite Sir Walter being positioned against him, considering a contrary approach.'

'Does the Earl really seek to usurp the throne and name himself King in her place?' demanded Kate, dropping her voice at the enormity of the question so that Tom could hardly hear her.

'Sir Walter would never countenance that,' snapped Forman. 'That or anything like it. He is Captain of the Guard. Even to discuss such things is a treason he must never be made aware of or we will all lose out heads over the matter. Having been broken on the rack first as like as not.'

'We'd be fortunate were it just our heads,' warned Poley drily. 'We'd likely go the way of Babington and his plotters - hung, drawn and then quartered while yet living.

*

'My Lord of Essex means no such thing as usurpation,' soothed Bacon. 'He thinks only of placing Her Majesty in protective custody, perhaps, at Drayton Basset with his mother and step father while the Council seeks a way forward that does not involve poisoning her mind against him.'

'A way that has to include him, however,' said Poley. 'He neither likes or trusts any of the men we represent, but still has his ambitions. You must admit as much, Sir Francis. He is as alert for perfidy as a naked soldier on the wrong side of a battlefield. And in any case, how would this protective custody work?'

'As it worked with the Queen of Scots,' said Bacon. 'As, so you say, it is working with Shagsberd at the Marshalsea now.'

'And look how the first turned out,' said Poley, 'though I cannot speak for the second as yet.'

'But in any case, said Forman, 'we all know that the Council and Sir Thomas Walsingham are both making love to the Queen of Scots' son King James in Edinburgh. Through the offices of Lady Walsingham, your sister, Mistress Kate, deny it if you can!'

'If it is so,' said Kate archly, 'they would simply be seeking a steady and appropriate succession. There are too many, especially in the North, who would see us all returned to the Old Religion the moment that she dies; those that still remember and revere the Lords of the North, the Nevills, the Dacres and the Percys, not to mention those at Hoghton Hall. Which brings us back to the Infanta of Spain as master Poley said. And, indeed, to the Lady Arbella Stuart - a lady all too likely by some reckoning to share the fate of Jane Grey, Queen for nine days and beheaded in the Tower.'

<h2 style="text-align:center">v</h2>

'But James of Scotland is by no means well suited to every taste,' said Forman. 'Has he not written *Daemonologie* anathematizing magic of all sorts? Has he not personally overseen the trials of witches? I fear that were he to succeed things would go hard for me and, I have to say, for Sir Walter were the king to misunderstand the debates held in the spirit of pure philosophical enquiry by our group called by William Shagsberd *The School of Night*.'

There was the briefest silence then Kate added, 'Heaven forefend that he should ever see the upper stories of your Billingsgate house, Master Forman.'

'Places of experiment,' said Forman, 'where we seek alternative truths and sources of power beyond the biblical. We speak no treason nor practice any forbidden arts up there…'

'My sister Audrey is bosom companion with Anne of Denmark James' queen,' said Kate. 'And Queen Anne is fully convinced that witchcraft is a powerful political weapon!'

'Was not King James nearly drowned at sea with his new queen at his side as they returned from Denmark together ten years ago?' asked Bacon. 'Was that not proven to be the act of witches?'

'It was, or so King James believes,' answered Poley. 'Witches given power and motivation by the Earl of Bothwell, against whom Sir Walter has written to our own Queen Elizabeth, for Bothwell escaped King James' justice - though his coven of witches did not - and he still visits London on occasion. As we talk of dangerous matters here in any case, I should suggest Sir Francis, that there is a disturbing similarity between the Earls of Bothwell and of Essex. Let us hope that My Lord of Essex does not share Bothwell's fate - banishment and penury.'

'Or a worse fate still,' said Simon Forman.'

'So,' said Kate, 'The case so far is this. If King James succeeds Her Majesty then it is likely that Raleigh and Essex will come off badly, which is no doubt why Secretary Cecil and my brother-in-law Sir Thomas are keen to see him seated safely on the throne. Despite the danger which we have not yet discussed - to wit, that of the Scottish courtiers he will bring south with him to usurp the men well-placed in court circles at the moment.'

'And that is also why,' said Poley, 'Essex and Raleigh have other plans in mind.' His voice sank almost to a whisper. 'Perhaps even in hand.'

*

Straining to hear, Tom crept closer to the window and stepped on a fallen branch. The wood was winter-brittle and snapped with a sharp sound almost as loud as one of Ugo's pistols. Poley was in motion at once, swinging towards the window like a wolf scenting blood. Tom was in motion just as swiftly. There was no chance of concealment - there were shadows nearby but the evening sky was frost-clear and a moon was on the rise. He caught Rosalind round the waist and all-but threw her against the nearest tree-trunk, pushing himself against her as though the pair of them were taking pleasure despite the cold.

'Can you see the window?' he gasped into her ear.

'Yes. They are all rising. No doubt to leave.'

'Poley. Where is Poley?'

'I cannot see him...'

'Run!' he swung her round again so that they were shoulder to shoulder with the Little Rose's garden stretching away towards Maiden Lane, the south wind blowing into their faces. She did not need more prompting. Side by side they took off like a pair of hares at a coursing. They covered the length of the garden and slipped through the thin beech hedge at the end of it. In Maiden Lane, Tom froze for an instant looking left and right, then he was in motion once again. Blessedly, the performance at the Rose Theatre was just finishing. The audience was streaming out. Within five minutes Rosalind and he were lost amongst the merry throng, whose numbers were swollen not once but twice as they passed the Bull Baiting Pit and the Bear Baiting Pit beside it. After that they attained Dead Man's Place and turned north towards Bank End. Then they turned left and retraced their steps a little before Tom led Rosalind into The Castel, the first stew house in the long row of such establishments. In spite of the fact that the place was bustling and increasingly busy as the audiences from the various entertainments came in for food, drink and frolics, Tom managed to find a table. They sat, face to face, fighting to catch their breath. One of the girls came up, 'What's your pleasure?' she asked Tom, appraising Rosalind coolly.

'A flagon of Rhenish,' answered Tom, looking around. 'And as to food...' There was a promising-looking pig on the spit with a line of good fat capons beside it. 'Rosalind?' he asked.

A tall figure loomed in silhouette against the firelight, drew up a stool and sat at the table between them. He leaned forward, his face dark with suspicion. 'The beef *chuet* pies with raisins, plums and prunes are good,' said Robert Poley. 'Bring three of those and trenchers, girl. Then leave us alone. We three have much to discuss, have we not my fine pair of eavesdroppers?'

Chapter 11: The Men with the Motives

i

'So,' said Tom plainly, for it was no use trying to prevaricate with Poley, 'the most powerful men in the land all have something to hide, perhaps from each-other and certainly from the Queen, which is a situation poor Spenser seems to have stumbled into when he re-issued his old satire of *Mother Hubberd's Tale*; desperate for money if Ben Jonson's right.'

'And so he disturbed not just these powerful men,' added Rosalind, 'but also their acolytes.'

'Acolytes,' said Poley. 'I like that. I don't think I've ever been called an acolyte before…'

'If that is so,' said Tom, 'it must be one of the few things you haven't been called…'

The conversation paused there as two of the Castel tavern's serving women brought the *chuet* pies, coarse bread trenchers and the flagon of Rhenish they had ordered, horn spoons and cups with which to eat and drink. Tom and Poley pulled daggers from their belts and Rosalind produced one from somewhere about her person, something that raised Tom's eyebrow but seemed to be accepted by Poley without a second thought. They all fell-to with a will and found that Poley was right. The combination of soft beef and sweet fruit was very tasty. The pastry was golden and crumbly, yet firm enough to hold the steaming contents safe until the pies were opened. The gravy soaked into the trenchers, softening and sweetening them for consumption later.

'But the fair Rosalind is right,' continued Poley after a while. 'One only has to think of Henry II - one of the few King Henrys your industrious friend seems to have overlooked - to see how dangerous acolytes can be. A simple word spoken in thoughtless anger: *who will rid me of this turbulent priest…* And *pouf*! Archbishop Becket's brains splattered all over Canterbury Cathedral. And I'm sure there must be more modern instances…'

'Who was it wanted rid of Marlowe, for instance?' asked Tom.

'Almost everybody wanted rid of Marlowe!' Poley finally rose to the bait. 'He was trading in state secrets alongside his penchant for illegally trimming silver coins, which he had been doing in Amsterdam, against orders. He was indulging - very loudly - in the kinds of sodomitical pastimes that Cicero so memorably accused Mark Antony of pursuing in his youth. He was at the edge of Raleigh's School of Night and keen to experiment further. He was not only dabbling in magic and witchcraft, he was also writing blasphemous texts and causing them to be performed. And finally, he was getting far too good at passing himself off as a Catholic - so much so that certain powerful observers believed he had changed sides altogether. I am frankly surprised that God Himself didn't strike Marlowe down.'

'Perhaps He did,' suggested Tom quietly. 'Only He used Frizer, Skeres and you as His instruments.'

*

'Twice in a matter of moments,' said Poley, his tone full of ironic amazement. 'First I'm an acolyte and now I'm an instrument of Divine Retribution! It's a pity poor Spenser could not have been said to have offended the Lord God - or you could likely accuse me of his murder straight away.'

'This is off the point,' said Rosalind. 'We talked of powerful men with potentially deadly acolytes.'

'Such as Sir Walter Raleigh, perhaps,' said Tom. 'Who is dangerously lampooned - even if by chance - as the Fox in the re-print of Spenser's poem; suspected of dabbling in unholy things himself. Possessor of large estates in Ireland which he would no doubt be happy to extend as far as the ruins of Kilcolman castle and almost certainly considering whether to join one of the plots to bring Lady Arbella Stuart or the Infanta of Spain to the fore - in place of James if not of the Queen herself. With his acolyte Simon Forman who fears the possibility of trial for witchcraft and the noose or the stake after the succession to the throne by a royal expert on witches and witchcraft. He is especially so if his master becomes sufficiently damaged by appearing as the Fox in *Mother Hubberd's Tale*. All of which might well motivate him to kill the poet thus stopping any danger of further publication as the most recent print run has been confiscated I understand. And, as I keep learning to my wonder and my growing horror, Simon Forman seems to have a disturbingly wide clientele that reaches from apprentice-boys and their lights of love to the highest reaches of the Court. He has power, therefore, which might indeed seem magical. Not to mention, of course, the suspicion that he supplied the poison, no matter who eventually poured it in Spenser's ear!

'So,' said Poley, 'you are telling me that you suspect Forman above all the others so far.'

'He had a motive to kill Spenser,' confirmed Tom. 'He also had the means, and is as likely as anyone else we have discussed so far to have had the opportunity.'

A short, thoughtful silence fell, emphasized by the raucous chatter all around.

'Well, you have read Spenser's allegorical fairy tale well enough,' allowed Poley as the women cleared the remnants of dinner away and brought another flagon of Rhenish. 'Though if you still possess a copy you are likely to see the inside of Newgate, the Clink or the Borough Counter Jail earlier than you might wish to. But, now I think of it, perhaps your friend Shakespeare has thrust himself further into the matter by penning another tale like *Mother Hubberd*'s full of fairy-folk, replete with Athenian dukes and Amazonian queens, not to mention the Fairy Queen herself and yet more characters transformed into animals, though into donkeys rather than foxes or apes! Had you thought of that? Perhaps I will raise the matter when I talk to him at the Marshalsea tomorrow. It is a conversation we could easily continue in the Tower with Rackmaster Topcliffe as a participant.'

ii

'*A Midsummer Night's Dream* has no hidden meaning, and you know it!' Tom snapped. 'And you only raise the possibility as a diversion from considering Forman further as a suspect. Thus illustrating, indeed, the possible motive we have discussed for bringing Will into the situation in the first place - as a potent distraction!'

'Perhaps; perhaps not.' Poley shrugged. 'I suspect it is all in how you look at the matter of his presence in the situation, his recent writings and his whereabouts before or after we all first met at the siege of Nijmagen and ultimately whether you believe he actually was the tutor at Hoghton Hall. But to return to *Mother Hubberd* and other powerful men apparently satirized within it... I do not think we need discuss The Ape and his acolytes - Poley gave a slight, ironic bow. 'And I have to say that I am bored to death discussing Robert Devereux, his shortcomings, failings and fantasies. Whether or not it is the Ape or the Earl of Essex in some other guise who would wish to steal the crown and scepter from Spenser's sleeping lion - to wit the Queen. Though I must admit his acolytes, Sir Anthony and Sir Francis Bacon would benefit from some close and detailed scrutiny, not to mention his ill-controlled Welsh roaring boy - Sir Gelly Meyrick.'

'Which brings us to the fourth man who was represented at that table tonight,' said Rosalind quietly, 'as represented by Kate Shelton.'

Tom's lips became a thin, pale line.

'Sir Thomas Walsingham,' nodded Poley, 'and of course represented by his wife's younger sister. Lady Audrey could hardly be seen here. The immediate alternative, the keeper of his accounts and general business, Ingram Frizer, is loaded with a little too much history, perhaps. As am I, but my master is more powerful still and cares less than Sir Thomas. Mistress Kate Shelton, however, may move more widely without too much impropriety.'

'But, independently of how he was represented, how could Sir Thomas possibly be mixed up in this?' asked Tom, much more concerned about Kate and her involvement than he was about her brother-in-law and his.

'Well,' answered Poley, 'he is the closest living relative of the late Spymaster nonpareil Sir Francis Walsingham, the Queen's 'Moor' and master of dark secrets. Heir to all those secrets, contacts, and, come to that, to many of his agents - Ingram

Frizer, whom we have just mentioned, works directly for Sir Thomas; while Nicholas Skeres is Essex's man still. But…' Poley held up one long hand and began to count his points on its fingers. '*Primo*, Sir Thomas, a master of subtle inactivity, is nowhere to be found in *Mother Hubberd's Tale* - and believe me, I have looked. *Secundo*, he has no lands in Ireland, nor is he covetous of any as far as I know. He owns the great estate of Scadbury which comprises a fair portion of the county of Kent and he owns Nonsuch House, the best property on London Bridge if not in London as a whole, excepting one or two great houses and the royal palaces. *Tertio*, he has never dabbled in unnatural acts nor blasphemous beliefs. *Quarto*, he makes no great secret that he is content for the succession to run a natural course - Lady Audrey, being popular both in the Queen's court here and King James' court in Edinburgh and travels between the two courts regularly. With a freedom, I must observe, which is the envy of many men of my acquaintance. Thus, *perorare*, to sum up, it is plain that Sir Thomas has no reason to fear a Scottish succession while he can easily afford to spend the rest of his life as a protestant recusant should the Catholic contenders the Infanta or Lady Arbella take the throne. Though what I know of the man suggests he is of *Le Roi Henri Quatre*'s pragmatic stripe and would happily take Mass from the Pope himself if things came to a point.'

*

'He has absolutely no reason I can see to be mixed up in the matter of Spenser's death at all,' said Tom, 'though now you have mentioned King Henry of France, raised as a Huguenot but lately converted to the Old Faith, I should point out that he and Sir Anthony Bacon are reputed to be close friends.'

'Almost brothers,' nodded Poley. 'But it is hard to see where that places either Sir Anthony or the Earl his master in any of this - unless there are poetry lovers in Paris murderously offended by Spenser's English usurpation of French *Fabliaux*.'

'Tempting,' said Tom, 'but unlikely.'

'I agree,' said Poley. 'The only other association with Sir Thomas that I can think of is that he is a great sponsor of poets. Shakespeare, Spenser, Donne, Chapman, all may be found somewhere in the weave of this like flies in a web, as well as half a dozen of the others that recited their dross at Spenser's funeral. And, as we are considering acolytes no matter how painfully, the Lady Kate Shelton seems to have a thoroughly unhealthy fascination with Simon Forman. And who knows where something like that might lead?'

'So,' said Rosalind after a moment or two more of silence as Tom, for one, fought to calculate the answer to that burning question, 'Apart from yourself, Master Poley, the two acolytes closest to the centre of this would seem to be Sir Anthony Bacon and Simon Forman. And Simon Forman appears to be not only involved in the political background but also in the practicalities of the murder: the first among suspects. He is an acolyte of one of the men most offended by the poem - Sir Walter Raleigh The Fox - but he is also possibly the man who supplied the distillation of hemlock used in the murder and played some part in the scheme to put the blame on poor Will through the use of Hal, Gerard's apprentice - for reasons as yet unclear unless Tom is right and it's all just a distraction. And it is certain that Hal died in his Billingsgate house, was hidden in his privy and - logic suggests - was placed in Spenser's grave by Forman and his associates, with the forged poem that put yet more blame on Will. George Chapman being one of the most likely men for that.'

'Of the *men*, yes,' said Tom. The emphasis on that one word showing his continuing disquiet at the part Kate seemed to be playing in the mystery.

iii

'Where does that get us?' wondered Poley. 'Sir Antony Bacon is far beyond our reach and would be even were he up and about as opposed to near bed-ridden as he is.'

'But Kate is not,' said Tom forcefully. 'I can sound Kate out one way or another.'

'And as Master Forman has no knowledge of who I am nor who my friends might be,' said Rosalind, 'it should be easy enough for me to become one of his most assiduous clients. As you know, I am adept at securing secrets from men.'

'Most especially men,' said Tom. 'However I would caution against using any of your particular wiles against Forman. I have seen his bedchamber and the room above it.'

'I'm sure the risk is smaller than you imagine,' said Rosalind. 'But the sooner we discover the truth underlying all this, the sooner we'll all be safe.'

'Besides,' suggested Poley, 'It would be a good idea for you to have something to occupy you while I hold Master Shakespeare in protective custody. The Lord only knows what mischief you might get up to in idleness.'

'How long will that *protective custody* last for?' asked Rosalind.

'I have not decided yet.'

'As long, perhaps, as unsubstantiated rumors as to the purchase of distilled hemlock and the possibility of its application to Spencer's ear are circulating,' said Tom. 'Rumors that remain unsubstantiated because of the lack of a witness, living or dead, and the disappearance of the accusatory verse. Meanwhile, in case further ways to ensnare Will might be generated, it is better to hold the potential culprit - whether he turns out to be the guilty man or not - than to leave him loose for others to take up and thereby do themselves and their masters some credit. Not to mention the risk that they might torture a confession out of him and let the real murderer walk free as Will goes to the gallows.'

'If you are right, young Tom,' said Poley, 'then your poetic friend is certainly safer where he is, no matter how long he might have to remain there. Besides, there is the other matter that my unfortunate predecessor Pursuivant Marshal Roe was looking into, concerning the tutor Shakeshaft at Hoghton Hall.'

'Master Poley,' Rosalind turned her most beseeching gaze upon the spymaster. 'Is there no way we can get paper, pen and ink to Will in the mean-time? He will run distracted if he cannot continue with his play of *Henry Fifth*.'

'The Marshalsea is not the most conducive location for creative writing,' said Poley. 'But I will see what I can do.'

'Will does not need a special place or situation,' said Tom. 'He never stops working on his imaginary forces.'

'Well,' said Poley, 'I will tell him you said so when I see him.'

*

'It is too late for me to get back to Blackfriars now,' said Tom as Rosalind and he walked out of the Castel into the bitter darkness of Bankside. Typically, Poley had disappeared into the shadows without a warning or a farewell as the three of them came out of the tavern's door. The weather was so wintery that neither the brightness nor the bustle seemed to alleviate it much. The southerly wind had developed such an edge that the pair of them gathered their cloaks around themselves as they walked back towards London Bridge.

'Besides, there is still much to discuss,' said Tom, 'particularly if you are serious about bearding Forman in his den. Will your reputation stand a night visitor if I come home to you?'

'In Maiden Lane? A night visitor will probably enhance it.'

Neither one of them mentioned the night they had spent together in her father's inn before it was burned to the ground by Gelly Meyrick and his roaring boys under the Earl of Essex' orders. There was no need to do so. It was a pleasant experience which neither had the slightest intention of repeating.

'You trust Poley,' said Tom. His tone made it plain that this was a statement and not a question.

'I do.' She peered at him, her eyes wide and dark in the pale glimmer of her face within her hood. 'I worked for him for long enough and he never used any double-dealing on me or my parents.'

'Just so.' Tom forbore to point out that this - if it was true - made Rosalind unique in the world of modern spycraft. 'Then we can stop worrying about Will. He will be treated well and may even be supplied with sufficient paper, ink and quills to enjoy the peace and quiet enforced by the jail's routine. Now I think of it, a prison cell might indeed prove an inspirational place for a would-be writer to spend some time. I must ask Will, and get Ben Jonson's view on the matter too.'

Rosalind gave a quiet chuckle. 'Stone walls and iron bars may limit the movement of Will's body but there is no chaining down his imagination. His arse may be going numb on the cold floor of his cell, but his mind will be away in the vasty fields of France, marching with Good King Harry to Agincourt.'

'So, you're not worried about him?'

'If Master Poley says he is safe then he is safe.'

'Very well. It will be doubly convenient for me to remain at your side when you visit the Marshalsea in the morning, however, so that we may test this faith and Humiliation Gauge's verisimilitude in passing Will the food you left.'

'But my gain, it seems, will be Mistress Shelton's loss. Were you not to start sounding her out tonight? Deeply and repeatedly, I would guess.'

'Tomorrow will do for that,' chuckled Tom. 'To be forthright, I am glad of the time and distance so that I can think matters through before I plunge in.' He paused, then added, '*willy-nilly* as you might say.'

This conversation was enough to take them through the bustle down to Bank End where they turned right into Dead Man's Lane. This, like Maiden Lane which turned off it, was little more than a rutted mud track, but at least the chill had turned the puddles to ice and the ruts to solid little ridges. They had to walk carefully, but their footwear and the hems of their cloaks remained relatively clean. The noise they made as they proceeded reminded Tom of his childhood on the Scottish borders for it was the sound his boots had made walking across the fields immediately after harvest, crunching the brittle close-cropped corn-stalks. It was a sound that seemed to echo.

iv

Until, as he whirled into action, Tom registered that it was not an echo at all but the sound of footsteps following their own. His laggard mind caught up with his body as his rapier hissed out. Beyond the arc of his sword-blade, three figures hulked, featureless black against the dim brightness of Bank End behind them. About the only things that were clear were the clubs that they each carried. 'Ho!' called Tom, 'welcome, masters. What's your business with us?'

There was no reply. The three spread out so that Tom could not engage them all together, and came on.

'So,' hissed Tom, his tone as cold as his icy blade. 'Who dies first?'

'The one in the middle dies first!' said Rosalind, and shot him in the chest. At least Tom, dazed by the explosion and flash of the shot as well as by simple surprise, assumed he was shot in the chest, for he went flat on his back as though clubbed in the throat.

'Who next?' Tom shouted leaping forward.

But it seemed that Rosalind had won the day for the two club-wielders still standing, stooped and grabbed their supine companion before staggering away down the alley towards the brightness of Bankside.

'Damnation!' swore Rosalind. 'Will said this would fire two shots. Now we have let them get away!'

'Probably just as well,' said Tom. 'What would we have done with two corpses and a prisoner?'

'I'd have got some answers!' snapped Rosalind.

'Easier said than done,' said Tom. 'Particularly half way down Dead Man's Place in the middle of the night.'

'Perhaps. But now we have two enemies with reason to come after us again.'

'Let us hope that they were simple *highlawyers* then, set on nothing more than robbery.'

'Let us barricade the doors when we get home nevertheless. In case they have more than robbery on their minds. And, come to that, in case they have friends and associates ready to help them.'

Tom sheathed his sword. 'Let me see the pistol,' he said. 'I have learned enough from Ugo to have some expertise in the matter of guns. If you were expecting a second shot that did not come, then the thing might still be dangerous. Might fire without warning when you least expected it.'

'I have been keeping it tucked into the waist of my kirtle,' she admitted. 'So the Lord only knows what might get damaged were it to fire without warning.'

This conversation took them to the corner of Maiden Lane where a guttering torch in a sconce just above head-height gave some extra light. Tom took the pistol and examined it. It was a double-barreled affair and one barrel had fired while the cock on the second had wedged, its mechanism stilled by a fragment of cloth clearly torn from Rosalind's skirt-waist. Within a moment, he was certain that it was safe, and he turned to return it to her, only to see her hurrying into the shadows outside her door - made impatient no doubt by the cutting wind. He shrugged and followed her. Both were so preoccupied with the pistol and the biting wind that neither of them thought to look up.

Rosalind vanished into the door of her lodging and paused to light a lamp just inside it. By the time he caught up, she was half way up the stairs to her rooms with the lamp held high to illuminate the way. He ran nimbly up behind her, hurrying in the hope that he would reach the top of the stairs before she - and the light - disappeared into her rooms. But the moment she opened the door, light flooded out. Tom froze and gasped a breath to call to her.

*

Too late. In spite of her experience in the intelligencers' world, she went straight in. Tom checked behind him, all too well aware that the three who failed to stop them on Dead Man's Place might well be confederates of whoever was waiting in Rosalind's room. There was no-one there. He took the stairs two at a time and arrived in the open doorway with his right hand on the pommel of his rapier and his left clutching Rosalind's pistol.

'So,' Gelly Meyrick was saying, the Welsh lilt of his accent identifying him even before Tom saw his all-too familiar face. 'I see you missed my little welcoming committee.'

'If you mean the three ruffians with clubs that followed us into Dead Man's Place, I didn't miss them at all,' snapped Rosalind in return. 'As at least one will tell you - if he's still alive.'

'*Us…*' hissed Meyrick. 'And where is your partner?'

'Will is safe from the likes of you,' said Tom stepping into the room, pistol leveled, one barrel primed with the cock now free. Swinging round as he did so to cover the rest of the room and put the solid doorframe at his back; just as though he were still on the battlefields of Holland.

191

'Ah. I was expecting a Shakespeare but I seem to have a swordmaster,' said Meyrick. He was leaning nonchalantly against the table, his buttocks just on the edge of it - ready to spring into action at any moment, but in the meantime alone and caught off-guard, his rapier safely sheathed and his arms folded across his chest.

Tom said nothing. He had bested Meyrick once in a hard-fought rapier bout and had no desire to repeat the experience.

'And,' continued Meyrick smoothly, 'from what I recall of your reputation, as dexterous with the left hand as with the right. Certainly the fist holding that pretty snaphaunce seems steady enough.'

'What do you want, Sir Gelly?' asked Tom.

'I had planned to extend an invitation to the lady here and her pet poet to visit Essex House with me. But I see I am no longer in a position to enforce my wishes. For the moment, at least.'

'What does the Earl of Essex want with Will and Rosalind?' asked Tom.

'Especially as he has entertained me already,' added Rosalind. 'At least his acolyte Sir Francis Bacon entertained me.'

'Acolyte,' Gelly Martin seemed to chew on the word. 'How amusingly religious; I must discuss it with Sir Francis. You make us sound like choir-boys, which, as you both know we most certainly are not. No. This time I was to extend an invitation on behalf of Sir Antony, who regrets he is too unwell to visit you in person at the moment. Ah well,' he pulled himself erect. 'I see my cohorts are not going to arrive after all. Another time, therefore. He crossed to the door and paused. 'Sometime soon, though. You may be sure of that.' He stepped past Tom, and ran light-footed down the stairs.

'Cohorts,' said Tom, coming right into the room and lowering the pistol. 'So much more military than acolytes…'

V

'I should have let him take me,' said Rosalind next morning, that of Friday 19th, after a night filled with talk rather than slumber. In the small hours they had lain side by side on the bed, both still clothed, their minds resolutely fixed on discussion rather than on fornication. Now they sat face to face over a breakfast of stale bread, cold milk and dry cheese. 'Next time I shall do so. It seems Sir Anthony Bacon is not so far beyond our reach after all, if I approach him as his apparent prisoner.'

'He plans - I assume - to question you, *peine forte et dure* as the Spanish Inquisition has it, not the other way round,' warned Tom who had emerged from their discussions worried by the recklessness of her plans as well as by her determination to enact them.

'What is planned and what is achieved are not necessarily the same thing,' she said, unconsciously echoing his thoughts, 'as Sir Gelly Meyrick and his associates discovered last night.'

'Very well. But Sir Anthony and Essex' cohorts are something for the future. More immediately there is the question of Simon Forman. And there I fear it is you who underestimate the danger.'

'How so? Do you suppose Forman will murder me when I will present myself as a client willing to part with coin in order to purchase his occult wisdom? Surely not! Rumor has it that he is visited by men and women of the highest rank - and you yourself have pointed out he is not above drawing up charts for more lowly folk. What did you call Gerard's daughter? An apprentice's light o' love? And yet there is no talk of murder...'

'Except with regard to the apprentice in question, of course.'

'You argue with yourself there, then, for did you not say he died through accident?'

'So I believed, but...'

'There you are, then. I will present myself in Billingsgate once I am certain Will is safe and settled. All I will ask of you is a purse. One that is weighty enough to attract attention without being rich enough to rouse suspicion.'

'The richness of the purse, surely, will depend on the part you choose to play - for you cannot tell the truth.'

'True. But Poley would no doubt advise that I stay as close to truth as possible. And it so happens that I can do that most effectively; my own character and situation hardly changed. My clothing is appropriate to my station and my purse is perhaps a little heavier than might be expected but only so because my lover, although not rich, is generous.'

'I see,' Tom was impressed and amused. 'And the part you will play?'

'Why, that of a poor country girl recently orphaned and rendered near destitute by a fire. Newly come to London from Saffron Walden where I was born and raised, fresh as a rose…'

'A rose that has not been plucked too often…'

'Who has no intention of letting Forman even scent, let alone pluck…'

'But what has brought you to Billingsgate, fair *Rosa - linda*?'

'Fear for my lover and our future. I have come Londonwards to join my family who are carters but I have fallen in with a troupe of players for whom my family works on occasion. And I visit Forman because my lover, Will Shakespeare by name, has been taken up by the Pursuivant Marshal and is currently held in the Marshalsea, for what reason I do not know. With what possible outcome I cannot guess. But in the meantime I am racked with terror. Does Will truly love me? If so, how will we fare together? When will he be released? Will he prosper? Can the stars advise me where to seek friendship and support in this dark hour should he be held for much longer or - Heaven forefend - found guilty of some terrible crime? My Will and my family have scraped together enough coin for us to set up house - coin I now must spend on finding what the future has in store. I must know or I shall run mad or die with the stress of ignorance…'

*

'I still think I should come in with you,' said Tom. 'Saying you are Will's woman should make you irresistible to Forman independently of the weight of your purse. But there are still terrible risks. Remember, we still debate whether or not Hal's death was an accident.'

'No! You have convinced me that it was an accident so I shall be doubly careful to avoid such things! And to be honest it was bad enough having you trailing along at the Marshalsea. Your verbal fencing with Poley was bad enough but you reduced Humiliation Gauge to such rage I thought all would be undone and Will chained in the furthest corner of the deepest dungeon because of you!'

'But all was well in the end. You must admit that!'

'Perhaps. By a whisker as the saying is. If you come in here as well, you will undo most of what I am trying to achieve before you even open your mouth. How can Will Shakespeare's lover be in company with Tom Musgrave?'

'The world knows we are friends. I taught Dick Burbage and Will the fencing moves in the Italian style for his play of *Romeo*…'

'A fact we would have Forman forget rather than have it emphasized!'

'I could pretend to be Martin Fletcher, your cousin the carter…'

'Dressed in the height of fashion and carrying a blade of that quality? Do you know nothing about playing a part? Besides, I'll lay odds you have some equally fashionable young men waiting in your school of defense, wondering where their master is and why no lessons are toward. Leave me. I will be safe. I have Will's dagger to protect me - and he will find that before he gets anywhere near my shift or my person. And if he finds it, then rest assured, I will use it!'

'I did not fear rapine. Or rather I did not fear *only* rapine…'

'I fear nothing else and am armed against it. Now go!'

Tom had no choice but to obey. Rosalind had made several telling points, prime amongst which was the probability that he had aristocratic students waiting at his school of defense in Blackfriars. Students all too willing to go elsewhere if he were repeatedly tardy. In earlier days, he had been one of the only masters of the Italian art of rapier-play in London. Now such masters were ten-a-penny.

Rather than waste time walking, he ran nimbly down Billingsgate stairs and hailed a wherry, 'Westward-ho!'

vi

The tide was rising beneath the stern of the boat that answered his call so that he was able to run up the Blackfriars stairs and into Water Lane little more than fifteen minutes later. The narrow lane led up the hill from the river towards St Paul's and passed Blackfriars on the way so that he arrived in the square outside his school above Robert Aske's haberdashery scarcely five minutes later still. He was hurrying towards the door when a familiar figure stepped out in front of him to block his way. It was his neighbor and professional rival Rocco Bonetti, also a master in the Italian method, but a student of the late Camillo Agrippa rather than Tom's master Ridolfo Capo Ferro. Tom's footsteps faltered. 'Signior Bonetti,' he said as he came to a stand and gave a slight bow. He glanced around. Blackfriars was unusually quiet. They were alone and apparently unobserved.

'I have been awaiting you,' said Bonetti. His Italian accent was thick but his English words were clear.

'I am flattered, Signior, but to what purpose?'

'I have been asked to give you a message.'

'Really, Signior? What message is that?'

'That it is your time to die.' As he spoke, Bonetti unsheathed his rapier and fell into Agrippa's first position, right foot forward, right arm held near waist height, elbow in and fist steady holding the point of the rapier unwaveringly towards Tom's chest ready for the opening lunge.

Just for an instant, probably governed by the unreality of the situation, Tom was struck by an illuminating irrelevance. Agrippa's method, lampooned at his suggestion in Will's play of *Romeo*, was all to do with numbers and their movement in space, time and relation to each other. Agrippa was not alone in believing that a man who truly understood the Aristotelian, Euclidian and Pythagorean theories of number could master anything, for they represented a language in which the macrocosm of the universe under heaven and the motions of men - both mental and physical in the earthly microcosm - could meet and communicate. In Bonetti's case, such numbers could be used in the perfection of fencing; in Forman's case in the magical control and prediction of both the present and the future.

But, as Romeo himself proved when facing Tybalt with his Agrippa-inspired *prick-song technique, keeping time, distance, and proportion with his minim rests - one, two, and the third in your bosom*, the practical power of Capo Ferro's more modern and less esoteric techniques could put one in your bosom just that heartbeat more swiftly.

*

Tom fell into Capo Ferro's favoured third guard which was a mirror image of Bonetti's. He settled on wide measure to begin with, meaning that either of them would have to move their feet to strike their opponent. There seemed little point in talking, though Tom was burning to know who had put Bonetti up to this. Talking would distract the speaker more than the listener who could disregard the words entirely and concentrate on his fencing. Bonetti was a master swordsman after all and no-one to be dismissed lightly. As he proved by thrusting with the speed of a striking snake, his point, as Agrippa dictated, flashing straight for Tom's chest as he stepped forward into the narrow measure where the killing was done. Tom parried, his blade turning Bonetti's off-line. Both men recovered.

As he settled into the third guard again, Tom's mind seemed to focus in a way it only ever did when he was fencing. He became almost supernaturally aware not only of his opponent, his eyes, his sword, his feet, but also of the makeshift *piste* on which they were fighting. Bonetti stepped sideways as he fell into Agrippa's guard once more, his movement moving the line along which the next section of the combat would take place. As he turned to face his opponent, Tom became aware of a wall behind him. If he retired at the end of the next pass he would be unable to take Capo Ferro's favored two steps back without hitting it. And, with Tom trapped against the brickwork, Bonetti could move from wide measure to narrow - almost chest to chest - whenever he wanted.

These thoughts occupied less than a heartbeat as Bonetti thrust again, his point flashing toward Tom's left eye. Tom parried but instead of simply knocking Bonetti's blade off-line, he stepped forward in riposte, sliding his blade along his opponent's so that as Bonetti's point passed harmlessly past his ear, his own point stabbed through the Italian's upper torso, in that triangle of thick muscle joining the side of the neck to the point of the shoulder. With both blades still in place, his own grating against Bonetti's collar-bone, Tom stepped forward and sideways, turning Bonetti like a lamb on a spit. The move placed Tom back in the mouth of Water Lane so that when he disengaged, he was able to take two steps back, his rapier held high, the point and a good foot of the blade covered in Bonetti's blood.

As Tom had expected, Bonetti jumped into the close ward and attacked again immediately. All the masters of defence, and indeed the masters of horsemanship, agreed - if you fall off, get straight back on. Furthermore, Bonetti was losing blood fast, and with it, strength, speed and concentration. Time suddenly became a matter of more than Agrippa's minim rests. Although he was expecting the attack and was focused on Bonetti's eyes and sword-point, the strike against his groin almost took him by surprise. He riposted again so that the Italian's blade passed the outside of his thigh while his own point went safely past his opponent's shoulder. Instead of stepping back, he pushed forward himself, tearing his rapier sideways and nearly disarming Bonetti. But the Italian kept tight hold of his rapier, snarling with pain and effort, and reached behind his back with his left hand.

In a flash, Tom did the same so that when Bonetti's dagger swung in and plunged towards Tom's throat, he was able to catch it and hold it back from doing any damage, blade against blade, quillions grinding together. He stepped forward half a pace once more until his flaring nostrils were filled with the Italian's garlic-scented breath. Then, without warning, he head-butted Bonetti full in the face as hard as he could, feeling his opponent's nose shatter against his forehead.

'I didn't learn that at the school in Sienna,' he said as Bonetti reeled back, bleeding and blinded. 'I learned that at university in Glasgow. A good education is never wasted.'

Then he lunged at the helpless man, sending his point through Bonetti's right arm, just below the shoulder. He was about to disengage and step back when the Italian threw himself blindly forward, his sword-arm useless, but stabbing viciously with his dagger. Taken off guard, Tom felt the cold steel pierce his own shoulder. Once again he was face-to face with Bonetti but now the Italian's eyes were wide with shock and surprise.

Only then did Tom realize what had happened. Bonetti had attacked before Tom could free his sword. The Italian had simply skewered himself upon it - the weight of his body thrusting the point of Tom's rapier not only through his arm but through his chest behind it. Both sword and dagger clattered to the ground. Bonetti fell to his knees, disarming Tom at last as his body-weight tore Tom's rapier from his grasp. Then, with a yard of Solingen steel reaching from one arm-pit to the other, the Italian pitched face down on the cobbles as a great gout of blood vomited from his gaping mouth.

'I came to Signior Bonetti for my accustomed lesson,' said a virile baritone voice with a west-country accent even stronger than Will's. 'But I did not think to see an exhibition bout as fearsome or fatal as that!'

Tom straightened, turned, and found himself standing face to face with Sir Walter Raleigh.

Chapter 12: The Dangers of Deception

i

'So,' said Simon Forman, 'you are William Shakespeare's mistress.' He leaned forward and licked his lips. The point of his tongue was surprisingly red. It pushed the ends of his greasy moustache to one side and then to the other as it cleaned droplets of wine from the ill-trimmed hairs while his bulbous eyes undressed his visitor with more license than normal.

She was clearly no virginal shrinking violet despite her apparent youth, he calculated - not if she was mistress to a player; a profession notorious for their lechery and that of their audiences. Forman himself often attended plays, well aware that other - female - members of the audience were alluringly loose in their morals.

Rosalind took a deep breath, suddenly uneasy at being here with him. She was used to lecherous gazes, but not many had been as direct as Forman's. If she hadn't heard a reassuring bustle of activity and muted conversations from deeper within the house, she might well have made an excuse and left. She would certainly never have accepted the glass of canary-yellow wine he offered, or taken a sip of its chilly, bitter contents. But it was done now. She was here and even though Hal's mysterious fate haunted her more poignantly than she had expected, it was time to continue building the deceptive character she was playing and press on with her investigation.

'That I am your worship,' answered Rosalind well aware of the veniality of his glaze. 'Rosalind Fletcher late of Saffron Waldon, orphaned by a terrible fire at my father's inn, The Crown.' She wiped her eyes, glancing secretly at Forman over the folded cloth of her kerchief, aware that she was performing in spite of the fact that the tears were real enough. True, she was playing herself as she told her own story - but a slower, much less intelligent, country-bumpkin version of herself. She was gambling on the belief that, like many clever men of her acquaintance, Forman was likely to patronize such a creature, underestimate her and overestimate his abilities in relation to her. A situation compounded by the fact that he obviously lusted after not only her money but also her body. She was counting on the belief that she could handle Forman and half a dozen like him - she just wished Tom Musgrave could have been somewhere close at hand after all. Her seduction of Tom himself and her acquisition from him of the information requested by Poley had been on another level altogether; more urgent and immediate, less coldly calculating; somehow less dangerous.

'Well, you're a pretty little thing,' said Forman unctuously. 'It's terrible that such misfortune should have overcome you.' He reached a sympathetic hand across the table at which they were both sitting, a hand that covered one of hers - the one that held her purse.

The table stood in front of a low-banked fire in the front room of his Billingsgate house. This was the room that was situated immediately within the front door; the one which contained his shop. Behind his right shoulder there was a counter and behind that a wall of shelves containing bottles of colourful powders and potions almost without number. Behind his left shoulder, a high window looked south towards the Thames and the fish-market but neither was actually visible. Behind Rosalind, broad windows flanked a door whose upper portion was also glazed. It all looked out onto Billingsgate, but little diamond-shaped panes of thick green glass made it difficult to see in. From each side, however, came the sounds of people passing or pausing to do business - which matched those reassuring noises from deeper within Forman's house itself.

Rosalind and Forman were alone in the room if not in the house and Forman had told her more than once already that she was lucky to have found him so. For, as he explained, - having listened to her as he poured out two glasses of white wine and carried them over to her - he had business all over London which often called him away and a list of regular clients and visitors long enough to have filled one of her lover's theatres. She took him at his word for the moment. She had not begun to find him much more than disturbing - certainly not frightening.

Yet.

*

She allowed Forman's hand to take the hand that was holding her purse as her other hand pressed her kerchief to her cheeks. She sobbed, hiccupped and looked up at him with the eyes of a starving puppy.

'Master Shakespeare has better taste than I would have guessed,' he said, supposing that this complimented her.

'Oh sir! Do you know my Will then sir?' She took his hand in both of hers, keeping firm hold on the purse for the moment as well as of the kerchief.

'Hardly, my dear,' his hands closed over both of hers. 'But I know of him.'

She gasped, even more wide eyed, wondering whether or not to flutter her eyelashes like a Bankside bawd. 'He must be famous indeed if someone as important as you knows of him!' Had she gone too far? she wondered at once, even though she had not fluttered her eyelashes after all. His eyes narrowed with suspicion. He pulled his hands free and sat back, observing her coolly. The purse was clearly no longer at the centre of his thoughts. Nor, for the moment, were the size and disposition of her breasts. Though, for some reason she could not explain to herself, her nipples had come erect beneath the heat of his earlier gaze. He pushed the goblet towards her and waited silently as she took another sip, and then a third, larger than the first two.

'Master Shakespeare and I are both known at court,' Forman explained more formally as she replaced her glass beside his on the table. 'Master Shakespeare and his company perform plays, jigs, bergomasks and so-forth for the entertainment of their betters. I map out the future of the country and those who rule it. My acquaintance with the players and therefore of Master Shakespeare is of the slightest.'

'You map out the future…' breathed Rosalind, keeping her eyes as wide as she could. 'Can you see it, then? Can you truly see the future, sir? Such a skill would be beyond price!'

'I certainly can!' he leaned forward once more, reminded about the purse, as she had planned.

'And would you be willing to look into my future, sir? Mine and my Will's? Though of course we will never rule the country nor ever be remembered after we die.' She squared her shoulders, thrusting her bosom back into prominence. 'I know we are people of no account,' she emphasized, 'but I have brought a goodly weight in silver coin, sir, and would make it worth your while.' She opened her hands as though her fingers were petals and there in the heart of the flower lay the little leather bag of coins.

'Worth my while, eh?' said Forman as he glanced at the purse apparently casually, his experienced eyes no doubt assessing its worth to within a farthing. Then they glanced up again, their gaze stopping well below the level of her own. Were the points of her breasts showing through her shift, bodice and jerkin, she wondered, for they tingled with arousal. 'And not only your future but also Master Shakespeare's though neither of you will ever achieve importance, let alone immortality? Why I think that could be arranged. Yes indeed.' He sat back. His demeanor changed. He became less engaging; more decisive. 'Let us go upstairs to my library. I have up there everything I need to begin to construct the charts that will predict how life and the occult powers that control it will treat you and Master Shakespeare in the future.'

He rose and she copied him. Tom's warnings about the man and his house flashed into her mind, but she pushed them back, even though she had not quite kept her word to Tom. She still carried the dagger but not the snaphaunce pistol. Even so, she thought, if she was going to find out what had happened to Hal, whether Forman had supplied the hemlock, what was the depth of his involvement in Spenser's death and - perhaps most urgently of all - what was his true relationship with Kate Shelton, she could not afford to be shy or fearful.

He turned and crossed to the door that led to the corridor and the staircase.

Feeling a little dizzy, she took a final draught of the wine to steady herself and followed him into the passage outside only to hesitate, horrified. The reassuring noises that sounded like several other people working and gossiping in the house were in fact coming from a cage containing two restless birds.

She and Forman were absolutely alone after all.

ii

Constable Banks, chief of the watch in the Blackfriars ward looked down at Rocco Bonetti's corpse then up at Tom. There was quite a crowd now but Tom and Raleigh had not moved - and neither had touched the corpse. It was clear from the outset that he was dead. No-one could lose that much blood and survive. Both Tom and Raleigh had been in enough battles to be certain of that. Bonetti had been dead for less than ten minutes before Banks and his men arrived - an arrival that Tom for one found suspiciously swift.

'He challenged you. He attacked you. He started the *duello*,' said Banks. Only his tone gave away the fact that these were questions. He was a man of slow speech with a cast in one eye. Tom knew that it would be a mistake to suppose him to be as stupid as he looked. And he also suspected it would be a mistake to suppose him to be absolutely honest.

'Yes,' said Tom. 'He said he was passing on a message. I have no idea why or who from.'

'And the message was…' Banks asked.

'That it was my time to die.'

'Your time to die.' Banks mulled it over. 'That sounds like a challenge right enough.' Then he turned. 'Sir Walter, did you hear this challenge?'

'No, constable. I arrived part-way through the encounter. I had come for my accustomed lesson with *Signior* Bonetti, as his assistants will no doubt confirm.'

'That you had a regular lesson, I should guess,' said the constable. 'Not that you arrived in time to see the beginning of the fight or, on the other hand, too late to do so. Unless they were standing outside too, of course.'

'Indeed,' nodded Raleigh. 'Though they were not. There was no-one else about when I arrived. Except for masters Musgrave and Bonetti.'

Constable Banks turned to the crowd which was being held back by his watchmen. 'Did anyone here hear or see the beginning of this matter? The onset of this fight? Did anyone hear the challenge?'

There was much shaking of heads in reply, even amongst the pale and shaken men that Tom recognized as Bonetti's assistants.

Then a new voice called, 'I heard it! I heard it all. It is precisely as Master Musgrave said.' They looked up to see Kate Shelton standing in the open window of Tom's rooms immediately above, with the shadowy figure of Ugo Stell a little way behind her. '*Signior* Bonetti challenged Master Musgrave just as he said and he drew his rapier first!'

Tom looked back down at Banks and then up at Kate once more. She was describing what had happened precisely enough but he knew she was lying. During that moment of preternatural focus before Bonetti made the first pass, Tom had registered everything nearby, including the fact that the windows to his rooms were shut. There was no way Kate could have heard anything except, perhaps, for the clash of blade upon blade. Had he not seen her at Poley's secret conference in The Rose tavern last night, he would simply have accepted her lies as a welcome attempt to help him and been grateful that she cared enough to do so. Now, he found that he was suspicious of her motives.

But the deed was done, the lies were told and their effectiveness could not be denied. He looked back at Bates as the constable shrugged. 'That's that, then. We will remove the corpus and hold it until his family or someone concerned claims it otherwise it goes to a pauper's grave. In the mean time I will report to the Queen's Crowner, for this death took place so close to Her Majesty it is well beneath The Verge. So you may find yourself summoned to Sir William Danby's presence, with the lady your witness; and perhaps even you along with them, Sir Walter. But then again, perhaps not: Sir William is a busy man on the verge of retirement and this looks open and shut to me.'

*

The watchmen took up Bonetti's corpse and carried it away, led by Constable Banks and followed by the assistants from the dead master's school. The crowd began to disperse. Walter Raleigh and Tom exchanged formal bows and the Captain of the Queen's Guard turned to follow the crowd. But then he stopped and turned back. 'Master Musgrave,' he said in his deceptively gentle west-country brogue. 'It occurs to me that I no longer have a master of defence to assist in the perfection of my style. And, further, that of all the men to whom I should refer for his replacement, the man who bested him in a passage of arms would be the wisest choice. Do you have room for another pupil, sir?'

'Of course, Sir Walter. I would be honoured. I warn you, however, we would have to do some work on rebuilding your technique - Agrippa will no longer stand against the more modern methods of *Maestro* Capo Ferro.'

'As you have just so ably demonstrated,' Raleigh nodded. 'Very well, I will send one of my attendants later today and we will come to an arrangement. Good day to you.'

As Raleigh walked away, Kate arrived at Tom's shoulder. 'Perfect!' she laughed. 'You have rid yourself of a competitor who was clearly suborned to assassinate you and have already poached his most illustrious student! Poley would be proud of you.'

'No doubt. But the method you find so effective - and I cannot disagree with you, it was - I found too extreme. And of course it robbed us of the chance to discover who it was that suborned him'

'Even though the choice appeared to be *kill or be killed*?'

'Even then. As we proceed along the passageway towards the heart of this matter, every death is just another door closed against us.' He would have said more, still vaguely dissatisfied with the fact that she had so easily lied to protect him not to mention last night's secret meeting and the unguarded comment about her possible involvement with Forman - and, perhaps even Hal's death - but he stayed silent instead.

Side by side, they went into the doorway beside the haberdasher's shop and climbed the stair to his rooms. As she often did when she was here during the day, Kate went through into his teaching room and took a rapier, practicing her technique in front of the long mirror that covered most of the inner wall. At times he wondered whether she did this so that she could revel in her own beauty and grace rather than study and perfect her technique.

The window at the far end of the long room stood open because that was the one Kate had called down from. Tom, still thoughtful, was about to join her when Ugo caught his eye and jerked his head. Side by side the two men went into Ugo's work-room. 'Don't tell me,' said Tom. 'She couldn't possibly have heard anything Bonetti said.'

'True enough,' nodded Ugo. 'And I know that for a fact because I was just behind her looking out of that window when Bonetti stopped you. Though I couldn't hear what he said either. But that's not what I wanted to tell you.'

'What then?'

'Raleigh was there. She knows it and I know it. I heard him say he only arrived part-way through the fight. He lied. He was there right from the beginning. He was watching closely into the bargain, as though he had something important invested in the outcome.' The Dutch gunsmith's piercing blue gaze met Tom's. 'As was Kate,' he added,' watching from the beginning through the closed window. But she was watching *him*.'

iii

Rosalind hesitated at the foot of the stairs looking down the corridor towards the door she guessed must lead into Forman's kitchen. The cage hanging just this side of the door was the better part of four feet high and well over two feet across. It was a tall cage with a rounded top, circular at the base. Even so it was crowded. Two large grey birds were confined restlessly within it, flapping their wings as best they could and grumbling to each-other in disturbingly human tones. She could well understand how, from a distance and through a shut door she had supposed noises these creatures made to be those of people moving and conversing.

Rosalind dragged her gaze back and looked up. Forman was eagerly mounting the stairs, as yet unaware of her hesitation. She just had time to make an escape if she turned and ran now, she thought. But that would undo so much. Flight would not only be cowardly, it would rob Tom and herself of a potent chance to discover what was going on behind these mysterious deaths. And that discovery would, she hoped and believed, cause Will to be freed from the Marshalsea and Poley's toils all the sooner. One moment of womanish weakness would rob them all of incalculable potential rewards of intelligence if of nothing else - and her lover of his freedom. At least, so she told herself, her mental tone scathing.

She squared her shoulders, looped the laces of her money-bag through her belt and wished once more that she was carrying Ugo's double-barreled snaphaunce as well as Will's dagger there. She tucked her kerchief between the buttons of her doublet where they strained to contain her breasts and stepped up onto the bottom stair. Her breath was short and her head span just a little - was it nervousness or something more? The memory of that last long draught of wine seemed to burn in her throat like the fire that comes from ice.

Forman turned at the stair-head, playing the perfect host. 'There is a bath room a little further along the corridor,' he said. 'It has a chamber pot within should you feel the need.'

At his words she did begin to feel the need, and hurried up the stairs in consequence. He stepped back to let her rush past, like a bull-fighter in a Spanish *Corrida* that Poley had once described to her. She reached the little room pulled the door closed behind her and began to search for the chamber pot. She found it behind the hip bath almost invisible in the shadows. As she pulled it out with a gasp of relief, something else came with it. She paid it no attention as her need for relief was almost overwhelming. She grabbed the chamber pot as she pulled her skirts and petticoats out of the way and squatted. Only to discover that with relief came the unsettling suspicion that she was being spied upon. She finished, rose and adjusted her clothing. No longer quite so certain she was being watched, she slid the vessel back behind the bath and the object that had come out with it moved again. She stooped and retrieved it. It was a lock of hair tied with a tiny red ribbon. Frowning, she slipped it into the little leather bag with the silver.

When Rosalind came out into the corridor again, Forman was standing in the nearest of two doorways leading one behind the other towards a window in the end wall which, she calculated, must overlook Billingsgate. Putting her suspicion that she had been overwatched to one side for the moment, she walked towards him.

'Welcome,' he said with a smile that looked genuine. 'This is my library where I work on such things as you would have me prepare for you.' He stepped back to let her enter but somehow in spite of his apparent gallantry she found that she had to push past him in an unexpectedly intimate manner. Then she was in the room, surrounded by the books. She didn't bother reading the titles - Tom had described them - but they still seemed to give off a strange and unsettling atmosphere as well as a dusty odour, such as she might have imagined coming from a long-lost tomb. Forman's proximity seemed suddenly more protective than threatening. When he came closer still she did not pull away.

'Now,' he said, 'We must begin with the basics. Place and time of birth.' As he spoke he led her over to a tall table at which they were forced to stand shoulder to shoulder hip to hip and thigh to thigh. He smelt of sweat and dust, not unlike his books, but she found the smell quite pleasant. Nor was she unduly disturbed by the way his limb pressed against hers, seeming to burn through the layers of cloth between them to feel disturbingly like naked skin on skin.

*

'I was born in Saffron Waldon which is in the county of Essex,' said Rosalind, remembering just in time to slow her speech and maintain her country accent.

'Location! Excellent! Now, as to date…'

'Well, sir my birthday has always been held on All Saints Day but my mother said as she could never be certain I did not arrive just before midnight on All-hallow-e'en. For she often said as I was growing up that I had more in me of a devil than an angel…'

'A most propitious birth date and hour when the forces of Good and Evil are in perfect balance - but with Good on the wax and Evil on the wane. And as to the year, fair one? The year?'

'Well, I've always reckoned as I was born ten year afore Armada Year…'

'Fifteen seventy eight. And you come to me even before your twenty-first birthday. Such sweetness!'

'But you can compose a chart sir, can you not?'

'For a woman born in Saffron Waldon at midnight on the thirty first of October fifteen seventy eight - I certainly can!' he slipped his hand round her waist and hugged her exuberantly as though his excitement was the most natural thing in the world. And some strange, distant part of herself observed her also responding as though it was the most natural thing in the world. A part of her that silently ordered her to reach for Will's dagger before things got out of hand. But she made no move at all. Forman's hand slipped down to her hip; round the back onto her right buttock.

'You see,' he continued, his voice growing throaty, like the purr of a big cat, 'now I can fit your birth into my charts and see what stars and signs govern you, your spirit, your character, your destiny and your body. With these charts I can uncover the deepest secrets of your desires.

Now! shouted that tiny but shrinking part of her. Go for the dagger now!

'Let us see… Your Sun is in Scorpio, and so I'm sure will several of your other governing planets. Scorpio is a secretive, calculating sign; a chess-player always thinking several moves ahead. It is a passionate sign with much power and little control, especially in matters of the flesh. The only sign or planet that might be more powerful in this area is Lilith. Now where is the black moon of Lilith in your chart; Lilith the mistress of even more hidden lusts…'

Forman's arm tightened around her waist even as his fingers clawed at the fullness of her buttock. Without apparent effort, almost, it seemed, without thought, he swung her away from the desk and began to guide her towards the door. She followed like a puppet despite that tiny, shrinking voice yelling at her that NOW was the time to draw the dagger.

The door opened almost magically and they were out in the corridor, heading towards the window at the end of the passage, the door into his bedroom on their left. She knew she was lost if she went in there with him because Tom had told her so. But she simply couldn't stop herself.

BANG! BANG! BANG! Three great urgent hammer-blows on the front door below echoed through the house. Forman hesitated. Rosalind stopped as though incapable of movement without his guiding hand on her hindquarters.

A distant voice bellowed, 'Forman! Forman are you there?'

The astrologer left her standing like Galataea awaiting her Pygmalion whose kiss would turn her from cold ivory to hot flesh. He went to the window at the end of the corridor and opened it. He leaned out. 'George Chapman!' he spat. 'What ails you, man?'

'Bonetti!' came the distant reply. 'Bonetti's dead.'

'Dead?' demanded Forman. 'How?'

'He and Musgrave fought. Musgrave killed him.'

Tom's name ran like iced water through Rosalind's bewitched consciousness. Her body twitched seeming to come to life. She found herself staring at Forman's back with an almost shocking intensity, as though her gaze could become lethal and do the work of the dagger she had never touched.

'Musgrave!' spat Forman. 'And how do you know this?'

'It is common gossip. But I'm told Sir Walter saw it. Sir Walter saw it all!'

iv

'Take me to see John Gerard,' Rosalind ordered Tom a couple of hours later after a wherry-ride westward-ho and a brisk walk up Water Lane.

'Certainly,' said Tom, looking askance at this harridan who had so unexpectedly and tempestuously arrived in Blackfriars without so much as a word to explain what was going on. It was fortunate that Kate had departed some time ago, he thought, and the next two lessons should have been with Spenser, for Rosalind clearly needed all his attention for the moment. 'But why?'

'Forman gave me some sort of drug' she explained, pacing across the room like a wild beast ill-caged. 'A love potion. It aroused me and would likely have led me to his bed had George Chapman not broken the spell with news of you and Bonetti.'

'A drug, you say?' Tom found that doubly disturbing. Forman's reputation with the women was such that he hardly needed to use love potions! And yet...

'Something.' Rosalind insisted. 'I cannot be certain. But it robbed me of my will and aroused me in a way I have never experienced before. It is incredibly dangerous. That is why I wish to see Gerard. To get his opinion on the likely source of the stuff and, once we have that clear, what he can do to arm me against it when I return.'

'You want to go back?' Tom didn't know whether to be impressed by her bravery or shocked by her simple madness.

'Of course!' she snapped. 'And as soon as I can tomorrow. Chapman's news distracted him even as it woke me up. I was able to leave without him realizing I had seen through what he was attempting. He expects me to return tomorrow and again later in the week as he completes the chart. I am keen to do so - I am certain there is more to learn and another visit or two will give me ample opportunity. But I will feel safer if I have a counter to whatever he had put into the wine he gave me.'

Tom thought for a moment, then he said, 'The problem with the fact that he does not suspect that you have seen through his plan being that he will try it again at the earliest opportunity.'

'And unless I am armed against it in some way, he might succeed next time. He is very likely to do so in fact, unless I am armed as I say.'

'Armed with the snaphaunce this time perhaps?'

'I fear not - he slipped his arm around my waist several times. It was lucky I hid the dagger so well. He would have discovered the pistol for certain and all would have been lost! I dare not risk it. And in any case, I had the dagger and somehow I could not bring myself to use it and I fear it would be the same even with the snaphaunce. It was as though whatever he gave me turned me into his doll... His poppet...'

'And you will not countenance someone coming with you.'

She shook her head decisively. 'If I am accompanied the chance of discovering anything new is lost. He must not suspect anything. Only when he is unguarded… Indeed…' Rosalind stopped talking and pacing. She stood still, her face folding into a thoughtful frown.

'What?' demanded Tom.

'Perhaps once Gerard has determined what Forman gave me and has given me an antidote against it he would be willing to give me something in turn that I might use on Forman. The biter bit so to speak.'

'He needs no aphrodisiacs, Rosalind! I am surprised he used such a thing on you but he certainly needs no aids to arouse himself.'

'Not something to arouse his lust, Tom! Something that might overcome his reserve; make it easier to get the truth out of him.

'Wine will do that! *In vino veritas* as the ancients say, is that not so?'

'I would need a butt of Greek Malmsey to break down his reserve were I only using wine! No. I need something swifter that will be efficacious by the drop, not by the barrel!'

*

'Mandrake root of course,' said John Gerard later that evening. 'That has quite a reputation but I must admit I believe it arises principally from the shape. And it is believed to be most efficacious in the case of men, especially old ones.' The three of them were closeted together in his shop. The rest of the family, including the temperamental Elizabeth, was in the kitchen noisily at supper. 'Blue thistles have a reputation too,' he continued. 'I have no idea why…'

'But would a potion made from blue thistles not be blue?' wondered Rosalind. 'Or green if mixed with yellow wine?'

'It would,' nodded Gerard.

'Was the wine green?' asked Tom. 'You didn't mention green wine to me…'

'No; it was yellow; quite deep yellow. I didn't mention it because I didn't think the colour was important.'

'Ah! It is important. And I have him because of it!' exulted Gerard. 'Deep yellow you say?'

'Yellow,' she confirmed. 'And darker than piss.'

'Saffron,' said Gerard. 'The yellow parts of a crocus flower - which may have given its name to you birthplace Saffron Waldon now I think of it. The yellow parts of the crocus picked and dried then either used as threads or as powder. Concocted into a potion they become almost the same colour as the skins of Spanish noranges. Mixing the potion with wine would lighten its colour but darken the wine's.'

'And what do you have that I can take to counter this saffron potion?'

'Why, more of the same,' answered Gerard. 'It is one of those distillations which need to be served in careful measure - too little or too much and the effect is lost.'

'That sounds like a risky stratagem,' observed Tom. 'We already know that Rosalind can be affected by whatever Forman gave her. If she goes into his house already aroused who knows what may come of it?'

'Forman dead of ravishment?' wondered Rosalind. 'But I'll wager I could make him reveal everything I want to know before he expires.'

'Entirely possible!' said Tom. 'Why I remember on my first visit to The Crown in Saffron Walden, Rosalind, when you…'

'But we will take your word on it Master Gerard,' Rosalind interrupted Tom. 'I will take a good measure of saffron potion. Now, is there anything I can secretly give to Forman that will break down his reserve as Will's King Henry breaks down the walls at Harfleur in his play?

Gerard looked at Tom. 'We are straying into dangerous territory here, Tom,' he said. 'I have such things but Rosalind would have to be terribly careful. The need would have to be very great…'

'Master Gerard,' Tom dropped his voice. 'Consider. What Mistress Rosalind seeks to find the truth of is - amongst other matters, true - the facts of Hal's fate. What Hal discovered when he went there. And, perhaps most importantly from your point of view, what Forman has done to your Elizabeth - who has been visiting him in secret, remember, as part of her campaign to ensnare the poet John Donne by magic if by no other means.'

'Very well,' capitulated Gerard. 'I have a potion made from the dried caps of the toadstool called Fly Agaric. You will have seen it in the woods - all bright red with white spots. Some say if you cook it carefully you can eat it without much harm. But if the red caps are dried and distilled into potion without using too much heat, the result can make a man lose control of his faculties. Too much and he might run mad - or even die - but just the right amount and he will behave as though he has consumed a bottle or so of French brandywine, Scottish usquebaugh or Holland gin.'

Rosalind looked at Tom with the wickedest of grins. 'As Will's King Henry says, *one more unto the breach, dear friends…*' She pulled the purse from her waist without a second thought and spilled the silver coins onto Gerard's counter. 'How much will all that cost, good sir?' she asked.

Before Gerard could answer, Tom reached across the wooden board between them and lifted the lock of hair Rosalind found in Forman's bath room and put in her purse without a second thought. It was the kind of talisman that a lover might wear next to the skin to bind them to their heart's desire.

'Where did you get this?' he asked.

'Beneath a bath at Foreman's house,' she answered. 'Why? Do you know whose it is - or whose hair?'

'I think so,' he answered soberly. 'It looks like mine.' He brought the curls closer to his eye and studied them for a moment then he said, 'No. This hair isn't mine at all, it's too red.' He frowned. 'I wonder whose it is and how it came to be there.'

'Something else for me to discover when I beard Forman in his den again,' said Rosalind.

Chapter 13: The Blame Game

i

'It is a well-known fact,' said Robert Poley.

'Well known,' echoed Parrot.

'That the best way to escape blame for some action is to blame someone else. Do you agree?'

'Do you agree?' echoed Parrot.

'Of course I agree!' snapped Will. 'It is one of the first things a boy learns at school - in spite of the master and his birch rather than because of them! Always assuming that he hasn't learned it from his brothers and sisters at home. And not just some*one* else, some*thing* else - almost anything else! Why do you think Richard blames his twisted form in my play of *Richard III* for the evil that he does? or Don John his bastardy in *Much Ado*? There is no end to it! In the play of *Romeo* Benvolio blames the heat for the fatal bout between Mercutio and Tybalt then Romeo blames Fortune when he kills Tybalt in turn. In Kit Marlowe's play of *Faustus*, Faustus even blames his books - "I'll burn my books - ah Mephistopheles!"' Will thundered, in full dramatic mode worthy of the great Alleyn himself. The Pursuivant Marshal's office in the Marshalsea seemed to echo his agonised cry. Parrot cringed a little and even Poley sat back. There was a rattling of chains from the great cell next door as the other prisoners stirred restlessly.

Will continued, at his most forceful, beginning to run out of patience after several days in prison. It was Saturday, 20th, though he was by no means sure of the date. 'It's not the good doctor's fault, you notice. It's the books - never the wicked use he made of them! Putting the blame elsewhere is the very coin of the man discovered performing evil acts!'

'I'm pleased to see you so willing to admit to it,' purred Poley.

'Admit to what?' Will sat up straight, squaring his shoulders to disguise the sinking feeling in the pit of his stomach. Talking with Poley was, indeed, a lot like conversing with the demon Mephistopheles.

'Why, to shuffling the blame onto Simon Forman when we have…'

'…had…' inserted Parrot earning a murderous look from Poley.

'.. a witness to the fact that you bought the poison from Apothecary Gerard yourself!'

Will sat back, his eyes narrow. 'I have admitted no such thing,' he said. 'I have not even admitted the possibility - in the real world. Note that the examples I gave in general discussion, were from plays. From things of fantasy.'

'So you say!' snarled Parrot, recovering from his fright and leaning forward belligerently. A gesture, Will noted, which was somewhat undermined by the louse that scuttled out of his straggling hair and across the balding dome of his forehead. Will's own scalp clenched and began to itch furiously.

*

'Yes,' persisted Will. 'So I say. So I have said at each of these meetings. I did not buy poison from Gerard's apprentice. The same apprentice who visited Simon Forman seeking news of Gerard's daughter whom he fancied that he loved. Tom Musgrave has gone further. Tom says the lying apprentice likely met his end there, and that's an end to it as far as I can swear. I know nothing more of Forman, the exercise of magic powers, the dead boy, the apothecary's daughter or anything else to do with Spenser's death. I have been working on my play of *Henry Fifth*. That has occupied my mind to the exclusion of all else.'

'And so we see,' observed Poley drily, 'that it isn't only Faustus who tries to blame his books.'

Parrot looked at his superior, his face blank so Poley deigned to explain. 'Master Shakespeare here is blaming a book he is writing where Faustus blamed the books he was reading.'

'Reading!' spat Parrot. 'A right waste of time that is!'

Will said nothing as he tried to kick his mind into analytical thinking that might rival Tom's. It seemed to him that Poley and Parrot were prodding the question of Spenser's death with more vigour than before. The fact that it was murder seemed to have been almost entirely lost in the great ritual of the funeral Essex had arranged for the poet four days or so ago. The investigation into the death seemed to have fallen out of importance after that

- Tom kept looking, of course, and Poley, desultorily - mostly, as now - into the question of who bought what poison from whom, an act in itself illegal both by seller and purchaser, as he had pointed out in *Romeo*. But now the fact of Spenser's murder seemed to have gained a renewed grip on proceedings. Whether he himself had purchased the poison, perhaps, was becoming of less immediate importance - unless they could prove that his was also the hand that had poured it into the poet's ear. He shivered with horror at the thought of the guilt and at the act itself.

'But,' said Poley, calling Will out of his dream-like speculation, 'it does lead us to another interesting avenue of enquiry does it not?' He leaned forward and stared straight into Will's eyes. 'Are you so desperate to complete your play because you are so desperate to be paid for it? Desperate enough to have done something in the mean-time to mend your fortunes?'

'What?' asked Will, utterly bemused by this sudden change of tack after so many hours of questioning.

'Let's look at your finances for a moment shall we?' Poley's gaze held Will's unflinchingly as the intelligencer proceeded along his disturbing new line of enquiry. 'Your acting troupe has been forced to steal their own theatre which is in process of erection upon a field owned by Sir Nicholas Brend within a mile of this place, leased at a pretty penny by all accounts. You are getting no income from that in the meantime even as a shareholder, though you may well be looking at an expensive law-suit when Giles Allen, who owned the field your theatre originally stood in, gets his case to the inns of court. Even should Mr Allen prove uncharacteristically laggard in that regard, you shareholders owe Peter Street the carpenter and his men a small fortune for taking The Theatre down and putting it up again as The Globe and in the meantime you also owe Martin Fletcher the carter an almost equal sum for transporting the entire building from one place to another. Sir Nicholas Brend awaits his first rent-payment on the new field that the Globe will stand in when it is finished, and I understand Richard Burbage is wildly seeking a thatcher who will roof the place swiftly and above all cheaply!'

ii

Will drew breath to refute some of the details in Poley's grim assessment, but before Will could continue, Poley held up a restraining hand and continued relentlessly.

'But this is only the beginning. You are also a shareholder in the Blackfriars theatre built on the old Dominican priory land purchased by your company for £600 three years ago. Built and fitted out at great expense as an indoor theatre meant to be available to your troupe during the months of inclement weather and also in the evenings. A fully dressed stage, lit with ruinously expensive candles - none of your tapers or tallow dips! Comfortable seating - no groundlings allowed! Investment with the original purchase of the land running well past a thousand pounds but this fabulous new theatre is still closed to you by petition of the good folk of Blackfriars. Not including your friend Tom Musgrave, I hope. They do not want such scum as common playgoers and the lower levels still that batten onto them - wine-sellers, orange girls, whores and actors - sullying their streets and driving down house prices nearby! Oh no!' Poley shook his head as though saddened at such folly.

Then he continued, 'On top of all this you have just left your rooms in St Helens and are seeking to settle with your mistress in larger, more expensive premises on Maiden Lane - all the while supporting wife and family back in Stratford! You must be as desperate for money as the perennially bankrupt George Chapman!'

'Well?' snarled Will, stung by the comparison with Chapman as much as by the accuracy of Poley's summation. 'What of it?'

'*Well*,' echoed Poley, 'it is important because it brings us to the other matter does it not?'

'The other matter,' echoed Parrot.

'What other matter?' demanded Will.

'Why, the matter of Spenser's pension, of course,' said Poley as though this was the most obvious thing in the world. 'The Queen granted him £50 out of her bounty at Christmastide. The exchequer filled a purse with fifty golden pounds and gave it to Spenser himself as Her Majesty directed.' Poley paused with a theatricality that easily matched Will's impersonation of Faustus. 'But now that purse is nowhere to be found.'

Back in the cell, in his familiar corner, wearing his familiar leg iron, Will tried to cudgel his wits into placing the new information - the new accusation - into the whole pattern of Spenser's death. No-one had mentioned money as a motive before; land holdings and rents, yes, but not coin of the realm. The fact that Poley and Parrot had done so now needed to be treated carefully. Was it likely that the Queen would grant Spenser such a large sum? Yes! For she admired him above all other poets, knowing as she did that she herself was The Fairy Queen. Knowing, and flattered by the fact above almost every other tribute laid down before her. But, granted that, was the Council - or their financial arm the Exchequer - likely simply to put fifty golden pounds into a purse and hand it to him? It frankly seemed unlikely in these impecunious and sometimes desperately debt-ridden times. And even granted those two possibilities, how would someone learn of the bequest and act upon it so swiftly that the man was dead and the purse vanished in a matter of days?

*

Will settled back into a less uncomfortable position and fell to thinking more deeply than he had done so far - and for once he was not thinking about King Henry. Instead he picked up his earlier train of thought and followed it. Something in Poley's manner had changed. Something more was going on now than had been going on when he was brought in here; something beyond the sudden revelation about the money. He began to go through the conversation he had just suffered with the Pursuivant Marshal and his lousy accomplice. They were clearly concerned about something and their focus on reassigning the blame possibly suggested more than they meant it to or, indeed, thought it would. Even those ephemeral pounds seemed to place an idea somewhere that completed a pattern. An idea he could not quite grasp yet; a pattern he could not quite comprehend.

Whoever had bought the poison - from whatever source - clearly wanted to put the blame on him for the murder and - now - for the theft. It seemed that Poley and Parrot believed them. But what of that? They had not used him badly beyond their relentless questioning. They and pursuivant Gauge had passed on the food and water Rosalind brought daily, had indeed allowed him to proceed with his work, which, he had to admit, fared better in here than it did out in bustling Bankside. Those facts alone spoke of something strange afoot.

Will extended, broadened, that original thought. Why should it only apply to him? he wondered. Perhaps Poley was testing the idea on one unimportant playwright - to wit Will himself - when his real focus was on someone much more powerful and important. Whoever had caused Spenser's death - rather than the mere executioner who had carried it out and paid themselves fifty golden pounds for the act. Someone who had believed they were sufficiently elevated to be able to have a life snuffed out with no personal consequences. Who now discovered that they had made a miscalculation. Like the Dauphin in the play of *Henry* who never thought his insulting jest of sending the young king Henry tennis balls would ever lead to the Siege of Harfleur, the Battle of Agincourt, his own ignoble death and the conquest of his country.

A powerful person who now somehow found themselves cornered and looking at some dire consequences, who now, in consequence was looking for someone else to blame: possibly someone with an equivalent level of power. How satisfactory it would be to pass the culpability for your unexpectedly catastrophic action onto your nearest rival or most dangerous enemy.

Had Tom thought of this? Will wondered.

And had Tom got even the slightest idea of what had caused everything to change in the way it seemed to have done?

iii

'Yes I have visited Simon Forman. What of it? You may own my heart, Tom, but the rest of me has other masters, you know that.' Kate leaned back into her chair, thoughtlessly smoothing her hands over a green velvet skirt Tom had never seen before. Her mind clearly elsewhere, she repeated the gesture, stroking the thighs of questionable mastership.

Tom, in the opposite chair on the far side of the fire in his day room, leaned forward. 'But what purpose could you or your masters have in your visits to Billingsgate?' he asked.

'None that I may readily share with you,' Kate shrugged. The fire-light gleamed off her red tresses as they stirred on her shoulder, arm and bosom. An emerald gleamed there, perfectly matching the new dress - and, now Tom thought of it - her eyes. 'There is sufficient danger in this for me, and I am protected as you know. I will not pass the danger on to you.'

'I cannot see what dangers lie in Billingsgate and Forman's house. Dangers to your person, I mean, unless you were to fall down the stairs perhaps. However, I can see dangers aplenty to your reputation and your chastity.'

'Ignorance is no sort of armour my love. And remember, when it comes to my chastity you are my lover not my father or my confessor.'

'And these secret things were what you and Forman were discussing with Poley and Francis Bacon at The Rose? Here, take a draught of wine.' Tom leaned further forward and filled two glasses from the bottle on the fireside table.

'Thanks kind sir!' Kate took the proffered glass and sipped. The wine gleamed like pale amber in the firelight. 'It is very good wine too,' she continued dreamily. 'To answer your question with another: if such knowledge was so dangerous would I ever reveal who I discuss it with, why or where? It seems to me that even that knowledge would be dangerous.'

'Perhaps and perhaps not. It is a matter of trust. No, more than trust - faith.'

'You mean that I have no faith in you to keep such matters secret? To weigh them judiciously and act on them wisely.' She cradled the glass in her cupped hands and looked into its depths, then raised her eyes to his. 'That I have no faith in you to survive the dangers such knowledge brings?' She raised the glass and all-but emptied it at one draught.

'Are you indeed like an anxious mother watching over me and keeping me from danger?' Tom asked, frowning.

'What I feel for you, Tom Musgrave - more wine, sirrah! - is nothing like a mother should feel. Unless she is Jocasta, perhaps, mother and lover to the doomed Oedipus of legend.'

Tom leaned forward and filled her glass again. 'Shall we put that assertion to the test?'

'God's bones, yes! I am of a sudden so *hot…*'

*

As Tom followed Kate through to the bedroom, he carried the two glasses - one untasted - and the bottle. When her back was to him, he allowed his face to fall into a deeper frown. He was angry with himself, deeply disappointed that he had chosen to go down this route. It was a massive betrayal of Kate's confidence and love. How easy is it, he sneered at himself, to betray those who love us most, for they would never dream we were capable of such perfidy.

When she found out what he had done - and there was no 'if' for him to shelter behind - the repercussions would be dire. He was tempted to blame her intransigence for forcing him into such underhanded action but he was far too clear-sighted to do that. He knew himself far too well for prevarication or equivocation. He was simply too impatient to wait while he wheedled it out of her. This method was swift, if it worked, but almost certainly fatal to his love affair as soon as Kate discovered what the wine contained. Whatever resulted, he knew he would deserve every bitter drop of it.

'Use this very sparingly,' John Gerard had said. 'It is a variant of the potion Forman seems to use as described by Rosalind, in its effects at least. The decoction of Fly Agaric will break down the natural reserve of anyone taking it faster and more efficiently than mere alcohol - *in vino veritas* as you observed. Then the concentrate of saffron will disguise and distract by arousing lust. A person consumed with desire is unlikely to question their increasing lack of reserve in other areas.'

'Quickly Tom! Oh Tom be quick! I must have you!' called Kate breathlessly. 'Help me unloose these strings or I shall be forced to tear them asunder! Help me quickly or I shall expire!'

As he placed the glasses and the drugged bottle on the bedside table, Tom salved his conscience with the knowledge that his tempestuous mistress had used words like these often enough in the past, usually - as would be the case in a moment or two more - while he was relieving her of her farthingale and untying the cords of her corset. He had been forced to learn how to do the latter blindly for she was always too impatient to turn her back on him and wait, so he was forced to reach round her and untie the knots while her eager hands were at his belt-buckle, galligaskins and codpiece, his boat-bellied doublet having come off with her kirtle and partlet.

At last he pushed her willing body back across the bed, thrusting his hands beneath her damp, fragrant shift as she slid hers beneath his shirt. She arched against him more wantonly than usual but he lay down beside her rather than easing himself on top of her - ready but not yet willing to proceed. He ran his nails up the inside of her thigh from stocking-top to hip, teasingly along the outer edge of the neat red forest part-way between one and the other. God, he thought; yes indeed she was hot.

She gasped as she felt his fingertips move. Her wide green eyes looked strange but enticing, their pupils huge and fathomless. Almost as though she was trying to see inside herself, he thought, for, as she often did at such moments she seemed to vanish away from him. But not from what they were doing. She pushed his hand back down to where she was hottest, thrust herself into his palm and the fingers tightened almost by reflex. 'Foreman and Poley,' he said as though he was whispering endearments. 'Tell me.'

'A mistake,' she whispered, her voice strange. 'A fearful miscalculation worthy of the whelp Devereux.'

Tom paused for a moment, lost in thought. Perhaps Kate had indeed somehow vanished within herself. These seemed to be words she had overheard - not that she was saying herself. Foreman's parrot sprang to mind. 'What miscalculation?'

'…so consumed with *Mother Hubberd* that the *Fairy Queen* was forgotten altogether.'

'Who forgot? Poley? Forman? What has *The Fairy Queen* got to do with it?'

'Changed everything! Of course it did! And that bloody boy! With his funeral. So public. So soon. So magnificent - almost as though he wanted to catch her eye! Which of course he did!' She took a juddering breath and continued, sounding a lot like Abdias Assheton. 'Does He not see the fall of a sparrow? Does she not see any less? And now she wants to know how and why this sparrow fell!' She stopped speaking, took a shuddering breath, then, it seemed, returned to the present and the current situation. 'Take me, Tom. Take me now!'

Preoccupied with her words, who she might have overheard speaking them and trying to fathom their full meaning, he did as she asked at last, thrusting into her with thoughtless urgency.

She gasped. 'OH! Do not hurt me Tom.' Her voice sank to a murmur as she continued, 'Do not hurt me any more than I deserve…'

iv

'Did they hurt you?' Rosalind asked Will. It was the first thing she said to him after he suddenly appeared at their lodgings on Maiden Lane early the next morning just as she was preparing to go to church. The bells of St Mary Overie chimed in the background but for Matins, not for Common Prayer with Eucharist. Attendance today was not mandatory.

'No. they treated me well enough,' he said, avoiding her attempt to hug and kiss him, putting the cloak he had carried carefully over one arm, wrapped round a bundle of papers in spite of the icy clarity of the mid-winter morning.

'Why was that? What did you tell them?' asked Tom at once. He had been visiting Rosalind to discuss what he thought he had learned from Kate after she had slept like the dead, awoken refreshed, dressed and departed cheerily enough to change for Matins which Sir Thomas and his household customarily attended at St Olaves on Seething Lane when he was in town. She was apparently none the wiser about what he had done to her. Remembering almost nothing about what she had told him as they prepared to make love - if *love* was the correct term now after such a betrayal. Tom himself felt an urgent need of prayer and wished that he could avail himself of the catholic confessional.

The plan Tom and Rosalind were debating just before Will appeared was that, after attending church if they chose to, Tom would return to Gerard's and talk further with the flighty Elizabeth while Rosalind would return to Simon Forman's, this time well armed with enough saffron water to counteract whatever he might plan on feeding to her. Still angry at his own behaviour, Tom was over-eager to see suspiciousness in much of what went on around him. And was at once made more suspicious by Will's strange behaviour.

'No,' answered Will innocently. 'I told them nothing. They told me a good amount, however.'

'Why would they do that?' wondered Tom, as Rosalind stood back, nonplussed.

'I don't think they meant to reveal as much as they did,' shrugged Will. 'Tom, where is the nearest bath? I feel soiled to my very soul by the Marshalsea and all within it. Stay away from me a little longer, my darling, or I fear I will pass on an infestation of lice and fleas as powerful as one of the plagues of Egypt. We will have my linen laundered but in spite of any risk of disease I must bathe or remain a walking feast for the six-legged denizens of the prison house that have battened onto me. I cannot attend matins in this state. Evensong will have to suffice if we wish to attend services.'

'This is Poley we are talking of,' said Tom. 'He never says or does anything by accident. Whatever he revealed, he let slip on purpose. At the very least to set hares running -to see what we would do with the information. Likely as not in the hope that we will either discover more of the matter than he can do or, just as good, incriminate ourselves.'

'Or reveal the criminality in others he suspects but cannot touch in person,' said Rosalind, 'just as I cannot touch my Will for the moment without some sort of strong protection.'

'The Rose has a good bath house,' said Tom after a moment. 'And with any luck it will be quiet at this time on a Sabbath if it's open at all. They have a laundry there too. Most convenient to those that need their clothes cleaned while they wash their bodies.'

Will put down the cloak and unwrapped the bundle of papers he had carried back from the Marshalsea. '*Henry Fifth*,' he explained. 'Nearly finished at last thank the Lord. As to the bath house, good enough,' he added. 'We will ask them to launder and dry my clothes into the bargain and we can discuss matters while I wash and wait for my clothes to dry. I believe the cloak is clear of infestation, but would be glad if someone else carried it until such times as I need it again.'

So Tom's and Rosalind's plans were put to rest for the moment. The three of them trooped out of Maiden Lane and through to The Rose, Will bare-headed, Tom and Rosalind cloaked and hooded with Rosalind carrying Will's cloak for the return journey rather than risking infesting it now.

*

The bath in The Rose was half a Brentford tun, lined with sheets. It stood so high that bathers needed to use a stool to climb into it and often had difficulty climbing out again. This early on a Sunday morning it had only been half filled but the water was hot - augmented on a regular basis by huge bowls carried still scalding from the fire. Soap was made from the fat of the animals cooked on the spit and the ash from the fires that cooked them. Famously, it was scented with petals from the roses the tavern was named for. Will stripped unselfconsciously in front of the laundry girl who took all of his clothes - the linen undergarments and the woollen outer layers, without turning a hair at their stench or their swarming visitors. 'I will boil them in lye,' she said.

'Do so,' said Will as he placed his boots as near to the fire as he dared, hoping to roast any visitors still scuttling around within them. 'I shall have to replace anything that does not survive.' Then he climbed into the bath which was fortunately otherwise untenanted, took a deep breath and sank beneath the water. After a few moments the insects he had been harbouring began to float to the surface. Tom and Rosalind leaned in, scooping as many as they could away and throwing them into the rushes lining the floor on the far side of the bath room. When he resurfaced, Rosalind passed him a handful of soft, rose-scented lye soap and he scrubbed himself with the stuff from head to foot, then washed his hair and belly again for good measure.

Tom looked down into the seething water as the playwright pulled his lean frame out of the bath. 'God help the next man in,' he said cheerfully. 'Unless all those creatures have had good time to drown, they'll just be passing from one feast to the next.'

'Their Easter will come early,' said Will. 'That's a moveable feast as well.'

Rosalind helped her lover get dry by rubbing him vigorously with linen cloths, her eyes busy seeking any remaining guests - her nails quick to dispatch them, bursting them like tiny lead-covered grapes. Then they all sat by the bath-house fire and, while they waited for those of his clothes that survived being boiled in lye to be returned, they broke their fast with manchet loaves, cheese, butter flavoured with winter sage and fresh milk still steaming from the udder while they held the discussion as they had planned.

'Poley talks of Spenser's pension,' Will started. 'Her Majesty granted him £50 at Christmastide. According to Poley, the Council directed the Exchequer to pay it in full at once - unlikely as that sounds - so there was somewhere about poor Spenser a purse with fifty gold pounds in it. Which purse has vanished or so they say. Poley supposes it has vanished into my hands for he knows that I am low on funds until the Globe is up, *Henry* finished, cast, rehearsed and on the stage, generating an income for all of us. And he knows how desperate things could become unless all these things happen soon - we cannot live on our payment from our last performance at court of *The Dream* over Christmas. Especially as Her Majesty preferred to dance on Twelfth Night and robbed us of an entire performance which we had hoped for.'

'Robbery, and of such a sum! An interesting conceit,' said Tom. 'Do you believe it?'

'That Her Majesty granted the pension? Of course. Spenser was her favourite poet.' Will said. 'That the Council paid it out in coin? And so swiftly? Less so. I have never heard of such celerity in all my dealings with them.'

'And yet, as you say,' mused Rosalind, 'If Spenser was her darling, perhaps she ordered it so.'

'True,' agreed Tom. 'And if - for once in his life - Poley speaks the truth, whoever really poured the poison into Spenser's ear as he slept, removed that purse and is now a rich man - for the moment at least. Though doubly endangered, of course, for even if he has carried out the murder unsuspected, the moment he starts spending Her Majesty's gold coin, he puts himself at the centre of suspicion once again. Not to mention at the top of every thief and cut-throat's robbery list, unless he is very careful indeed.'

'Or,' added Rosalind, 'unless he is very well protected.'

Tom sat silent for a moment. Rosalind's phrase chimed with something in his memory.

'But there was more,' said Will after a moment. 'Poley and Parrot spent some time examining with me a possibility in parallel. That whoever lies at the root of this, someone of great power which he wields without much thought, supposed that he could crush Spenser as easily as Rosalind is crushing the fleas from the Marshalsea. But then the Earl of Essex, with his gaudy funeral full of poets and his positioning of the grave next to Chaucer's somehow changed matters, though it seemed they could not fathom how this was so.'

'But surely it is obvious,' said Tom. 'We have been discussing it without assessing the full import of our words.' He looked at the other two, his eyes shining. 'And what Kate told me last night makes the whole thing seem clearer still.'

'How so?' asked Will.

'Consider,' said Tom. 'Spenser upsets one of the most powerful men in the land, perhaps with *Mother Hubberd*, perhaps in some other way. The plot to kill him is thrown together with little more planning but with equal effect to Henry II's execution of Archbishop Becket.'

'But how would that work?' queried Rosalind. 'Are there men so powerful and are the court and the council so corrupt that such things can be done on a whim?'

'Poor Kit Marlowe was murdered on little more than a whim,' said Will. 'All the world knows that! And by your evil genius Robert Poley into the bargain!'

'Let us suppose,' said Tom, 'that the offended man is Sir Walter Raleigh, The Fox. He stands high in the Queen's favour but remembers all too well the result of his marriage to Bess Throckmorton.'

'Some time in the Tower then banishment to Dorset,' explained Will to Rosalind.

'A fate likely to be repeated if he becomes a figure of gossip and of fun!' said Tom. 'He would face ruination at the least, if not yet another sojourn in the Tower. Particularly as he sits on the outer limits of those who consider the Infanta of Spain has a strong case to succeed to the throne after Her Majesty dies. One of the few things he has in common with his mortal enemy the Earl of Essex.

'To his bruised pride and dangerous politicking, let us add some other matters. We know him to be ruthless. His execution of so many men at the Siege of Smerwick proves that. Despite his position at court, he is not rich - his adventures in the Americas have brought fame, restoration of Royal favour, but little else - certainly no great fortune. The demands of his position call upon his purse as well as his time and loyalty. His mansion in Sherborne is a costly indulgence.'

'But a safe refuge,' added Will. 'Word is that he sent his family and household there after Twelfth Night and the riots on the Strand.'

'So he did,' nodded Tom, 'But for him as a skeleton staff, Durham House stands empty.' Then he pushed on with his argument. 'His lands in Ireland generate little income while there is a war going on there - but they stand close enough to Spencer's for a ruthless man to be tempted, especially as there is a chance that the Earl of Essex will bring peace to the province and thereby prosperity to all - and twice the prosperity to a man who can add Spencer's lands to his own.'

'Very well,' said Will, 'I can see how he might be tempted, wounded pride and all. But how would he go about it?'

'With surprising ease,' answered Tom. 'He has at his beck and call the School of Night - Forman, Chapman, Thomas Harriot to name but a few, but all godless and desperate men: Forman we have discussed; Chapman is perennially desperate for money to fight his case against John Wolfall, to whom he stands in considerable debt, if for nothing else. So Forman could generate the poison - and probably did, no matter who he was really working for. Chapmen could well have delivered it and would have stolen a purse containing such a sum without a second thought. And Chapman could well have worked to put the blame on some other man - preferably a poet and playwright whose writings were eclipsing his own. You see how well it all might fit together?'

'Except for that one element you have not yet mentioned,' said Will. 'The one I descried this morning - the one that appears to have changed everything.'

'Just so,' said Tom. 'Let us move on with our trail of logic therefore. Consider this. The task is done - and, perhaps, the purse with £50 taken. The originator of the murder rubs his hands and stands back, task completed, satisfaction achieved. He observes Essex as Earl Marshal and as the poet's sponsor looking into the matter. Essex warns Forman to be circumspect as to the true cause of death though Will's accusation is left hanging as insurance should anything go wrong. As it does when Hal falls to his death and their witness is gone, necessitating some quick-thinking. To what end, we know. Meanwhile, Essex declares himself satisfied and arranges the funeral.'

'Why would he do that?' asked Will and Rosalind almost together. 'Why would he wink at murder and let it pass?'

'For the same reason that has dictated his every action for weeks and months past,' said Tom. 'He is too firmly focussed on his ambition to get to Ireland to risk a full investigation into a murder and robbery slowing him down, distracting his attention, trapping him here in London when he burns to be in Dublin.'

He looked at the pair of them, took a breath and continued, praying somewhere at the back of his mind that this final step of logical reasoning, based on what his drugged lover had revealed last night, would be worth the price he must inevitably pay.

'But the funeral in itself attracts the notice of the one person in the whole realm more powerful still. Who loves the poet and his poetry more than any other in the entire kingdom. The Fairy Queen herself. She is informed of Essex's rush to judgement - his business in Ireland keeps him very much under her eye - and the speed with which the dead man is interred. She may not have many spies of her own but she is surrounded by men who have spies in similar numbers those poor Will brought fleas from the Marshalsea. And so, inevitably, she hears a rumour about hemlock distilled into Spenser's ear.

'So it transpires that things are not settled after all. She does not turn to her Crowner Sir William Danby who looked into Marlowe's murder with Poley, Frizer and Skeres for he is old and nearing retirement. She turns to the Earl Marshal and orders him to re-open his investigation, to uncover the truth and unmask the plot - and its originator - all before she will permit him to set out for Ireland himself. His nightmare has become fact so his actions go into reverse and all of a sudden, here we are.'

'The Queen,' said Will. 'Of course! The Queen. She will have changed everything, for if she believes that it was murder then she will want a murderer unmasked. The man who laid the plan and those that carried it out. And at her command, heads can roll, even if they are affixed to the most powerful and important shoulders in the land!'

Tom nodded. 'All four of the men we most suspect must know that, and the guilty man must now get busy to shift the blame elsewhere; to put any other head but his at risk of the headsman's axe.'

'Which is why,' concluded Rosalind, 'the entire game has changed.'

Chapter 14: The Guts and the Heart's Desire

i

Rosalind hesitated on Billingsgate looking up at Forman's house. She had never felt like this before. All around her the noisy, malodorous bustle squeezed between the coal market and the fish market on a chilly Monday morning continued but she was hardly conscious of it. She was far too aware of her own body to spend any of her attention on her surroundings. She felt as though she was terrified though she was not - her heart was hammering and her breath was short. Her mouth was dry and her nostrils flared. She would have supposed herself fearful of some appalling monster or event rushing towards her through the crowd, had the truth of the matter not been so overwhelmingly obvious. She had sipped John Gerard's saffron potion in preparation for Forman's own concoction and the effects were coming close to overwhelming her.

The tips of her breasts were so sensitive that even the light linen of her shift sent thrills through her as it moved across them while she panted. And if she was aroused above the waist, that was nothing as to how she felt below. Once or twice with her Will, in that brief time between one bout of love-making and another when completion had simply led to further arousal rather than satisfaction she felt this stimulated. But to experience such a thing on a crowded street part way through a workaday Monday went far beyond any experience she had ever undergone. She took another deep breath, tried to still her fluttering heart, and stepped forward carefully - fearful that the motion of her thighs might bring things to a crisis.

The shop door was closed but not locked as she discovered when she turned the handle and pushed. The shop inside was empty, the counter untenanted. She hesitated for a heartbeat. Images of flies approaching spiders' webs and moths fluttering near flames replaced the erotic pictures in her imagination. Perhaps her heart was pounding with more fear and less lust after all. Once again she was torn - Forman had no idea she was here: she could still escape. She took a deep breath to steady herself and then moved forward. She had no sooner reached the counter than the door into the rooms behind it opened and matters were settled for it was too late to escape now.

Forman emerged, looking over his shoulder as he talked to someone behind him. 'We no longer conceal, we reveal; but only what we are ordered to reveal; what we are still able to reveal. It is, as I said, a new game…'

The man he was talking to emerged and Rosalind recognised him from the funeral - it was the bankrupt poet George Chapman. He tapped Forman on the shoulder with a warning finger and the astrologer turned, frowning. Almost immediately, however his expression cleared.

'Ah, George,' he said. 'Allow me to introduce Rosalind Fletcher, late of Saffron Walden, who has come to me for spiritual advice.'

'Spiritual advice - from *you*? said Chapman, his tone one of amusement rather than surprise.

'Indeed,' chuckled Forman, 'but guidance from my spirits, rather than my guidance of hers.'

'Well,' said Chapman, 'I'll leave you and Mistress Fletcher to your guidance, spiritual or otherwise. I'm for the Strand as we discussed.'

'Very well,' said Forman. 'We'll meet later.'

Rosalind, still caught up in the departing skirts of that erotic reverie, watched him leave as though in some kind of a dream. Then she turned to find Forman at the counter immediately behind her, that bottle of dangerous Rhenish standing erect between them.

'Now,' said Forman, 'where were we?'

*

'Alas,' said Forman, 'although your details could hardly be clearer, the chart to which they give birth remains obscure.' He looked down at the birth-chart lying open on the desk in the library beside his bed room and beneath the occult chamber as he slid a conciliatory hand round her waist. The wine bottle stood beside the chart and two goblets stood beside that, all part empty now. The first couple of sips had not helped matters for Rosalind. She had started to slip out of her sensual state with the nervousness she felt at coming into the shop and, further, there was an unexpected distraction of a riddle on the way up here. For the half-open door to the room at the rear of the house above the kitchen that contained the chamber pot and the bath revealed that the room was full of steam. The bath was clearly filled and ready to be used. But, once again, whoever had filled it was absent, as all Forman's servants seemed to be.

However, first draught of Forman's wine had pushed her back into the state which had held her in her grip as she arrived. She was once more so aroused she couldn't think straight and she certainly had seen no chance as yet to pour the distillate of fly agaric into his. The only thing keeping her safe at the moment, she thought, was the fact that Forman had no idea of the state in which she arrived so he was waiting for his own saffron-enhanced wine to take effect. His hand slipped down to clasp her buttock once again and she returned the pressure with sensuous abandon before she realised what she was doing. She really needed to get a grip on herself, she thought, before Forman got a far more serious grip on her.

'The character revealed is as I described at our last encounter,' Forman was saying. 'Secretive, determined, insightful and forward-looking. But the future remains obscure…'

'Oh sir,' she breathed, maintaining her character as a country innocent by the skin of her teeth. 'How could that be?'

'In my experience,' he answered, lifting her glass to her lips so she was forced to take another sip, 'and my experience is wide…' he put down her glass and picked up his own, 'such vagueness comes from one reason only. That you have not yet found your heart's desire.'

'I have so, sir,' she protested. 'I have found my Will!'

He gave a knowing chuckle. 'And you do realise, do you not that a *will* or *willy* is a love-name for a man's parts, especially when aroused. Perhaps Master Shakespeare's is not the *will* you really desire after all…'

'And is there nothing in all these fine books, sir, that will - that *would* - guide you further?' she gestured broadly at the packed shelves and succeeded in knocking the bottle over. The wine splashed onto the floor, missing the chart by inches. Forman tutted and caught it by the neck as Rosalind portrayed slightly tipsy horror at what she had done as effectively as any of Will's actors. 'Oh sir! Forgive me I beg! That was so clumsy…'

'Think nothing of it,' Forman soothed, clearly pleased at the speed with which his adulterate Rhenish was taking effect. 'Wait here and I will fetch a little more.'

The minute the door closed behind him Rosalind poured John Gerard's concoction of fly agaric into his glass then she slapped herself round the face, twice with each hand. Four times in all. Hard.

ii

Sir Walter Raleigh was just as tall as Tom and Bonetti had schooled him well. Faced with almost anyone else, the Captain of the Guard would have easily prevailed, despite the fact that he worked within the bounds of Agrippa's minim beats. His style was fluid, almost as though he were performing an energetic pavane, dancing to the rhythm in his head. His blade reached out from all of Agrippa's guards, rock-steady, with fearsome speed both in solidly founded thrusts and light-footed, well-balanced lunges.

Tom stepped back from their final bout, stripped off his gloves and reached for one of the towels beside the ewer of warm water that stood between the piste and the long mirror on the inner wall. Raleigh also mopped his face, sweeping the cloth back over the red curls of his hair where they were darkened almost to mahogany by sweat, watching himself do so in reflection. 'Truth to tell Sir Walter,' said Tom. 'I have little to teach you. Your grasp of Agrippa's method will stand you in good stead unless you face a true master or a loaded gun.'

Raleigh gave a grunt of laughter then turned. 'Even so, I will persist until I have reached mastery myself - the lessons are worthwhile even were I doing nothing other than going through the moves while watching myself in that glass. It is a revelation, sir. Poor Bonetti never thought of such a thing.'

Still watching his every move in the huge mirror, Raleigh slid his long blade home, pulled on his outer garments and swung his cloak over his shoulders. 'Does this hour suit?'

'It does, Sir Walter.'

'Well then I will come at this hour on Mondays, Wednesdays and Fridays while I am at court and in the country. I will send a man with the fee as agreed and see you the day after tomorrow.'

The two men crossed to the inner door that led to Tom's office with its second door out onto landing at the top of the stairs. No sooner had Raleigh thundered down them into Blackfriars than another, lighter footstep came pounding upward. Tom waited, eyebrows raised, for he was expecting Will as his next student and this was definitely not the poet's footfall. The young man who eventually appeared seemed familiar, but Tom couldn't place him until he began to speak. 'Master Musgrave, I have not come for any lessons in the art and science of defence, but on the orders of the Dean himself.'

'Ah, the scholar from the Abbey. I don't believe we have been introduced.'

'Hugh Bunton, sir. The Dean himself, The Reverend Master Gabriel Goodman, has sent me to seek you out - though your name was raised at my suggestion...'

'To seek me out with what purpose, Master Bunton?'

At the mention of the Dean of Westminster, Ugo came out of his workroom and joined Tom, all ears.

'Why, so that you can explain the plagues that overcame the Abbey during services yesterday, Master Musgrave,' continued Hugh Bunton eagerly. 'The Dean of course thought first of exorcism but I suggested that there might be an earthly explanation rather than a demonic one and were that so, you would be the man to settle matters.'

'You flatter me. And if I fail, there is always exorcism. I see. But the next step should be clear to you Master Bunton. If I am to try and explain these plagues then...'

'...then I must tell you what they are!'

'Indeed! Well reasoned.'

At this point Will came thundering up the stairs. 'Am I late?' he gasped.

*

'It was at Evensong yesterday that it really started,' said Hugh. 'There was the beginning of a stench at Matins and one or two flies, but by Vespers that is to say Evensong, both the stench and the infestation were more pronounced and at the Evening Service later still it was stronger. And when we opened the Abbey this morning...'

Tom listened attentively as the four of them were rowed along the familiar stretch of the river between Blackfriars and West Minster. He couldn't see any way out of this which wouldn't enhance his reputation undeservedly because he knew very well what must be happening but at the same time the Good Lord was offering him a chance to tie up a loose end that had been worrying him ever since last Tuesday night. 'And the stink is near the Choir, you say?' he probed, exchanging a glance with a disapproving Ugo.

'Yes, Master Musgrave. It is near the Choir and hard by Master Spenser's new-made grave. There is a good deal of speculation that it might be Spenser's spirit rendered restless by the manner of his death manifesting itself in the Abbey. Hence Dean Goodman's thoughts of exorcism of course.'

'The manner of his death?' asked Ugo.

'Why yes, sir. Had you not heard? It is an almost certain fact that he was murdered. Her Majesty's court is all a-buzz with speculation, and as the Dean reports directly to the Queen herself, such speculation is carried down to us with great rapidity. It seems certain that poor Master Spenser was somehow poisoned! The Earl Marshal is fully engaged with the case by all accounts, and there is talk of bringing Sir William Danby the Queen's Crowner out of retirement to assist him!'

Tom glanced at his two companions once again and was pleased to see that they were giving nothing away. 'A restless spirit, you say,' he turned to the wide-eyed Hugh. 'If he sends forth stenches and plagues of flies during the day, has anyone waited after midnight to see whether this spirit walks?'

'No-one sir! Such things are said to harrow up the soul and freeze the blood of anyone that dares to look upon them!'

'But perhaps,' suggested Ugo, 'you could try that, Master Musgrave, if you cannot plumb the depth of this mystery before sunset.'

iii

The silence of the Abbey immediately inside the North Doorway was indeed disturbed on an almost inaudible level by a droning, buzzing hum which became evident the moment the great portal shut out the workaday world outside. Once the ear picked it up, thought Tom, it seemed to come from everywhere and nowhere. No wonder the Dean's men reacted to it with superstitious awe. But that was as nothing compared with the shock of looking upward to discover that the shadows immediately above were alive. Swarms of flies in numbers Tom had never experienced whirled above, threatening at any moment to settle on his upturned face. It certainly explained why, apart from themselves and their guide, the Abbey seemed utterly empty - of men at least. 'Jesu,' he said quietly, 'I have never seen flies of such size and in such numbers. Have you Will?'

'Not above the greatest midden at midsummer,' said the playwright. 'Nor following the Fleet, be it never so full of dead dogs and putrefaction! Though now I call it to mind, the Marshalsea prison was almost as badly infested with the things.'

'Ugo?'

'I have heard that Venice on occasion and some lands in the far North near to Russia are plagued. As was Rome of course before the swamps were drained; and sometime along the borders of the Zuyderzee we have midges and mosquitoes. But never like this nor in winter.'

'And there is the stench,' added Hugh enthusiastically. 'That emanates from Spenser's grave for certain!'

'Let us explore, then,' said Tom and he strode along the transept with the others close behind him.

'Should have brought a dog,' said the ever-practical Ugo.

'We'll try and follow our own noses,' called Tom, 'and see where they lead.'

'I'd start at Spenser's grave,' suggested Hugo. 'Our noses won't lead us far from there, I'll be bound.'

Indeed, the stench and the flies which seemed to be born from it grew almost intolerable as they passed the tombs of King Henry and Queen Katherine, heading towards those of Spenser and Chaucer. As they approached, however, Tom grew ever more certain where both the stench and the swarms were coming from but he was worried that too swift a revelation would make Hugh suspicious - for the lad was clearly no fool.

Tom spent a good quarter of an hour examining Chaucer's grave, then twenty minutes more looking at Spenser's before he declared that his sensitive nose wanted to lead him elsewhere. Fifteen minutes later again the three of them arrived at Queen Katherine's tomb. The first thing that Tom noticed was that the top did not quite fit properly. There was a gap less than a finger's width at the very top. Had they left it open when they hid Hal's body? he wondered. He had no idea. He thought he had overseen perfect placing but it had been dark and he could not quite remember where Kate was standing when they finally slid the tomb's massive lid into position. But even had they been uncertain as to the source of the stench, there was no arguing with the way the flies were coming crawling through the tiny gap.

Tom looked up at the others. He needed to say nothing. Will and Ugo joined him in swinging the tomb's lid round so that it balanced across the tomb and revealed its contents.

*

The most terrible transformation had come over Hal's corpse. Tom might have supposed, had he thought about it, that the body would have lain safely and relatively free of infestation in a cold marble tomb in a chilly Abbey in the midst of a freezing winter. But clearly something had happened to upset the normal processes in this case. Tom remembered the body he had raised from Spenser's tomb being slack and flaccid - head rolling, brains just contained in the battered skull, everything below the chest sagging and pendulous, almost as though held together by his clothing. But he had supposed this to be nothing more than the natural outcome of time spent in the outside privy days after death.

But now it was clear that something else must have been going on. Had Hal been a shoulder of mutton, Tom might almost have sworn he had been poached. Seethed. Boiled. A kind of revelation hit him. There was no doubt in his mind that

Hal had been kept in Forman's hip bath after he fell down the stairs. But what if the bath had been filled with scalding water which remained boiling-hot all the while the mess on the stairs and at the stair-foot was being cleaned? What if Hal's body was in that state when he was put in the outside privy and left there for day after day, night after night? Steaming at first and offering welcome warmth to any of the creatures usually found in a privy. Warmth and, as Will had discovered at The Marshalsea, sustenance. The outcome, he supposed, might well be just like this. The corpse was falling to pieces. The rotten clothing might have held it together for a while but it had failed now. Just as his jerkin had burst, so had the belly beneath it, releasing more than just that dreadful stench. Hal's intestines lay between his legs like offal in a butcher's. Much of the skin and a good deal of the flesh on his upper body and face were gone. His eyeballs were as white as poached eggs. And, from top to toe he was crawling with fat white worms, which had clearly been feasting on him while the flies which had been born from that stunning, sickening stench, multiplied in enormous numbers and escaped out into the Abbey itself.

'Not Spenser's ghost after all,' said Tom to Hugh, but the Dean's young associate was nowhere nearby. He had staggered away, fighting to avoid the ultimate sacrilege of vomiting in Westminster Abbey.

The three friends looked at each-other. 'Well,' said Tom, 'at least this means we don't have to move him ourselves.'

'That's good in some ways but less good in others,' warned Ugo. 'We'll have to stay well clear of any speculation as to how he arrived here - and in this condition. And, frankly, Tom, it opens another question that we cannot avoid by pretending ignorance.'

'Which is?' asked Tom, though he knew the answer well enough.

'Who moved the lid after we sealed it - and why.'

'That's strange,' said Will who had not really been listening, consumed by the grotesque sight of a man being consumed by worms, 'look at his left arm. Could he have been reaching up?

Trying to push the lid aside? Fearful that he had been buried alive?'

'No,' answered Tom shortly. 'He was long past being alive when we entombed him.' But then he saw what Will was talking about. Hal's right arm was raised, the white, near-shapeless excrescence of his hand - looking more like one of John Gerard's fungi than anything of flesh and blood - rested against the side of the tomb, high above the rest of the body. Without a second thought, Tom reached down and pulled the fist higher still. With a brutality arising from disgust, he closed his fingers round the cheese-like coldness of the thing and pulled the fingers open with surprising ease. To reveal nothing. The digits were like white sausages he had once consumed in Germany. The creases at their joints were correspondingly deep. Their roots vanished into the plump waxiness of the palm. 'Someone's been here before you,' said Ugo. 'Searching for whatever he held in that fist.'

'Indeed,' Tom agreed, bending the fingers back and spreading them as wide as he could. Still nothing...

And yet...

Tom leaned forward, eyes wide, seeking the minutest detail. And there, almost lost within the deep dark creases of that swollen hand there was something: hair. There was a curl of dark hair which might be of any colour from chestnut brown to foxy red.

iv

'Why, you're blushing!' Simon Foreman paused on the threshold of his library, bottle in hand, looking at Rosalind's bright red cheeks. 'What thoughts have brought such colour?'

'None that are improper, sir, I assure you,' whispered Rosalind not very convincingly. The slaps had cleared her mind and she watched her would-be seducer as he preened under the weight of her flattery. 'I merely thought what would my poor parents say, God rest them, if they knew I was living with a famous play writer and visiting such important men as yourself. There is no-one such as yourself in Saffron Walden, sir, that's certain!'

'Well, well,' he said coming fully into the room. 'I'm certain-sure your poor parents - whose sad end is clearly demonstrated in your chart just before it becomes so hazy - would approve of your visit here, whatever they might think of your association with a mere actor!'

He topped up both the glasses and reached for his own at once.

'Can you show me more of what this wonderful chart reveals?' she asked, taking a judicious sip of her own wine - relieved to feel no ill-effects this time.

'Well,' he said expansively, leaning forward to gesture at his calculations with the base of the glass in his left hand while his right hand returned to her hip and then slid down, 'here you are, born where and when you told me. These charts tell us that the Sun is in Scorpio with Leo ascendant. Giving you the determined character we have discussed. All is as it should be until here, the square between the Sun and Lilith. This may warn that your self-reliance and determination can spill over into the taking of dangerous risks and, perhaps even self-destructive ones. Further on we see that your moon is in Libra - meaning that you are always looking for steady and reliable relationships - so, perhaps, your current liaison with a simple actor lies at the root of the vagueness I see in the chart over-all.'

'But what can you see of my life, sir? Before it becomes misty as you say?'

'Of your past, I can see a happy childhood without brother or sister to distract your parents from you. Yet you were not indulged. Your father and mother ran an establishment - an inn perhaps - and you grew up helping them. Then it seems that a dark figure enters your life - all of your lives in fact. He brings good things and bad things. You learn much from him, so much that you can continue educating yourself, perhaps; but the price he exacts from both yourself and your parents is high; ultimately the highest price of all. See here where it shows death and destruction all around.' He took a sizeable sip from his wine and then another.

Rosalind sipped hers before she asked, intrigued in spite of herself and wondering how much of this was truly revealed by the chart and how much came from gossip and research, 'And did this dark figure cause all this destruction?'

'Not directly,' answered Forman. 'The chart shows the dark figure in conflict with others far above your reach. It is these others who bring destruction. I see your escape, here,' he gestured at a section of the chart which meant no more to her than if it had been written in Greek and was lucky not to slop wine over it. 'And your flight to London. Where the dark figures all seem to be congregated, the one who influenced you so deeply in Saffron Walden most powerful of all - with regard to your chart that is though I cannot speak for his true power in the world.'

You don't need to, thought Rosalind. I know all about his power in the world.

*

Forman swung round to look more closely at Rosalind, making her jump out of the reflective moment that had claimed her while she thought about Poley. The sorcerer's pupils were beginning to widen as the fly agaric took its effect on top, she supposed, of a good dose of saffron to sharpen his own lust in anticipation of meeting hers. Certainly, they were both drinking from the same - drugged - bottle now. 'This is not the chart of some helpless country girl,' he said suspiciously as if he was only seeing it for the first time. As perhaps he was, reasoned Rosalind. In all probability he had just drawn the chart paying little attention to it other than as a way to get a gullible country girl into his bed; but that surely meant he had not researched her background. Though, to be fair, he worked for the most powerful of the 'dark forces' affecting her - Gelly Meyrick, Francis Bacon or Essex himself could have let slip any number of facts about her.

'In fact I have drawn only a very few charts like this.' He continued as he put down his glass with a decided *click*, released her waist and swung away, reaching up to the shelf above their heads. He pulled down another chart and spread it in front of her, careful to conceal whose chart it was. 'You see?' he said, slurring the 's' very slightly. He picked up the glass again, took a draught and continued to use its base as a pointer. 'Sun in

Pisces, gives her a mutable character, able to change almost as effectively as your actor friend Shagsberd. In spite of appearing open and friendly, she also has a secretive side to her nature. As you would expect from a water sign, she has an affinity with the colour green.' He took another swig. 'But I digress. The chart shows us a woman, the younger of two sisters, born to loving parents. In this case they saw to her education, but dark and powerful figures cluster round her from infancy; really powerful ones; royalty or near-royalty. She is one of two sisters admittedly, but see how the elder one also falls under the influence of dark forces, dark individuals, who add to both girls' knowledge and understanding but only at a price. You see how, especially in later, more recent, sections you and the woman belonging to this chart have much in common. And indeed, your futures in both cases are difficult to descry with any clarity or precision even though they seem, for the moment at least, to run in parallel.' He paused, then folded the chart and returned it to the shelf. 'This woman also has found it hard to see clearly her heart's desire despite her fullest efforts to do so,' he concluded, emptying his glass with a single gulp.

Rosalind nodded, wide-eyed, her mind racing: Forman had hidden the name of the other woman, but not her date or place of birth: Wednesday February 29th 1576; Shelton Hall, Norfolk.

v

So it seemed that, in spite of her affair with Tom, Kate Shelton had not yet found her heart's desire and was still actively searching for it. Unless, like Rosalind herself, Kate was on a mission to find out the truth of Forman's involvement in Spenser's murder and the circumstances surrounding it. For Sir Thomas Walsingham, her brother-in-law and spymaster, no doubt; which, if so, reflected interestingly on Sir Thomas' position. Now there was a fascinating possibility, mused Rosalind momentarily distracted once again. Perhaps after all the lingering effects of the saffron were undermining her powers of concentration. 'But how do I discover the truth of my

245

heart's desire?' she asked after a moment, frowning as though she had difficulty understanding the concept.

'I can help you discover it,' Forman promised airily. His pupils looked like black moons. Like Lilith, perhaps, thought Rosalind coming back into the present and remembering his explanation of her chart from yesterday and the place of the mysterious dark moon within it. 'I can do this through the use of magic.'

'Magic, sir? Not witchcraft surely…' She gave a convincing shudder - then realised she hardly need to have bothered. Forman was *away with the fairies* already, as the good folk of Saffron Walden said. His eyes, his speech, his gestures - and most of all his airy overconfidence and willingness to discuss matters he would presumably have kept secret - all demonstrated this.

'No, no my dear,' he explained, his face settling into a look of theatrical cunning, She was reminded of Mercutio on Will's play of *Romeo*, wildly - almost madly - planning to break into the Capulets' party as he babbled about Queen Mab the fairy. 'I speak of natural magic, of good spirits who can be contacted and put to work through certain simple rituals.'

'What spirits, sir?'

'Have you not seen your lover's play of the *Midsummer Dream*?' he asked. 'As I believe Puck, servant to Oberon and Titania, king and queen of the fairies says: "If we spirits have offended…" Those are the kinds of spirits I speak of.'

Rosalind had never seen the play but she had seen the players' copy and was fairly certain that Puck spoke of *shadows* rather than *spirits*, but that was not the sort of distinction a simple country girl would make, even one surrounded by dark and powerful forces and going to live with the playwright.

'Oh, sir! You mean goblins, hobgoblins and sprites? Country spirits?'

'Like that rogue Robin Goodfellow! Yes indeed. And I have a way of calling upon them that is certain sure!' He frowned, doing his best to appear reliable, poured himself more wine and took a swig.

'And this other woman whose chart you showed me, sir,' probed Rosalind, hot on Mistress Kate's trail. 'Did she call on Robin Goodfellow and his friends for guidance as you suggest?'

'She was a little more... ah... desperate than you, perhaps,' allowed Forman. 'She called on spirits that were darker and more powerful. But she called them in the same way you would call on Robin Goodfellow and his friends - and she plans to do so again soon!'

'Did she not succeed in getting the guidance she sought, then?'

'On the contrary! She gained such potent insight that she wishes to commune with her guiding spirits once more and learn even more about her heart's desire and how it might be achieved!'

'Oh sir, take me wherever this lady went and show me what to do as well.'

'I shall, my dear. We must mount to my occult chamber which is on the next storey up above us.'

'Occult chamber! What is that? It sounds like a place of danger!' she trembled once again - but this time did her best to force an unmissable thrill of sexual excitement into it.

And, as she had planned for him to do, Forman ran out of patience with her vapid country bumpkin hesitation. He emptied his glass, thrust out his hand, took hers and led her out into the corridor. 'Come,' he said, 'and you shall see everything.'

*

Rosalind would have hesitated in the corridor outside Forman's library but he didn't give her the chance. She was able to orientate herself however. Immediately behind her the library door was swinging closed. Behind and to her left, the next door led, she knew, into his bedroom - the spider's parlour to many a lust-drugged female fly. Away on her right, the corridor ended in the bath chamber where she had used the chamber pot on her last visit and discovered the ribbon-bound curl of hair; that strange little room which was filled with steam this time, as though Forman was preparing to bathe as soon as she left.

And, straight ahead, with Forman already on the lower steps, the rickety staircase where Tom deduced that Hal had fallen to his death. She shivered again but this time it was no act. As she stepped onto the lower stairs, her eyes were busy examining the broken balusters as she calculated how best to get a closer look at them without Forman nearby. A rudimentary attempt had been made to repair them by binding the broken ends together with rope, the tightly wrapped coils reminding her of the knot above a hangman's noose or the rope-work on a ship. Even so, they didn't look all that safe and so, although she examined them as she passed, she stayed well clear of them, rubbing her left shoulder against the wall opposite. Just like Tom's imagination, she guessed, her head filled with images of the young apprentice tumbling backwards, reaching out in a vain attempt to save himself.

Forman reached the door at the top of the stair and threw it wide, stepping up and pulling her in, all in one fluid movement. His grip on her hand tightened as she too stepped into the room. One long glance revealed a tall stand on her right with a cage at the top of it even larger than the one outside the kitchen. But it only had one occupant. The colourful bird put its head on one side, observing her with bright eyes astride a black, fearsomely hooked bill. 'Don't be fearful my lady,' it said in a voice disturbingly similar to Forman's own.

'Don't be fearful,' echoed Forman, pulling her clear of the door before she could step back - though, pre-warned by Tom, she was not actually frightened by the bird and its ability to speak. Nor by the circles on the floor - nor by the five-pointed star at their heart. Nor, in fact, was she scared by the huge crocodile and the massive serpent wrapped around it; by the candle-crested skull, the mummified corpses of the jackal, the monkey and the much abused cat. But her carefully calculated performance continued. 'Oh, Lord, sir, what monstrous creatures are these?'

''They are familiars of great age and almost limitless power,' he assured her, releasing her hand and crossing to the wardrobe at the far side of the room. While she gawped like a hayseed, he pulled on long black robes edged with strange symbols in silver, put on a square hat such as she had seen doctors wearing, and took out a long staff with a silver skull at its head.

'Now,' he said, his slurred voice ringing with authority, 'before I release the puissant powers to do your bidding, I must ensure that you are both protected and positioned so as to command them. You see the star in the midst of the circles?'

'I do sir,' she breathed, apparently awestruck.

'You must enter that star. More, to gain the greatest possible benefit, you must lie down in it with your head and your limbs reaching toward each of its points.'

'Lie down, sir! But the floor is mortal dirty! I cannot afford to soil my dress so…'

'Ah,' he said. 'I had not considered that. Though now you mention it, the lady whose chart I showed you was also solicitous of her dress.'

'What then, sir?'

'Why, she took it off! And her underclothing. Even to her shift - then, after the magic was done, she bathed.'

'A *lady* did this?'

'A lady indeed! And one, I might tell you, who is well-known at court, at one time even as playfellow with the Queen.' Having delivered himself of this, the magician turned and rummaged in the wardrobe once again.

Rosalind paused, nonplussed. This was not quite what she had expected. Perhaps it was fortunate that the simple, gullible country maiden she was playing would also have hesitated in the face of a situation in which, it seemed Lady Katherine Sheldon had charged ahead regardless. And naked - or nearly so.

*

'Help me unloose the strings of my dress,' said the parrot. Forman turned, apparently believing Rosalind had spoken.

'Certainly,' he said. 'And, look! Here is something to hang your clothing from to guarantee its cleanliness.'

The combination of the situation, the apparent error arising from the parrot's words and a belly-full of saffron - spiced wine would surely have overcome everyone other than a nun, thought Rosalind as she began to loosen her clothing. Within a moment, Forman was behind her, helping. And a few moments after that, Rosalind was standing shivering in her shift. The room was cold. This, combined with the lingering effects of the saffron, made various parts of her flagrantly visible through the sheer linen garment and, she realised at once, if she followed his directions and lay spread in the star shape on the floor, she might as well have been naked in any case. A vision popped into her head of the poor girl in the Tower spread on one of Topcliffe's racks convenient to his lust. Would she be in any better case? Especially were she really a maiden fresh from the country full of Forman's aphrodisiacal saffron wine.

On the other hand, she wondered, what more could she learn by proceeding? Little or nothing, except, perhaps, close acquaintance with his bedroom. Unless she could find a way of wringing a few more drops of unguarded revelation courtesy of John Gerard's distillate of fly agaric.

'And is it only great ladies who come to you for guidance?' she asked, as she crouched, ready to sit at the very heart of the star.

'Of course not! Have I not said? Great men of the court, great men of business and of politics, soldiers and sailors, all come to me for assurance that their various businesses will proceed.'

She sat. Through the flimsy tissue of her linen shift, the floor was icy against the heat of her buttocks and those places nearest to them. She found that she was breathless - either with shock or nervousness.

'And do men as well as women come here, to your occult chamber, to lie within the magic star seeking to know their heart's desire?'

'It is a pentacle, not a star. But it is certainly magic. And yes. Men have sat where you sit now. Great men - though not so many perhaps.'

'Courtiers? For I know many such men have great matters in hand in Ireland and the New World as well as at court. I can hardly imagine Secretary Cecil relying on such things from what little I know of him. But surely there might be others: men who look beyond the commonplaces of everyday philosophy; beyond the Good Book even. *Explorerateurs*, brave soldiers and fearless sailors perhaps, men who have voyaged far afield to the honour and benefit of their country and returned to establish great positions at Her Majesty's side, who hold great estates and great ambitions to accompany them, who might yet need to know how secure their situation is and how future ventures might fare…'

This was far beyond anything a mere country girl might want to know, thought Rosalind, her heart pounding even faster as Forman stood silently looking down at her, his figure strangely inverted as she looked up at him in turn from the floor in front of his toecaps; seeing his strange eyes shining in the shadow beneath his magician's headgear. She spread her arms, feeling her breasts moving on the arches of her ribs. She spread her legs.

'Indeed,' said Forman, his voice strangely constricted, 'men such as you describe have come to seek guidance from the spirits just as you are doing. Three such men within the week that followed Twelfth Night.'

Rosalind wondered whether the drugged and lust-driven sorcerer realised that she had just, in careful detail, described not only Robert Devereux, Earl of Essex but also the red-headed Fox Sir Walter Raleigh and wrung from him clear conformation that one of them - perhaps both of them - had lain where she was lying now. But there had been a third man. Who under Heaven could the third man be?

Chapter 15: The Cunning Fox

i

'I can't see Essex submitting to such a ritual,' said Tom. 'No matter how desperate he is to learn about his heart's desire and the best way to achieve it. To begin with, I think he sees his future clearly. He will take an army to Ireland, defeat Hugh O'Neil and the Irish rebels then return like a modern Henry V to the adulation of London, the thanks of the Queen and limitless addition to his power and standing in the face of the near-destruction of his enemies, especially Secretary Cecil and Sir Walter Raleigh. He's far too proud to go lying on a dirty floor reaching into the points of a star with head, hands and feet; and the idea that he might remove any of his clothing while doing so goes far beyond anything I can conceive of.'

'He might send Gelly Meyrick or Francis Bacon, though,' suggested Ugo. 'Particularly as there are elements of the future you say he sees that are nowhere near as clear as he would like. When will he be commissioned as Lord Lieutenant of Ireland? How large and powerful an army will he be able to assemble? How will the campaign against O'Neal actually go? What will Cecil, Raleigh and their coteries have done to destroy him in the Queen's favour while he's away? You know that all of them can rise or fall on a royal whim; one wrong move and they're banished from her court, company and favour. What will he find when he returns, whenever or however he finally does so? Essex or his representative must be one of the three men who visited Forman.'

'I agree. Francis Bacon's more likely to be sent than Essex to come himself,' said Will. 'The intelligencer Anthony Bacon is too unwell, though he would be the best man to give a glimpse of the future to. Francis Bacon's a pragmatist; he doesn't stand on his dignity like his master does. Besides, he's at least willing to explore beyond the bounds of the everyday; perhaps even of the Bible though I take your point about the clothes, particularly as he follows Tom here in his taste for fashionable black.'

'You know very well,' said Tom, 'that removal of clothes is something Forman reserves for his female clients; the colour of the clothing in question is absolutely irrelevant.'

'The problem is, surely,' added Rosalind, 'that whoever lies in the star - the pentacle as Forman called it - is likely to see their own future rather than that of their master, unless, of course, the two are inextricably intertwined. To the extent that he sees anything in particular at all,' she added as the only person present who had undergone the experience. 'I certainly saw nothing in my future beyond the likelihood of immediate ravishment.'

'Walter Raleigh,' said Tom, 'Walter Raleigh is a different proposition altogether.'

'What,' chuckled Will, 'do you suppose that because he so famously laid his cloak over a puddle so the Queen would not soil her shoes that he would be willing to remove the rest of his clothing in order to see his future?'

'No,' said Tom. 'Rosalind is right. Forman has no interest in causing his male clients to remove one stitch of clothing. It is the women he's after. But, as you mention Raleigh's cloak, would he not happily lay it down in the midst of the pentacle and lie on it himself if some powerful good was promised him because of it? And logic suggests that, men or women, someone must have seen - or believed they have seen - some future good promised to them. If no-one had seen anything Forman would not have such a bustling business with women in particular lining up to have their charts drawn, their potions distilled, their charms blessed or cursed and to take part in his occult practices.'

*

'But again I agree. Raleigh is our second man. Then who's the third?' added Will. ''Tis a shame he did not let more information slip before he moved on with his attempted seduction. Or ravishment, rather. Rosalind was lucky to escape him.'

'It's a wonder,' said Rosalind, 'what can be achieved - even at the door into his bedroom - by a woman suddenly going frantic.'

'You said frenetic, when you first got back to us,' observed Ugo.

'Indeed,' she answered cheerfully. 'There was a sizeable amount of both conditions. When I fell to the floor and started screaming as though in a fit, I thought the man would faint. Clearly all the other poor fools he has conducted through that particular portal either went willingly - addled by wine and saffron or not - or they were too nervous to refuse him at the last moment.'

In the instant of silence that followed, Rosalind took a sip of the fresh water that Will had bought from a local water-seller to celebrate her return and meet the overpowering thirst generated by the concoctions she had been consuming. Tom, meanwhile, filled the silence with wondering whether Kate had followed Forman into his bedroom after her sessions in the occult pentacle and, if so, whether she had done so of her own free will or because she had been entranced by his saffron wine. He could not envisage her submitting to Forman through nervousness at the final moment. On the other hand, Heaven alone knew what she might be willing to do were she acting under orders from Thomas Walsingham or even Robert Poley. Her loyalty, once won, was truly fearsome.

Rosalind cleared her throat then continued, 'He almost fell over himself retrieving my clothing, then he helped me into it with more alacrity every time my screaming quietened, until at last I was dressed and silent, except for the occasional sob. Then he showed me to the door and issued me into Billingsgate as though I had only just *popped* in as the saying goes, for an elixir or potion. But Will is right, there was no further mention of the third visitor.'

ii

It was late afternoon on that same busy Monday. When Rosalind had returned safely from Forman's, Tom and the others had left the Dean's men to take care of the infested body that had miraculously appeared in Queen Katherine's marble tomb. They were all seated round the table in Will and Rosalind's lodgings. Will was more relaxed than Tom had seen him in a while. Not only had Rosalind returned from Forman's safely but his play of *Henry* was now out at the copyist's being put into the character sections and prompt-books that the cast would use as the basis of their rehearsals and performance. He would not become tense and short-tempered again until the actors from Dick Burbage down the cast-list began to suggest improvements to their lines, additions to their importance and augmentations to their parts. But the rehearsal process was still some days off and the mentally exhausted dramatist was content to bask in the glory of a job well done and a woman willing to indulge him. Once, that is, the friends and colleagues gathered here finished talking and left - hopefully before all the effects of John Gerard's saffron potion Rosalind had consumed wore off altogether.

But Tom was not quite ready to let Will and Rosalind have their way with each other yet. 'How did you describe the men whose identities you sought?' he said to her, then answered on her behalf as she was looking longingly at Will, momentarily distracted: 'Brave soldiers, men who hold great estates and great ambitions to accompany them, who might yet need to know how secure their situation is and how future ventures might fare…'

'Indeed,' she confirmed turning back to face him. 'But surely such a description could refer to many men at court and I got no impression that Forman was flooded out with worried courtiers. Men of business yes: men of war, explorers - people whose futures might contain ruin or death on the flip of a coin all seemed to come to have their futures read. But no courtiers apart from the three he failed to name.'

'So we need to look for someone who has either recently arrived at court or someone who has suddenly found themselves in a desperate situation.'

'Or both,' nodded Rosalind.

'Someone recently arrived at court seeking to redress their desperate situation?' suggested Ugo.

'Could it be that obvious?' wondered Will.

'Indeed it could,' said Tom. 'Now how can we establish with some certainty that Edmund Spenser was visiting Simon

Forman in the weeks before his death? He visited me often enough, but only for lessons and although we saw a good deal of each-other, he had ample time alone to do whatever he pleased when we had parted.'

'Forman will know,' said Ugo, 'and there's more than one rack in London if he's hesitant to tell us.'

'But Forman, like my Kate Shelton, is protected,' said Tom, 'not least by Walter Raleigh but probably by others of similar power. Else he would need to have no fear of King James the Witch finder assuming the throne because he'd have gone to the stake already like half of the occultists in Europe or be rotting in jail like Giordano Bruno.'

'But,' said Will, 'as we found out a week or so ago, Forman is surrounded by men of poetical disposition who are by no means noted for their taciturnity.'

'Well thought on, Will,' said Tom. 'I wonder whether John Weever or George Chapman has shared a good supper and a friendly drink with anyone recently.'

*

George Chapman stared across the table at Tom. The poet's face was an interesting mixture of expressions. Largest amongst them - hardly surprisingly - was suspicion. Chapman was not used to being offered free dinners by relative strangers, especially not men involved in situations which also claimed some of the poet's time and loyalty in opposition to those of his would-be host. Then there was the amalgam of personal dislike which lay between them, man to man for no particular reason but potent nevertheless. All this combined with the natural arrogance of a man who considers himself a great artist unrivalled in the fields of poetry and classical translation except, perhaps, (grudgingly) by Will Shakespeare or Sir Thomas North, whether his genius has been recognised yet or not. Further, he was an Oxford man confronted by a graduate from the University of Glasgow an institution he reckoned to be incalculably inferior to his own.

But all of this was more than counterbalanced by the expression on the face of a starving man confronted with a large and fragrant umble pie, and the promise of a haunch of venison from the deer whose umbles - heart, liver and lights - filled the golden crust before him. As the serving woman brought trenchers and horn spoons, Chapman reached for the tall glass of dark yellow Rhenish which Tom had already poured for him. They were seated, aptly enough in the White Hart on Cheapside, though Tom had spent the late afternoon and early evening tracking Chapman to a much less salubrious institution the Black Bitch on Thames Street which seemed to be serving spit-roasted dog and cat not very convincingly disguised as hare and rabbit.

'Surely you saw as much of him as I did towards the end,' said Chapman. 'He came to you for lessons in fencing and referred to you again when other problems arose. Was it not you who referred him to your friend John Gerard when his ear was damaged in a brawl?'

'All that is true enough,' Tom cut into the pie and ladled some of the contents onto Chapman's trencher, heaping the golden crust beside it. Chapman took a draught of wine, watching the feast being piled higher and higher. He wiped the back of his hand across his watering mouth. His stomach growled like the dog he was going to have for dinner before Tom found him. 'But I was not with him every hour of the day,' Tom continued. 'I supposed him to have spent most of his waking hours waiting in the draughty corridors of White Hall and West Minster, hoping to place his proposals before the Council or, once he had done so, praying for a swift and positive response.'

'And what makes you think otherwise now?' Chapman took his spoon and started shovelling the contents of the pie into his mouth. He hardly seemed to chew before he swallowed, washing the mouthful down with the contents of his wine glass. Tom filled it again at once.

'Something Simon Forman said,' he answered.

Chapman frowned. His spoon hesitated half-way to his mouth, but only for an instant. 'You have been talking to Simon Forman? I don't believe it!' he said indistinctly, spraying a little gravy as he articulated the 'b' and the 't'.

'He said it not to me but to a friend of mine,' Tom explained. 'She was consulting him on another matter.'

'Oh!' said Chapman, picking up a solid section of piecrust. 'I *see…*' He leered knowingly. 'A *friend…*' he pushed the pastry into his mouth and continued speaking round it. 'We all know which of your friends most assiduously visits Master Forman!'

'Well,' said Tom easily, though he had not expected this. For it seemed Chapman had automatically assumed they were discussing Kate rather than Rosalind. As was logical - he should have seen it coming. But, he found himself wondering, was this a path he really wanted to pursue? God alone knew where it might lead - or how dangerous it might become.

iii

'Indeed,' said Chapman, airily unaware of Tom's dilemma, 'it seems a certain lady is more often at Forman's than she is anywhere else nowadays.'

'Searching her heart's desire,' said Tom, unable to stop himself. He immediately regretted the words - this was the Tom Musgrave who had fed Kate with John Gerard's fly agaric potion to get information from her at any price. It was not a side of himself that he approved of at all. He considered himself briefly with a good deal of guilt and self-loathing. But here he was, doing the same thing once again.

Chapman smirked; almost gave a knowing wink, picked up a sizeable portion of steaming deer's offal piled on a slab of crust, stuffed it in his mouth and reached for his wine glass. 'It almost makes you wonder, does it not, whether she has in fact discovered her heart's desire - and found it under Simon Forman's roof.' *And perhaps in Simon Forman's bed* remained mercifully unsaid, but even the implication was deadly dangerous.

In the recent past, such a suggestion would have led to a challenge and a swift death for the poet who had impugned the lady's honour. But Tom had engineered this in more ways than one - by searching for Chapman throughout the late afternoon; by finding Chapman at last, by feeding Chapman, by guiding the conversation along that unexpected byway and, most of all, by plying him with wine laced with fly agaric.

In vino veritas - in wine the truth, Tom thought; it was not Chapman's fault if he didn't like the truth he seemed to be hearing. *Seemed to be hearing* because of course, Kate's visits to Forman's might be, as he had already considered, at Sir Thomas' behest or on Poley's orders or even - it now occurred to him - on the orders of the Council. Consider the roles that Poley and Parrot played in the Marshalsea, equivocating confessions out of catholic sympathisers by pretending to be of the Old Religion themselves. Could not Kate be equivocating information out of Forman? But what information? To what purpose? And at whose behest?

'There's the rub,' he whispered to himself.

'Don't be downhearted,' said Chapman with very evident enjoyment. 'It has happened to better men that us. Consider Menelaus, his Helen, she of the face that launched a thousand ships, ravished away by another voyager; even Zeus was cuckolded by Hera who bore Hephaestus as a result...'

*

'Your sympathy would be moving were there any need for it,' said Tom, keeping his voice level with an effort. 'But I am here to discuss other matters. You wrote and recited a moving elegy to Edmund Spenser a week ago...'

'A great poet; a dreadful loss...' Chapman schooled his face into a mournful expression which for Tom simply did not ring true.

'Especially now he's dead and cannot eclipse you or any of your friends,' spat Tom, mildly surprised to discover that Chapman had managed to goad him after all.

The poet drew himself up, trying for an aspect of righteous outrage but he was defeated by the gravy dribbling copiously into his beard and the fact that he was reaching for more pie before the performance was anywhere near complete. He hesitated, spoon in the air and reached for his glass with his free hand.

'You and Forman organised the eulogies,' said Tom. 'Under direction from the Earl of Essex I assume, as he was in over-all charge of the funeral.'

'Indeed,' Chapman nodded, perhaps a little too energetically. His stool rocked and his backside came close to sliding off it. He steadied himself against the table with his spoon hand. The contents of the spoon ran unnoticed over his hand, onto his wrist and into the already grubby lace of his cuffs.

'I had heard,' continued Tom, 'that the Earl's request was particularly apposite because Spenser had been consulting Forman in any case.'

'Once or twice,' Chapman waved his spoon hand airily. This time the braised offal it had contained landed on the table where it started to congeal.

'Only once or twice?' said Tom. 'I had heard that his visits were quite regular - almost as regular as his visits to White Hall and West Minster.'

'To begin with, perhaps but not so later on.' Chapman leaned forward conspiratorially. His elbow went into the mess he had dropped on the table-top. 'Not after the incident and the accident, you see.

'Ah yes, the accident,' said Tom. 'The poor apprentice… Hal I think his name was…'

'No! NO! Not the stupid boy! The accidental discovery! The discovery of the secret! Don't you understand? The secret! If word of *that* had got out, he would have been ruined. He came so close to it the first time...'

Chapman's mouth closed even as his eyes widened. His nostrils flared. Now that his hunger was at least partly assuaged, the look of suspicion returned to his face. A third trencher arrived, this one piled with slices of venison. 'Water,' said Chapman to the serving woman. 'Bring a jug of fresh water.'

The interrogation was clearly at an end.

Tom sat back, mind racing. Elements of his investigation were falling into place now but not in a way that he liked. He refused to tie up any more loose ends without checking the truth of what Chapman was saying and of the disturbing conclusions he was beginning to draw from them. In the meantime, he had paid for dinner and he wanted to enjoy it. 'I read your *De Guiana*,' he said. 'A fine work. Did Sir Walter gain much support for his adventures in the New World through it? More adventurers keen to start new lives in the Roanoke settlement?'

'Less than he had hoped,' said Chapman grudgingly. 'And there's something amiss at Roanoke in any case. But he agrees: it is a fine work.'

'And your translation of Homer. How does that proceed?'

'Well enough.'

'That is where your true immortality will lie, I believe, though I see *The Blind Beggar of Alexandria* which played so well at The Rose last year is in print at last on Jaggard's stall at St Paul's.'

'But not my poetry, you believe?'

'Your work for Sir Walter is as fine as any I have seen in print and I know you have completed Marlowe's unfinished *Hero and Leander* to much acclaim. But in my mind your work on Homer towers over even Sir Thomas North's translation of Plutarch.'

'Which he culled out of the French by Bishop Amyot of Auxerre as I suppose you know. I however, have reached back to the original; as is required to my mind by *true* scholarship such as Sir Walter truly appreciates…'

iv

Tom walked back along Cheapside from the White Hart deep in thought as the night settled down all around him. Chapman's assumption that Kate was a regular visitor to Billingsgate because Forman had somehow managed to add her to his long list of seductions rankled. Tom could only see three ways of finding the truth of the matter for certain. First, he could ask Kate herself - with or without feeding her fly agaric first. Then he could ask Forman either in person or by rifling his library to search out something such as a journal containing the truth. Thirdly, he could ask whichever spymaster was currently controlling her - Poley or Sir Thomas Walsingham - for the facts as far as they knew them. None of these approaches seemed in any way satisfactory for, with the possible exception of Forman's journal - if such a thing existed - he could not guarantee that anyone he questioned would actually tell him the truth.

That was as far as he had got in his deliberations when he was disturbed by a commotion down a darkening side-street. Without thinking, he turned aside and walked towards the melee. As he drew nearer, he could see that a small group of boys had cornered a cat and were doing their best to stone it to death. But the cat wasn't going down without a fight, a fact that was illuminated by a torch blazing in a sconce above the battlefield. Yowling and screaming defiance, the creature dodged as many stones as it could and hurled itself forward at the skipping, jeering boys. A couple of them had torn stockings and clawed shins, which certainly explained why they were stoning rather than clubbing it. As he drew nearer still, he saw the explanation of the cat's bravery. In the corner behind it, just visible in the shadows, cowered a kitten. The tiny creature had been lucky to escape injury so far but Tom had little doubt that as soon as its protector - probably its mother - was disposed of the boys would make short work of it.

Culling the wild cats that infested the city was a popular enough sport, though it ranked below cock-fighting, ratting and dog-fighting in the majority of public houses and, of course, the grand public spectacles of Bull- and Bear-baiting. But tonight at least, Tom was minded to put a stop to this particular cull. 'You boys!' he bellowed. 'Be off with you before I summon the watch!'

They were young enough to believe that he would bother to carry out such a threat - or that the watch would turn out to save a mere cat if he did so. They took to their heels and Tom strolled over to the objects of their cruelty. The mother was not quite full-grown, he guessed, for she was thin but not scrawny and there were still muscles defined below her sleek black pelt. But she had already suffered many of the hurts she fought to save her kitten from. Her face had been clawed. One eye was missing, as was the ear above it. The remaining ear was tall and pointed; the eye beneath it as green and clear as the ocean. There were scars on her shoulders and flanks - put there, he guessed, by whichever tom-cat had mounted her most recently. The boys' stones had done further damage to her face and flanks. And one of her forelegs was clearly hurt. As he stooped to look at her more closely, she attacked with all the ferocity of which she was capable, spitting and snarling as she clawed at his boots. He stooped, reached behind her, picked up the kitten by the scruff of its neck then walked away carrying it. The kitten spat and snarled and clawed as fiercely as its mother, but it could only claw the air, for it was facing away from Tom. After half a dozen steps, Tom looked back. The mother cat was limping silently along behind him, vanishing from sight now and again as her totally black shape was consumed by deepening shadows, leaving only that one green eye to gleam like an emerald floating magically six inches up in the air.

*

'Does she really need a name?' asked Rosalind. 'She's a stray cat. The Lord alone knows what prompted you to bring her and her kitten home…'

'But now that he has,' interjected Ugo, 'she's adopted us. She knows a soft bed when she finds one and she won't leave it until she's made to.'

It was mid morning next day, Tuesday 23rd. Will had already visited The Globe and discovered that rehearsing *Henry* took second place to thatching the roof - and in any case the copyists had not quite finished yet. So he had retired to his lodging and resumed work on *Caesar* - though he had vouchsafed to Rosalind that he also had some promising ideas for his new version of *Hamlet* - which she had taken as a plea to be left alone while he got on with his work.

Rosalind arrived at Tom's fencing school not only looking for company but also because Will was due to have a lesson there just before lunch and she planned to watch the lesson then spend the afternoon with him - if he remembered to turn up in the first place. She had become involved in the debate about the cat almost at once.

The subject of the discussion was curled on an old cloak in the corner with her kitten at her side. A partly-consumed saucer of milk lay in front of them above which that one green eye gleamed, daring anyone except Tom to approach with anything other than food.

With her mind still full of yesterday's adventures, Rosalind said, 'Very well. If she stays you should name her after a demon. Look at her - not one white hair amongst the black; that face; that one-eyed glare. And yet there is something about her, recent motherhood perhaps or the scars of the kitten's begetting. I think she should be called Astaroth.'

'*Astaroth*,' Ugo echoed. 'You name her for the demon of Lust? Let no-one hear you call her that or it's the ducking chair, the pricking and the stake or the noose for you! Astaroth is the name of a witch's familiar if ever I heard one! Dear God in heaven and we're due to have a Scottish witch-finder as our king when Queen Elizabeth dies!'

'Were I you,' said a new voice, a virile baritone with a soft West-country burr, 'I'd be a sight more careful about discussing the Queen's death than about naming a cat after a demon!'

The three humans and Astaroth looked up. Rosalind caught her breath. The man in the doorway who had come upon them almost as soundlessly as the cat could have done was tall, lean, wearing some 47 years as easily as he wore his fashionable clothing and his long rapier. The red curls of his hair and beard were without a trace of grey; his keen brown eyes were edged with the wrinkles that only come from smiling broadly and gazing on far horizons. His cheek bones were high and sharp, his nose long and straight. His full lips were twisted in a slight, ironic grin. Rosalind knew well enough who he was but she had never been this close to him before. Never felt the power of his personality; almost the heat of his presence bringing a blush to her cheeks. She wondered for an instant whether the saffron was still coursing through her veins shortening her breath and moistening her lips even as it dried her throat.

It was Walter Raleigh.

V

'I apologise for appearing thus unannounced, Master Musgrave,' said Raleigh. 'But I bring our agreement written down and payment for our work so far. I know my next lesson is not until Wednesday but I had an hour to spare and wondered, Master Musgrave, whether you are available…'

'Until Will Shakespeare's lesson at noon,' said Tom rising. 'I am at your service, Sir Walter.'

The two men strode shoulder to shoulder into Tom's fencing room. Under Rosalind's lingering gaze it seemed that they were equally matched - broad shoulders, trim waists, long, muscular limbs. But then her view was blocked as Tom closed the door behind them.

Both men stripped off their upper garments, piling them on chairs convenient for the purpose, hangers and scabbards on the top. In a matter of moments they were in shirt-sleeves, broad belts supporting galligaskins whose wide turn-ups brushed the tops of tall leather boots. Ugo appeared with a pair of practise foils but Raleigh waved him away. 'I prefer to practise with my true blade,' he said. 'I have always done so. If a master such as this and a pupil such as myself cannot avoid hitting each-other, then at least one of us is in the wrong place.' He eased his shoulders as he crossed to the chair and slid his rapier out of its scabbard, cutting it through the air as he eased his wrist and forearm, making it hiss and sing.

Tom, who was pulling on his fencing gloves, caught Ugo's eye and motioned for him to leave before slipping his own hand into the Ferrara silver basket around the hilt of his own rapier, reaching past the heavy pommel that helped to balance the long steel blade, curling a finger round the spur of metal that felt almost like a trigger, and sliding the German-made Solingen steel blade free. Capo Ferro said that the sword should be the same length as its owner's arm, and so this one was - made especially for him. Frowning with deepening concern, he went through his own stretching routine; he knew the late Bonetti only slightly but he could not believe the Italian sword-master would have allowed lessons with naked blades.

No matter how Tom considered meeting Raleigh's request, he could see nothing but ill coming from it. But refusing the demands of a new student - especially one such as the man preparing to face him now - would damage, perhaps destroy, his business. Just as, he thought, falling foul of the Queen's favour

- as he had done to great cost in the past - could destroy Sir Walter himself. He looked up, caught a glance at his reflection in the long mirror and swiftly schooled his face into a more amenable expression.

So at last he turned to face Raleigh, who had already assumed the *terza* guard, hilt level with the top of his thigh, pommel in front of his hip, blade pointing upward and inward. Those steady brown eyes met Tom's bright blue ones, neither man able to read the other's intentions as yet. Tom took up the same guard, keeping back in the *mesura largo* wide measure from which the blades could be engaged with a thrust, but the opponents could only strike each-other with a lunge, moving forward one step or skipping forward two.

Feet planted firmly - to begin with at least - the two men thrust and parried increasingly swiftly. Once again Tom was impressed with Raleigh's technique. He used the *debole* or more flexible part of the blade behind the point for his attacks and the stronger *forte* nearest the handle to turn aside Tom's attacks in *riposte*. Both men, it seemed, were fortunate in the strength of their wrists the clarity of their vision and the speed of their reactions. The *phrases d' armes* became swifter and the rests between them shorter. The guards from which the attacks were launched varied from middling *terza* to high *prima* and low *quarta*, from *open* to *closed*. At last Raleigh stepped back. Tom straightened and courteously stepped back in precise measure to his opponent's movements.

'This will get us nowhere,' said Raleigh. 'We need to come to narrow measure, or at least put aside mere thrusting to liberate the lunge. Come to *close quarters* as we sailors say. That will test our mettle will it not?'

'And quite possibly show us the colour of our blood.'

'I've seen enough of my own blood in the past,' said Raleigh. 'And a great deal more of other men's.'

'I've seen enough of mine as well,' nodded Tom, 'but not as much of other men's as you, Sir Walter.'

'You are young,' said Raleigh after a moment's pause as the ghost of the slaughter at Smerwick lay between them. 'You'll see more as you grow older. If you do grow older, of course.'

*

Tom returned to the wide measure, assumed Capo Ferro's preferred *terza* guard and waited, every fibre of his being focused on Raleigh. Raleigh also assumed the *terza* guard but only for a heartbeat. No sooner had he settled than he leaped forward, his right foot reaching out while his left foot and left hand balanced the lunge that sped the point of his rapier straight for Tom's right eye.

Tom collected the *debole* on his blade's *forte* and turned it aside but the point sped so close to his right ear that he heard it hiss through the air. Raleigh disengaged and stepped back - but only half as far as he had stepped forward in his lunge. They were close together now, in the measure Capo Ferro called *strettisima* where either man could wound or kill the other with a thrust without resorting to the lunge. This close, thrusts were not only deadly but also dazzlingly swift once more. Raleigh and Tom were of similar size and reach. Their blades also similar in length and temper - Solingen steel against the finest Toledo metal. The first part of the bout had proved that they were equal in speed and technique - save that, as Tom already knew, Raleigh favoured the school of Agrippa, who was particularly popular with the older generation; or those not seduced by George Silver's fanatical patriotism and rabid defence of English weapons and techniques even though they were little changed from the battlefield at Bosworth.

The only real difference was that Raleigh seemed to be trying to kill Tom while Tom was working hard to extend the bout for as long as he could in the hope that the older man would tire. As Raleigh had already calculated, Tom was in no position to do his new pupil any serious damage. No damage at all, in fact, whereas Raleigh could do what he liked to Tom and walk away unquestioned.

Even though Raleigh was of the Agrippa school, he was impetuous and impatient; he soon resorted to an *attaccare di spada*, pushing the *forte* of his blade against Tom's with all his might in the hope of shoving it out of line and out of the way. This was unexpected, for it was a technique Agrippa disapproved of. No doubt therefore Bonetti had warned against it as well. But given the closeness of their bodies and the speed of the bout, it was a logical move to use, especially if Raleigh was at last beginning to tire. Even so, it nearly took Tom by surprise.

Tom answered with a *cederi*, apparently yielding to the pressure, but then *voiding*, or stepping out of line as he had with the first attack. Raleigh was surprised in turn and stepped forward, his own sword out of line now. Tom thrust almost automatically, his blade a streak of steely lightning. Which would have laid Raleigh's face open along the left cheekbone had he not turned it aside at the last moment. Then he stepped back, resumed a high *prima* guard and waited.

'You see?' said Raleigh softly, his voice steady, his breathing easy. 'I have you *over a barrel* as we sailors say. You cannot afford to hurt someone as powerful as me while I can crush you as I would crush a worm in ship's pork. If I die, the Queen will demand full justice. If you die no-one will notice.'

'Why?' asked Tom.

'I thought you were the Master of Logic. I'm sure you can work it out!'

Raleigh attacked again as he said the last sentence, this time *sotto mano*, an underhand thrust rising dangerously under Tom's blade towards his chest. It was delivered *dalla spalla* from the shoulder with enormous speed and force. Tom saw it coming, however, and moved an inch or so to the side, allowing the blade to graze his ribs while he answered with an *imbroccata* downward thrust that would have opened the great blood vessels near the groin, high on the inside of the Raleigh's thigh. It would have, had Tom not allowed the point to waver.

Raleigh gave a shout of laughter. He disengaged. Stepped back. Stepped back again, all arrogant overconfidence, then, with amazing speed, from a position that seemed closest to the *quarta* low fourth guard he hopped and stepped lithely forward into the *passata sotto*, lowest of the lunges, his point aimed unwaveringly at Tom's groin in a dangerously accomplished reflection of the sword master's last attack.

Tom twisted out of the way so the point of Raleigh's sword just missed the outside of his thigh as the blade hissed across his stout galligaskins. But he had dismissed all thoughts of the blade the moment he understood the nature of Raleigh's counter-attack - one that his own high guard made more tempting, particularly as he had just demonstrated how to do it. Now he twisted back again. Raleigh, fully extended, had his chest on his right thigh, his thigh low to the floor with his leading foot surprisingly close to Tom's. The point of his beard, therefore, was level with Tom's hip; his head less than an arm's length distant, and caught in that position until Raleigh, dangerously overextended, found a way to recover.

Which Tom was not about to allow him to do; instead, he brought the pommel of his sword down onto the back of Raleigh's red-haired skull with all the force at his command and the weight of the vertical rapier above it. Then he stepped back and allowed Queen Elizabeth's Captain of the Guard to collapse onto the floor, completely unconscious.

PETER TONKIN

Chapter 16: The Angry Ape

i

Lord Robert Cecil, Secretary to the Council, Chancellor of the Duchy of Lancaster, MP for Hertfordshire and the Queen's most trusted advisor, drew himself up and squared his shoulders. He was seated in a high chair so the movement was more effective than it might otherwise have been. Certainly it reduced the effect of his hunched back and disguised the fact that his legs, which were invisible beneath the table, didn't quite reach the floor. For a moment it seemed that his twisted, stunted frame was equal to that of the figure seated opposite him, as though an ape was managing to mirror a man.

Lord Robert's face was folded into a thunderous frown, his slightly protuberant, fiercely intelligent eyes seemed to glint with anger and the bejewelled fingers on the table-top folded into surprisingly large fists. 'So, that's what I'm to tell Her Majesty is it?' he snarled. 'That her favorite poet might have been murdered by her favorite playwright using poison apparently purchased from my own personal horticulturalist - as witnessed by an apprentice who has just turned up as though by magic dead and rotting in the tomb of Henry Vth's wife Queen Katherine in Westminster Abbey!'

The man opposite, the intelligencer Robert Poley, nodded. His mouth opened and closed but no words came out.

'It's a tale worthy of Mother Hubberd herself,' continued Lord Robert angrily. 'But I fear the Queen will not be amused by it - any more than I am!'

'Shakespeare seemed to be a likely culprit at first,' said Robert Poley uneasily, 'though the accusation was little more than rumour in the absence of the witness Hal'.

Poley had in fact been uneasy ever since Cecil had told him to sit down - something unique in his experience and somehow, therefore, threatening. A threat compounded by the fact that the meeting was being held for the first time in the intelligencer's experience, in Cecil's newly-built mansion Salisbury House, overlooking the Thames on the southern side of the Strand, immediately across the road from his childhood home Burghley

House which now belonged to his tall, straight-backed, good-looking elder brother.

Everything looked new, smelt new, felt new. There were distant noises suggesting strongly that some parts of the great mansion were so new that they hadn't actually been finished yet. The only old thing in this room was a portrait of Lord Robert's father in his robes as Lord High Treasurer painted by Marcus Gheeraerts the Younger in a massive gilt frame that towered behind the twisted, dwarfish, simian form of his second son.

'It was rumoured that this Hal, Gerard's apprentice, would have been able to identify Shakespeare as buying herbal poisons that killed Spenser, and - as the involvement of the Earl Marshal and his pursuivants seemed to make clear - there appeared to be a Catholic connection,' Poley continued.

'A secretly Catholic or Catholic-leaning Shakespeare killing a stoutly Protestant Spenser - the recently dispossessed landlord and Crown official very active in the Irish war whose home may well still be smouldering above the corpse of his slaughtered child. And performing this murder on secret orders from Hugh O'Neal and his rebels, who would have been damaged - to say the least - had Spenser's proposals been adopted by the Council and the revolting population simply starved into submission. Or their women and children starved at least: famine as a weapon of war - an interesting reinvention of an old idea, but Spenser was always a classicist and Shakespeare has always been suspect. Given his links to the Earl of Southampton whose father at least had dangerously Catholic tendencies - a Catholic wife and family - Shakespeare is clearly open to suspicion, then there are his activities in the North. That's a convincing case at first glance - almost enough to call in Topcliffe and his racks.'

*

'We took Shakespeare to the Marshalsea instead, my Lord. Pursuivant Gauge, Parrot and I all questioned him, formally and informally; our undercover priest and equivocator tempted him without result. He refused to celebrate mass and be granted absolution on three different occasions. It's all noted in my report to the Council. All we established was that he is almost certainly not the Shakeshaft who tutored children in Catholic households across the North - before serving in the Low Countries and moving to London on his return as we know Shakespeare did. We know that the third Earl of Southampton, Shakespeare's patron, has been brought up as ward of some of Her Majesty's most trusted courtiers and scrubbed clean of the sins of his father in the process. And we established that he did not purchase any poison from anyone and knows absolutely nothing about Spenser's death.'

'Not this Shakeshaft, tutor to the Hoghton children you say? Despite the similarity of the name?'

'Shakespeare is a common enough name in the West Country and in the North, with a range of local variations - Shakeshaft, Shakebolt, Shackle, Shakleton, Shakehell, Shaddock - Shakehands and Shakepizzle for all I know… '

'Enough!' snapped Cecil and Poley regretted the unfortunately-timed levity of his last two suggestions. Nervousness was the only explanation. He took a deep breath and fought for more self-control. 'So, if not Shakespeare, then who killed Spenser?' Lord Robert demanded.

'This is where it becomes more delicate, My Lord. Our discussions and explorations reveal quite clearly that there are likely to be two levels of guilt: to wit, the man who ordered it done and the man who did it. The men likely to have given the orders being courtiers of great power and influence.'

'Of which I can readily call to mind a hundred or so. I presume you managed to create a short-list?'

'Of four, Lord Robert. Yourself…' Poley paused for a heartbeat expecting an explosion. When none came, he proceeded. 'Sir Walter Raleigh, the Earl of Essex and Sir Thomas Walsingham.'

'I assume my name was on the list for the briefest moment and then your sanity returned?'

ii

Poley gritted his teeth. But he was Lord Robert's chief intelligencer and the Secretary expected nothing less than the truth. A tantrum from Lord Robert now would lead to a generous apology later - as long as Poley was not imprisoned, deported, murdered or beheaded in the interim. 'You and Sir Walter were first on the list and remained there longest,' he said. 'Our thinking being that you were both mocked in *Mother Hubberd's Tale* even through chance and ill fortune given the poem is so old that its original targets are long dead. However, we thought you might, understandably, desire revenge for the insult, especially if it threatened to cause damage to your standing and favour in Her Majesty's eyes.'

'So I am still on the list am I?'

'Not really, my Lord.'

'A great relief! May I ask why? My honest, open nature? My famous aversion to unnecessary violence? My notable Christian charity and reverent lifestyle? My trusted position at Her Majesty's side?'

'Because if you were to proceed with Spenser's murder, then I would be the man commissioned to perform it, my Lord. And if not me, then someone of my acquaintance - Ingram Frizer perhaps or Nic Skeres. But I didn't do it. No-one I know did it. Therefore you did not order it, my Lord.'

'Logical, if singularly unflattering. This was all your own reasoning was it?'

Uncharacteristically, Poley sought to shuffle off a little responsibility, though he had a twinge of conscience recalling his conversation with Shakespeare in the Marshalsea about blaming others for your own transgressions. 'Thomas Musgrave was first to come to that conclusion, my lord.'

'And he became involved *why*?'

Poley explained, at some length.

'And Sir Thomas Walsingham? What good could he pretend?' Lord Robert took up the inquisition some time later.

'None that we can see. And certainly his representative, Kate Shelton, is as firm as adamant that he could never be involved. He has no ties to Ireland and he is as you know, active in courtship of King James in Scotland through Audrey his wife who is bosom companion to the Scottish Queen Anne of Denmark.' Poley decided not to remark upon the fact that Lord Robert and the Privy Council to which he was Secretary were exploring a Scottish succession themselves, and often via Lady Audrey into the bargain. Open discussion of such things, as he had already observed, could come close to being treason. 'Sir Thomas' power and position are assured if the succession goes that way,' Poley continued. 'But he is also proof against any other eventuality. Nor is he mocked in any part of *Mother Hubberd's Tale*. He is inviolate - no harm can come to him from any of this. We can see no reason at all for him to bestir himself in the matter of Spenser's death.'

'Which, to a cynical mind, might suggest that we should place him at the head of the list. Not, I have to say, that I would trust one word proceeding from Kate Shelton's mouth. But let us proceed...'

*

'The Earl of Essex does not seem to feature in *Mother Hubberd's Tale*, but he has other motivation and also has access to a range of men ready, willing and able to carry out any murderous act he wants: Sir Gelly Meyrick, the Bacon brothers to name but a few. As to precise motivation, we wondered, for instance, whether he might be desperate enough to think that Spenser's death could prompt the Queen into moving more decisively in the matter of confirming him as Lord Lieutenant of Ireland and allowing him to lead his army there. There was an added element of course as Spencer was Sheriff of Cork. If a Catholic plot to carry out the murder could be established, then Her Majesty and her Council might well be moved to retaliate by confirming Essex' commission.'

'And he has been all afire and increasingly desperate to get to Ireland for these last six months at least. But is that all your reasoning for this?'

'No my Lord, we though there was more. The supposition we have just discussed that Shakespeare has Catholic leanings.'

'You would have to work harder to convince me of this, especially after what we have just said on that matter. Perhaps you need The Master of Logic to help you as Thomas Musgrave seems to be involved already.'

Poley chose to ignore the jibe. 'Furthermore, if that was Essex's plan, he certainly added power to it by the public spectacle he made of the funeral. This unquestionably succeeded in attracting Her Majesty's attention - but not, perhaps, in the way he intended. His two major responsibilities clashed, it seems. His responsibilities as putative Lord Lieutenant of Ireland were overridden by those as Earl Marshal. Instead of granting him his coveted command, she has simply demanded that he find the truth of what happened to Spenser. And, it now appears, that he will not be allowed to depart for Ireland until he has cleared the matter up to Her Majesty's satisfaction.'

'Not only Her Majesty's,' purred Lord Robert. 'To the Council's as well.'

'But my Lord, if you, the Council and her Majesty are relying on Essex as Earl Marshal to bring everything to light, why am I still employed in the matter?' wondered Poley.

'You know very well that there are several reasons. First, you as Pursuivant Marshal, a viper in his bosom, are a good measure of how desperate the Earl is and I am happy to keep reminding him of that fact.'

'Furthermore,' added Poley, 'if he is sufficiently desperate to gain your support that he continues to let me assume the post of Pursuivant Marshal, then we should keep careful watch for other favours he might be willing to do for other powerful men?'

Cecil folded his hands, right over left on the table and leaned forward above them. 'Precisely. But even more importantly, because, no matter what Robert Devereux discovers - or pretends he has discovered - I want to know the truth. It is like something I learned during my studies at the Sorbonne - a good lawyer never asks a question he doesn't already know the answer to.'

iii

'Finally,' said Robert Poley, 'we come to Sir Walter Raleigh…'

'Currently nursing a sore head all alone and lonely in Durham House if my information is correct. As of course it is. His household may have gone to Sherborne with his wife but there are still one or two servants remaining who I keep fee'd to watch him.'

'I know nothing of his sore head, my Lord, but I am well aware that Lady Raleigh, the family and almost all of the servants set out for Sherborne soon after Twelfth Night. Other than that, nothing. Except that, like Essex, he has a circle of men around him - the School of Night - any one of which is capable of the act and at least one of whom might well have supplied the poisons used.'

'Well, let us start with Raleigh where we started with Sir Thomas - what good would it do him to see Spenser dead?'

As succinctly as possible, Poley ran through the burden of the various discussions he had been party to.

Raleigh's finances - which were not quite as desperate as Chapman's but under enormous strain. His Irish estates that currently yielded so little - so convenient to Spenser's which Raleigh therefore coveted both together being worth a great deal as capital and as regular income if Essex could settle the rebellion.

His absolute reliance on the Queen's good graces, still by no means guaranteed after his time in the Tower and years of effective exile because of his marriage to Bess Throckmorton - now, as Lady Raleigh, removed from London altogether.

Those good graces possibly further strained - and to the breaking point - by his identification as The Fox in *Mother Hubberd's Tale*; the cunning backstabber willing to do anything to gain preferment - including stealing Royal robes, accoutrements and power. In this case, stealing them not for his own use but for Lady Arbella Stuart or the Infanta of Spain, both of whom he was considering as worthy, Catholic, successors to the throne.

Finally, to come full-circle, Sir Walter stood at the heart of a coterie of dangerous free-thinkers, whose discussions were at least impious, perhaps heretical and who could certainly be murderous if called upon. The group christened by Shakespeare as The School of Night - a name that clung - to the increasing damage of all concerned. Especially if King James did succeed

Queen Elizabeth to the throne with his famously negative attitude to anything smacking of the occult or witchcraft.

'Well,' said Lord Robert after Poley had finished. 'I could hardly separate Essex and Raleigh by the thinnest sheet of parchment. Both could be equally guilty in my eyes. Both have means and motivation - and a host of acolytes willing to obey their every wish. And, now I think of it, I do not discount Sir Thomas Walsingham because of his seeming innocence. He is equally powerful, equally capable and equally well-served - dear God, Ingram Frizer is his man of business as Nicholas Skeres is one of Essex' household and you above all know that they are capable of killing without a second thought.' Cecil paused, looking calculatingly at Poley who was equally as capable of murder as the other two. And Poley was being careful not to mention that all this was equally true of Lord Robert - who might, in fact, have access to murderous men beyond Poley's acquaintance.

Lord Robert broke into the intelligencer's thoughts. 'What is your next move in the matter?'

'I must continue to discuss what we already know, my Lord, while searching for yet more clues.'

'I'm afraid you cannot discuss it with me. The Tuesday meeting of the Council will be in session within the hour and I'm bound for West Minster.'

'In that case, my Lord,' said Poley who had had no intention of discussing anything further with Lord Robert anyway, 'I will have to find someone else to discuss the matter with.'

'If I were you, Poley,' advised Lord Robert, 'I'd talk to Tom Musgrave.'

*

'What are the motives for murder?' wondered Tom. 'It stands high amongst the greatest sins and leads straight down the primrose path to the everlasting bonfire. Why do people do it?'

'For reasons as many and various as there are men and women committing the crime,' said Will. 'History provides a million examples all bound together by one thing - to wit the presence of Evil in the world.' He looked over his shoulder and surreptitiously crossed himself as though naming Evil could

277

summon the Devil. But the only things behind him were the fireplace with Astaroth purring contentedly beside it at his right shoulder and the door though to Tom's class-room immediately at his back.

'A logical place to start,' said Tom, seated at the table beside him, his back to the fire and the somnolent cat. 'Go on.'

'Evil entered the world through the Garden of Eden when the Serpent tempted Eve and she tempted Adam,' said Will. 'Original Sin as the Old Religion has it. Total Depravity according to the new philosophy - according to Calvin at least. Through the fault of a woman.'

'But murder did not enter the world until Cain slew Abel,' countered Rosalind sitting at Will's left hand, across the table from Tom. 'Murder is therefore the province of men.'

'Though women might also prove capable of it,' said Will, 'if they overcome their natural natures - by appealing to the Devil or the Powers of Darkness to… I don't know… *unsex* them somehow.'

'And so we arrive at witchcraft,' said Poley, who sat at the inner end of the table beside Ugo. 'That didn't take long.'

It was later that afternoon, approaching day's end and suppertime. Poley's arrival at Tom's lodging had prompted the discussion they were currently having but it was Tom who had suggested that rather than go over what little evidence they had in the matter they should go back to basics - to Aristotle's *primum movens* or first cause. And the closest they could come to that was the Bible.

'But why did Cain kill Abel?' wondered Rosalind.

'God preferred Abel's sacrifice of a lamb to Cain's sacrifice of fruits from the harvest,' said Ugo.

'So he was motivated by envy and rage,' said Tom. 'I see what you're driving at.' He looked down at Astaroth who was purring contentedly as she suckled her kitten, some scraps from Tom's long-consumed luncheon on the saucer in front of her. 'Then there's lust. King David's sin and the reason he had Uriah the Hittite murdered so he could come to his wife Bathsheba.'

'That's King Claudius' motivation in the old play of *Hamlet*, added Will. 'Or part of it at least. He kills his brother the King

278

so he can take his throne as well as his wife and sister in law to his bed. I'm still working on Prince Hamlet's motivation for killing the old advisor Corambis, though. Mad rage seems likely…'

iv

'Leaving the Bible and the wisdom of the theatre, sane or otherwise, to one side for the moment,' suggested Poley. 'Machiavel suggests in *Il Pricipe* that a Prince should seem peaceful and supportive in public while in private or in secret he murders a range of subjects who are or could be opponents to his reign.'

'As King Claudius does in *Ham*…' Will began then he caught Poley's eye.

'That is murder, not through fear as such, but through policy,' the intelligencer continued. 'And yet, I would suggest we could call it fear of opposition.'

'So,' said Tom, 'we have rage, envy, fear and lust.'

'And we have Cicero's *cui bono*,' said Will. 'Murder for benefit…'

'By which I guess we could mean money,' suggested Ugo.

'More than that,' suggested Rosalind, 'someone who has committed an act in secret that they fear will be unmasked in public might benefit from security - the knowledge that the dead victim can no longer expose him; an ordinary mortal might well think that as well as any king or prince.'

'There's probably a sub-section on that in *Il Principe*,' said Tom. 'Not to mention an entire act in *Hamlet*. How a king - or any man, indeed - with secret murders hanging on him must keep on killing to avoid discovery. Though of course kings and other men of power would suborn others to do the deed rather than wielding the knife themselves as we have already discussed. What do you think, Poley?'

'I think we are building quite a list,' answered Poley smoothly. 'Rage, envy, fear, lust, political ambition and security against discovery. And, of course security against poverty which is just another term for greed - or, as Ugo pointed out - money.'

'That more or less covers the seven deadly sins,' said Ugo.

'Except for Pride - Satan's own sin,' said Tom. 'And the one that many elders warn is the most deadly of all. Consider how any one of our suspects could be so proud that he would think nothing of snuffing out an inconvenient life as though it were indeed the merest candle-flame.'

'Well, now that we have the list, what should be the next step?' wondered Will.

'To order them in such a manner as to put at the head of the list those motives that seem most likely - both in theory and in our specific case,' said Tom.

'Pride,' said Poley, recounting the list in no particular order, 'then rage, envy, fear, lust, greed, political ambition and security against discovery. Any of the men on our list could be motivated by one or more of these. They are all proud, most are easily provoked to rage; lustful, politically ambitious; greedy for power as well as desperate for money - though some more so than others; envious of others who appear to have more of these things than they do; desirous of being protected against discovery having committed various sins and solecisms that must never be brought to Her Majesty's attention.'

*

'So,' said Tom, perhaps it's time to re-approach the problem more directly. We are looking for a man who is proud, easily provoked, lustful, politically ambitious; greedy for power as well as desperate for money; perhaps envious of others who appear to have more than he does; desirous of being protected against discovery having committed some act that must never be brought to Her Majesty's attention.'

'Both Essex and Raleigh fit that description,' said Poley. 'As Lord Robert observed, no more than the thinnest sheet of parchment separating them.'

'The similarities do not stop there,' continued Tom. 'They have both - either directly or indirectly and in deathly secret - been seeking occult guidance from Simon Forman.'

'Which means that either one could have easy access to the poisons he concocts,' added Rosalind.

'The only problem being,' said the ever-practical Ugo, 'that if they have a fearsome secret that they will kill to keep from the Queen's ear, it will take a deal of reasoning and logic on our parts to work it out.'

'Essex is easy,' said Poley. 'He has been making preparations to recruit an army that will follow him to Ireland through the good-offices of Sir Thomas North who is famous for translating Plutarch. Who is also a renowned and effective Captain, having fought in the Low Countries as well as in Ireland. Who is so well-thought of that he was put in charge of the defence of the South Coast when Essex' pursuit of treasure together with the fleet at his command left the Channel open to another Spanish Armada.'

'But,' continued Tom, 'I thought Essex was using North as his muster master because he doesn't trust Sir Ralph Lane the Muster Master General as he is one of Raleigh's closest associates. That he is hoping therefore to get a larger, better trained and better equipped army than has ever been sent to Ireland in the past.'

'Indeed,' said Poley. 'But remember that Lord Robert is not the only Councillor worried that such an army might follow Essex back again, no matter how things turn out in Ulster, and be the backbone of an attempt to snatch the throne.'

Tom nodded. 'Essex' concern at the conclusion of either of these enterprises is more than enough to explain the visits from men of his camp to Simon Forman seeking assurance of the outcome. Is it possible that Essex himself could have visited Billingsgate in secret or in disguise?'

'I would think it just possible,' said Will. 'Unless Master Poley has had a close watch kept on Forman's house, anyone might have come or gone in secret.'

'But I think we can all agree that even if Essex did visit Forman there are limits to what his dignity would allow. In which case, all that secrecy would effectively come to nothing. It remains far more likely that Sir Francis Bacon visited on Essex' behalf.'

'Very well,' said Poley. 'Let us turn to Sir Walter…'

'Mercy!' cried Rosalind. 'It appears there may be a lengthy set of deliberations in prospect. For God's sake let us fetch in sustenance to give us strength. Is there no local hostelry whose food is worth carrying home?'

'The White Hart on Cheapside is scarce ten minutes' walk from here,' answered Tom. 'It is where Kate and I always get our food - either to eat there or to carry home.'

'Umble pies and venison,' elaborated Ugo. 'Winter fruits and vegetables. They do a fine eel pie, too, on Fish Days.'

'If there's a fish pie, I'd be happy with that,' said Rosalind.

Tom looked around the room. 'Venison, pies and trenchers it is,' he said.

'And as much Rhenish as you can carry,' added Poley with a straight face - and a twinkle of wickedness in his eye.

'Very well,' said Tom. 'Ugo, are you happy to help?'

'As ever.' The Dutch gunsmith gave a theatrical sigh and pulled himself to his feet. 'Food for five and, by the sound of it, drink for ten.'

v

'When are you going to bring out the two actual clues in your possession?' wondered Ugo as the he and Tom strode up Knightrider Street towards St Pauls.

'If you can call them clues,' said Tom. 'A love-lock curl of hair tied with a ribbon such as a lover might carry next to their heart in reminiscence of the beloved. And a few threads of hair pulled from the fist of a bloated corpse.'

'The one dropped by someone bathing at Simon Forman's and the other from a man we are certain died at Simon Forman's and was kept in that same bath for a while before being secreted in the garden privy.'

'The fact that they both come from the same place adds some weight to them as clues - especially as they come from that particular place. Where almost all of our suspects or their representatives have been at least once and many more than once between Twelfth Night and Saturday week ago, including both of our corpses.'

This conversation took them through St Paul's churchyard, past New Change and onto The Cheap. Then it was only a matter of moments before they were pushing into the White Hart. The tavern was as busy as usual but Tom and Ugo still managed to find a table and place an order for venison pies, eel pies, trenchers and Rhenish. Everything soon arrived, together with a couple of pot-boys to help carry the food back to Blackfriars. But, Tom was regretfully informed, there were no eel pies, salmon pies or fish pies of any sort.

The four men set out, laden with the best that the White Hart could offer, Tom and Ugo bemoaning the lack of fish pies for Rosalind. But as chance would have it, as they came out of Knightrider Street into Blackfriars, another two men joined them. Tom recognised them as being servants from Nonsuch, Sir Thomas Walsingham's great house on London Bridge. The servants recognised Tom too, for he was a frequent visitor. 'Master Musgrave,' called the taller of the pair, 'well met, sir. We come bearing gifts. Sir Thomas has sent you a pie of lampreys from his fish ponds at Scadbury as were brought up fresh this morning then killed and cooked this noon but they're cold and well set now!'

'That solves all your problems,' Ugo observed. 'The lamprey pie is probably Scadbury's greatest dish.'

Tom agreed. It was by far his favorite, though there was little enough to the making of it, especially compared to some of the other culinary delights prepared in Sir Thomas' kitchens. A case of robust, buttery shortcrust sealed on the inside with more butter, stuffed with gutted, washed and chunked lamprey, layered with shallots and bay, seasoned with salt, pepper and nutmeg, and brimming with yet more melted butter before the shortcrust lid went on and the whole was gently baked to a golden perfection. All in all a heavenly case with a firm, flavoursome filling set hard and best eaten cold with mustard, which Sir Thomas had been thoughtful enough to supply as well.

Tom, Ugo and the four laden servants crowded into the room and put the various pies on the table. There was more food than they needed now, but they were willing enough to do their best in the matter of consuming everything in front of them. While Ugo opened the wine, Tom cut open the venison pie and piled the steaming contents on the trenchers which immediately began to soak up the rich, sweet gravy. As he worked, he became aware of a soft, serpentine movement around his ankles. Astaroth had smelt the lamprey pie, he thought. Then he sectioned Sir Thomas' gift and the hungry group arranged the cold, fragrant wedges on the bread trenchers behind the venison, the better to eat the hot food before it cooled and leaving the cold pie until later. Before he sat down to say grace and start eating, Tom piled some of the fishy filling onto Astaroth's plate - a gesture that had become habitual in a mere 24 hours or so. The cat sniffed it delicately, then began to wolf it down.

*

'So,' said Poley round a mouthful of venison pie, you have two hanks of hair. Lord Robert keeps saying that he could not separate Essex and Raleigh with a sheet of parchment but perhaps, Master Musgrave, if you have a sheet of paper we should lay these items side by side upon it.'

'The white of the paper will allow us to see the true colour of the hair more clearly,' agreed Tom, his voice thick and his gullet mired with venison pie-crust. He reached for a glass of Rhenish and cleared his throat with a lengthy draught. He rose, left the table, found a piece of paper that he had been recording the names of those who had booked lessons and the time he was expecting them and returned, turning it over so that the clean side was uppermost. Then he reached into his pouch and carefully removed the two lengths of hair. He put them on the paper and they all craned forward to look more closely at them.

Tom had, of course, examined them before but never on white paper and never side by side. Both were red, both lengthy - the keepsake winding the curls into a circle before tying them together with a short length of narrow red ribbon. Without undoing this it would be impossible to judge their length with any accuracy, though their russet colouring was clear enough. The colour of the curls emphasised not only by the whiteness of the paper they were lying on but also by the vivid scarlet of the ribbon binding them together. The strands from Hal's hand also tended to curl but it was difficult to judge whether they were the same colour as the love token beside them.

'For a proper comparison,' said Poley, stirring the strands with a dismissive finger, 'we need more of these.'

'Or perhaps, 'said Tom, pointing towards the beribboned locks, 'fewer of these.' He wiped the blade of his dagger and used the point to cut the ribbon then, again with the point, he separated a few strand and moved them to lie beside those pulled out of Hal's cold dead hand. They were strikingly similar.

'But are they identical?' wondered Poley. 'And even if so, what does that prove?'

'That Hal did not die alone,' said Tom. 'As he tumbled backwards down the stair, there was someone standing in the doorway of Forman's occult chamber. Perhaps they pushed him or perhaps the surprise was enough to make Hal step back. The boy reached up as he fell. Whether or not the person in the doorway tried to help him or hurt him, the boy reached out and caught these hairs from that person's head. These remained in his closed fist throughout the experiences that his corpse went through. It is tempting to suppose this stranger to be a man but we have already established that even a restless parrot can cause enough shock and surprise to send someone back out through the door, so - man or woman: someone watched him fall and die.'

'But why attack Hal?' wondered Ugo.

Tom turned to Poley. 'You said something about my lady impatience when talking - in secret as you supposed - to Kate Shelton at the Rose. What did you mean by that? What do you know that you have yet to share?'

'Little enough, except that my pursuivants keeping watch on Forman's house kept warning me that she was the most regular of his visitors. Even after he had sent his household to the country just as Sir Walter has done.'

*

'And did your pursuivant spies tell you of any other regular visitors?'

'None who were regular. Many who visited once or twice - Spenser amongst them - and one or two whose faces they could not see. Also, being men whose intellect stands even lower than Humiliation Gouge's, they kept watch on the front of the house - not the back. So there might well have been visitors coming and going through the garden as well as through the front-door with their faces muffled.'

'Like the man who called himself Will Shakespeare and bought poison from young Hal in John Gerard's shop,' added Rosalind. 'But wait a moment, surely I saw hairs like this bound up in the rope that repaired Forman's broken banister. A fancy piece of rope-work designed to hold the broken halves together. Such as a hangman puts above his noose or a sailor might use aboard ship.'

'Well,' said Poley, 'we have a sailor on our list true enough. And a fox-haired one at that.' He stirred the hairs spread across the white paper sheet once more.

'But none of your watchers saw him coming or going,' said Tom.

'That doesn't mean he wasn't there,' said Ugo.

'But if he was there in secret, he might well have a powerful motive to murder anyone who discovered him.'

'Depending on why he wanted his visits to be kept secret,' said Will. 'What damage could the opening of the secret do? That he was having his birth chart drawn and his future predicted? Why he'd be one among hundreds. That he wanted a love philtre or token - such as the lock of hair curled here? Again, one amongst many. Almost any of Forman's occult practices in the way of showing or controlling the future might embarrass a man if known - but hardly do him damage enough to merit murder as a response.'

'Unless,' said Tom, 'Forman's lodging was not being used as a place of magic. What if the most important room in the place was not the shop, the *laboratorium*, the library or the occult chamber. What if the important room was the bedroom? All the men on our list are happily married. Their reputation and standing at court depends upon it for the Queen's disapproval of secret liaisons has led to the Tower in the past and may well do so again. The Tower followed by years in the wilderness of royal disapproval and exile from court. If Spenser somehow discovered one of our suspects *in flagrante* or nearly so, that might well make a man fear utter ruin if it came to the Queen's ears. Make him so worried that the only way forward might be murder.'

Tom paused and there was a moment of silence as the others digested his words, testing their logic and probability.

The silence was broken by a choking yowl and they all turned to look at Astaroth. She was dancing wildly in place, her one eye a black gape with the finest green edge around it. Suddenly she lost control of her bladder and flooded the old cloak with urine.

Tom reached over and caught Rosalind's wrist, stopping her first spoonful of lamprey pie half way to her lips. He glanced round the table - everyone else was still on the venison pie with no ill effects. Only Astaroth had eaten the fish.

'There's hemlock in the lamprey pie,' he said.

Chapter 17: The Doubting Thomas

i

'Lord Robert suspected that it would be Sir Thomas,' said Poley as he, Will and Tom walked briskly out of Blackfriars, heading for London Bridge. 'But his logic was not of the strongest.'

'What argument did he employ?' asked Will.

'That Sir Thomas did not feature anywhere on the lists of suspects,' Poley explained. 'That he appeared to be absolutely innocent.'

'Therefore it could be argued he had been so careful to keep himself free of suspicion that its very absence was in itself suspicious?' asked Tom.

'Just so.'

'Only a man who studied law at the Sorbonne could chop logic like that! And, now I think of it, the same reasoning could be applied to Master Secretary himself - not only has he ensured that his name is kept well clear of this situation, he has even arranged for one of his most trusted lieutenants and intelligencers to be involved in every likely aspect of the case either as Chief Intelligencer or Pursuivant Marshal. It's a situation with *guilt* written all over it; yours as well as his.'

'Most amusing!' said Poley. 'But you both know the guilty man must be Walter Raleigh.'

'I do,' said Tom. 'Sir Walter must stand at the heart of the matter at least.'

Will frowned, trying to work out the other men's logic.

'Or rather it seemed so until Sir Thomas Walsingham started sending you poisoned pies,' said Poley thoughtfully.

'It seems so still. I fear the poisoned pie simply confirms matters,' replied Tom grimly.

'How so?' demanded Will but there was no reply.

The three of them were hurrying down Water Lane but instead of hailing a wherry *Eastward Ho!* Tom chose to turn left and follow the River. They walked along White Lion Hill into Paul's Walk, then up by Broken Wharf to High Timber and along Upper Thames Street to Fish Street then down onto the Bridge.

It was a brisk walk of twenty minutes through a clear, frosty evening and they soon became too short of breath for conversation so they each dwelt on their own thoughts as they shouldered through the bustle, leaving great clouds of breath behind them as though they were all smoking pipes of Sir Walter's new-fangled medicinal tobacco.

On their right for much of the time, the River also bustled with shipping of all sorts from the wherries they decided not to hire to the tall ocean-going galleons which had sailed past London Bridge at the turn of low-tide while the drawbridges were raised and the incoming surge was beginning to push upriver behind them. The tide was full at the moment, and just beginning to turn once more, so that, as they came down Fish Street, they felt as much as heard the great rumbling as the massive water wheels between the northernmost starlings of the Bridge began to turn and the Thames started to form that six-foot cliff of water beneath the Bridge itself that Rosalind so wanted to ride.

*

The massive edifice of Nonsuch, prefabricated in Holland and shipped here to be reassembled piece by piece, straddled the bridge half way along its length. The central roadway led beneath its great arch, with access into the house from either side. The rear of the great building faced north and the front faced south. To the north, other houses and shops crowded close behind it but to the south, facing the South Wark, the Great South Gateway and the church of St Mary Overie beyond it, there was a broad expanse that included one of the drawbridges and so was clear of shops. The house stood near twelve stories to the great onion cupolas above its four square towers. Although the house itself - erected here using only wooden pins to hold the whole together - reached from one edge of the bridge to the other, there were added sections on each side overhanging the river that contained the privies which served the house's occupants and their numerous servants. Though, like the public privies to the north and the south of them, they were little more than long rooms containing holes cut into stout boards raised

289

knee-high that reached out conveniently over the water. They made excellent fishing-holes when not employed in their primary purpose, for hungry fish congregated here awaiting the food that rained from on high. Whereas the public facilities were open, those in Nonsuch were enclosed, with tall windows looking up-stream and down-stream behind the seated occupants' shoulders.

Tom, Will and Poley stopped beneath the Nonsuch arch and rapped on the door that led into the massive building. A footman answered at once and even as he ushered them in, taking their cloaks as he did so, Sir Thomas' butler Bates appeared. 'Is it Sir Thomas, Lady Audrey or Mistress Kate you wish to see, Master Musgrave?' asked Bates. 'They are all at home, I believe.'

Although he spoke to Tom as a familiar visitor and nodded to Will as an occasional guest, his wise eyes were taking the measure of Poley who was standing at Tom's side. Tom began to wonder whether his companion was also a regular - clandestine - visitor.

'We are here to see Sir Thomas, to begin with at least, thankyou Bates,' said Tom.

'Very well, sir. If you would follow me…' Bates led them deeper into the house at bridge level, to the stairs leading up above the stories filled by the household servants, brewers, butchers, mongers, cooks and cleaners. Then, a little laboriously further up storey after storey until they reached the lower family apartments. Here, where the floor reached from side to side of the house well above the arch, there was a strange sensation of space, as though they were entering the Royal palaces of West Minster, Hampton Court or Greenwich. Or, thought Tom, remembering more recent experiences, the Royal chambers in the Tower - the Queen's fourth London palace.

Sir Thomas met them in his study, the book-lined sanctum whose one tall window overlooked the River downstream almost as far as Deptford, a vista of maritime activity that matched the bustle on London's streets. As the tide was beginning to fall and the current of the mighty river was following the withdrawal of the water out towards the sea, many of the vessels in the anchorages of Deptford and Greenwich were getting ready to sail, though one or two - for whatever reason - were doggedly beating upriver against wind, tide and current.

Sir Thomas' study was where he retired in the evenings - when not at Parliament in West Minster - to do his business, meet his responsibilities as MP for Rochester in Kent and oversee his extensive network of spies. Because of the latter - thought Tom - he had no difficulty in recognising Robert Poley, regular visitor or not.

ii

Looking at Sir Thomas before they began to explain their presence and mission, Tom was struck by several facts that he had never really noticed before. To begin with, Sir Thomas shared much of his physical make-up as well as his mental acuity with his close relative the late spymaster Sir Francis Walsingham, the Queen's dark-hued *Moor*, rather than with his bluff landowner father Sir Thomas after whom he had been named. Not yet forty years old, this Sir Thomas was a lean, dark-haired man whose pointed beard and swept-back hair framed a long, intelligent face as smoothly as an otter's pelt. But Tom noticed for the first time how strong the reddish tinge in those sleek dark locks appeared to be. Which, he wryly thought, explained the fact that Sir Thomas could be every bit as quick-tempered and unforgiving as his red-haired sister-in-law.

For a disturbing instant he wondered whether Sir Robert Cecil's French chopped logic as presented by Poley might have some merit after all and Sir Thomas rather than Sir Walter somehow stood at the heart of this.

'Well, gentlemen, how can I be of service?' Sir Thomas asked, moving his papers aside so that he could give them his full attention.

'Sir Thomas, did you send a lamprey pie as a gift to Blackfriars tonight?' asked Tom.

'Not to my knowledge. We did in fact have lamprey pie this evening and very fine it was, but you would have to ask Audrey, the butler or the cook whether there was more than one made and whether the extra one was sent to you. Or, I suppose, you could ask the men who brought it to you - for I imagine it did not arrive at Blackfriars by its own occult motion. But it must have been especially tasty to have called you, Master Shakespeare and Master Poley right across London to show your gratitude.'

'That is not quite our intention, Sir Thomas,' said Poley.

'What brings you to my door then?' wondered Sir Thomas.

'Perhaps if we could talk to Lady Audrey as you suggest,' said Tom, who was in no rush to give anything much away. Despite his ironic conversation with Poley, he actually thought that Sir Thomas was innocent of any wrongdoing, for he still believed the guilty man really was Raleigh, but even so, a cautious approach could do no harm - especially as an open accusation could all too easily lead to confrontation and ejection from Nonsuch with the enquiry only part-done. For it was vital to his mind that he establish how the poison in the pie - if it originated with Raleigh's associate Forman like all the other hemlock in the case so far - got from Billingsgate to Blackfriars in the guts of that lamprey pie.

Sir Thomas nodded and picked up a bell from his desk. It made a piercing, silvery jingle as he shook it and even before the echoing tintinnabulation died, Bates was back in the doorway, waiting for his master's instructions.

'Ah, Bates. Would you see whether my wife is free to grant us a moment or two of her time?'

'Of course, Sir Thomas.'

Moments later he returned and ushered in his mistress. Lady Audrey Walsingham was an older version of her sister Kate. The difference in their ages added several subtle strengths to Audrey. Physically, she was slightly fuller of figure, but she carried herself almost like a queen while something of the tom-boy still lingered in Kate. Audrey's hair was darker than Kate's flame-red, almost the colour of autumn leaves. Like her husband's it contained no trace of grey as yet. Likewise her eyes had less of the emerald and more of moss-green about them. Her nose and lips were straighter and thinner than Kate's and, although her chin was determined, there was no dimple, as there was with Kate's. When she smiled, however - which she did

292

often - there were dimples in her cheeks just as there were in Kate's as well. Her voice when she spoke was quiet but carrying and several tones deeper than Kate's.

*

'Good evening Tom, this is a pleasant surprise. Master Shakespeare and Master Poley - to what do we owe the pleasure of this visit?' her tone and demeanour made it clear that this was a woman well-used to walking and talking with royalty. But she had always had a soft spot for Tom - partially but not entirely because of his steadying influence on her wildcat of a sister.

'They have come across London from Blackfriars to say *gramercy* for a lamprey pie which we sent them earlier this evening,' explained Sir Thomas.

'Are they indeed? That is strange, for I sent them no pie.' Lady Audrey frowned slightly. 'What makes you think it came from my kitchens, Tom?'

'I recognised the men that brought it, Lady Audrey. They are from the household here.'

Lady Audrey looked at Sir Thomas. The silver bell chimed once more.

'Bates,' said Lady Audrey when the butler arrived immediately, 'did we send a pie to Master Musgrave this evening?'

'Indeed we did, My Lady. Cook made one for the household and another, as ordered, to be sent to Master Musgrave.'

'Who ordered the second pie?'

'Why, you did My Lady. I was there when the message arrived, together with the extra fishes straight from Billingsgate.'

Lady Audrey looked at Sir Thomas. His eyebrows rose. She turned to Bates again. 'And who delivered this message and the extra lampreys?'

Tom answered before Bates could: 'It was Kate, Lady Audrey. It could only have been Kate.'

'And so it was indeed, Master Musgrave,' Bates confirmed. 'Miss Kate brought Lady Audrey's message and the great basket of lampreys fresh from Billingsgate wharf herself.'

'I see,' said Sir Thomas, though his tone made it abundantly clear that he did not see at all. 'I am at a loss to explain this in any way. I had no knowledge that Kate was out. She had not approached me for money - and lampreys are ruinously expensive items. Audrey, had she come to you?'

Lady Audrey simply shook her head, her lovely face folded in a frown of confusion to match her husband's.

'Bates, if you could ask the Lady Kate to spare us a moment or two…' said Sir Thomas.

'Of course, Sir Thomas.' Bates bowed and exited.

'So, Tom,' said Lady Audrey. 'What is this about a lamprey pie?'

'My Lady,' asked Tom gently in reply, 'are you aware of the part played by lampreys in the history of our kings and queens?'

Lady Audrey, like both Queen Elizabeth of England and Queen Ann of Scotland, not to mention a good number of their ladies in waiting, was very well educated. She knew her English history and her Holinshed as well as she knew her Plutarch and her Homer. 'Was it not Henry the First,' she asked, 'who had troubles with Archbishop Anselm of Canterbury - though as nothing compared with those of Henry the Second and Archbishop Becket. But when Henry the First died, he is reputed to have done so through consuming *a surfeit of lampreys*?'

'Just so, Lady Audrey,' said Tom.

'A coincidence, surely?' said Sir Thomas.

'I think not, Sir Thomas. There has been a great deal of focus on various Kings called Henry of late.' Tom glanced across at Will. 'And, although not at the centre of things, this last gesture is perhaps the most telling.'

'In what way?' asked Sir Thomas, his intellect as clearly engaged now as that of Lady Audrey.

But before Tom could answer, Bates was back, his normally open face folded in a frown. 'Miss Kate is not in her rooms, sir, though her waiting gentlewomen say all of her clothes are there, including the dress she wore to dinner this evening. Still warm, apparently. But none of them have been summoned to help Miss Kate get changed. Furthermore, Sir Thomas, your personal valet is in a state of outrage because your private *garderobes* have been opened and rifled.'

iii

'Lock the doors and search the house!' snapped Sir Thomas. 'I want Miss Kate found! Meanwhile, Tom, will you kindly tell me what all this is about. And don't tell me it's all about lampreys!'

'Very well, Sir Thomas,' said Tom. 'Let us begin with something else.' He turned to face not only his host but also Poley and the Lady Audrey who stood beside him. 'Which of you set Kate to spy on Raleigh? I take it for granted that Sir Francis Bacon is beginning to waver in his support of the Earl of Essex and provides intelligence from Essex House and I suppose that Lord Robert Cecil, being the spider at the heart of this web, is competent to keep a close watch on himself while he sets Poley here to keep close watch on everybody else except, perhaps Sir Walter. But which of you set Kate to watch on Durham House and its master when *Mother Hubberd's Tale* began to stir up trouble for the men newly lampooned within it?'

'Lord Robert suggested it,' admitted Poley after a brief pause. He looked across at Sir Thomas. 'I had no contacts either in Durham House or in the School of Night.'

'And I expedited it,' Sir Thomas admitted. 'I gave it my blessing at least. Lady Audrey and I discussed it with each-other and with Kate herself. We needed her close to Sir Walter - but not too close.'

'Close enough, however, to gauge his reactions should his standing at court begin to suffer as a result of the satire - would he contact the Infanta in Spain in the same way that you, through Lady Audrey, are in contact with Queen Ann in Scotland. Or would he instead lean towards Lady Arbella Stewart in his attempts to shore up his future under the new monarchy should the Queen banish him once again in the short-term - while she was still alive, at least?'

'Just so,' nodded Sir Thomas.

'But Kate's work would have been complicated by the involvement of The School of Night - though they hate that name and refuse to use it of themselves. And especially the involvement of Simon Forman, to whom Raleigh - and eventually Kate herself - increasingly frequently referred, seeking assurances as to the future. And I suspect that it was there, at Forman's house in Billingsgate, that things began to go seriously wrong. For there is no doubt in my mind that Kate became besotted with Sir Walter and he with her. Like Romeo and Juliet in Will's play; or rather, perhaps, like Antony and Cleopatra out of Plutarch.

'While Lady Raleigh was in London for the Christmas season their liaisons remained chaste - at least I hope so, for I was Kate's lover at that time as well. But immediately Lady Raleigh left, their affair became much more intense - nearly all-consuming. Kate visited my bed only once thereafter and that was at least in part through a love potion I had given her, while she spoke of guilt and punishment as much as she spoke of love.'

'If this is true then it was madness!' said Lady Audrey. 'Sir Walter lost the Queen's favour once through his affair with Bess Throckmorton the best part of ten years ago. How many years did it take him to regain it? Seven? Eight? If Her Majesty ever found out he was deep in an affair with Kate she would expel him and never forgive him. It would ruin him.'

*

'My point precisely,' said Tom. 'They carried on their liaisons at Forman's house, therefore, rather than at Durham House or his house at Blackwall - Kate leaving by accident a love-token such as one she once wore of mine after she bathed there, to wit a lock of hair bound with a ribbon. But this was not my hair - it was Sir Walter's, though it took me long enough to fathom whose it was and reason where it came from.'

'So,' said Poley, 'they carried on their dangerous liaison. But they did so in secret. With no-one any the wiser, they were safe enough.'

'Or they were to begin with,' said Tom. 'Only Forman - and perhaps Chapman - were aware of the truth. Forman reliant on

Sir Walter to stand between him and the witch finder should King James ascend the throne; Chapman perennially bankrupt and starving - reliant on Sir Walter for life itself. But then, by accident, everything changed.'

'How so?' asked Sir Thomas. He looked up at Lady Audrey and across at Poley. If they had worked out the truth, they chose to keep it to themselves. 'Spenser visited Forman without warning; unannounced. Frustrated by the constant delay he met at the Council, suspicious that he had made a terrible mistake in republishing *Mother Hubberd*, and growing ever more concerned about the state of his wife and children in Cork, he went to see whether Forman and his occult predictions could reassure or even guide him. And instead of the assistance he had hoped for, he discovered Kate and Sir Walter *in flagrante*, and so he signed his death warrant.'

'That's it?' demanded Sir Thomas. 'That's all? Nothing, really, to do with the satiric verse, with the Fox and the Ape, with the Irish question, with enemies coveting his lands and income, with his proposals to starve O'Neil and his people into submission? They killed him just because he found them *fornicating*?'

'Both Spenser and the lad Hal. Both just in the wrong place at the wrong time, and that was all it took. But you see, it all played a part; everything you have just itemised from the poem to the proposal - just not the part we supposed at first.'

'Wait,' said Sir Thomas. 'Let's take this a little more slowly. Whatever his reason for going there, Spenser found Kate and Raleigh at Forman's house…'

'Probably in Forman's bedroom,' agreed Tom.

'Very well, if you say so,' said Sir Thomas. 'He discovered them in Forman's bedroom. What then?'

'He would have promised never to reveal their secret,' said Tom. 'Sworn on everything he considered holy - on the lives of his wife and remaining children as like as not. But the suspicion would be there in their minds that he would give their secret away - to Essex, to the Council, to Sir Thomas here - to anyone who could profit through Raleigh's downfall. Either on purpose or by accident.'

'But they did not act at once…' observed Lady Audrey.

'They trusted him, My Lady; or Raleigh did at least. Raleigh and he were old acquaintances. Their lands were close to each-others in Ireland. He had given his word as one honourable gentleman to another…'

'But then something happened to upset their trust,' said Poley. 'What could have done that?'

'The Queen and Council did it,' said Tom.

'The Queen and Council?' demanded Sir Thomas. 'How so? What did they do?'

'They gave Spencer his thirty pieces of silver,' said Tom. 'His £50 pension. In gold. In a purse. What else were Raleigh and Kate to think? He had sold their secret and unless he could be silenced, they were on the verge of ruin!'

iv

'But he hadn't sold anything, surely,' said Lady Audrey.

'That is true but they didn't know it,' said Tom. 'So they took action at once, perhaps without thinking the matter through.'

'You keep saying "they",' said Poley.

Tom was silent for a moment. Then, 'You are right,' he admitted. 'I should have said "she".'

'"She" being Kate,' whispered Lady Audrey.

'Kate was an habitué of Forman's, her visits frequent - both as observed by Poley's pursuivant watchers and in secret through the garden they never watched. No doubt on many occasions, while awaiting her lover, she learned a good number of the secrets the astrologer was keeping as well as some of the treatments the herbalist was discussing. He kept a journal and recorded everything in it - even his own liaisons. Spenser came to him for pain-relief as well as for more occult guidance but must have told Forman that he also saw John Gerard, no doubt giving some details about his hurt - and how he could often taste the medicines designed to heal his ear in the back of his throat. While detailing of course, what those medicines were. As fate would have it, both Gerard's daughter Bess and his apprentice Hal were also occasional visitors - she legitimately though without her parents knowledge and he through burglary in search of her at first and then of her birth chart. These were the very people who were treating Spenser. And so Kate's plan was drawn, with or without Raleigh's knowledge or approval.'

'*With or without*? Are you sure?' asked Sir Thomas.

'I have assessed the details time and again since the pattern began to come together and I can see no necessity of his involvement. Once it becomes clear that Kate was the prime mover, his participation becomes questionable to say the least. We know how Raleigh goes about killing. He might set his fencing tutor on to confront me when my suspicions started to become clear, arriving in secret to observe my execution - and with Kate at my window watching him. But when that failed he set about killing me himself. He kills with blades and face to face for the most part. I cannot see him using poison. Had he decided to kill Spenser he would likely have contrived a confrontation, an insult - a duel. Even the playwright Ben Jonson got away with that.'

'Poison is a woman's weapon,' observed Lady Audrey. 'Think of Lucrezia Borgia, Julia Tofana…'

'It was in this case, My Lady. On the night of Friday the 12th, she took desperate action. She knew where Forman's poisons were. She took hemlock and sped through the storm to Gerard's where she knew Spenser would be at the end of his long day waiting at White Hall. She saw Spenser being treated and waited until he had left. Covering her face with her scarf she bought more poisons in the name of Will Shakespeare.' He turned to his wide-eyed friend. 'Avenging, as she thought, Will, your anathematising of her beloved Raleigh's circle of poets and philosophers as the *School of Night*. Then she followed Spenser to King Street, observed him consuming Kentish ale in such quantities as Gerard advised against. Saw him stagger drunkenly up to bed. Followed him on silent feet, managed to remove his bandage so she could pour her hemlock into his ear. And so the deed was done.'

'And the apprentice, Hal?' asked Lady Audrey. 'Did Kate kill him too?'

*

'Ah. Now that, I believe, *was* Sir Walter, though Kate may well have been with him. They must have heard Hal breaking in and disquieting the parrots outside the kitchen which make a shocking noise if disturbed. While he was downstairs, they ran up to the occult room to hide, perhaps taking clothing with them - but perhaps not. But Hal's inquisitiveness was aroused - he found the birth chart and tucked it into his jerkin, he saw the bed chamber and felt stirring in his codpiece. He thought perhaps even greater excitements lay higher still. He climbed the stair, he opened the door and discovered - Sir Walter Raleigh framed in the portal with Kate close behind no doubt. He stepped back. Felt himself falling. Reached out automatically and caught some of Raleigh's hair. Raleigh could not - or did not - save him. The hair tore out and was closed in the poor boy's fist as he fell to his death.

'I assume the bath had been filled with hot water to allow the lovers to wash after their love-making. They put Hal in it instead as they cleaned up. Raleigh would eventually mend the bannisters with the sailor's knot that reminded Rosalind of a hangman's noose. In the mean-time, when they were finished in the house, they put Hal in Forman's privy. When he returned he took over the task of getting rid of Hal while agreeing with Kate's scheme to leave poor Will as a major suspect in the matter. So he and Chapman concocted the poem and the dagger pinning it in place. They used Sir Walter's good offices and, no doubt, the cutter from one of his vessels docked off Deptford to transport the corpse to West Minster then the cutter's crew carried it on up into Spenser's grave; one of them, not very expertly picking the lock on the Great North Door. It was from that grave, by another twist of irony, Kate herself helped us move Hal later that same night, all without showing any surprise or horror for of course she felt none. That adventure was the price she paid for coming to find out from me how my investigation was proceeding. And at that stage it all seemed to be proceeding quietly. Essex had called on Forman to assess the body. Forman announced that he saw nothing wrong of course. Kate must have told Raleigh where Hal's corpse had ended up but, apart from checking the corpse and leaving the lid of the tomb open an inch, there was nothing they could do. But Kate's attempt to involve Will blew up in her face like a sapper destroyed by his own mine. The rumour she started that poison - purchased by Will here - had been involved in Spenser's death reached the Queen's ears courtesy of gossip arising from the funeral Essex had arranged for him. And suddenly a guilty party was required. Her Majesty had to be satisfied or Essex could not go to Ireland - and Essex in Ireland is something upon which almost everyone has some hope of a great fortune riding.'

Tom had no sooner stopped speaking than Bates threw the door open and staggered into the room. Walter Raleigh strode in behind him, rapier drawn. 'Where is she?' Raleigh demanded.

'We don't know, Sir Walter,' answered Tom, as though this were an everyday occurrence. 'She is, we believe, still somewhere about the house most likely dressed in man's attire.'

That brought Raleigh up sharp. But only for a moment. 'We must find her,' he said. 'I have arranged matters as she wanted, but we must be quick!'

Tom looked back at Sir Thomas who was still seated at his desk, as though frozen with surprise. But as the Master of Logic looked past the spymaster, the last piece of the puzzle fell into place.

There, flat across the window, as though painted upon the glass, was a flag. It was a square of cloth with edges of more than a yard long. A cross of St George stood red and proud in the foreground and two broad green stripes below two white stripes sat behind. It was the masthead pennant of a galleon. 'I know where she is,' he said. 'Quick! We must get to her…'

v

They all moved together, Raleigh sheathing his sword as they left Sir Thomas's study, leaving hold of Bates and falling in with the leaders. As they passed small groups of servants hunting for Kate, they joined the larger group until Tom suggested to Sir Thomas that they hardly needed the entire household following in their footsteps - particularly as their way led down staircase after staircase. Those in the family's section broad and accommodating enough but those in the servants' quarters lower down were little better than the flight at Forman's which had claimed Hal's life.

Tom led the way with Raleigh behind one shoulder and Poley behind the other. Sir Thomas and Lady Audrey were behind them, then Bates and several strapping footmen bringing up the rear. 'All to try and catch one young woman,' said Audrey, her tone making it clear that she could hardly credit what was going on.

'A woman disguised as a man,' added Sir Thomas. 'Dressed in my clothes! Like one of your players Master Shakespeare!'

'Except that this drama is real,' added Poley. 'There are no actors here!'

'I would dispute that Master Poley, having seen you and Master Parrot at work in the Marshalsea,' riposted Will bitterly.

'But it is not so much a disguise I believe,' explained Tom before the exchange became heated. 'It's just that she couldn't climb through the window in whatever finery she wore to dinner. And going places without clothing has got her into a deal of trouble already.'

It was perhaps just as well that the conversation paused while they tried to catch their breath. But because they did so a strange vibration made itself audible. It was a deep note that seemed to hover somewhere between being heard and felt and to come from every direction at once, like the bass rumbling of the waterwheels beside the north bank.

One of Bates' men touched a bannister and jumped in surprise. Tom did the same and frowned. It seemed that the entire building was trembling, almost thrilling, under the spell of this strange sound.

'So, Sir Walter,' said Tom after a moment as they clattered on downwards, his voice raised above the strange vibration, 'it was none of your doing but all for love.'

'It was as though she was possessed,' he shouted in reply. 'I have known men become like that on the battlefield or in close encounters at sea but never a woman. I would never have done so much or even dared so much.'

Tom paused for a moment, all too well aware that Raleigh was far too experienced a courtier and politician to say anything that would condemn himself in from of men like Sir Thomas Walsingham and Robert Poley. Any final facts he wished to clear up would be severely limited in scope, therefore. But Sir Walter was clearly happy enough, like Adam coming out of Eden, to blame his woman.

*

'And yet you stand by her,' he observed. 'You will not see her brought to book.'

'How could I? Even though none of this is my doing - I even reached out to catch the boy as he pulled my hair out before he fell back down the stair, I have been active at the edges, trying to make everything right again.'

'But Spenser and Hal are both dead because of the pair of you.'

'Because of my weakness, perhaps, but through none of my doing.'

'"*The woman tempted me*,"' quoted Will, '"*and I did eat…*"'

'Well, Adam stood by Eve in the end and she bore him sons, away in the Land of Nod which was east of Eden,' answered Raleigh.

'And that's what you are doing, isn't it?' said Tom. 'Sending your Eve *west* of Eden so that you can face your Queen rather than your God with your hands clean even though your conscience might be stained.'

'My conscience is as clean as my hands,' said Raleigh. I but do what the woman asked.'

During this conversation the ten hunters at last closed with their quarry - in the most unlikely place of all. The latrine was secured to the side of Nonsuch with wooden pins as strong as any others used in the house's frame. But, unlike the rest of the house it overhung the river with no support beneath. Tom and the others stepped down into a long room, perhaps thirty feet from wall to wall. Three yards in, there was a raised platform standing at knee-height the better part of a further yard deep in which there were ten round holes. Behind the raised section, above a foot or so of outer wall, there were windows reaching from one side to the other, each perhaps a yard in width and a yard in height.

Kate, in Sir Thomas' ill-fitting clothes, was kneeling between two of the holes, leaning out of an open window. Her knees were spread and her left fist was closed tight on the frame. For the whole room was shaking increasingly fearsomely. Tom had experienced more than one earthquake during his time in Italy, but never anything like this. A quick glance around established that the quaking had reached such intensity that the room was beginning to come apart.

'*Kate*!' Both Tom and Raleigh called her name and leaped down onto the straining floorboards of the room. No sooner had they done so than the floor began to tear apart. Spaces opened between the floorboards, some revealing the roiling river, others revealing more planks sitting distantly below. Tom's logical assumptions had proved right. There was a ship there, hard up against the bridge, being shaken like a rat in a terrier's jaws by the power of the rushing River - waterfall and all. The mast was wedged against the side of the building, passing the vessel's violent motion straight into the wood-pegged structure, the weakest part of which - the latrine- was coming apart. Kate cared nothing for that. Her plan was to climb through the window onto the rigging that held the shaking mast in place.

Kate had not heard them, so when they reached her and grabbed a shoulder each she jumped with shock. Tom got a glance through the open window she was leaning out of that confirmed everything he suspected since seeing the flag pressed flat across Sir Thomas' study window. But no sooner was everything confirmed than everything really began to fall apart. The entire wall, windows and all, sprang free and started sliding downwards like a headsman's axe. Kate reared back, no longer paying any attention to the men holding her shoulders. Then she threw herself forward again, tearing free of their fists.

*

Immediately outside the room the cause of its destruction stood fully revealed - the foremast and rigging of an ocean-going galleon. The topmast and crow's nest were an easy leap away. A brawny sailor was standing in the crow's nest reaching out for Kate but even were he and she to miss each-other, there was a web of rigging for her to cling to, reaching higher up still, to the pennant at the masthead that had been pushed flat across Sir Thomas' window, and down to the deck far below.

Without a second thought, she hurled herself outward, leaving her two would-be rescuers standing. The man in the crow's nest caught one arm and swung her onto the rigging. She clung for a moment then she began to scramble down. She spared not one glance for her two latest lovers standing in the slowly-collapsing latrine from which she had just escaped, nor her family standing in shocked silence behind them.

A distant voice bellowed, 'Let go all!' And, with a whip-snap of parting ropes and groan of timbers, the great ship slowly edged back downriver as she turned, pushed away by the six-foot wall of water underneath the Bridge. Turning further as she moved to head downstream she passed between the other shipping like a swan among ducks. Sailors swarmed busily all about her masts and spars so that by the time Kate stepped onto the deck, she was under full sail, heading for the North Sea and all points beyond.

Tom and Raleigh did not stay to observe Kate's escape. They turned, side by side and pounded back across the disintegrating floor. Tom made it back to the safety of the doorway first and turned to catch Raleigh, heaving him upwards and wryly thinking that Raleigh had failed to perform exactly the same service for the unfortunate Hal. Raleigh said something - perhaps in thanks - but the noise of destruction made everything else inaudible. Then they all stood crowded on the outer edge of the main house's solid flooring and watched the wreck of the latrine fall away into the wake of the departing galleon.

The wind backed, sending the cold breeze that had pasted the flag to Sir Thomas' window to make them shiver and that in turn broke the spell that had held them so that they began to move. They climbed silently up to Sir Thomas' study and the servants were dismissed - though Bates was ordered to bring a bottle of the best *usquebaugh* recently brought south from the Scottish court. Seated around the fire-bright room overlooking the bustle of distantly departing ships they sipped the golden liquid and discussed the situation. Raleigh confirmed what Tom had worked out, even apologising - as far as his honour would permit - to Will and forgiving him for giving his circle of poets and philosophers the name they all associated with the death of their friend and colleague Christopher Marlowe - and hatred in consequence. There was an opportunity there for Poley to apologise for his part in Marlowe's murder - which he chose not to take. Then matters turned almost exclusively to Kate. Her murder of Spenser had not only settled matters for Raleigh in her mind but also furnished her with a great deal of money when she stole his purse and pension. She bought new clothes - and a complete wardrobe that was aboard with her now - under the watchful eye of a waiting gentlewoman she had also hired. Such trifles as a basket of ruinously expensive lampreys stood neither here nor there in her new world of riches.

So they finally came back to the lamprey pie she had poisoned and sent to Tom: 'A complexity,' he explained. 'At once a revenge for my taking advantage of her trust and drugging her, a way of closing any further inquiry into the business from myself - as the man she feared might come too close to the truth too soon; soon enough to stop her at any rate. Which, as it turned out, was a close-run thing. And a kind of confession.'

'How so?' asked Raleigh, but it seemed he spoke for them all.

'Lady Audrey touched upon the heart of the matter,' said Tom. 'Lampreys were what caused the death of Henry the First. She was well enough aware that Will was hard at work on his play of Henry the Fifth. But the pie was a reminder of our conversations about Henry the Second - how a thoughtless word from him had caused his followers to act without his knowledge and perform a murder he was later to regret.'

'At once a means of murder and a confession in itself,' said Will.

'Perhaps you can find a way of putting that in a play,' suggested Lady Audrey.

'But no more pies,' said Sir Thomas. 'There were pies enough in *Titus Andronicus* full of the flesh of murdered children.'

'So, she planned to sail away tonight,' said Tom, returning to the subject in hand. 'Allowing Sir Walter here to inform the Earl of Essex as to the facts of the murder - so that he can satisfy the Queen and she will sign his commission at last. Then he will be off to Ireland and that will be that.'

'She asked me to send her far away, Sir Walter confirmed. 'To a new land west of Eden as you guessed.' Raleigh paused. Sighed. 'And I have in this as in all the rest, granted her wish. The vessel is captained by my friend and associate John Watts. She is bound for the settlement I founded some years ago in the New World. We have found it hard to stay in contact with the settlers and there are rumours that they may have moved on. But John is going to discover the truth if he can and Kate will join the colonists if there are any still there.'

'I see,' said her sister sadly. 'And what is this settlement she is bound for called, Sir Walter?'

'We called it Roanoke,' he replied.

The End

Epilogue: The Facts of the Case

On Saturday 13 January 1599 Edmund Spenser was found dead in his bed at his lodgings on King Street, Westminster, London. The bells of the local churches rang that afternoon to mark his passing. The Earl of Essex claimed the body, prepared it for burial and arranged the funeral, as described, on Tuesday 16th (though there was no Sin Eater and some of the poems have been 'adapted'). Ben Jonson later claimed Spenser died of starvation - his castle at Kilcolman had been destroyed by Irish rebels and one of his children had died in the battle. His family was hiding in Cork, where he was Sherriff. His income from his Irish estates was negligible. On the other hand the Queen granted a pension of £50 (the equivalent of many thousands of pounds today) though it is debatable how much of this he ever saw. He also re-released many of his earlier poems hoping to generate income from them. These included the previously banned satire *Mother Hubberd's Tale*, the main characters of which are The Ape and The Fox. Queen Elizabeth habitually called Secretary Cecil her 'Pygmy' and her 'Elf' and - occasionally - her 'Ape'.

Sir Walter Raleigh and several associates tried to found colonies in America. The most famous of which was Raleigh's Roanoke settlement. Roanoke is one of the great unsolved mysteries of early American history. The entire settlement vanished. No-one knows why (though failure of supplies and starvation probably featured) or where they went to. By the time John Watts got there in the early 1600's there was hardly any sign of them and even nowadays their fate is a matter of speculation. Raleigh himself was to become involved in the Main Plot (July 1603) to replace King James with Arbella Stuart and spent many years in the Tower as a result. He was released in 1616 just in time to join the (long, strange) list of men suspected of having murdered Shakespeare. He made one final voyage to the New World but was tried and condemned on his return. He was beheaded on Monday, 29th October 1618.

Essex left with an army of 16,000 for Ireland on Tuesday, 27th March 1599. As he exited the city, a bright, sunny spring day was transformed into a thunderous downpour - an ill-omen that proved true. Will Shakespeare added an extra element to the Chorus in *Henry V* which was playing at the Globe that day, praising the earl, wishing him well and predicting a happy return. The campaign was a disaster. Fearing his enemies at home (led by Cecil and Raleigh), Essex returned against the Queen's specific orders, invaded her dressing room and literally threw himself on her mercy. She never forgave him. Little more than a year later, he led his infamous 'rebellion', having asked his friend Southampton to get the Chamberlain's Men to perform *Richard II* at the Globe hoping the story of a weak king's replacement by strong usurpers would rouse the City. It didn't. When Raleigh was being sworn in as a witness against him, Essex said, 'What booteth it (good will it do) to swear (in) The Fox!'

Robert Devereux, 2nd Earl of Essex was the last person to be beheaded on Tower Green, just before 8am on Sunday 25th February 1601.

My main source once more is Shapiro's *1599*.

Avid readers of Bernard Cornwell will note my debt to *Fools and Mortals*.

The post of Pursuivant Marshal is my own creation - unlike Earl Marshal and Knight Marshal, it never existed.

*

Printed in Great Britain
by Amazon